MW01136946

The Bogside Boys

A Novel
By Eoin Dempsey

Acknowledgments

Massive thanks to my beta readers Chris Menier, Sarah Lepro, Liz Slanina, Orla Dempsey, Nicola Hogan, Brian Dempsey, Conor Dempsey, Jack Layden, Jill Dempsey, Morgan Leafe, Chelsea Barrish, Alison Reynolds, Eric Kvelums, Matt Coppa and Ed McDuell. Special thanks to Betsy Frimmer and Carol McDuell who both went above and beyond.

Also huge thanks to Paul Doherty from Bogside History Tours, and 'Sam', from Belfast Black Cab Tours who both lived through the Troubles I merely researched and wrote about.

Copyright © 2015 Eoin Dempsey
This book is a work of fiction based around true events. Most of the characters are fictitious, except for those that are not.

This book is for my son, Robbie.

Other Books by Eoin Dempsey

FINDING REBECCA

Table of Contents

Contents

Foreword

The conflict between the Catholic and Protestant communities in Northern Ireland has its roots in the 17th Century, when Protestant settlers from Scotland and England were given land confiscated from the native Catholic Irish by King James I. This was an effort to subjugate what had previously been the most rebellious part of the British occupied island of Ireland. Protestant domination continued over the following centuries through laws put in place by the British Crown. The polarization of the communities centered on the loyalty of the Protestant population to the occupying British forces and the desire of the Catholic population for a united Ireland, free of British rule.

In 1922, following the Irish war of Independence that led to the formation of the Irish Free State, Northern Ireland was partitioned from the rest of Ireland, remaining a part of the United Kingdom. Although meant only as a temporary solution to satisfy the Protestant majority in the six counties of Northern Ireland, the partition remained.

By the 1960's the Catholic people of Northern Ireland, sick of years of underrepresentation through gerrymandering and struggling to break free from the yoke of poverty imposed on them by sectarian policies of the Northern Irish government, began to march for their civil rights. Dr. Martin Luther King Jr. was their inspiration. The march on January 30th 1972 in Derry would signal the end of the civil rights movement in Northern Ireland, and an escalation of the violence known as the Troubles, which began with the battle of Bogside in Derry in 1969. That day would become known as Bloody Sunday.

8

List of TermsList of Terms

Bogside – a majority Catholic area outside the city walls of Derry, west of the River Foyle. A focal point of the Troubles, it was the scene of Bloody Sunday in 1972.

Cityside – the traditional home of the Catholic majority in Derry. The segment of the city west of the River Foyle.

Derry/Londonderry - a point of political dispute, with unionists advocating the longer, Anglicized name and nationalists advocating the shorter.

DUP – Democratic Unionist Party. The larger of the two unionist parties in Northern Ireland with strong traditional links to Protestant churches.

Fenian – a demeaning term for Irish Catholics.

Gardaí – the police force of the Republic of Ireland.

Huns – a demeaning term for Protestants in Northern Ireland.

Ian Paisley – the founding member of the DUP. A highly polarizing figure in Northern Irish history.

IRA – refers to the Provisional Irish Republican Army, the biggest and most active paramilitary group in Northern Ireland during the Troubles. Its goal was to remove Northern Ireland from the United Kingdom and bring about a united Irish republic.

IRA Army Council – the decision making body of the IRA.

Irish War of Independence – a guerilla war fought between 1919 and 1921 between the occupying forces of the British Crown and the IRA that resulted in the formation of the Irish Free State in 1922.

Loyalists – a group of people typified by militant opposition to Irish Republicanism, loyal to the British Crown. See also Unionists.

Nationalists – a group who support the idea of a united Ireland. See also Republicans.

NICRA – the Northern Ireland Civil Rights during the late 1960's and early 1970's. They organized the march on Bloody Sunday, which effectively ended their activities.

Orange Order - a Protestant fraternal society with strong links to Ulster Loyalism.

Prods – a derogatory term for Protestants in Northern Ireland

Republicans – a majority Catholic group who believe all Ireland should be an Independent Republic, independent of Britain.

RUC – the Royal Ulster Constabulary, the police force in Northern Ireland from 1922-2001. Held by Republicans to have strong bias toward, as well as colluding with, loyalist paramilitary groups.

The Troubles - the common name for the ethno-nationalist conflict in Northern Ireland from the late 1960's until it was deemed to have ended in 1998.

Unionists – a predominantly Protestant group who favor the continued union between Northern Ireland and the United Kingdom. See Loyalists.

UVF – an Ulster loyalist, anti-Catholic paramilitary group.

Chapter 1

The city of Derry, Northern Ireland, January 30th, 1972

Father Daly urged calm, but the surge of disquiet spilled through the crowd unabated. British soldiers were putting up barbed wire barriers on William Street and Little James Street. Armored cars packed with Parachute Regiment soldiers were lined up on Clarence Avenue. Snipers had set up along the walls of the old city, and overhead Mick could hear the sound of a helicopter circling. Mick's mother muttered something to her husband about an invasion. Pat looked at Mick, shaking his head. Paratroopers with camouflaged, blackened faces idled outside the cathedral in full combat gear. Father Daly, still speaking as the crowd shuffled out the doors of the cathedral, urged the crowd to attend the march that afternoon despite the attentions of the Paras. He would be there in case anything went wrong. The march was too important to let the Paras intimidate anyone into staying away.

It was a crisp and clear day. The sparkle of winter sunshine filled the air. Mick tried to rub the tiredness from his eyes. None of the Doherty family spoke as they filed out of the cathedral and past the British soldiers milling around on the corner. Fifty yards away, a young boy, around ten years old, broke away from his parents and kicked one of the soldiers in the shin. The soldier picked him up and began pacing away, the boy under his arm, his legs flailing like an animal in a trap. The boy's parents, incensed and embarrassed, followed the soldier as he carried the child away to be arrested. Celine Doherty waited until they were around the corner, before speaking to her husband and twin sons. Her Parisian accent was barely diminished, even after twenty-five years.

"Who was that boy? Do you know him?"

"I know him, aye. I know his brother, Thomas. Tom's one of the regulars down at Aggro Corner. One of the regular stone throwers," Pat answered.

"How do you know him then?" Peter, their father, interrupted. "How many times have I told you not to get involved with those bloody idiots down there? They think they're going to bring down the British Empire with a few stones."

"Relax, Da, I only know him to see is all. I played football with him a few times. I know better than to get involved in all that nonsense."

Three armored cars rumbled past, each filled with Paras. Mick stayed quiet. He knew his parents were worried about the march scheduled for that afternoon. Mick was sure that if Father Daly hadn't given his assurances at the end of Mass they would have tried to forbid him and Pat from going.

"What's the march about today?" Celine asked.

"Internment. It's NICRA," Peter replied as they turned the corner onto Creggan Street. They nodded to the masked men by the barricade erected to block off the street. The barricade was an old minibus with twisted metal girders and concrete blocks strewn on the street either side of it. The windows of the minibus had long since been broken in on any one of a hundred occasions. There was a sign daubed on the wall in white paint. YOU ARE NOW ENTERING FREE DERRY. It was a new one, mimicking the original, on the corner of Lecky Road and Fahan Street.

His wife looked at him, withdrawing her hand from his. "You never used to care for politics."

"I still don't, but the people who come into the shop to get their hair cut certainly do. I care about the people of this area."

"It's all people talk about. All day long," Mick said. "Just one day it'd be nice to not have to talk about internment, civil rights, RUC no-go areas or British soldiers."

"What do you expect, son?" Peter countered. "We live in an RUC no go area." He sighed and ran his hand over his cheek. "It's still hard to believe."

"You're in the wrong profession, little brother." Pat was 18 minutes older. He was smiling as he spoke now. "We've got to get you off to university like you're always going on about."

"I look forward to the day I get away from you." Mick was smiling too. "It'd be nice go one day without being mistaken for my brother, particularly when he's got a face like a badger's arse."

Peter and Pat both laughed, but Celine scowled. "Don't say that about your brother."

"I mean how is it possible, Mam, weren't you gave birth to the two of us and I'm so beautiful and he looks like that."

"Exactly like you, you mean?" Peter said, "I'd say you were about twelve by the time even I could tell you apart."

"Make that sixteen," Pat said. "In fact, what age are we now? Twenty? Make that twenty."

"How can you make jokes at a time like this?" Celine was verging on anger as she spoke.

"It's always times like this now," Mick said looking around. Every day there's something. When was the last time you left the house and you weren't reminded of all this going on?" He shook his head. "If we can't make jokes now, when can we?"

The crowds from Mass were dissipating. Mick wondered how many of them he would see later, how many wouldn't be intimidated by the presence of the soldiers. The soldiers on the city walls were visible, overlooking Bogside like vultures. Mick wondered what they could be expecting. Word was that the local IRA would stand down today. The masked gunmen they had become used to seeing in the last few years, defiant on top of the barricades, openly brandishing ancient rifles and pistols from World War II and before, would not be around by the time the march began. Mick knew most of them, to see at least. Most of them came into the barbershop. Some of them were boys he'd grown up with. Others were older republicans brimming over with hatred for everything that the British, or Protestants in general, represented.

As they reached Rossville Street, Celine and Peter said their goodbyes. Their mother hugged each one of them in turn, holding them just a little bit longer and more tightly than usual. Soldiers were scattered all over the area surrounding Bogside, the Catholic, republican area outside the city walls the IRA had cordoned off as Free Derry.

"Are you sure that you boys want to go on this march today?" Her face was lined with worry. "There are so many soldiers around."

"What are they going to do, Ma, start a war?" Pat asked. "They're only here for a show of force. It's all bluster."

Celine brought her eyes up to her husband. "There's always soldiers around now. I can only imagine that they're looking to make some arrests if things get out of hand," he said and looked at his sons. "Now, you two boys be careful. If there's trouble, you get out o' there. Don't be the ones hauled off. The Paras will be nothing on what I'll do if you get arrested." He embraced his sons, kissing each on the head before he let them go. "Remember, be careful, and we'll see ye both home later for dinner."

"Aye, of course," Mick said. "When have we ever gotten involved in all the stone throwing stupidity?"

"I know you haven't, but some of your friends, Jimmy and Noel. And Paul McGowan, every time I see his poor mother...with fourteen children to feed and no husband. Him getting arrested again will do nothing to put food on the table for that family," Celine answered.

Peter laughed. "Don't worry boys, I'll get this one home. You two be careful or you'll have me to deal with." He pointed a finger at them and then put his arm around his wife calling her a 'crazy French woman' as they walked away.

The run down tenements of Bogside seemed to close in around them as the twins walked together. An open door to a house revealed the squalor inside that three families shared. Crowds of people were starting to gather. It wouldn't be long before the march began. Somehow making the marches illegal had had the opposite effect. People who never would have marched before were out. Mick looked at his watch. There would be time, and she was waiting for him now. He turned to his brother. "I gotta go down the town and meet someone before the March."

"Who're you meeting? Not this mystery girl is it?" he smiled.

"Soon to be a mystery no more, my brother." Mick stopped and put his hand on Pat's shoulder. "She wants to come along with us today."

"She wants to come along?" Pat shook his head, the smile still on his face. "Why? A God-fearing Protestant girl like herself? What would she want with us Fenians? Come to infiltrate has she? She's a spy. That must be it. There's no other way she'd touch you anyways."

"Yeah, that's it. You've hit the nail on the head there, brother. She's been sent on a personal mission from Ian Paisley. That's what the Prods are trying to do, breed us out one by one." They both laughed before Mick continued. "Nah, she wants to come on the march. She's interested in the civil rights movement. Martin

Luther King. One man one vote, and all that stuff. She also wants to meet you."

"All right, I'm off to meet the boys." Pat reached out to shake his brother's hand. "I'll see you down at Bishop's Field at about 2.30."

Mick shook Pat's hand and walked away, past Aggro Corner, where youths would battle the British soldiers on a daily basis. The only thing that stopped them was the rain or dinner. There was a general agreement between the rioters and the soldiers that six o'clock was designated as teatime. Both sides would take a break for an hour before resuming hostilities at seven. Mick had been down there a few times, mainly when he was younger, but it all seemed so futile now. A horde of boys was already gathering there, angry at the troops, with stones in their pockets and frustration at their useless, unemployed lives seething through them. Getting hit by rubber bullets was an occupational hazard. The gaudy bruises that the bullets left were a mark of pride, an illustration of their commitment to the cause. The luckiest would show off the bullets that had struck them, big as a can of beans in their hand. Mick's cousin in Paris had asked for him to send over a rubber bullet as a memento. Not a good idea. Best not to get involved, as his father always said.

Mick passed over the rubble barricade strewn across the middle of Rossville Street. The intimidating red brick colossus of the Rossville flats hulked on his left. His thoughts turned to Melissa Rice, from Waterside, oldest daughter of the unionist councilor, Reginald Rice and he laughed to himself.

Pat raised a hand to greet the boys in the corner of the pub, priming themselves for the march. They cheered as he approached the table they were sitting around. Phillip was there with Noel and Paul and their neighbors Jimmy Kelly and John Gilmore. Jimmy was only 17, and still in school, but had a beer sitting in front of him. The pub was packed, but there was just enough space to squeeze in beside Noel on the end. Pat had enough for a pint but wondered where the other boys were getting the money for theirs. Apart from Phillip, whose uncle had gotten him a job in the DuPont rubber plant, they were all unemployed. Everyone under the age of 25 seemed to be. Pat and Phillip were the lucky ones but were always expected to buy the pints too. A palpable sense of excitement filled the smoky air. Everyone was talking about the march. They would all be there. Pat was sure of that. Today was going to be important. Everyone sensed it. To the boys, that was everything. Trapped in the ghetto of the Bogside, the autonomous nationalist breakaway state surrounded by British troops, the march was all they had to cling to that day. Tomorrow there would be something else.

"So boys, we gonna start some trouble today or what?" Jimmy said. "We'll show them Paras a thing or two, eh?"

"You're gonna show the Paras a thing or two, are ye, Jimmy?" Phillip shook his head. "They're carrying assault rifles. You know what one of them could do to your head?" He brought his fingers into a fist and then exploded them outwards. "Like a watermelon, my friend."

"They're not gonna start shooting live rounds," Noel said. "They never use real bullets. Well, almost never."

"What about that fourteen-year-old girl, shot dead last year, out gathering stones for a school project? That fifteen-year-old? He was coming out of the chip shop and got two bullets in his head. No reason for it. The Paras are complete bastards. Don't think they won't shoot you down," John said. His words were met with solemn silence, broken only when Noel changed the subject to girls, specifically Mick's new mystery girlfriend they were all so eager to meet.

She was waiting on the corner. They had developed a system where he would throw stones at the window, but this was the middle of the day, so they had arranged to meet on the corner of her street. There were no soldiers, no crowds milling around and there would be no march in this area of the city. The Bogside, across the River Foyle in the Cityside section of the city, seemed far away. But Melissa had agreed to take part in a civil rights march in the most staunchly republican area in all of Ulster. He could walk a little to meet her. Melissa's green eyes looked dewy and tired but seemed to brighten as he approached. Her flawless skin stretched over high cheekbones. Her long brown hair curled on the ends. She was wearing a red jacket and tight bell-bottom flares which showed off her long, slender legs. Her pristine make-up indicated the time she'd spent readying herself for him, polishing the perfection of her face. That felt good, a validation of him and their relationship. He was taller than her, about six inches taller, and he had to reach down to kiss her on the lips as she ran her hands through his shaggy blonde hair. No Catholic girls ever said hello like this, not the ones he knew anyway.

"How are you doing?" he began. "Are you upset about something?"

"Just the usual, all this sneaking around." She exhaled some of the stress inside. Mick watched her lips as she spoke. "I think my sister suspects something. If she knows, my dad is next."

"How would she know?"

"One of her friends must have told her."

"Told her what?" Mick went to hold her hand, but she pushed it away. He wasn't insulted. "How many Catholics from Bogside does your sister know?"

"About as many Protestants from Waterside as you do."

"I know a few," Mick smiled. "They're salt of the earth people, some beautiful girls there." They walked around a corner and off the street. Melissa pulled him close to her.

"Beautiful girls? Plural? You're chasing other girls from Waterside then are ye?"

Mick moved his face down to hers and spoke as her lips were touching his. "No, there's just one girl from the Waterside for me. One Prod is enough for anyone." He started laughing.

Melissa poked him in the ribs. "Cheeky monkey," she said with a wry smile.

They walked on, over the Craigavon Bridge and the great platinum blue expanse of the River Foyle that separated his side from hers. He felt the warmth of her hand in his as they moved through the army checkpoint and across. It was hard, hard for them to be seen in public together, but every time he thought it wasn't worth it, she did something or said something to draw him back in. Everything seemed so easy when it was just them.

"So, are you nervous?"

"About what?"

"About going on the march. About meeting my brother for the first time."

"I'm excited to meet your brother. The way you talk about him, I feel like he's a part of you. I thought I was close to my sister."

"It's different with twins."

"And he looks exactly like you?" She smiled. "Maybe you're the one who should be nervous. Maybe I'll run off with Patrick. Who knew that the best-looking boy in the whole city of Derry came in duplicate? That's what I call a good deal. If something happens to you, then I have him to fall back on."

Several cars full of people moved past. They were approaching Bishop's Field, where the crowds were congregating to go on the march. Internment without trial had been introduced less than six months before. Mick knew several men who had been scooped up in the nighttime raids that followed. Several regulars in the barbershop had been taken.

"How do you feel about the march? About marching in Bogside?" he asked.

"I feel great about the march. What the government is doing is wrong. You don't have to be Catholic to see that. I don't think that the government is handling the situation correctly at all. I'm delighted to be a part of something that's a force for good."

"Even if it's illegal?"

"Just because it's illegal doesn't make it wrong. And just because the RUC and the soldiers have the law on their side doesn't make everything they do right. Although if I get arrested today my dad is going to kill you." Mick started laughing again. "Oh, no, don't laugh, my friend. He will literally kill you. No joke about that."

"I'll have to make sure to keep you safe then." Mick thought about the warning from Father Daly and the build-up of Paras around the Bogside and the snipers on the city walls. "I should tell you that there's a pretty substantial army presence in town today." A helicopter appeared over their heads as if on cue. "Paras. They're tough bastards. Not known for their gentle manner."

"There's no way they'll open fire on UK citizens, their people," Melissa assured him, or possibly herself.

"If you say so," Mick muttered under his breath. He looked at her and she back at him. They stopped on the road.

"This is going to be safe, isn't it Mick?" Her voice was wavering. "I can meet your brother some other time."

"No, let's do this. It's going to be fine. As you say, they're hardly going to shoot down their own citizens, are they? And anyway, I'll protect you." He took her hand as they strolled on to join the people walking up toward the large crowd that was already gathering.

Chapter 2

The crowd was in high spirits, the atmosphere as if there were a big game that afternoon. Laughter and even excitement seemed to be everywhere in the multitude of people, lighting their eyes like lanterns. Everyone was there, old people, young families, accountants, doctors, barmen, plumbers, painters, lawyers, and they all seemed to have brought their kids along, running all over. It was hard to say how many people, maybe three thousand, or maybe five, or ten. Mick thought of his parents and began to wish that they'd come along themselves. Mrs. McGlinchey, there with her eight children, was the first person Mick recognized. She greeted him with a broad smile as he ambled past, hand in hand with Melissa. It wasn't right to introduce Melissa to anyone yet. Best to test the waters first. Pat wouldn't be a problem. Some others might be. But let them hold on to their bigotry. Mick didn't care. He took Melissa's hand as they walked up the hill toward the boys, who were waiting for them. Some people had already started singing 'We Shall Overcome.' The blue and white civil rights banner was blowing in the now stiff breeze. It seemed like there was magic in the air, and Melissa's smile widened with every step they took.

Mick saw his family and friends gathered in a group at the top of the hill and gestured to Melissa. Mick felt her try to let go of his hand, but he gripped hers even tighter. They walked as one. Pat was first to see them. "So this is her?" He stepped forward with a massive grin on his face and, ignoring her outstretched hand, hugged her. "You've done well, little brother," he said glancing at Mick.

Melissa stepped back. "Wow, identical twins. You weren't joking were you?"

"Can you tell the difference?" Pat asked.

"I think so." Melissa motioned for them to stand side by side. They were wearing different clothes, which they had always made a point of doing. Melissa put her finger against her lips as she looked at them. "Yes. Mick, you've got a thinner face," she nodded her head, backing her assertion.

"Excellent."

Philip stepped forward. "The way I tell them apart is that Mick's a dickhead while Pat's just an arsehole," he said, and Melissa started laughing. "So it's pretty simple really."

"Thanks, Phil," Mick said, "I wanted her to figure that one out for herself."

"I think I already had," she answered.

"Already figured me out?" Pat said. "That's a new record then." He held his arms up in the air in faux shock.

Noel was the next to step forward to introduce himself. He held out a hand, his face uncertain. Mick stared at him. Jimmy was no better, but John smiled as Mick introduced her. There would be time to talk to Noel and Jimmy later. There were always going to be people who didn't approve of this, although Mick had expected them to be older, and not his friends. He stepped back and put an arm around Melissa's shoulders. "So, quite a crowd for the march today, eh? Where's Paul?"

"He's going to come along later," Noel answered.

"Let me guess, you're gonna meet him at Aggro Corner?" Pat asked. Noel didn't answer. Paul, Jimmy, and Noel had taken to throwing stones at the British soldiers on Aggro Corner almost every night. They didn't have much else to do with their time. Saturday afternoon was an institution now, nicknamed 'The Saturday Matinee' by the locals. That was when the real crowds came. People were off work, kids were out of school, so they came to Aggro Corner to riot. They threw stones and bollards, paving stones and return any CS gas that might have been pitched their way. Mick could see the handkerchief soaked in vinegar, protruding from Jimmy's pocket for when the soldiers tried to gas them later on. There was no point talking to the kid, not when grown men rioted every day themselves. It wasn't just the norm, but the most commonly accepted free entertainment available in Bogside. Jimmy, Paul, and Noel had nicknames for each other. Jimmy was 'Firebomber,' Noel was 'Hammer' and Paul was the 'General.' Their mission that day was to get revenge on the soldiers for something or other that had happened a few days before. They'd said what, but no one listened anymore.

A flat-topped coal truck pulled up, and the leaders of the procession got on, their loudspeakers in their hands. Mick turned around as he heard his brother's shout.

"You made it," Pat said and as Mick turned around, he saw his father standing with two of his brothers and several friends. Melissa looked frightened now. Too much, too soon, Mick smiled to himself, and at her.

"Best to get them all out of the way at once, you'll love my dad, he's a legend around these parts." She seemed reassured, the confidence returning to her eyes. "Let me introduce you."

Mick led her over to where his father, uncles, and brother were standing, about twenty feet away. They were wearing their Sunday best clothes, shirts, and ties, pressed and laundered. Most of the marchers were.

"I couldn't miss this, Pat," Peter was saying as Mick walked over. "This means too much to the community. I couldn't just sit at home, not today."

"What did Ma say about that?" Mick asked. "I wouldn't say she echoed your sentiments."

"Nah she didn't, but she'll get over it." His eyes fell onto Melissa. "Who's your friend, Mick?"

Mick smiled and looked at Melissa. She stepped forward, holding out her hand. "My name's Melissa, Melissa Rice. It's lovely to meet you, Mr. Doherty."

Peter took her hand, looked at Mick, and then back at her. "The pleasure's mine. I don't believe I've seen you around before."

"I'm from Waterside, my father's a counselor there, Reg Rice."

"Well I'm delighted to meet you, Melissa Rice from Waterside, and welcome to Bogside." He was smiling now. "I'm so glad you've decided to join us on our march today."

"So am I, it's been wonderful so far."

"The information you shared with me just there, about your father? Let's keep that to ourselves for now, OK?" He winked and turned around to introduce her as 'young Mick's beautiful new lady friend,' to his brothers; Frank, Donal and Kieran, and his sisters, Ciara, Lisa and Deirdre. Mick and Pat said hello to each in turn. It took a while.

"You have a large family," Melissa said to Peter after she'd shaken their hands herself.

"Not around these parts. Around here anything less than a dozen is hardly worth mentioning. And me, with only two? The shame of it." He reached down to Melissa, his hand over one side of his mouth. "It's all down to me wife, you know, French, so she is." He shook his head, a fake puzzled expression on his face. "They're different over there, but I wouldn't change her."

One of the organizers on the truck said something indecipherable over the loudspeaker and the vehicle began to move and the people behind it. Exhilaration lifted the crowd, driving them forward in the coal truck's wake and the march started. Some of the stern women at the front with Belfast accents were trying to shepherd people into rows, but the young people didn't pay any attention and ran to the front. Jimmy, Noel and Paul with them. Pat knew the real reason Paul had been late; he had been getting the unexploded CS gas canisters that he'd picked up a few days before. Time to send them back.

The crowd was spread out; the atmosphere laid back. It was very hard to tell how many people were out. As they moved down through the Creggan, more and more people came out of their houses to join the march like streams running into the vast river of people, and the crowd began to tighten and swell. Mick, Pat, their father, and family were walking together with Phillip and Melissa, about fifty yards back from the lorry. The organizers of the march spoke through their respective megaphones, and the crowd was beginning to sing. The soldiers from earlier weren't to be seen, but the helicopter still circled overhead, buzzing like a vicious insect. Melissa moved toward Mick's father and asked him how he'd met his wife. Mick looked at the two talking and smiled. Peter had met her when he'd fought for the British Army in World War II. He'd been among the men who'd landed on the beaches of Normandy with the Royal Ulster Rifles and had met Celine when he was on leave in Paris. If you believed her stories, he'd harassed her until she finally agreed to go out with him and then eventually after the war was over, move back to Derry with him. But, in fact, they fell in love the first time they met. Mick and Pat had heard the story enough times, from both sides.

"So you've heard my story? What about yours?" Peter asked. He made sure no one other than Mick was listening. His family members were directly in front of them, but with the noise of the crowd, out of earshot.

"It's simple really. He found my wallet." Melissa looked up at Peter and then straight ahead, at the flat top truck moving in front of them at about five miles an hour. "He ran after me on the street and tapped me on the shoulder."

"So you did the old, steal the girl's wallet and then pretend you found it trick, eh, son?" he laughed. "I hope you thoroughly checked the contents after he handed it back to you."

"Da's the comedian in the family as you can see," Mick said to Melissa, who was red-faced with laughter.

"Where were you when you met?" Peter asked after they'd stopped laughing. "No offense Melissa, but I can't see you crossing the barricades into the Bogside too often."

"I was running down by the Guildhall," Melissa answered.

"I saw her drop her wallet, gave it back to her, and I had to ask her for a pint, I just had to." Mick continued.

"I can understand that I just can't understand why she said yes."

"How could I say no, to this face?" Melissa said, pinching Mick's chin.

"Well, the good news is that if you get sick of this one, I've got another that looks just like him."

Mick shook his head, but they all laughed again. "We've been seeing each other ever since. Six months now."

"And you never mentioned it?" Peter raised his eyebrows, tilting his head a few degrees. "I can see why. I had enough raised eyebrows myself marrying a foreigner. Being with someone from the other community? It's never going to be easy." There was silence for a few seconds. "This is a good way to meet people. On a day like today, people will see you for who you are."

"Aye, I did hope that, but that's not the reason I'm here. I do want to support the cause."

"I know that," Peter answered. "You've done well here, son. Now we'll just need to get your brother set up with someone who could stand him." He turned to Melissa again. "They look the same, but they don't act the same. Very different people."

The demonstration moved down William Street, passing the pool where Peter had taught his boys to swim. An excited, hopeful, almost carnival atmosphere prevailed among the crowd as they approached the junction of Rossville and Little James Streets. The waste ground of Aggro Corner came into view. A once busy shopping area, now destroyed. Rubble lay all over the street, thrown down to be used again in the next riot. Charred buildings and hulks of burnt out cars dominated the landscape now. And the Paratroopers were there, their faces painted black, their camouflaged jumpsuits in stark contrast to the distinctive red berets some wore though most had combat helmets on their heads. All had their rifles pointed at the crowd. Melissa grabbed onto Mick's arm. He tried to reassure her, but couldn't find the words. He patted her hand. Pat, who was standing beside Uncle Kieran, looked back at his father as if looking for an answer to this. Still they shuffled forward. Snipers surrounded them. Some on the wall by the Presbyterian church, some on the flat roof of the Post Office, some in derelict buildings. Mick could see the barrels of their SLR rifles poking through broken glass windows now covered with sheets of corrugated iron.

Some of the usual stone throwers took their opportunity and reached down to pick up whatever they could hurl at the soldiers. The teenagers at the front of the procession began to whistle and shout abuse. Not one soldier moved. Jimmy and Paul raced over to Aggro Corner and picked up the largest stones they could find. Paul almost hit one soldier, but he raised his shield in time. Noel just stood there, roaring abuse. There was a crowd of youths around them now. They had gotten what they were here for.

"I dunno what they're doing here, aiming their guns at the crowd like that. I can only assume that they're expecting some IRA action, but everyone knows they were to stand down today, surely the Paras do too?" Peter said out loud to no-one in particular though everyone heard.

"They've gotta be trying to intimidate us, trying to get us to call off the march," Mick answered. Melissa was still holding his hand. He could feel the sweat in her palm.

A barrier lay in front of them, a few hundred yards away at the end of William Street. The lorry leading the march turned right, down Rossville Street and away from the barrier. The young men at the front of the procession, including those who had been throwing stones on Aggro Corner raced down to the barrier, ignoring the path of the march. Suddenly a hundred, two hundred, of them were down there, Paul and Noel with them. Jimmy was still on Aggro Corner, but would follow them on. Mick looked at his father. The lines of worry were starting to appear on his face. On the lorry, the organizers shouted through their loudspeakers, trying to get the stone throwers to rejoin the march, but if they heard them, they paid no attention.

One of the organizers jumped down from the lorry to try to steer them back on course, back down Rossville Street but was ignored. More and more marchers rushed down to the barrier, which was manned by about twenty soldiers. The regular soldiers were dressed in the more usual riot gear, as opposed to the Paras, who were dressed for combat. More Paras stood a few yards behind the riot soldiers at the barrier. Waiting. They seemed everywhere, the vise tightening.

The crowd down at the barrier was thick with people. Jimmy couldn't find the others. He was beside one of his neighbors, John O'Neill, there with his three sons, all under ten years old. "English bastards, come out and fight like men!" Jimmy shouted, but his screams were lost in the cacophony of shouts aimed at the soldiers on the barrier. The crowd was so thick now that everyone was being pushed and shoved and crushed. Jimmy knew that rubber bullets would come soon. He intended to get one as a souvenir. An RUC officer shouted through a loud speaker, but once again no one paid any attention to his words. He may as well have invited the barrage that came as soon as his words ended. Chunks of paving stone, loose rocks, bottles, bricks, planks of wood, and whatever came to hand, rained down on the soldiers manning the barrier. The army officers took cover behind their armored vehicles. Several of the soldiers seemed to be hit, but as always most of the riot was ineffectual; for show.

A few hundred yards back, at the turning for Rossville Street, Mick and Melissa were standing with Peter, watching the rioting. Melissa seemed shocked.

Mick and Peter were calm, as were most of the marchers around them.

"I can't believe this," she said.

"I wouldn't worry about it," Mick assured her. "This is nothing unusual; this happens every day here. Sure, the army hasn't even used rubber bullets or CS gas yet. This is nothing to get worried about." He took both her hands. "Don't worry, we won't be joining in with that rubbish. We're going to stay well away from that."

Patrick and the rest of the Doherty clan had moved, barely even bothering to watch the melee as it developed down at the barricade. Mick looked around. British army barricades were all over, halfway up Little James Street and on Sackville Street, forcing the marchers into a bottleneck down Rossville Street. If the Paras moved in, there would be no escape. Mick called forward to his brother, who slowed down to wait for them as they moved down Rossville Street after the flattop lorry.

Back at the barricade, the British soldiers had moved in with the water cannon and soon the rioters at the front were all drenched in purple-dyed water. Everyone within a hundred yards was soaked and began to fall back, away from the barricade. Noel shook his head and sat down, tying his handkerchief over his face in case CS gas was next. Within seconds, there was no one within fifty feet of him. As Paul was running backward, drenched in water and purple dye, he ran into Jimmy, coming down from Aggro Corner. It was time to start exacting some retribution.

Chapter 3

Jimmy and Paul made their way down Chamberlain Street, lighting the CS gas canisters. Jimmy counted, one, two, three and they heaved them up and over the roofs of the houses between themselves and the soldiers guarding the barricade. The throws were good, and the crowd in front of the barricade cheered as the two gas canisters exploded among the soldiers, who scrambled for their gas masks. Jimmy and Paul ran around to survey the chaos they'd created. A thick fog of white gas was spreading over the barricade, enveloping the soldiers underneath. But the wind changed and the cloud of gas began to drift back toward the rioters themselves. Within seconds, some of the young men at the front were bent over, scrambling away through pools of their own vomit. Noel got up from his sitting position and ran backward. They all knew what was next in this game they played, and as soon as the gas cleared the first volley of rubber bullets came, answered by a hailstorm of missiles from the rioters.

All but the hardcore rioters fell back from the barricade and began to rejoin the peaceful protesters, who formed a large majority. Noel, Jimmy, John and Paul fell back towards Aggro Corner where rioters were congregating again to attack the other barricades. But these barricades were different. Mick looked back over his shoulder at the rioters and saw the Paras, lying in their shooting positions, the barrels of their rifles pointed down at them. He saw Jimmy and the other three boys as they reached Aggro Corner and then lost them in the crowd. He looked at his father and then Melissa. The thought to go back, to warn them, came into his head, but he dismissed it. The Paras would never open fire with real bullets. The marchers ambled forward.

Paul had been carrying a lemonade bottle, waiting for the right moment. "Watch this," he said and left the other three standing in the middle of the crowd. Several Paras had holed up in a derelict house, long since abandoned and subsequently burnt out, the barrels of their high-velocity rifles poking through the windows. Another volley of rubber bullets hurtled down the street as Paul ran towards the derelict house. Paul had just reached the house and hurled himself up against the wall when he heard a loud bang. But this bang was not the sound of a rubber bullet. It was something else. The noise rang loud in Paul's ears, and he grimaced in pain at being so close. As he looked up, he could see the barrel of the rifle poking out. Seeing a hole in the wall he jumped up and threw the bottle in. As he was in the air, he saw the Paras inside and saw the bottle strike one on the arm. Elated, he ran back towards the boys. More shots cracked. A crowd gathered in the middle of the waste ground, and as Paul pushed through, he heard the cries of pain. A young boy around his age, seventeen or so, was holding his leg as blood poured out through a round hole above his knee, his face etched in agony. Just beside him was a man in his fifties, seemingly shot several times. His movements were slow, his breathing checked. There were no bombs or guns in their hands. "What the hell happened?" he said out loud. "Is this my fault?"

The main body of the march was a few hundred yards down Rossville Street when they heard the shots. Peter jerked his head backward toward the noise, wide-eyed "That was no rubber bullet. They were SLR rounds. They came from the British soldiers."

Melissa gripped onto Mick's hand. "Are we safe?" She was shaking, and he put his arm around her.

"The best thing is to stay with the march now," Peter assured her. "I'm sure they were only warning shots. They're not going to use live rounds on the crowd."

Mick wanted to believe him but knew that he didn't believe the words himself. His eyes spoke a different truth.

Breaking off from the crowd now might be even more dangerous. So they kept walking, down Rossville Street toward Free Derry Corner. The lorry at the front had stopped just in front of Free Derry Corner and the organizers of the march were preparing to speak the crowd. There might have been around three thousand people or so. It was hard to tell with stragglers crossing over the rubble barricade that bisected Rossville Street to join the main body of the march at Free Derry corner. The organizers made their speeches, the crowd reacting with roars of support and cheers. Melissa stood there rapt. The civil rights leaders were becoming heroes to her, particularly Bernadette Devlin, the youngest female Member of Parliament in UK history.

John and Paul helped carry the bodies of the wounded men to safety. Jimmy and Noel were in the crowd, still chanting, still shouting, and throwing whatever they could at whatever British soldiers they could see. Without warning the barricade at the end of William Street opened and the Paras rumbled through in the armored vehicles they and the locals knew as 'pigs'. The crowd ran for cover, down Chamberlain Street, down Rossville Street, toward the main body of the march. John emerged from the building where he had carried the wounded young boy. He was arrested immediately, thrown up against the wall and searched by Paras with blackened faces. Paul saw his friend being taken, and knowing there was nothing he could do, ran as fast as he could, past the troops and down Rossville Street. It wasn't the first time John had been arrested. It wouldn't be the last. He'd be fine.

Jimmy ran down Rossville Street, with dozens, perhaps hundreds, of others. As he looked over his shoulder, he could see the advancing Paratroopers and more getting out of pigs as they pulled up. They were swarming all over now, and another shot rang out. The boy running beside Jimmy let out a gasp and fell straight down on his face. Jimmy assumed he had been hit by a rubber bullet and ran on. Another shot and Mrs. Gilmore, one of Jimmy's neighbors, clutched the back of her leg, screaming out, a pool of blood forming around her. The boy was dead. Someone was over his body, screaming. Jimmy stopped, and Mrs. Gilmore looked him with terrified eyes. "Get out of here, Jimmy, before they kill us all." Another shot pierced the air, and as they looked back, they saw a Para about fifty yards away take dead aim at them. Mrs. Gilmore waved her arms, "No, no, don't shoot, I've nine children, and I'm all they have!" The Para brought his rifle to his side and started to run toward them. Mrs. Gilmore grabbed at Jimmy. "Run, boy, get out o' here." Jimmy patted her on the shoulder and ran after the crowd down towards the rubble barricade on Rossville Street.

Every person in the crowd at Free Derry corner had heard the shots. The organizers of the rally were telling everyone to try to stay calm. The pigs came onto Rossville Street, stopping short of the rubble barricade, about five hundred yards away. The Paras jumped out and fanned across the waste ground that made up most of the area on either side of the broad street. Jimmy was just ahead of them and made it over the rubble barricade as the Paras took up their positions, sheltering behind walls or under any cover they could find. Panic began to spread through the marchers at Free Derry corner. "What's going on?" Melissa asked. "Do the soldiers usually come down here?"

Mick shook his head, staring back at the Paras. "No, they don't."

There were more shots, followed by the sound of shots being returned.

"That wasn't a high-velocity round," Peter told them. "That was an IRA shot." Peter had told his sons about the weapons the local IRA used, the same type that he had used in the war, almost thirty years before. Many of them didn't work, and bullets were rare. But there was always one. Mick saw marchers struggling with a local IRA man, wrestling an antiquated rifle out of his hands. The only shots now were from the Paras.

Jimmy saw Noel crouching under the cover of the rubble barricade, about thirty yards from where he was hiding himself. "They're shooting!" Jimmy shouted. "They're killing people!" More shots. A few hundred yards away a man running down toward them was flipped around by the impact of a bullet, yet still limped on. At the rubble barricade, Noel cursed out loud and stood up to look. Another gunshot shuddered the air, and he immediately fell backward, a spurt of blood coming out of his mouth as he hit the ground. He lay there for a few seconds, his chest heaving with his fading breaths, pumping crimson blood into the dirt.

"Jimmy, I'm shot." The words gurgled through.

Jimmy bent down to his friend, boiling tears in his eyes, molten anger within him. "Noel. Oh, Jesus, Noel."

Noel went to reach out to his friend, but his hand dropped. The shrill breaths emanating from his chest slowed and stopped, and he was dead by the time the three other boys came over to take his body away.

"Jesus, they're firing real bullets," Peter said, raising his voice with each word. "They're firing live rounds, take cover, take cover."

Fear spread through the crowd like an infestation. Everyone around them, hundreds of people, were crouching low to the ground, and everywhere the air shook with the sound of screaming and gunfire. Mick heard a yelp escape from Melissa's mouth as he put his arms around her shoulders, dragging her down.

The organizers of the march began to scream warnings to the crowd and threw themselves down on the flat surface of the lorry as more shots sliced the air around them. Another boy went down at the rubble barricade. More and more soldiers were pouring out of armored cars, scattering across Rossville Street.

Bullets were bouncing off the rubble in front of them, and another boy went down, about ten feet from where Jimmy had seen Noel die. A middle-aged man, seemingly the boy's father, ran to him and was hit by a bullet in the arm. There were no weapons anywhere on the barricade.

"Oh, sweet Jesus, what the hell is going on?" Pat yelled as he ran to where Mick and Melissa were crouching. The Paras were advancing toward them, rifles in their hands, almost at the rubble barricade two hundred yards away. "We've gotta the hell outta here!" He heard himself roar. Screaming marchers started to run, tripping over their own feet, bumping into one another. Some of the Paras shouted to cease-fire but still came the sounds of more bullets.

"What the hell are they shooting at?" Peter shouted. He grabbed onto Patrick and Mick and motioned back up the street. "Let's go." The crowd was fleeing in every direction. Peter, Melissa, Pat and Mick ran back towards the Rossville Flats for cover. Complete chaos reigned on Rossville Street. People were leaping over the rubble barricade, bumping into each other and falling. The Paras were arresting marchers, throwing them up against walls and still more shots, and everywhere the panic spread like fire through a parched forest. The organizers of the parade were still cowering behind the lorry. Several were trying to yell at people to get down, or in some vain attempt to tell the soldiers that the people were unarmed, that this was murder.

Jimmy and Paul, who had met again among the main crowd, ran to the right, in the opposite direction of the Dohertys. A large crowd, numbering in the hundreds, ran with them, desperate to escape the Paras' bullets. Everywhere there was screaming, shouting, blind hysteria. Shots rang out, and another man went down, and then another and another. They ran across a courtyard, but the Paras appeared around a corner thirty yards away and immediately started firing indiscriminately into the crowd and more people dropped. Jimmy and Paul reached a wall, four feet high and took cover behind it with several others. The Paras were following about fifty yards away. Jimmy peered back. Horror overtook him as he saw a Para shoot a man prone on the ground. He got up to run. He'd barely made three paces when a shot hit him in the back, spinning him around as he fell. Paul was frozen, barely able to breathe. Jimmy squirmed and then went still. Another man got up, holding his arms in the air as if to surrender, trying to help Jimmy, who was lying prostrate on the grass about ten feet away. "Don't shoot!" the man roared, but another shot hit him in the chest, and his body collapsed onto the grass beside Jimmy. The sound of screaming was everywhere, and the crying had begun.

Peter, Mick, Pat and Melissa were crouching down by Joseph's Place, a pair of small apartment blocks with thirty or forty other marchers around them. The forecourt of the Rossville flats was just a few yards away, and that's where they saw him, crawling on his belly, a trail of blood behind him on the asphalt below his body. The man, who was in his early thirties and wore the white handkerchief of a steward at the march, had plainly been shot and was trying to crawl to safety. He was about thirty yards from where they were hiding. Peter looked at the man, who was crying in pain. The man stopped. "Please, please, I don't want to die alone." He stopped as if to take a breath and then began again, his voice fainter now. "Somebody help me, God help me," he wailed.

Melissa was crying. "Can't someone help him?"

Peter bit down on his lip, anguish staining his eyes as the man cried out again. "I can get him," he said.

"No way, Dad, you're not going out there." Pat put his arm on his father's shoulder.

"It's too dangerous," Mick added. "He's stopped moving, he must be dead already."

"He's not dead, and I can get him." Peter reached into his pocket for a white handkerchief. "If I wave this, they won't shoot. I can get him. I can't let that man die alone." He pushed Pat's arm away. "I have to do this."

"No, Dad, no. Don't do it, please." Pat shouted, as his father stood up and began to inch his way out into the forecourt. The man was lying twenty feet away, now deathly still. Mick could feel his heart thumping like a hammer in his chest and hear the sound of people screaming and more shots in the distance. Peter held up the pathetically tiny handkerchief he'd take from his pocket, which licked the back of his hand as it fluttered in the breeze. No more gunshots rang out, and it seemed like the carnage was over. But then Mick saw a soldier run to the corner of the flats, fifty yards away and kneel to shoot. Mick tried to shout to his father, but his voice was lost in the sound of the shot that thundered through the air. Peter was ten feet from the man on the ground as the bullet hit him in the head spewing blood into the air around him. Pat roared something incomprehensible. Mick jumped to his feet, forgetting where he was, and any sense of danger as Peter collapsed onto the forecourt, his legs bent underneath his body in an ugly, ungainly pose. Melissa screamed. Mick tried to run to his father, but Pat was on his feet, holding him back. "No, they'll kill you too!" Mick tried to fight him, but Pat was on top of him, resting his entire weight on his body. Mick's face was pressed against the concrete and from where he lay he could see his father's lifeless, bloodied eyes and the pool of dirty crimson extending out from his corpse. The shots faded, and Mick and Pat ran out to their father, pushing through the small crowd already gathered around him. Mick fell to his knees, grabbing at his father's lifeless body, the tears uncontrollable, the pain like nothing he'd ever thought possible. He felt Melissa clutch him, could feel her body shuddering against the numbness of his. Pat crouched down over his father's corpse and fell on the asphalt clutching at his father's body. A few minutes later, after the gunfire and death had finally ended, someone laid the NICRA civil rights flag as an impromptu shroud across Peter's lifeless body.

Chapter 4

A hush descended, a blanket of mourning covering the Bogside. The next morning offered no escape. Gray faces came to the Doherty's house melding into one. They all came, young boys with the sleeves loose in their father's suits, old men with spit-shined shoes and jackets older than Peter had been when he died. Little girls wore their Sunday-best dresses, adorned with black ribbons. The ladies who'd seen times like this before wore black mourning dresses, although there'd never been any time quite like this. All tried to say something to douse the inferno of pain. But what was there to say? Mick longed to be away from the crying and handshakes, the well-meaning neighbors and friends, the vain attempts at some form of consolation and the cold talk of revenge. Pat was stoic, acting now as the man of the house, the man Mick wished he could have been, strong and resolute. Pat wore his father's suit and tie. They fit perfectly. Mick had his own suit but wished he didn't. He wished he could have worn his father's suit. He wished he could have felt the touch of his father against him one last time.

Mick saw Phillip at the bottom of the narrow staircase as he came down. Phillip made an attempt to smile at him but couldn't. He couldn't fake it. Neither spoke as Mick gestured for him to come out the front door. The two young men walked out into the cold gray outside. "Did John get out?" Mick began.

"Aye, last night."

"We should head over to Jimmy's house."

"What about Pat?" Philip's words came as a whisper. "He'd want to come along wouldn't he?"

"He's got too much to do here." Mick closed his eyes and shook his head. "Let's get out of here."

Some of the terraced houses had limp Irish flags hanging out the windows, even though flying the Irish tricolor was an illegal act in Northern Ireland. Others had pretty flowers in window boxes, splashing color out of the gray. Every house was familiar, a story, or a moment in time fixed to each one, some reference point to their community and their youth. They walked in the middle of the road, as there were few cars. Cars were a luxury few could afford.

"Paul's already gone and joined up." Phillip said.

The answer took a few seconds to come. "How d'you know?"

"I saw him this morning. He did it last night. He said there was a line of local lads queued all the way around the corner. Tommy Malone, Peter Sutherland, James O'Leary, Kevin McCourt. They all joined."

Mick didn't answer for a few seconds. The shock he had felt was giving way to the barbs of anger spreading inside him. "I can understand that."

Jimmy's house was a three-bed in a terraced row, unremarkable even though a family of seven lived there. A smaller crowd was filing through the front door to stand around inside, not knowing what to say. Only a few dozen. The two boys hugged Jimmy's mother, reserving handshakes for his father and four brothers. They sat in the tiny back garden, drinking warm bottles of beer, in the middle of a swarm of mourners. Melissa drifted through his mind. Why couldn't she come to offer her condolences? Who made these rules? Why couldn't he see the person he craved most? They stayed another hour before going to Noel's house to see the parents of another dead son.

Night came, and Mick was home, had been for hours. Pat stayed with their mother, held her as they sat on the couch together, but Mick was in his room, smoking, staring out into the darkness that had descended outside. Sleeping was out of the question. An impossibility. It was after midnight, and he needed to see her. He pulled his jeans on, his undershirt, a warm sweater and then his shoes. The door made no sound as he closed it behind him. Outside, the wounded Bogside was sleeping, only the ghosts and the drunks haunting the empty streets. Mick turned back to face the house and stood there for a few seconds. His mind filled with memories before the hurt inside drowned them out, and he lit a cigarette to distract himself as much as anything else.

The narrow street they lived on was entirely empty. There were no cars parked, as hardly anyone owned a car. There was no life, barely any lights on in any of the houses. Mick jogged down and onto Rossville Street. The barriers were still in place, and rubble still strewn all over the street. A few drunks stumbled around. Mick went forward toward the rubble barricade where Noel and the others had died. Flowers lay interspersed among the rocks, and the bullet holes were visible in the rubble even in the half-light. Over to the left, the lights of the forecourt where his father had died illuminated where he and the other man had fallen. A large pile of flowers marked the spot. He stood there for a minute or more, waiting for something, a whisper, a sign, a comfort from somewhere, but none came. Nothing. Another man walked over and mumbled something. Mick didn't even acknowledge his words. He just turned and walked away.

Soldiers stood on the street, not Paras, regular soldiers. The Paras had disappeared as quickly as they'd arrived. They weren't stationed in Derry and had been brought in especially all the way from Belfast. Why? To break up the march? To kill the civil rights movement? They'd done all that, but they hadn't brought the people of the Bogside and Derry to heel. The actions of the day before had been a deliberate attempt by someone to reinstate the status quo, to subjugate the people of the Bogside once more. Mick knew they'd reap a whirlwind of fire for what they'd done. He didn't spit at the soldiers or call them names, he didn't tell them that they would each die on this island or threaten their families like he'd seen done so many times. The hatred inside him remained taciturn. He didn't look at them as he squeezed out the one-word answers he had to give to prevent himself from being arrested. He thought of his father, not as the dead body on the ground outside the Rossville Flats, but as the vibrant, kind man he knew. The man who'd sheltered his family from the madness around them as best he could in life, but in death had brought them into the eye of the storm that was engulfing them. Mick wanted to talk to the soldiers. He knew contrition was beyond them but did they know who his father and the other marchers were? Did they know that the Paras had killed innocent men? Innocent boys? He moved past the barricade, his heart boiling, and as he turned the corner, he had to rest against a wall to contain the venom inside him.

It was almost one o'clock in the morning by the time he arrived at Melissa's pretty four-bedroom detached house. He immediately began searching for stones on the pavement outside. A well-aimed throw hit her window with a loud clack, and he ducked behind the bushes in front of the house. She was used to this, but rarely this late. The light appeared in her room. She opened the window and gave him the signal to stay where he was, and that she'd be down in a few minutes. Mick crouched down in front of the hedge, the memories of the previous day like hornets in his head. He didn't notice the front door opening and barely heard her whisper to him over the sound of his breath and the beating of his heart. He stood up and held her close to his body. Her heart was tranquil and slow compared to his. He kissed her.

"I love you," he said, surprised at the words as they leaped out of his mouth.

She was shocked, unsure if he meant what he was saying, but she felt it too. "I love you," she replied, and a single tear fell down her cheek. "I'm so sorry I couldn't be there today. My father would have disowned me. I've never seen them so angry as when I got home from the march yesterday."

"Who did you say you were there with?"

"Some of the girls from college, but I'm not sure they believed me." She breathed out hard. "They asked me for names. I'm not a good liar."

"What did they say about the march, about what happened?"

Melissa looked at him, wondered if he was ready for the truth. He wasn't. "They thought it was terrible, that the army was insane, that they should be brought up on charges, each one of them."

He took his hands away from her face, dropped them down to his side. An ugly sneer came over his face. "You're right, Melissa," he said stepping back. "You're an awful liar."

"I'm sorry." Her face seemed to turn red under the light of the lamppost outside her house. "I didn't think it was right to tell you what they said."

"What did they say?"

"They believe what the army said, that the people killed were IRA bombers and gunmen, that the Paras were only returning fire."

Mick gasped. "My father? You were there, Melissa."

"Of course I know, Mick, of course. They just believe what they heard on the television. They weren't there. I can't tell them."

"So, I suppose that's what everyone around here believes, what all the unionists believe."

"I don't know. Not me," she whispered. "I know the truth. It's just not the right time to tell them."

"My father was innocent. He had nothing to do with any violence or politics." Mick was trying not to cry, ashamed in front of her, but the tears were rolling down his cheeks. "Jimmy and Noel too, they were just kids, throwing a few stones, they'd no jobs, nothing else in their lives."

She hugged him again. "It's OK, my darling, it's OK. I love you."

Her words soothed him, and he stood there in her arms as she held him, running her fingers through his hair.

Chapter 5

The hearses were lined up outside the church, ready for the short drive through the rain to the City Cemetery. So many people choked the streets that it wasn't possible to go more than five miles an hour. Mourners crowded everywhere, onto lampposts, on top of buildings, and in every window along the route, many draped in Irish flags. Each of the victim's families was showered with the hugs and handshakes of strangers as they emerged from the hearses that carried them. Celine was quiet, draped in grief. Mick searched the crowd for Melissa. Even though she'd told him she couldn't be there that it was too much, he'd still hoped that she was somewhere in the ocean of people standing out in the driving rain.

Melissa watched at home that night, as the boy she'd told she loved, carried his father's coffin through the black iron gates of the graveyard. Jenny, her younger sister by four years, asked if they could change channels. Melissa snapped back at her, and Jenny walked out of the room muttering something incomprehensible. Melissa was still watching as her mother sat down on the couch beside her. Her mother lit a cigarette and stared on for a few seconds before she began. She was as beautiful as her daughters, with chestnut brown hair past her shoulders and hazel green eyes.

"I still can't believe you were on that march the other day." Her voice was colored by the anger Melissa could see in her eyes. "If your grandfather knew."

"What, Mam, what? What would he say?"

"He'd be worried, pet, worried as I am." She took a deep pull off her cigarette. "You could have been shot, caught in the crossfire between the army and those terrorists." The sound of the front door closing interrupted her. "Here's your father now, I'd turn that television off right now if I were you."

Melissa's mother greeted her husband with a kiss in the hallway. Melissa didn't move, even when she heard him come into the room.

"I see you're watching the funerals then?" he started. "Bloody traffic on the way home because of them was something awful. Have they started rioting yet? It's all they seem to bloody well do." Melissa turned around to face him but didn't speak. The lines on his forehead seemed to be deepening by the minute. "Change over the channel. I've had quite enough of the civil rights march for one week, thank you."

"I wouldn't have to watch it on the TV if you'd let me go as I'd asked." And though she wasn't looking at him she could sense the disgusted look forming on his face, could feel it.

"Are you serious, are you bloody serious?" He raised his voice, not quite shouting, not yet. "Have you go up the Creggan, for the funerals of IRA terrorists? After what happened?"

"They weren't terrorists, Dad." She stood up, her eyes slicing into his. " I was there. You weren't. I saw what happened. The soldiers cut them down..."

"And you know, do you? You know who all these people were?" He was shouting now, and Melissa's mother reappeared at the door. "Those soldiers are the best the Crown has to offer, the very best."

"They murdered them," she said. Her voice was cold as the bodies in the ground. "None of the people I saw were armed. The Paras just shot them down."

"Nonsense, utter nonsense, I won't hear this in my own house." He hadn't taken off his coat yet, and his umbrella was still in his hand. "Who were you at the march with? Who's filling your head with this rubbish?"

"I told you; I was there with some girls from college." Her voice was cracking as she spoke now.

"What girls, what are their names?"

"You don't know them, Da, you don't know any of my friends."

"And you wonder why?" He brought a hand up to his forehead. "What is this cause you're taking on, going to these marches?"

"I've only been on one," she screamed back, forgetting herself.

"Yes, yes, and look how that turned out." He stepped closer to her, only about a foot from where she was standing. The lines around his eyes were much deeper than she remembered. "This cause, this IRA mayhem that you're subscribing to. What do you know about that?" He dropped the umbrella and turned to take off his coat. She could hear the raw breaths coursing in and out of his lungs. "You know my Uncle Charlie was killed by IRA thugs, not twelve years ago."

'This has nothing to do with that," she replied, her voice weaker.

"This has everything to do with that." He pointed a finger at her and let it hang in the air. He took a breath, seemingly trying to calm himself. "These terrorists have been trying to destroy our community, questioning our very right to be here, ever since the inception of this state, and before. Your participation in these activities, which propagate the ideas and activities of these murderers, is a betrayal of all that we stand for as good, hard working British people."

"It wasn't about that, Dad, it wasn't." She was crying as she spoke and as she looked across she saw her mother was too. "It was about giving the people the right to represent themselves."

"Do you hear yourself, Melissa?" He turned around and then back to face her. "Do you even hear what you're saying? These people don't want us here. Have you seen what it's like down south? Have you seen that 'paradise' down there? It's a third world country. They proclaim their hatred for all things British but then go begging to Her Majesty's government for their basic needs. If the Catholic people of this city want that life, then they're welcome to it. The Republic is only three miles away."

"Why should they leave? This is their home."

"Well, then, they should learn to live in their community without rioting and killing. They should learn to use the ballot box like we do." He turned to walk out of the room and had taken a couple of strides before he heard her answer.

'They can't," she said. "That's the whole point of the marches. The process of gerrymandering means that they're not represented."

Reginald turned around again. "So they think that firing on Her Majesty's soldiers is going to get them these rights that they're looking for?" He clasped his hands together, his knuckles pink and white. 'This is not your fight, Melissa. There are so many problems in our community, so much that I see in my job every day. Why are you taking their side?"

She took a step towards him. "It's not about sides. It's about standing up for what's right."

"Who are these people you're hanging around with these days?"

Every muscle in her body was oak, her pulse thundering in her ears. Melissa's gaze drifted to the television. Mick and Pat carried their father's coffin through the lashing rain. She had to leave, had to get away from this man, and she threw her hand in the air and rushed past him, outside into the deep chill of the night. Union Jacks hung out of several of the windows on the street that hadn't been there the previous day. Her breath was cold condensation, clouds of white forming and disappearing in front of her. The rage surging through her faded and died. Uncle Charlie's funeral had been on a day like this, back when she was eight. She'd cried then though she barely knew him. It seemed like the right thing to do. She thought of Peter, the march, the shooting and the death and began to question her own mind, her own memory. Was there any way that the Paras might have thought they were armed? She ran the pictures of his death through her mind again like a home movie, each shot fading into the next. The man on the ground was crawling, and they'd shot him again. Perhaps he had been shooting at the

Paras but where was his gun? Why had she only heard the shrill cracks of the Paras guns and not the dull sound of the IRA's? How much did she really know about Mick and his family? No, that was ridiculous, she knew Mick. She felt her love for him like a precious essence inside her.

She went back inside and flopped down on the couch beside her father, who had changed the channel. She smiled at him and put her hand on his. It took him a few seconds to look at her, but when he did, a smile broke out on his face.

"I just want you to be safe," he said.

"I know."

"I'm just trying to do the best for my community, for the people most important to me. If we don't stick up for ourselves, no one else will. The British government would just as easily cast us aside if we don't cling onto them. They won't want their soldiers dying for this part of the country. Not now that the economic importance of this province is fading. They'd get out of Ulster altogether if they could and leave us in a civil war."

"I know that too." She hugged him and then got up to go into the kitchen. The phone was hanging on the wall. Melissa hesitated. This wasn't something they usually did. Phone calls were meant to be for emergencies only. Surely this constituted that. Seeing him on TV and not being there for him was more than she could bear. She needed to hear his voice, to offer some measly part of herself to him. The flowers she'd sent were no doubt lost in the avalanche he'd receive. Her mother was in the lounge with her father. Her sister was in her room. The receiver felt heavy in her hand as she dialed the number. The phone rang twice before an unfamiliar voice came on.

"Hello," she started, "is Mick there?"

"He's not available right now." It was a man's voice. An uncle?

"Can you tell him that it's Melissa? I do think he'd want to speak to me, I think I met you at the march on Sunday."

"I wasn't on the march. Nice try." It wasn't one of his uncles. "Can't you hacks just leave us in peace for one day?"

The phone went dead.

Chapter 6

Three days passed, and Mick had run out of reasons not to open the barbershop again. Celine came into the shop with him that morning and placed a large framed picture of Peter on the wall. She didn't cry, just stared at it for a few seconds and left. Mick opened up. A steady line of men came in that day, not all in need of a haircut. It was easy to nod and chime in with the right answers at the right time because they all said the same things. The pain inside him ground their good intentions to dust. Lunchtime came as a relief, an escape. The phone rang. It had rung several times that morning, each time a concerned voice on the other end offered commiseration or support. No one said what he was thinking. Was it because they didn't dare say it out loud or that they just didn't know? More and more boys from the neighborhood had joined, John and Phillip among them. But Pat wouldn't discuss the possibility. He said that they should wait, that it wasn't their role to hand out justice, that they should wait for the results of the inquiry and let the government handle it. Mick agreed with his brother. They would wait.

The phone was still ringing. Mick took his head out of his hands and looked at it. He walked over and picked up the receiver.

"Hello?" It was her.

"Melissa," he breathed out hard. "Oh my God, it's so good to hear from you." Her voice was enough to drag some light into the black reaches inside him.

"Where have you been? I feel like it's been months since I saw you."

"I tried calling your house, but I couldn't get through."

He savored each syllable she uttered, waiting a few seconds to reply. "My house is full of people. Most of the time when the phone rings we ignore it. Everyone calling is a journalist or worse."

Melissa wanted to ask what he meant by 'or worse' but decided not to. "I've been thinking about you all the time. I wish I could be there for you."

"I wish you could be here."

"How have you been?"

"As bad as I ever could have imagined." His voice was diluted, hollow, a carbon copy of a carbon copy.

Thoughts raced through her mind. What to say? How could she make this better, or at least bearable? "How's your family? How is Patrick? How is your mother?"

"My mother is tough, but this is so much. I'm trying to be strong for her, but it's difficult." His father was looking down at him, the serious face in the black and white picture on the wall. It didn't suit him. He should have been smiling. Pictures and memories were all he'd ever be now. "Pat is a rock. I don't know what we would have done without him. He's back at work since yesterday."

"Don't think that he's any stronger than you, Mick. We all deal with things in different ways." Mick didn't answer; just stared into his father's eyes. Pat was a better man than he was. He always had been. "You've both got great qualities..." Melissa continued.

"People think because you look the same, you are the same. They've thought that about Pat and me our whole lives. But really, I'm not half the man he is." He was glassy-eyed as he spoke, not exactly conscious of seeing anything or being anywhere. "I want to handle this the same way he does, with the same strength."

"I love you, Michael James Doherty. I don't love Patrick. You look almost exactly the same, but I know you're not and I love you."

Mick let the words caress him, swirl around him like a sweet aroma.

"I want to see you. I need to see you."

"OK, I'll be able to a little bit later. I'll get away then."

"Come and see me in the shop, after I close, about six."

"That's great. I'll see you then." She went to hang up, but he caught her attention one last time.

"Oh, and Melissa, I love you too."

He heard her laugh before the click of the receiver.

He felt her with him for the rest of the day. Her words were like a lantern thrown down into the chasm of pain within him, its gentle flame flickering through the deep darkness.

The rains poured down that afternoon. The shop was empty. Mick turned up the radio to full volume as he tried to focus his attention on the wrinkled pages of the newspaper in his hand. The bell above the door chimed. A man stood in the doorway, shaking the rain off. Mick helped him take off his coat and led him to the chair. The man was in his early forties, small, but solidly built with a round face leading up to an egg-shaped head. He wore a full brown mustache. His thinning hair didn't need the trim he asked for, but Mick didn't question him. Mick began in silence, not really in the mood for conversation. The sound of the radio and the soft rain on the glass outside was the only noise in the otherwise empty barbershop.

"This is my first time in the barbershop. I'm from Creggan, myself."

"Welcome," Mick smiled but stopped there.

The man in the chair caught eyes with Mick in the mirror in front of them. "I see the picture of your father over there. I hear he was a great man, a respected man in the community. I wanted to offer my sincerest condolences."

"Thanks," Mick coughed. "It's strange not having him here. It's a hard time."

"I can only imagine." The man shifted in the seat. Mick withdrew his hands.

"I wasn't on the march last week. That's not my struggle," he said.

Mick looked at the man staring back at him in the mirror. "It's not my fight. It wasn't my father's fight either. We're not the types of people to get mixed up with politics."

"Sometimes politics gets mixed up with you."

Mick didn't answer. An uneasy silence settled in the barbershop. Mick wished he'd closed the shop today, wished that Melissa had come early, wished that his father was here, the person he needed to speak to most. The silence grew. It was huge. The man looked up at Mick again.

"I heard about your father," he said. "I spoke to a lot of people who were there. They told me how he died."

"I don't need to speak about it, sir, I saw it myself." His words were sharp as the scissors in his hand.

The man ignored Mick's tone, pressing on. "I can't tell you how sorry I am. There can't be many worse things that could happen to a man." Mick didn't answer. It was too hard. He stood back, wondering if he could finish, could get this man out of the shop now, but there was still some to do at the back. "A lot of people around here have suffered the same grief as you did, and not just on that day. Everyone knows someone who's been affected in the last few years."

"It's been a hard time."

"It has. It's been a very hard time for the Catholic people of this city. Mass unemployment, lack of housing, a political system that doesn't recognize them as the majority that they are."

"And then Bloody Sunday happened," Mick added.

"Yes, it did. And who's there to stand up for the Catholic people of this city? Who's to stand between them and the British Army next time they decide to use Catholic people for target practice? The RUC? The politicians in Stormont?"

The anger flamed inside Mick. "Don't make me laugh. They don't care a jot for the Catholic people here." The words sounded strange coming out of his mouth; as if he were listening to someone else speak through him, his same voice, and his mouth. The other man seemed encouraged.

"There's no police force for the people of this city, no government that speaks for them. Why else was Free Derry formed? You think people would have barricaded off Free Derry if there weren't the need?"

"Of course not." He felt fortified by the man's words. It felt good to agree with him.

"There's only one organization that is in place to protect the Catholic people of this city and this whole province."

The clamor for revenge, or some measure of justice that had driven John and Paul to join up began to grip him, choking him from the inside. "The IRA?" he said. It had only been a matter of saying it out loud.

"Of course, the Provisional IRA."

"Who are you?"

"My name's David McClean. Apart from that.... I'm just a concerned citizen getting a haircut. If you lock that door, we can talk. If you want to help your community, to strive to improve the lives of the Catholic people of this city and this province, then we can talk. If you want to make sure that the perpetrators of the killings on January 30th don't go unpunished, lock that door and we can talk."

Three seconds passed with no words. The invitation hung heavy in the air. Mick put the scissors down on the counter. His father's face on the wall remained unchanged. Mick went to the door, his steps slow and deliberate. The raindrops were still running down the window, leaving silver trails. He brought down the sign saying the shop was closed and locked the door. "All right, I'll see what ye have to say."

The man didn't move, was still sitting in the barber's chair. "I'm a member of the Derry Brigade. In the six days since the murders on Bloody Sunday, we've seen our membership almost triple. I'm sure you have friends who've joined."

"Aye, I do."

"The young people of this city have realized, have seen with their own eyes, the utter contempt the unionist government in Stormont and their masters in London hold them in. They've realized that they need to take the situation in this province into their own hands."

"Why are you here, talking to me about this, if you've so many new recruits?"

"One of our new recruits asked that I speak with you. He told me that you have a twin brother and that you're both very smart, capable young men, and he told me about what happened to your father."

"My father didn't approve of violence, or the Provos."

McClean smiled, seemingly amused at the nickname Mick used, but the smile melted, and his face was stern determination once more. "When we were talking earlier, I mentioned the fact that sometimes, even though we've no interest in politics, it drags us in. Well, these are the times we live in, Mick. Can I call you Mick?"

"Aye, of course, a lot of people do."

"You can't avoid politics living where we do. The simple fact of it is that we're at war. You didn't believe that before, but you believe it now, don't you, Mick?"

Melissa came into his mind, her smile, and her touch. He felt the picture of his father behind him, could feel the energy from it without even looking. His father had fought for what he believed in, even though fighting wasn't his way. "Aye, I suppose I do believe it now."

"What the Paras did last Sunday was an act of war, no doubt about it. We can't allow that to happen again. We can't as Irish Catholic men, stand by while soldiers of the British Empire murder our people in front of us."

"What about the inquiry into the killings?"

McClean reared back in his seat, almost as if the words had burnt him. "Are you serious, an investigation by an English Lord into killings by the Parachute Regiment of Catholics in Northern Ireland? Are you seriously expecting anything other than a whitewash? The Ministry of Defense has already come out backing their troops. Widgery can't do anything but corroborate their stories. Anything else would be an admission of guilt. Anything else would be an admission that their whole sectarian system in Northern Ireland is wrong. How would that look for the British Empire on the world stage?"

Mick thought about what Pat had said. 'I think the British deserve a chance to dish out justice.' But those words seemed more absurd with every passing day and Mick wondered if Pat had only uttered them for the sake of their mother.

"You're expecting justice from a government who sends in those animals, who subjugates the Catholic people of this city? You're just plain wrong, Mick. The only justice we'll get from the British government is justice we take." He had balled his fingers into a fist. "The only reason our people in the south got their Independence was that they fought for it. But they sold us out and left us in the hands of the Protestant ruling class. The British Empire doesn't give anything away. If you want something from the British, you have to take it, by force."

"My father deserves justice."

"It's not just about your poor father, God rest his soul. Your dad was an honest man, a good person, trying to raise his children and make a half-decent living. Not one of those people murdered on Bloody Sunday was a terrorist, but the government has lied with every statement they've made about the march and that's not going to change. It's not only about taking some concept of justice; it's about providing peace and security for our people so that good, honest men like your father don't get murdered in the streets. It's about providing freedom for our people and the only way the Catholic people of this province will ever be truly free will be if the British are thrown out."

Mick sat down, ingesting McClean's words, his legs suddenly heavy. What would Pat say to this man? "So, why did you come to see me today?"

"Just what I said before; I heard about you and your twin brother, your identical twin brother. I wanted to offer you my sincerest condolences, and then tell you that there are options. There are things that you can do to help the cause of your people both here, in this city, and throughout the province as a whole."

"You want me to join the IRA, to fight for the rights of the Catholic people?"

"There are plenty of ways to help the cause. That would be one of them." McClean's stare was so intense Mick thought it might burn a hole through him.

"I don't know. I couldn't leave my mother, or my brother, I'd have to see what he'd say." Mick shuffled the newspapers on the bench, tidying them into an orderly pile.

"Everyone's got their own path in life, Mick," McClean said, his tone softening. "Your brother's path might be different than yours, but if you did want to join us together, we could find a lot of uses for you both, together and separately. As for leaving your mother - you wouldn't have to. You could stay right here in the city."

Melissa. How could he be with her and be with them? Not now, not ever. He looked at his watch. She would be here in the matter of a few minutes. A knock on the door sounded through the shop.

"There's someone else here to see me," Mick said, his voice betraying his nerves.

McClean stood out of the chair. Mick brushed him down, fully aware that Melissa was stuck in the rain outside the door. She knocked again.

"Who is that?" McClean asked. "Your girlfriend? She seems pretty eager to see you."

"Just a friend, no one important really," he smiled. "I'd better let her in though." He paced to the door, unlocked it.

"What are you doing locking the door when you knew I was coming?" Melissa began. Mick tried to quiet her with his eyes, but she didn't take the hint. "I walk all the way up here from..."

"Melissa, I was having a conversation with my friend here." Mick interrupted, and some realization came over her.

McClean stretched a hand to Melissa. "David McClean, pleasure to meet you."

"The pleasure's mine," she smiled. "Melissa O'Hara."

"It's nice to meet you, Melissa. Look after your man here." He slipped into his coat as Mick handed him the umbrella. No words were spoken. No glances exchanged. "Goodbye folks," he said as he strode out into the rain.

Melissa waited until she saw McClean running across the street before turning to Mick. "Who the hell was that?"

"No one, just one of the organizers of the march last week, come to get a statement from me. No one to worry about." The weight of the lie slowed the words as they came out of his mouth, but she seemed to believe him, merely nodding her head before she leaned in to kiss him

Chapter 7

Dawn came as a tender mercy to Celine Doherty. Sleep was beyond her. The loss of Peter was still fresh inside her, an undressed wound. The dark ocean of the rest of her life without him spread out in front of her. The letter her mother had sent her, urging her to come home, was on the bedside table. The boys were old enough now, she'd said, they could find their own ways if they didn't want to come too. With Peter gone, what was left to keep her in a city where 'innocent people were mown down by Imperialist British soldiers.'? Celine picked up the letter again, read the impeccably written words on the most expensive paper her mother had. Celine's father still worked six days a week in the grocer's shop he'd run since 1925, the year she was born. Her mother had suggested that she could help him with the running of the store. Age had withered him, only his grim determination keeping the store afloat now.

Celine was forty-six. Her parents had never fully approved of her moving to this troubled town. They hadn't been able to make it over for the funeral. Peter had never been the man they wanted. They'd wanted a doctor from Auteuil, a lawyer from Neuilly, a captain of industry from the 16th Arrondissement, not a barber from Derry. They never visited. Not for the birth of the boys back in '51 and not for her husband's funeral.

Celine placed the letter back into the envelope and back onto the bedside table. The red-orange light of sunrise was leaking in through a chink in the curtains.

She was so used to waking first, seeing him there asleep beside her. His pillow was fresh, unused. The clothes in his closet were neat from where she'd put them away herself. There were no shoes strewn across the bedroom floor, and there were no shirts or ties hanging off the chair at the end of the bed. The room was clean, horribly clean. Silence had replaced the noise of life in the house.

The house was still quiet an hour later as Celine sat at the kitchen table with her sister. It was a pleasure to speak in French. The boys had been fluent once and could be again, but it was a long time since she'd spoken to them in her language. It felt like home.

Melissa ate dinner in silence, concentrating on chewing her food. What was the worst that could happen if they knew about Mick? What law said that she couldn't be with him? Jenny was talking about school, her mother and father's faces a picture of rapt concentration. Melissa put down her fork, watching her sister's mouth moving until she realized she was talking to her. Melissa shook her head and asked Jenny to repeat the question, something about a neighbor of theirs. Melissa was short, almost dismissive with her, but then immediately apologized. Her father's glare was like the rays of the sun through a magnifying glass. She felt it burning through her. The mood was suddenly different now.

Melissa smiled at him and apologized to Jenny again. Reg began to talk about something else, one of those anecdotes from work he always told. They all laughed, as much from the familiarity of his facial expressions as he told the stories they'd heard before as anything else. As much from the love they felt for him.

Dinner ended. Melissa volunteered to do the dishes with her mother. What she'd seen was like an open wound inside her. The crushing need to tell someone bobbed to the surface of her mind. She looked across at her mother. Could she trust her not to tell her father? What chance did her relationship with Mick have if she could never tell her parents?

Melissa's mother, Carol, had been engaged by the time she was her age. Melissa knew what she was thinking. She was a local busybody, in the nicest possible way. "So, a lot of my friends ask me about you, and why you don't have a boyfriend, a beautiful young girl like yourself." She reached through suds and into the murk of the water in the basin, fishing out knives, forks, and spoons.

Melissa had been deflecting this one for a while. It didn't seem to matter what she said; her mother kept asking. It seemed so trivial now. What did it matter if she were going out with a Catholic boy from the Bogside when people were being shot down in the streets? Really, what did it matter?

"Well, I have been seeing someone for a while now."

Carol smiled to herself, only looking at the cutlery she was washing. "Thank you for admitting that at last. I've had my suspicions for a while."

"You have?" Melissa stopped, put the plates down on the sideboard. "How?"

"A mother notices these things. You think I don't know you?"

Melissa smiled and nodded her head. Melissa tried to gauge how much she knew from the smile on her mother's face, the light in her eyes. She wished she knew everything. She wished everyone did. Melissa peeked into the living room, to make sure her father wasn't listening. "Does Da know anything?"

Melissa's mother shook her head, still smiling. "No, love, men don't notice things like that. You've been so happy, even happier than usual. There's a look in your eyes. It's hard to explain, I just knew."

Melissa leaned back against the counter. The dark of night had descended outside. There was nothing else to do but tell her. "It's funny that," Melissa said and turned around, picking up the plates again. She picked up a kitchen towel to dry them, but they were already dry. She could feel the weight of her mother's stare, the expectation. There was no avoiding this now. "I've been seeing him for a while. His name's Michael." The name was neutral, not giving too much away, perhaps she could avoid the details, leave them for another time.

Carol held her gloved hands out flat to the sides. "And? Where did you meet this Michael?"

Melissa smiled, as much to herself as outwardly. The memories of that day were a warm, safe place. "I met him on the street, believe it or not." Her mother was fascinated. "I was walking down by the Guildhall, doing some shopping and he came up to me. I'd dropped my wallet, and he brought it back to me. It's pretty silly."

"It's not silly at all," Carol said. "You know when your father first saw me he tripped me up in the restaurant to get my attention."

"I know, you told me, how he got past that is beyond me."

"With a lot of charms, but enough about us. What about Michael? Where is he from? Is he a local boy? Does he go to college with you?"

"No, he doesn't go to college, not yet, anyway. He wants to study engineering, but he's still saving his money."

"And..." Carol said, waving her arms. She didn't suspect anything. "Is he from around here, do I know his mother?"

"No, you don't know his mother." Melissa felt sweat on her palms although it was quite cold in the kitchen. She glanced around again to make sure her father wasn't listening.

"He's from the Bogside; he's a Catholic."

The smile on Carol's face was still there, but her eyes betrayed it. "Oh." She turned around, back towards the washing up, processing what her daughter had said. "So I suppose that's why you were at the march last Sunday?" Melissa didn't answer. "Melissa," her mother began. She seemed to be grasping for the right words. "How long have you been seeing this boy?"

"Six months now." Melissa was working scenarios in her mind, wondering how much of the truth she could reveal, how much would be too much. "He's sweet and..."

"Where do you see him?" his mother interrupted her.

"Where we can. I go to see him where he works. He comes to visit me at college."

"I'm sure Michael is a wonderful young boy, but I think you need to stop seeing him before things go too far." Her voice was low but in no way calm.

"Before things go too far?" Melissa's whisper bit at the side of her throat. Her father still hadn't heard them. "What do you think is going to happen?"

"You were with him on the march last Sunday? The march they're calling 'Bloody Sunday'? That was him, wasn't it?" Melissa could feel the tears welling in her eyes. She nodded, afraid to say more. "What if the soldiers had mistaken you for one of the terrorists they shot that day?"

"They didn't shoot any terrorists, none that I saw. I only saw them shooting innocent people."

Carol brought her hands out of the water and took off her gloves, throwing them down. "You see what being around these people has done to you, already? Are you siding with them over the government? You're siding with those.... people?"

"Why do I have to take sides? Why can't I just see who I want to see?"

"Melissa, I'm not telling you who you can and can't see. I'm just telling you that I'm worried about you, that I'm concerned for your safety, for your life."

Melissa stopped herself from saying what felt natural to say, afraid of the truth of what had happened, knowing what it would do to her mother. "What do you want me to do from here, then?"

"I want you to carefully consider what you're doing. I want you to carefully consider your father's feelings, how important our culture is to him and how something like this could affect him." Carol walked toward her daughter, was inches from her as she spoke. "We love you, Melissa, so very much. We just want the best for you."

"What about what I want?"

"You think you know what you want right now, but in a few years time, in a few months time you'll realize that I was right. There are so many handsome boys around here who'd love to take you out."

Melissa thought of Michael, how no one had ever made her feel like he did, his eyes, the kindness in his heart. How could she leave him now when he needed her most? She had seen what had happened on the march. Her parents had not. Lying was her only recourse, for now.

"I know you want the best for me, Ma. I'll think about what you said. Just give me a little time, and don't tell Dad, please?"

"I won't breathe a word, believe me, it's better that way." Carol hugged her daughter. "You know we've nothing against Catholics, nothing at all. It's just you're making your life so much harder than it needs to be." She stood back looking at Melissa as she held her at arm's length. "I wish things were different. I wish the two communities could live together. I wish they'd accept us, that they'd recognize that this is our country too, but they don't, so we have to look after ourselves."

"I know," Melissa muttered and picked up the plates to finish cleaning up.

It was two hours later, and Melissa was sitting by her bedroom window, wishing for him, when he came to her. She watched him draw his arm back to throw the stone, opening the window just before he threw it. She raised a finger to her lips and signaled him to go down the street to wait for her. They would have to be especially careful now. She was already fully dressed. Her parents were in bed, the light in their room off. There hadn't been any more talk about Mick and her mother hadn't told her father. There wouldn't have been any hiding the fact if she had. She crept down the stairs to the front door. The night was cold, and her breath plumed white clouds in front of her as she ran out the front gate and down the street. Her heart was hammering in her chest. Mick was waiting for her around the corner, away from the streetlight. It was a cloudy, starless night above. The street was quiet. She could barely see him, standing alone in the dark. She threw her arms around him, surprising him with the force and weight of her kiss.

"I love you, Mick," she whispered.

"I love you, Melissa."

"My mother knows about us. She got it out of me."

"What did she say?"

"Exactly what we knew she would, that it's too much for us to be together, that she's nothing against Catholics but that she doesn't want my life to be difficult."

She was expecting an argument, for him to fight for her like he always had. But he didn't. He just stared back, not saying any of the things she wanted to hear.

"I have to talk to you about something." His voice was low, distant. "This could change things."

Melissa held her hand up to her mouth. "What are you on about? Is there someone else?" The words came out as a reflex, instinct. He didn't even need to answer.

"Of course not. It's not that. Are you nuts?" Mick fumbled in his pockets for his cigarettes, took out the pack and offered one to Melissa. She shook her head, and he lit one for himself, taking a deep drag.

"What is it then?" Melissa asked after a silence that lasted several seconds.

Mick let out a pathetic laugh. He felt deflated, his insides torn out. The usual joy he got from being around Melissa, from seeing her beautiful face, wasn't there. Not tonight, no matter how much he searched for it inside him. But he had still needed to see her, to have her hold him, to try to feel normal again.

She held him again, and he felt the ice inside begin to melt. He needed this all the time now. He needed her around, and she couldn't be.

It took him a few seconds to find the words. They were jagged in his throat, painful to say. "My grandparents in Paris wrote my ma a letter. They want her to come over and help in my grandda's shop. He's getting old now and could use a hand. My ma wants to leave, to move the family there."

Each word was like a tiny knife, and her tears were almost instantaneous. "She wants you to go with her? You both?"

"Aye, she wants to get out of Derry, says there's nothing but trouble here for us now."

"I'm here. I'm here for you."

"I know. God, I know that, you're all that I have that's good in my life, but with us... it's not the way it should be." Mick said. "Where do we go from here now that your mother knows about us? What future do we have here? I think we've both known this."

"It doesn't matter, none of that matters. I love you."

"And I love you. I need you now, more than ever." He reached into her hair, felt the softness of it against his rough palms.

"And I want to be there for you, more than anything." She reached her arms around him again, pulling him tight against her.

"But you can't be. You can't call around and see my family. They'll say exactly what your parents did. It's ironic, isn't it? The opposite sides think exactly the same way."

Melissa's eyes fell, and she took her arms away from him. He took a drag on the cigarette and looked away.

"If you don't want me, ..." she said, playing for the answer she wanted.

"You know that's not it. God, you're the one thing in my life I've no doubts about. You're the one thing I know I want, but you were wrong when you said that none of the other stuff mattered. It does matter. You know that."

"So what did your ma say? When does she want you to go to Paris?"

"She wants to go soon, very soon, this week if possible."

"What? This week?" She felt her heart freeze in her chest.

Mick threw down the cigarette and put his arms around her again. "She said that there was nothing left for us here, nothing good."

"What about your dad's shop? What about Pat's job?"

"We'll just shut the shop down. That place is haunted for me now. Pat will get work wherever he goes. He can look after himself."

"What about you? What will you do?"

"Something else. Not get shot at in the streets, not walk past burnt out cars and barricades every day. Not see soldiers who murdered my father parading around. I'll do something else."

"What about us? Am I just meant to forget about you now? That's it then, is it?"

"No, of course not."

"What are you talking about? I live here."

His demeanor changed like he'd been infused with a new energy. " Don't you see that this is what we needed? It doesn't matter who you are there. No one cares if you're Protestant and I'm Catholic. No one cares about loyalists and republicans, the IRA or the UVF. We could be together there with no disapproving looks, no prejudices. Don't you see? This is our chance to be together, actually together." His energy was back in his eyes. She fed off it and the feeling of hope it brought to her.

"What about college? What about my studies?" she said, almost smiling now.

"You're studying to be a teacher, why not try teaching English for a while? You could transfer, or else just finish your course. You've only fifteen more months, and in the meantime Paris is a beautiful city to visit." He kissed her. "This isn't the end of anything. This is just the beginning."

"What about my family? Their attitude isn't going to change, no matter where we are, no matter where we run to."

"I think you should give your family a little more credit. I've not met them but from the way you talk about them I feel as if I know them. When they see the real me, away from all this, away from this city and the ridiculous conventions we're all slaves to here, they'll like me. They'll accept me at least."

"It's amazing." Melissa smiled. "After everything you've been through, after everything that you've seen, you're still an optimist, you still see the good in people."

"You think that I think that Protestants are bad people? That Catholics are the innocent victims of the Protestants? Maybe I did once before I learned to think for myself. You're the best person I've ever met, Melissa Rice. I want to be with you for the rest of my life."

"I want to be with you. I don't want anyone else." They kissed again. "My father will never accept you," she said, almost looking through him as she spoke. "My dad's a good man. He loves his family more than anything else in this world. He's done so much for his community, has dedicated his life to the people around him, but he'll never accept you. The traditions he was raised on, the stories his parents told him, the beliefs instilled into him through the generations are just too strong. I think he'd disown me rather than bring you into our family." Her arms were weak around him and fell away. He still held her.

"My family will accept you, though. I'm sure of it. You're going to need to think about this. It's a huge decision."

"You're wrong, Michael. I don't need to think about it. I've been thinking about it every day for the last six months. I choose you."

Chapter 8

Mick pushed back the black gates of the City Cemetery and started up the hill. A rainbow arched over tranquil green hills across the river. Mick stopped for a few seconds, just to feel the breath rolling in and out of his lungs. The graves of the other victims of the march were heaped in flowers, bright, shining colors against the dark of the headstones, the gray of the sky. Relatives of the other victims said hello to him as he passed, people he'd never known before last week but who were now bound to him forever. They all knew the twins, the sons of Peter Doherty. People shook their heads as he walked by. His mere presence was enough to make grown men cry. He turned up the collar of his coat in a vain attempt to ward off the encroaching chill in the air, held up a hand to greet dozens of straggling mourners. Still he walked on, and the figure of his brother came into view.

Pat was standing over their father's grave, smoking a cigarette, didn't see Mick approaching, and didn't turn as he stood beside him.

"Did you see Jimmy's grave, and Noel's?" Mick began.

"I did, aye."

"Your boss came into the shop looking for you." No answer came, so Mick spoke again. "He was wondering where you were."

"I was here."

"All day?"

"Aye."

They stood in silence for a minute before Mick spoke again. "Should you be smoking, here?"

"Da doesn't seem to object."

"Did you tell Fergus that you weren't coming in today…?"

"I was standing here praying. I've been praying most of the day. Have you ever heard of Saint Rita?"

"No, I can't say I have."

"She was one of Da's favorites. She's the patron saint of impossible causes. She seemed like the appropriate lady to pray to."

"For what? What are you praying for exactly?"

"Justice." He brought red eyes to his brother. "There's no bringing him back but it's up to us to make sure he didn't die for nothing."

"We're leaving Derry," Mick said reaching over to his brother. "Maybe that's what Da died for, to give us the better life he always wanted for us."

"So we could turn tail and run? Leave our people? I don't think that's what he died for, little brother."

"You agreed to come to Paris, Pat."

"Aye, I did, and I will, for now."

Mick thought to tell him about the conversation he'd had with Melissa on Sunday night, about her coming to Paris eventually. Not here. Not now. Another minute or so passed. Neither man spoke, just stared at the words on the headstone as if they could unwrite them somehow.

"I think it's best we get away while we still can."

"I spoke to Paul last night." His eyes were fixed on the grave as he spoke. "He's off to begin training in a few days, around the time we run away to France." He threw down the cigarette.

"That's his choice."

"And John too. A lot of boys from around here, a lot of boys who saw what happened, what happened to Da."

"You said yourself, Pat. You said yourself that the police would deal with it."

"I felt awful for that little girl the soldiers murdered last year, and the fifteen-year-old coming out of the chip shop after he got his first week's pay. I felt awful, but it was a situation for other people to deal with." He looked at Mick, straight in the eyes now. "Da always said, '"best not get involved boys, politics isn't for us,"' but where does that leave us now? How can we put our faith in the government, the same system that murdered our father?"

"What are we supposed to do? Take down the entire British Empire?"

"Something, Mick. We're supposed to do something. Something to get justice for our father, something to protect our community, so no more Peter Dohertys or Jimmy Kellys or Noel Wrays have to die."

"This whole house of cards is gonna come down anytime now, Pat. Free Derry isn't going to last much longer. The Brits won't stand for it. Who knows what'll happen? We can be free in Paris. We can live the lives we should have been born into. There's no jobs there solely for Protestants or Catholics, no restrictions on housing or voting dependent on what religion you happen to have been born into. We can be who we want to be there, be with who we want to be with."

"Is that who this is about, that girl?"

"If you're referring to Melissa, aye, yes, in part, but it's also about our Ma. Her husband's dead. She needs us."

"You don't think I know that? That's why I agreed to go to Paris with her in the first place."

"What are you planning, Pat?"

"I don't know. I'm making it up as I go." He reached into his pocket to fish out a pack of cigarettes, but didn't open it, just stared at the writing, holding it in his hand. "I just wish I didn't feel like this, all the time. I just wish I could get rid of this emptiness, this vacuum inside me. It's like nothing I've ever known."

"You were so strong those first few days."

"I always was a good actor. I don't remember any of it. The days between the march and the funeral are already gone. I barely remember the funeral itself."

An elderly woman in a black shawl came to the graveside to lay a fresh wreath alongside the others. Mick prayed that she wouldn't recognize them, wouldn't try to offer some crumb of comfort. She looked up at them with a kind smile and ambled away. The rains began to come again, just a few drops, spitting down on them.

"You're wrong, Pat. There's an uncommon strength in you. That strength is what got this family through the last week. I don't know how we could have done it without you." No answer came. "I feel the same way as you do. I feel the same anger, the same frustration, but if the government inquiry uncovers the truth, then justice will be done. The soldiers who murdered Da will pay for what they did."

"You believe that, do you?" It was Mick's turn not to answer now. "I didn't think so. I know we're different, but I'd hoped we wouldn't be that different. I'd hoped you wouldn't be that gullible to believe what they told you now."

"Where do we go from here then, Pat?"

"What do ye mean?" The smoke billowed leaden clouds around him as the wind lifted.

"I mean what do we do, for justice for Da?"

"Well, they say living well is the best revenge. We can go to Paris, make lives for ourselves there, look after Ma into her old age. You can have your Melissa. No one there will care if she's a Protestant." His voice was flat. Mick had never seen him like this before, so devoid of joy. "We could have our lives there in peace. Paris isn't perfect, but there's no war there."

"That doesn't sound so bad."

"If we do that, we desert our father, and our people. We leave our community in the worst place it's ever been, like rats abandoning the sinking ship."

"No one would think any the worse of us if we left."

"I would. Wouldn't you?"

Mick grimaced as the frustration bubbled up from within him. "Why are you asking me that? Why can't you think about our mother?"

Pat ignored the questions. "You have Melissa to think of. How serious are you two?"

"Serious."

"I told you I was praying to St. Rita."

"Aye, ye did."

"She's the patron Saint of impossible causes. She lived in Italy five hundred years ago. She was married off at age twelve and had two sons. When the boys were about sixteen, their father, Rita's husband, was killed in a local blood feud. Her sons swore revenge." The rain thickened around them, and people began to put up black umbrellas. The boys didn't move. "But Rita wouldn't have any of it. Being the pious person she was, she tried to convince them to forgive the killer and even publically pardoned the murderer at her husband's funeral."

"So what happened?"

"They didn't listen to her. They swore vengeance. Even after what their mother had said at the funeral, even after she begged them not to. So she prayed to God to stop them Himself."

"Did He?"

"Well, yeah, He did. Before they had a chance to gain their vengeance, they died of dysentery. Both of them."

"So God answered her prayers by giving them both dysentery?"

"It was an impossible cause. Dysentery saved their souls before they had a chance to commit the mortal sin of murder."

"Do you think Ma is praying for something like that for us?"

"Dysentery? Nah, I'd say more like a nasty case of syphilis."

"That would solve our problems, all right."

"It'd certainly solve the problem of you falling for that Protestant girl, little brother." A fleck of color returned to Pat's voice, drawing a smile from his brother.

Mick looked at his watch. It was almost four o'clock. "Are you ready to leave? Do ye want to go for a pint on our way home?"

"Just give me a little while longer," Pat replied. Neither spoke as they stood there for a few more minutes. Several men shook their hands and a woman even handed Pat a bouquet of fresh flowers as they turned to walk away. He placed them down on the grave of one of the other victims. Melissa appeared in Mick's mind like an apparition, the picture faint. Nothing was going to be easy for them. The thought of letting her go was as jagged and painful as anything else he'd felt. They stopped into the first pub they came across on the way home. The conversation was almost normal. Pat seemed to be returning to some version of himself. When they arrived home, their mother had already packed most of her clothes into suitcases by the front door.

Chapter 9

The letters he sent were all she had of him now. It was surprising that her parents never questioned those letters with the Parisian postmark that arrived two and sometimes three times a week. She'd told her mother that Mick had moved away. It was easier not to lie. She was a terrible liar. The feelings she had for him had not dimmed, had not been diminished by the distance between them or the two months he'd been gone. She felt that he was with her all the time, and she with him, in all her thoughts and actions, as if they were one now, like the water in two separate streams, indistinguishable once joined together. Michael Doherty was the first thing that came to her as she awoke and the last thing that hushed her to sleep at night. Her mother was puzzled. Melissa hadn't shown any sign of the heartbreak of a breakup. Melissa assured her that he was in Paris but neglected to mention her plans to travel there in the summer, neglected the plans they'd made for her to move there permanently the year after.

It was a sunny Tuesday in mid-April. Roger Dalton had taken to walking her home, at least as far as his house. None of the boys knew about Mick and only some of her girlfriends. Some of her friends thought the same way as their parents, voicing quiet disapproval, some did not. But it didn't matter. Soon no one's opinions about their relationship would matter except their own. Roger was a nice boy, good looking and fun. Melissa knew he wanted more, just pretended not to. It was easier that way, more polite. She said goodbye to Roger and her thoughts immediately turned to Michael. She smiled to herself as she ambled up the garden path towards the front door of her parent's house. She pushed open the front door. Jenny was home from school already, and their mother was in the kitchen, the aroma of newly baked bread filling the house. The letter was on the hall side table. Mick's messy handwriting brought a smile to her face and deepened the longing within her. It was a funny feeling; funny to be in love with someone you never saw. Melissa picked up the letter and slipped it into her bag before making her way upstairs to her room. She had a routine, a ritual for reading his letters. She sat up on the bed, took out the old shoebox she kept them in, took off the lid and opened the letter. She took the single sheet out of the envelope and lay on her back to read it.

Melissa,

Life in Paris is still good, although it would be much better were you here with me. I miss you every day. It's a strange mixture of joy and pain that I feel when I think of you. But I remind myself that the future is ours, and now that we've found each other, that we have each other, our whole lives together are laid out in front of us. One day we'll see each other so often that you'll be sick of me! I'll make our children tell you stupid jokes (in French accents, who knows?) and annoy you while you're trying to concentrate on more important things. You think that's funny right now, but just you wait!

Working in the shop is fine. I never thought I'd miss staring at the tops of men's heads so much. I suppose I miss the feeling of my dad being there with me. I knew he was there with me in the shop. It's different now. There's no link to him here. He feels far away or even gone. Ma is okay. She's keeping busy and enjoying the way of life that she grew up with. Grand-mère is fabulous. She is eternally sweet, completely wonderful. Grand-père, not so much, but he's not such a bad old guy.

Pat is the problem. I miss my brother because the brother I see with me every day isn't him. You must be sick of me telling you this, but it's on my mind all the time. I don't know what to do. He never smiles or laughs. He used to laugh all the time. He seems to have built Derry up in his mind to be heaven on earth. He talks about moving back there all the time. I could never let him do that alone.

I love you,

Mick

Melissa let the paper rest against her chin. She'd not voiced her opinion to Mick, but it was clear that Pat had only moved there as a temporary measure to moderate his family's grief. A selfish flame of hope lit within her, but would they be better off back in Londonderry? Pat was still suffering. Was the path back to Londonderry a path to happiness or just the revenge that most of the Catholic boys who Mick had grown up with now sought through the medium of joining the IRA? If Pat joined, would Mick? Surely not, if only because of her and the love they shared. Surely he would value that above revenge or the false hope of 'justice' that the IRA recruiters spouted to willing throngs of young men with nothing but anger and disillusionment and pain seething through them. How had Mick checked his anger? Was it her? Was it the love he felt for her? Was she the reason he wasn't succumbing to the same sickness that had seemingly taken hold of his twin brother?

*****

Patrick picked up the wooden crate of tomatoes and placed it on his shoulder. Grand-père gestured to him to put it in the corner. Grand-père didn't speak any English, flat out refused to, and Pat's French was short of where Grand-père expected it to be, so the two men rarely spoke, rarely even attempted it. Working helped. It was a way for Pat to escape himself and the thoughts that haunted him. But there was no real escape, even in sleep. The image of his father, dying on the pavement outside the Rossville Flats permeated every dream, holding dominion over all else. That was most nights, and how he awoke most mornings. They'd spoken about it many times, but Pat wasn't healing, not like his brother was. Mick seemed to have some inner fortitude that Pat didn't. It was hard to fathom. All their lives he'd been the big brother, the one to make the decisions, a born leader.

Mick was behind the counter trying to talk to a customer. Grand-père stood beside him, observing with judgmental eyes. The man thanked Mick, happy with the service. Grand-père shuffled away without a word. Pat sat on the crate of tomatoes, his weight on the corner so as not to bruise the fruit. Mick walked over and sat down on the floor beside him.

"What'll the old man say about us knocking off work?" Pat said.

"Do you care? Whatever he's thinking, he'll get over it." Mick looked at his watch. "The shop's closing in ten minutes anyway. We'll close up for him then."

"How's that wee girl o' yours back home?"

"She's doing great, still planning on coming over to see us here this summer."

"Aye, right, sounds like fun. Going out with a Prod doesn't matter here, nor should it."

"A lot of things that matter back home don't matter here."

"That doesn't mean they don't matter though, Mick."

"Aye, you're right."

They helped Grand-père close the shop. Mick brought in the vegetables from outside, stacking them in tidy rows at the back of the shop as Pat rolled up the awnings. It was a fine spring evening, the likes of which were all too rare in Derry. It was a beautiful evening to sit out in the sun, smoking a cigarette and drinking beer. Mick and Pat took off their aprons and sat at a table outside on the street. The street the shop was on was magnificent, a feast for the eyes, as was almost the entire city. The high buildings on each side of the road were stately, lending grandeur to the cobbled street below. Each shop window was sumptuously ornamented with fresh goods as if specifically chosen for their color, their beauty. But it was the people who were the truest adornment. Almost every person that passed was like a wonderful melody for the eyes, immaculately dressed as if wandering down a catwalk. Mick fixed his eyes on a gargoyle sitting atop the building across the street, and Pat sat down opposite him. With no rubble, no barricades or burnt out cars anywhere, it was hard to imagine these people had any idea what was going on just a few hundred miles away.

The narrow sidewalk provided enough room for the table and two chairs but little else. People walking past had to step one foot into the street as they passed, but the boys had long since stopped worrying about Parisians grumbling. They always seemed to have something to complain about.

Pat opened the beers as Mick lit up a cigarette and passed one across to his brother. People stared at them, the identical twins sitting together on the side of the street. It was normal. The boys were used to it.

"How are you doing?" Mick began, meaning each word in the question.

"I'm feeling guilty."

"Guilty about what precisely?" Mick asked although he knew.

"Guilty about leaving our friends and family to deal with the Brits. Guilty that the likes of John and Paul have dedicated themselves to protecting our community and gaining justice for our father, not to mention Jimmy and Noel." He pressed his lips hard together before opening them to speak again. "Honestly, I feel as if I'm wasting myself here, beautiful city that this is and all."

"You're looking after your mother, is that not noble enough for you?"

"It's not a question of nobility." He stopped himself, taking a mouthful of his beer. "It's a question of duty. Ma doesn't need me here. She has her parents, her sisters, her nieces, and nephews. I feel I need to be there more than she needs me here."

"Is it duty or is it guilt?" Mick asked.

"Is that what you feel?"

"Sometimes."

"Is it that wee girl? Is it her you want to see?"

"Yeah, that's always there. It's ironic, but we've more of a chance with me living over here. With me over here the only thing we have in our way is the distance between us. That doesn't seem like much compared to what we have against us back home."

"Yeah, that does seem kind of an irony all right." Pat looked up and around him. "What's wrong with me, Mick? Why do I miss the bloody Bogside so much when I'm here?"

Mick knew that his brother was expecting a joke back but wasn't going to give him one. "You're loyal. That's a rare thing. You love your community. You can't let go of what happened to Da."

Pat looked across the table at him, took a drag on the cigarette and blew a plume of white smoke into the warm air above his head. "I just can't get him out of my mind. I seem to dream about him every night."

"D'you ever have the one where you save him?"

"Aye, that one's the worst. Waking up is misery after that one, when you realize it was only a dream."

They were silent for a minute or more, just sitting there, the smoke from their cigarettes wafting around them.

"Do you think that there's anything we could have done to save him?" Mick asked.

"Not really, he wanted to help that poor man on the ground, didn't want him to die alone. Once he'd decided to help him, there wasn't much we could do to stop him."

"Do you really believe that?" Mick asked.

Pat just stared back. He stubbed out his cigarette and looked away.

"No, me neither." Mick murmured.

"We can do something now though, make up for what we didn't do then," Pat answered.

"You want to be one of those guys in the balaclavas standing on top of the barricades with a gun that doesn't work? What good is that going to do?"

"Things have changed. It's a full-blown war now. Those days are gone, and anyway Free Derry's days are numbered. You think the Brits are going to stand for Free Derry much longer? That revolt is going to be put down. I'm surprised it hasn't been already."

"It's only a matter of time."

"Aye."

Mick thought of Melissa and the impossibility of their being together. Pat was halfway home already, even further. Neither of them used the explicit terms, but they both knew why. The only chance of a future with Melissa, the future he wanted, was to stay here, to wait, to let Pat go back alone, to abandon his father's memory and the plight of his community and his people. Could he let Pat go back alone? Could he live with abandoning his brother, his father's memory?

"Is your mind made up?" Mick asked.

Pat took a drag on his cigarette as Mick stared at him, waiting for him to answer. "I don't see any other way for me now. I can't stay here. The pain is too much. I can't take it," he said, focusing his gaze on the ashtray as he stubbed out his cigarette. A beautiful young girl sauntered past in massive sunglasses and heels clacking on the concrete pavement, oblivious to their eyes.

Mick waited until she'd gone to speak again. "There could be one last chance for us."

"What?"

'The government inquiry. The Widgery Report. It's due out any day." The only real chance he and Melissa had was in the hands of the British government. An exoneration of the victims of the Paras and a full investigation was the only thing that could assuage his brother, and douse the fires of pain within them both.

"You're putting your faith in that?"

"You did once too when they launched it."

"I was a different person then."

"No, you weren't. And if they do admit responsibility, if they do admit that Da was innocent, that they murdered him, what then?"

"I don't know, I just don't know."

The English speaking newspapers reached the newsstands at teatime. The Widgery Report, the official government inquiry into the Bloody Sunday killings, had been published. It was April 18th, a Tuesday. The soldiers were cleared of any wrongdoing. The blame for the deaths was placed on the shoulders of the organizers of the march. The anger burned inside Mick and he closed his eyes, crumpling the paper in his hands. It was the whitewash that Pat had said it would be and Mick knew that any hope for a life with Melissa, the life he wanted, was gone.

Chapter 10

Loneliness crept through her gradually until it consumed her. She had come to rely on the letters, two or three a week, as life rafts for the emotions within her. The last letter had arrived nine days before. There had been no sign to that point of any impending break, no indication that his love for her had faded. Her feelings for him were the same. They always would be. She lay alone in her bed, darkness all around her. She held a hand up to the curtain by her bed and brushed it back to let in a sliver of silver light from outside. She sat up and looked out onto the street. The range of possibilities raced in front of her. Maybe he was busy. Maybe he had met someone else, was trying to let her go, to set her free. Perhaps he had listened to those who'd said that they were impossible, that they could never be together, that the world around them was too strong to overcome. Maybe, but she didn't believe it. If Derry couldn't kill what they had, nothing he could have encountered in Paris would have dimmed his determination to be with her.

The noise at the window jarred her from sleep. It was after two AM. Another stone hit and her heart began to gallop in her chest as she realized that it was him. She bounced up on the bed and threw back the curtain and saw him waving to her from behind the bush. He pointed down to the corner where they usually met and slipped away. Her first thought was that her hair was a mess and that she wouldn't have time to brush it properly or put on any makeup. It had been two months. This was important. Leaving the light off, she drew back the curtains to illuminate the room just enough to make out her clothes. Her favorite pair of jeans and a tight sweater would have to do, and she slipped them on as quickly as she could before going to the mirror to make herself somewhat presentable. She was ready in three minutes. Pretty good. Repetition had made her journey down through the house silent as the night itself. No one had ever woken up. The front door closed behind her with a barely audible tap, and she was out in the cold of night. The stars were bright above the city, casting an ethereal beauty over a place where such a thing was rare as gold.

She ran the last few steps to him, unable to contain her joy as she threw her arms around him. He swept her up, momentarily able to forget the heaviness in his heart and what he knew he had to say. He leaned in, felt the softness of her lips on his, and ran rough fingers through her hair. They took a few seconds to kiss away their two months apart but even through the bliss of seeing him again she felt it. She brought her head back. Something had crept in between them. Something was wrong.

"What are you doing here? Why haven't you written to me for so long?"

"I'm back, just me and Pat, my mother is still in Paris."

"Why didn't you write to let me know?"

"I was so busy trying to get things in order before I left. It wasn't easy leaving Ma, and the travel itself took a while between ferries and trains."

"Why did you come back? What happened to our plan?" The bitter irony of seeing him was that she knew it wasn't for the reasons she would have wanted. His smile had already melted, the stresses underneath bubbling through. She was still looking at him, waiting for an answer. He leaned his head back and reached into his pocket for the pack of cigarettes. He drew one out and lit it, taking a deep pull.

"We got back in around two hours ago. I'm sorry to wake you like this. I'm sorry it's so late, but you're all I've thought about for the last few days. I had to see you." Nerves swamped him, his practiced words fumbled and awkward. "I know I didn't write to you, but you were with me all this time." He stopped, unsure of how to proceed, unsure of how to say what had to be said. He knew that everything would be different in the matter of a few minutes. He longed to delay this, to be with her for as long as possible. What had to come next was already tearing at him. "You look so beautiful, even better than I remembered." She smiled but didn't take the bait. The expectant look on her face deepened and he knew that there was no avoiding it now. "It was Pat, mainly. He's not been the same since the funeral. There's been something gnawing away inside at him. But I'd be lying if I said it was just him. Paris was fantastic, but it's not home."

"What's gnawing away at you, Michael?"

"You know. Nothing's been the same since Da died. Everything's changed. Everything's worse. If it wasn't for you, even the thought of you, I don't know what I would have done. And I suppose that's the difference between me and Pat - the reason he broke first."

"What are you getting at? What are you doing back in Derry?" She asked the question, though she knew the answer and she caught herself taking a step back, away from the man she loved, whom she'd pined for, begged to see all the weeks he was away.

"Pat couldn't…. we couldn't stand being away any longer. Did you read the government report that came out? I haven't written to you since then. That's when things changed."

"I saw it and I see it for what it is." Her voice was hollow now, her body tensing. She wanted to go on, to voice her support for his reaction to the report but was afraid of what she might end up voicing her support of. So she cut herself off, allowing him to continue. Neither of them knew what to say or how to react to what they both knew was to come.

"When the report was released… we both realized that…" he took another drag on the cigarette, hiding behind it. She was staring at him and, even in the darkness of the night, he could see tears welling in her eyes. "There was nothing left for us to do but join up with the other boys who went on ahead of us. It was the only alternative we had left. Not one of those soldiers will ever face trial for what they did."

"So you're looking for justice? Like when the IRA set off that bomb in England, when they tried to bomb the headquarters of the Paras? When they killed six tea ladies and a Catholic chaplain? Is that the kind of justice that you're trying to serve out?"

"That operation was a mistake, and at least the IRA admitted that. What did the Paras admit to when they killed thirteen innocent people in Derry on Bloody Sunday when they murdered my father?"

Melissa placed her hands on his arms, calming him. "Don't do this. This isn't going to bring your dad back. This isn't what he would have wanted. You told me so many times that he never wanted you involved in this."

"Maybe it's what I want, maybe it's what I need to do."

"I don't believe that." She took her hands away. "We had a plan. I was going to leave my home, for you. I was prepared to give up everything to give us a chance. I thought that it was worth it, that you were worth it. What happened to that?"

"We can still have a future together."

"Are you joking?" She turned away. "You want to be with me, a Protestant girl, and be in the IRA? Are you serious?"

"This isn't forever. I can leave whenever I want. I just need to..."

"Just need to what?"

"I just need to see that Pat's gonna be OK. I can't let him do this alone."

"So that's what this is about? Your brother?"

"He's my twin brother. There's two of me. It's hard to explain. I can't let him do this alone; I can't be the one who doesn't go. I have to honor my father."

"I gave up my life for you because I thought you were worth it, that you were the happiness in my life, and God bless me, I still believe that. I was prepared to choose you over everything else. Why aren't you prepared to choose me?"

"It's nothing to do with my feelings for you, Melissa. You're the only thing holding me back. You're the only reason for me not to do this."

"But not reason enough, is that it?" She was crying as she spoke now. "You're going to choose your brother, your dead father over me?"

"It's not a case of choosing. You're the one who's turning this into a choice. I realize that this is hard for you, but I have to do this." He stopped, searching for the words to rescue this, or her. "I was trying to fool myself, that somehow I could have you and the life I wanted, and serve my father and my community too. But I know I can't. I agree with everything you say. But you have to see that I've no choice. I have to do this. If I ran away with you, and something happened to Pat, I'd never forgive myself."

"So you'd rather something happened to you too, that you were killed or sent to jail too, not just him. I see the twin ethic there, one for all and all for one. I understand you want to serve your community, but there are other ways."

"Like NICRA, the civil rights movement? That died along with my father, shot down by the Paras. There's nothing else for me to do now. Most of my friends and most of my peers have joined. Some of my friends that you met on the day of the march are already volunteers, assigned to the Derry Brigade."

"So that's it for us? All our plans ruined?"

"I never wanted it this way. It's killing me to do this. Don't you see that I can't win, no matter what I do?

Go with you and I desert my brother and my people; desert the memory of my father. If I go with them, I desert you."

"I know that this is hard for you, but I think you're making the wrong decision. Not just for my sake, for yours. The IRA is an illegal organization. You could end up in jail, or worse." Her words were measured, precise.

"I have to do this."

"I suppose that's it then." She stepped back, her voice cold as the night air swirling around them.

He reached forward to hug her and though she didn't want to, she wrapped her arms around him and cried as he held her. "I love you," he whispered.

"I can't do this," she said and stepped away from him, wiping the last tear from her face. "I have to say goodbye now." She turned and ran, all the way back to the house.

Mick sat alone on the pavement after she had gone, shaking. A waterfall of grief gushed over him. The walk home took him almost an hour, the city absolutely quiet as he moved through it. Each building, each street, seemed built exactly to the specification of his own memory as if they existed only to remind him of his past. It was after four in the morning when he reached the Bogside. There was no one around except a few of the regular drunks, babbling pathetic drivel. He didn't even look at them. They were completely useless to anyone, a hazard even to themselves, yet they were alive and his father was dead. He avoided Rossville Street, walking around instead. Pat was asleep as he arrived home. The house was a shell of what it once had been. Once it had been full of laughter, full of life. Now it held only death and mourning, longing and regret. The tears came when he was alone in his bed when the pain became more than he could bear.

Pat was awake in the other room, had heard him come in as well as the sound of his crying through the paper-thin walls of the old house. Pat didn't get up to go to him. His own heart was steeled for what was to come. His crying was done.

Chapter 11

McClean came on a cloudy Tuesday morning at the beginning of May. They had been told to pack a light bag, and that they were going on a trip. Nothing more. McClean pulled over to the side of the road once they were outside the city, past the army checkpoints littering the roadways in and out. McClean explained that they were being taken across the border where they'd be transferred to a training camp. Mick's blood was ice as McClean spoke. The finality of leaving her was like a knife in his chest. This was right, though. No other alternative remained. Sacrifices would have to be made. He'd heard as much in several dingy, smoke-filled rooms with Irish flags strewn along the walls since he'd joined. There could be no freedom, no justice without sacrifice. Hadn't all the great revolutions in history been born from people like him, wronged and thirsty for freedom and peace? What difference was there between him and Eamon de Valera, Padraig Pearse or James Connolly? Even the heroes of foreign wars like the French Revolution or the American struggle for freedom against the burden of British Imperialism? This was bigger than just him. This was life and death, freedom or oppression for the Catholic people of Northern Ireland. Only one problem always remained, to gnaw away at him. The IRA men, in all their nationalistic fervor, never mentioned what was to become of the Protestant people of Northern Ireland. They were never brought. Would half of the population just fade into oblivion once the socialist republic came about?

"There can be no peace in Ireland until the foreign oppressors are ejected from Ireland, until the Irish people are allowed to govern their own affairs, separately and distinctly, culturally, physically and economically from the British Empire," McClean said. He seemed excited. He never talked about anything else. Pat wondered how good he'd be with the Brits bearing down on them. Would he spout philosophies at them? Pat was proud of how far they'd come in so little time. Their physical similarities seemed to intrigue the local leadership, and, in a time where so many new recruits had joined, their training had been fast-tracked. Their father would have understood what they'd done, and would have been proud. He tried to convince himself of that. He thought of their mother, still in Paris, how she'd begged them not to go back. They hadn't told her the full truth of why they'd left her, but she knew. The time to be with her would come again. But even with all the false bravado he exhibited in front of himself and others, the truth of it was that he was scared. He was scared of jail, scared of dying and scared of how he'd view himself if he did nothing. There was no escaping it. It was with him all the time. No one knew, not even Mick. He couldn't show any weakness. Weakness had killed his father.

Neither brother spoke at all as McClean took the opportunity to give them another lecture on republican history. His voice was light as he spoke. He almost had the air of a storyteller, regaling them with mighty tales of ancient heroes. It was clear that he romanticized the histories in his mind, and the enthusiasm he had for them was infectious. He only stopped talking when they reached the border. He was pleasant and polite with the soldiers at the checkpoint. The boys got out of the car as the soldiers searched it, but there nothing to find but the light bags the boys had brought with them.

The terrain in Donegal was exactly the same; lush rolling hills pockmarked with stones. The roads were markedly different however, and the car bounced up and down through potholes in the road as they went. It was only the second time the boys had ever been over the border, and they peered out like children expecting to see some sign of the unusual freedoms the people of the south enjoyed.

They had driven half an hour past the village of Castlefinn before McClean pulled off the road to a farm, remote and private. He told them to stay put as he went inside, his feet crunching on the gravel path that led up to the large farmhouse. The farmhouse was old but well kept, freshly painted, with neat rows of flowers in front. Neither spoke for the two minutes that McClean was gone. He emerged from the farmhouse with a tall, elderly woman, perhaps seventy years old. She was wearing an old-fashioned shawl with long gray hair spilling over it. Her striking blue eyes bore testament to a beauty that had faded with time but a strength in her that remained. She strode toward the car. They both climbed out. McClean introduced the woman as Sorcha Uí Bhraonain. They both knew the name and stepped forward to greet her with a firm handshake. She gave them a friendly if serious look as she greeted them.

"Welcome to my home," she began. "This has been a safe house in a republican stronghold since before even I was born. It was burned down by Black and Tans during the war of independence in reprisal for IRA activity in the area back in '20. The Free State government executed my brother here during the Civil War, almost right where you're standing. I saw it with my own eyes. This is where your training and initiation into the Provisional Irish Republican Army will take place. You will address me as Bean Uí Bhraonain." Mick didn't speak much Irish but knew that 'Bean', pronounced ban, was Irish for Mrs.

"Yes, Bean Uí Bhraonain," they said in perfect synchronicity.

Sorcha smiled to McClean. "So they even speak together, do they?" McClean didn't answer, just flashed a grin back.

"You will be here for several weeks until we feel that you're ready for the field. You will train with the thirty-four other recruits we have here at the moment. Have you any questions?"

They didn't, so they were directed to a large barn with rows of bunk beds lined along the side. Each bed was made perfectly. The boys left their bags on the spare bunks they found. McClean brought them out the back and up a narrow trail, surrounded by high, overgrown hedges. The three men walked in silence for ten minutes until they reached a clearing where the other volunteers were sitting in front of a chalkboard, listening to a lecture on gun safety. Each volunteer was dressed in green combat fatigues. The man giving the speech had a black beret on his head. He motioned them to sit down at the back. There were no introductions made. The volunteers turned to look at them as they sat, several doing a double take. The lecture was similar to what they'd heard in the previous weeks in their meetings with McClean, who'd slipped away after they'd sat down. Mick looked through the faces as best he could, some were familiar, and some were not. All were in rapt attention. The lecture took another twenty minutes. When it was over the volunteers were instructed to stand. None spoke, their hands by their side as they began to march behind the instructor. They walked for a mile or two until they came to a small shed. All was quiet, except for each man's breath and the whisper of the wind through the hedgerow. Other than the shed there was no sign of human life, only mountains and craggy, stone filled fields, unsuitable for any kind of farming. Each volunteer was given a rifle taken from a wooden box in the corner of the shed. Mick, after first checking the safety and to see if it was loaded, let his hands run over the smooth wooden frame, worn down from being passed down from volunteer to volunteer countless times. He felt history in his hands, the feeling of belonging, being part of something, and the undeniable grace of fighting for a cause that he now truly believed in. He felt connected to these strangers around him. They were his brothers now. Pat looked across at him, his weapon in hand and both brothers smiled. The volunteers broke up into small groups. Mick and Pat were put together along with three other recruits from Donegal. The instructor took each group in turn, going through the basics of firearms and then explosives training. Melissa and the old life back in Derry felt like years ago. Yet she remained as if tattooed inside him.

Pat excelled at weapons training. He was a natural marksman and by the second week was helping to instruct the new recruits, who seemed to come in almost on a daily basis. It was hard to get to know anyone as one day they were training alongside them and the next, they were gone, off to fight the war against the imperialist invaders. They came to know the training camp as 'Teach Uí Bhraonain', Irish language for the house of Uí Bhraonain. Mick wondered how many of these camps were dotted across the rugged Donegal landscape, or indeed the whole country, but knew better than to ask. The other volunteers seemed slow to offer any of themselves, perhaps worried about not looking the part or the ever-present obsession of the informer. As a result, Pat and Mick didn't mix much with the other volunteers as they came and went. It was plain to see during training who each volunteer was and what they might amount to. Some were ungainly and stupid, unfit for anything other than light administrative duties. Others seemed born soldiers, cold and fanatical, infected with hatred the likes of which the boys had never seen before. Under the tutelage of the instructor, this hate was encouraged, nurtured, channeled. It was the vital life-blood of the organization and Mick felt it, felt it spreading like black tar inside him. Only she stopped it. Melissa was his only defense against it.

In the second week of training, after their run up the mountain and weapons drill, Mick saw Bean Uí

Bhraonain sitting alone by the fire. Most of the other recruits were in bed, reading through the green book of IRA philosophies or the republican histories they'd been issued. Her old blue eyes flicked up at him and she offered a rock to sit on, worn down by innumerable young republicans in the past.

"Ah, Mick isn't it?"

"Aye, it is. You can tell me from my brother?"

"You're the one with the shaggy hair. It's not too difficult." She smiled, staring into the heart of the fire. "Your training's almost finished now?"

"I think so, Bean Uí Bhraonain."

"Aye, it is." Her words were slow and deliberate. "You know what you're fighting for?"

"Aye, I do."

"There was a bomb outside a pub in Belfast last night. A car bomb was set off. It was a Catholic area and when the civilians outside came out onto the street the snipers that the UVF had set up opened fire. Five civilians killed, including one Prod. The stupid bastards got one of their own. It was the local IRA who showed up to stop them, to fight back. The soldiers showed, sure, but they were working with the loyalists. If it weren't for the IRA, more Catholics would have died." The orange flames of the fire burned deep in her eyes as she spoke. "Without the IRA, without brave young men like you and your brother, and the rest of these volunteers, the Catholic people of Northern Ireland are defenseless."

"My father was killed, in Derry, on Bloody Sunday."

Bean Uí Bhraonain reached into the fire to poke it with a long stick she was holding. "We've all suffered at the hands of the British, and because of the traitors in the south who deserted the cause. My father fought in the war of independence, in '19 along with both my brothers. My father survived, but both brothers died, one at the hands of the Brits, one at the hand of the Free Staters. Yes, this war has been going on a long time. I've met just about any republican you could care to name, from Michael Collins to Eamon DeVelera to Cathal Goulding and Sean MacStiofain. They were different men, who wanted the same thing, the only thing that can provide justice for the people of Ireland - complete separation from the Imperialist British. There's no other way. Cold steel, that's all the Brits and Prods understand. The cold kiss of the bullet."

Mick nodded but felt outmatched, unable to respond. He stayed silent. Her soft-spoken words shielded a violent, bitter tradition behind them. She'd never known anything else, he thought. She was an inspiration and a warning in one.

"It's up to you," she continued. "It's up to you and the rest of the volunteers, here and throughout this beautiful country to seize this chance that's arisen to throw out the foreign invaders. They've inflicted eight hundred years of misery on the people of this country. If I were thirty years younger, I'd be right beside you."

The next morning McClean came back, and the boys left with him. Their training was over. They were ready to join their unit, ready for duty.

Their first action as IRA volunteers was a raid on a quarry two weeks later to appropriate Cordtex detonating wire for the cause. They had met Ken Wall at training camp. It had been his idea. His father had worked there until he'd been laid off the year before. The quarry had been unguarded except for one security guard who slept as Pat sliced through the padlock on the shed. Mick had stood back and watched, then helped carry the rolls of detonating wire, precious as gold to an underfunded IRA, back to the van where Ken was waiting for them. McClean was delighted with the proceeds of the raid on the quarry. He didn't care about the details, and no one felt the need to fill him in.

Mick opened the barbershop again. Being a volunteer in the IRA was not a paid position. Only full-time members were paid, and even then it was no way to make your fortune. Most of the people who came into the barbershop knew who he was now, what he'd become, and he felt the respect that went along with his new station. He was dedicating his life, sacrificing the certainty of the happiness he would have had with Melissa for them. It felt good to be part of something, to stand with his brother in fighting for the rights of their community. But he still pined for her. The feelings inside wouldn't die. He would sometimes close the doors of the shop at the end of the day and sit down in front of the picture of his father, still hanging exactly as his mother had left it. He found himself speaking to it, even asking questions. He had no one else to talk to about Melissa.

Chapter 12

Melissa finished her makeup, rubbing her little finger across her bottom lip to even out the pink lipstick. The brush ran through her fine brown hair as the T-Rex single wound to an end. She reached across with a deft hand to take it off the record player before it scratched and replaced it with Elton John. It was Friday night in late June. It had been almost two months since she'd seen Michael, and she was trying to throw out the memories of him, to extricate them from her mind. But he had infiltrated every part of her. She had tried to change who he was in her memory. She attempted to remember him as a bad person or to pretend that he hadn't been good to her, to pretend he hadn't loved her. It didn't work. Lying to herself was a waste of energy. The fact that he was in the IRA now was unavoidable. So many of her friends had boyfriends who lied and cheated and abused any trust placed in them, but somehow none of that was worse than what Mick had done, even though she understood why.

The doorbell rang. She was ready. The record ended, and she could hear her mother greeting her cousin downstairs. Melissa evaluated herself one last time in the mirror. She had some doubts about her earrings but forced herself out the door. Melissa's cousin, Victoria, had promised to bring her out on the town, and not in Londonderry either. She needed to get away. Victoria's hometown of Limavady, twenty miles away on the Coleraine Road, would have to do. Melissa's mother kept Victoria at the door for ten minutes before they made their way out toward the car. Victoria didn't put the headlights on as they drove out of the city, the summer night as bright as the afternoon even at almost nine o'clock.

They drove to Victoria's house where they dropped off Melissa's bags and after a quick conversation with her parents, made their way to the pub. Victoria's friend, Jenny, was waiting for them in The Royal Arms, but she wasn't alone. Several boys were with her. A tall, handsome boy stepped forward, proffering a hand to Melissa.

"Hello, I'm Clive," he said, his southern English accent as noticeable as a red apple among the green. He was tall and handsome with black hair and tanned skin. "Can I buy you a drink, miss?"

Victoria stood in between them. "Now, if you're going to buy my attractive cousin a drink, surely you can get us all one?" Clive smirked and left for the bar. Two minutes later he returned with one drink, which he handed to Melissa. He scanned the expectant eyes on him with a smile before going back to get the drinks he'd bought for everyone else in the group. No one said it, but everyone knew they were soldiers. Soldiers were the only English people around. This was a pub soldiers felt comfortable in. There weren't many like it in Londonderry.

*****

McClean had told them to expect something that night. It was after ten o'clock and still nothing. Mick came into the kitchen, where his brother was by the phone, cigarette in hand. This was to be their first real operation. They wouldn't be stealing explosives from any tin huts tonight. They weren't talking much. The ashtray was almost full. Pat thought about their mother, and the torturous process of reading her last letter. She cried for them every night now, dreaded for their future. It wasn't too late; she'd written. But it was, Pat knew that. It was too late for him the moment their father had ventured out to help the man crawling along the ground, and those shots ripped through the air. The harsh sound of the phone cut through the silence.

"Hello," Pat answered.

"I'll be at your house in ten minutes. I'll need you both." He hung up.

Pat replaced the receiver. The silence came again. His brother was looking at him.

"That was McClean. He'll be here in ten minutes. He needs both of us." Mick didn't answer. "You ready for this?"

"I'm ready," Mick replied.

*****

The English boys were buying the drinks. Victoria was talking to Clive now, but Melissa could see him peeking at her over Victoria's shoulder. She felt the heat come to her skin as he smiled at her. It didn't feel right, having these feelings about someone who was probably a soldier, but wasn't she trying to move on? Not all Catholics, not all Protestants, not all soldiers were the same. Norman and Robert, the two other boys with Clive, were in front of her, and she began the conversation.

"So, where are you from in England?"

"Leeds," Robert answered. "Me and my little brother here have been over here a few months now," he put his arm around Norman, who was already swaying from side to side. It was only half past ten.

Norman managed to nod in agreement. "It's been so bloody hard trying to deal with these Paddys," he slurred. "We thought we were here to help the buggers, but they don't want it. At least you people appreciate what we're trying to do for this god-forsaken place."

The insult bit at Melissa, but she brushed it off with a smile.

"Forgive my brother," Robert answered as he clipped Norman over the back of the head. "He's had a few too many. This is what happens when you let eighteen-year-olds out of the barracks in the middle of a Saturday afternoon for the rest of the night."

Melissa smiled again, unsure what to feel. Robert had a kind face. It was hard to fathom how someone like him could open fire on innocent people. Was he so different from the soldiers who'd fired on the crowds on Bloody Sunday?

"What's it like for you over here?"

"It's a lot of different things," Robert said, looking directly into her eyes. "It's very boring when we're not doing anything. We were in Londonderry for a while. The only excitement we ever got was during those bloody riots, getting stones and petrol bombs chucked at us. It must sound strange, but in a way we came almost to look forward to those riots."

"You looked forward to them?"

"Those riots were the only break in the boredom."

"What else is it like being here?"

"It's intimidating. There's a lot of history here that's nothing to do with us, and we're here to try to sort it out. Nobody knows what to do. We're all trying to get through each day as it comes, and get home. I'm going to get married when I finish my tour of duty next year. Do you want to see a picture of my fiancé?"

"Aye, of course, I do."

Robert took out a brown leather wallet and produced a black and white photo of a girl, about her age hugging a golden retriever. "Her name's Charlotte," he said. "I need to write to her; I've not written to her yet this week."

"You do that tomorrow."

*****

McClean pulled up outside the Doherty house in a red Ford Cortina. They'd been waiting, watching for him since the phone call ten minutes before. Mick hugged his brother. "Let's do this."

"We'll be home in a few hours. Let's just not do anything stupid." Pat replied.

"Sounds good to me."

Patrick got into the front seat, with Mick behind him. McClean started the engine without a word. They were on the road when he finally spoke. "There's a pub we've been monitoring in Limavady for a while. We want to hit it, tonight. You boys are ready for this. That's why we got the job."

"We're ready," Mick said, his response hollow, devoid of the fear that he was trying to suppress.

*****

Clive was slightly older, about twenty-two, and he was handsome, not beautiful like Mick, but handsome. She cursed at herself for thinking about Mick, even as Clive was talking to her. She fought to get him out of her head to listen to Clive and his smooth southern English accent.

"...it is beautiful. I just wish I could get a proper chance to see it."

He didn't seem to notice that she'd not heard a word he'd said. Melissa took advantage of the break in conversation to look around. Victoria and her other friend, Jenny, were alone at the bar. Norman and Robert were talking to some other girls she'd never seen before. One of them was cradling Norman's head. The other girls motioned to Clive to come over. He looked at Melissa as if to ask should he go.

"I'd rather stay here and talk to you."

A thousand thoughts flew through her head, most of them to do with Michael. She had no idea what she wanted. "You go and talk to your friends. I'll be over here. I'm not going anywhere. I'll see you later on."

Clive smiled and walked over to the other group, where one of the girls greeted him with a flirtatious arm around his shoulder.

*****

McClean stopped off at a farmhouse as the night began to edge in. The boys didn't talk as McClean went inside, the fear within them wrenching their lips tight as scars on their faces. Two minutes later he emerged carrying a black plastic bag, bulging under the weight of its contents. He placed it into the trunk of the car, and they started out again. Both wanted to ask what was in the bag, what they were doing, where exactly they were going but knew better. They drove on.

*****

Melissa's gaze wandered over to where Clive and the others were talking. The girls seemed to find everything that the boys said hilarious, their raucous laughter scything through the air even over the loud music.

"I've never seen them before," Victoria said. "They're not from around here."

"They certainly seem to be enjoying their first time here," Jenny answered. "They're all over the soldier boys like a cheap suit."

A bead of jealousy simmered inside Melissa even though she wasn't ready for anything, and knew that she wouldn't have acted on any feelings. It just felt good to move on, or at least try to. She turned around and ordered more drinks.

*****

The sign for the town of Limavady flashed past. No one spoke in the car, the silence weighing on each of the boys. Pat's hands were clammy and cold, Mick's nerves jumbling his stomach into nausea. Both had their hands in their pockets – anything to hide the shaking. The narrow, clean streets of the town were lively, and there were people outside all of the pubs taking advantage of the warm night. There was no rubble strewn around from rioting, no burnt out cars or IRA men brandishing weapons. Union Jacks hung from lampposts, limp in the light breeze. They passed the Royal Arms pub and pulled into a parking space on the main road. McClean turned around. His face was granite determination.

"Three operatives are in the pub at the moment. This pub is a popular spot for soldiers from the local British Army barracks to come for a drink on a Saturday night. There should be several off-duty soldiers in there. We're going to make contact with the operatives inside to find out what our next move is. I can't show my face in there. It's a long story. I need one of you boys to make contact."

"I'll do it," Mick said. Pat felt the words of protest forming in his throat but swallowed them back. He patted his brother on the shoulder. "How am I going to recognize them?" Mick asked.

McClean reached into the glove compartment and took out a brown envelope. He opened it and took out three black and white photographs, each of a young girl, about their age. "This is Maggie," he said, pointing at the attractive blonde girl in the photo. "Got it?"

"I got it," Mick said and got out of the car.

*****

"Why don't you go over and talk to him?" Jenny said, nudging Melissa. Before she could protest, Jenny had taken her by the elbow. "I'll go over with you. Come on Victoria, we'll all go."

The three bustled their way through to where the soldiers were standing. The Irish girls looked them up and down as they melded into their circle. The boys were drunker now, Norman barely coherent. Melissa returned Clive's smile and took the opportunity to begin.

"Hi guys, you never introduced us to your new friends."

Robert answered her. "Oh, hello, great to see you ladies again. This is Sharon, Diana, and Maggie. Say hello, ladies."

An icy hello came back from aloof lips, daggers from sharpened eyes.

"Are you from around here?" Melissa asked Maggie, a pretty blonde with far too much eye makeup.

"No, just out for the weekend, you know?" Robert had one hand around Maggie's waist, and Sharon seemed to laugh at every word that came out of Norman's mouth. The girls had marked their territory. Clive slithered out of Diana's grasp and moved to Melissa.

"I was wondering when you were going to come over," he said.

"Can you hold my drink for a minute please?" she asked. The beer was starting to have its effect. She needed the bathroom and a few minutes to think. He took the pint glass she handed him.

"I'll guard it with my life," he assured her.

"You off to the loo? Victoria asked. "I'll come too. Come on, Jenny."

Mick undid the top button on his shirt as he neared the pub. Around twenty people stood on the patio outside. His nerves were jangling like wind chimes in a hurricane, but he forced one foot in front of another until he was inside. The pub was packed. Saturday night. Finding them wasn't going to be easy. He kept the picture of Maggie in his mind as he scanned the tops of heads in the crowd for her blonde hair. Several English accents stood out as he pushed through the throng of people. He was leaning against the bar, dismissing the thought of ordering a quick pint when he saw them, talking to three young men. Maggie was laughing with a guy who looked about twenty, had her hand in the back pocket of his jeans. Suddenly it was real. Every decision he'd made since his father died had led him to this moment. He could pretend he didn't see them, walk out of there and drive back to Derry with the others, or he could do his duty, what was perceived to be his duty. It was his choice to make, here and now. He began to move through the crowd, holding up his arms as he neared them.

"Maggie, how the hell are you? Long time no see."

Her eyes flicked up to him, offering no recognition until she realized. "I'm doing great, how are you?" She stepped forward to hug him. It felt bizarre, to embrace a stranger like that. "You remember Diana, don't you? But I don't think you've met Sharon."

He held out a hand to Sharon. "No, we've not met. Nice to meet you, my name's John." He could feel the weight of the stares from the boys standing around them.

"Who are your friends?" Mick asked.

"These lovely boys are, Clive, Robert and this wee fella here is Norman." Norman raised his hand to say hello, a ridiculous, cartoon-drunk haze veiled across his entire face. The other two just looked on. Mick thrust an arm forward and shook each of their hands.

"Nice to meet you," Clive said in return.

Mick pointed a finger toward Maggie. "Can I speak to you for a second? Something happened with Charlie Smith, your neighbor."

"Oh no," Maggie said. Her acting was good. "Poor old Charlie. Let's have a chat, come on." She put a hand on Mick's shoulder as he led her back in the direction of the door.

"So, what do you think of Clive?" Jenny asked. The three girls were at the mirror in the bathroom, fighting for space.

Melissa stared into her own eyes for a few seconds. No answers there. "He's a nice guy."

"He's gorgeous, and he definitely likes you."

"Maybe." She applied a little more eyeliner and pushed out a deep breath. "I just don't think I'm ready for this. I'm still hurting from…"

"Ah come on, would you? The only way to get over the last fall is to jump back on the horse and keep riding."

The two girls exploded with laughter. Melissa did too, despite herself. "Come on, let's get back over there and see what happens."

"I fancy a wee bit of fresh air. I'm just going to pop outside for five minutes. I'll see you girls back there."

"Clive's holding your drink," Jenny answered.

"He'll wait another five minutes for me. If he doesn't, he's not worth it."

The night air was cool, the sun only finally succumbing to darkness at almost eleven o'clock. It felt good outside, fresh, invigorating. Maggie took Mick away to the side and, once she'd made sure no one was listening, lowered her voice to speak.

"Who are you here with?"

"There's three of us, parked a hundred yards up the street in a red Ford Cortina."

"Where?"

Mick pointed toward the car. "Just up there."

"All right. We've got three Brits inside. They're pretty well oiled, so this shouldn't be too difficult. We'll get them in the car, you boys follow us, we'll pull over out of town and leave the rest up to you."

Melissa arrived outside and found a bare patch of wall to lean against, a few feet from the main entrance. She didn't know what to think, her thoughts like glue. She wished she'd brought her drink outside. Her love for Mick was pointless now. It would never amount to anything. It could only bring her pain, so why couldn't she leave it behind? She didn't smoke but thought of asking one of the people beside her for one. She looked at the crowd around her until her eyes fell upon him. Electricity surged through her body. Her bones seemed to turn to granite within her, her stomach a boiling sea. Mick. It was definitely Mick, and he was talking to Maggie. Melissa was soaked in shock, her knees about to buckle. What the hell was he doing here, talking to Maggie of all people? She was frozen.

Mick's blood was ice in his veins. Maggie's eyes were utterly convincing and left no room for the doubt in his heart. He went to speak but found himself unable to form the words. He thought of McClean and his brother in the car, the republican history lessons, the lectures, the constant reminders of the march, of the injustices concreted into the system, of the intentions of the unionists to subjugate his people. He thought of his father, dead on the asphalt, murdered outside the Rossville flats.

"Are you OK?" Maggie asked.

"Yeah, sure I am. I'll relay the message."

"Right," she nodded. "Give us a few minutes to get them into the car. It's a powder blue Vauxhall Viva. Be ready."

"Got it."

Melissa watched as Maggie walked back towards the door and inside. Mick brought two hands to his cover his face, letting his head drop into them. Maggie had stopped inside the door, was still watching him. And Melissa was in front of Mick, before she even realized she'd made the decision to go to him. He pulled his hands from his face to reveal red, desolate eyes.

"What the hell are you doing here?" His whisper was tinged with panic.

"I could ask you the same thing." She wanted to ask him how he knew Maggie, but at the same time didn't want to seem as if she cared.

"I'm in town visiting some friends. I heard that girl was in the pub and decided to come down and see her."

"Is she your girlfriend? You looked pretty upset after she left."

"You were watching me?"

"I was just standing there and I saw you. You expect me to look away?"

"She's not my girlfriend. There's been no one else."

She was beautiful. More so every time he saw her, more so now than ever before. He still loved her, still thought about her every day. Shouldn't he tell her? The only antidote to what he was feeling was standing in front of him. Was there a chance left to leave this behind, to honor the love he felt for her over the duty he felt to his brother, his father, his community? He reached his hand to hers and she took it.

"I can't be with you anymore, not with the life you've chosen," she said, immediately grabbing her hand back, annoyed at herself for letting him hold it in the first place.

"There was never any choice about it. I never wanted it like this. The only thing I ever wanted was you."

The anger in her began to boil over and just for a second she had the thought to go back inside and kiss Clive just to get back at him. "You can't just breeze into my life. You've made your choice. Did you think I was going to wait around for you?"

"I never thought you would. I just hoped that..." The words dissipated and died. "I love you. I always will."

A single tear burst out and fled down her cheek. He was amazed he didn't cry himself, but the truth of it was he was dead inside already. The moment of being there, of seeing her, was like a memory. It was as if it had happened already and he was reliving it, unable to say or do anything to affect the outcome.

"You can't say that to me. You can't just say that to me outside a random pub in Limavady. You can't just reach inside of me and pull my heart out like that." A few feet away Maggie was leading the off-duty English soldiers out of the pub, her arm around Robert. Sharon was holding Norman's hand, leading him. Maggie glanced over before laughing out loud at something Robert said to her. "I know the hell you've been through over the last few months but what you're doing isn't the answer. It's only the road to even more pain. Nothing good can come of this," Melissa continued.

"I have to go now," Mick said, his timid voice barely above a whisper, lacking any authority or conviction.

He was pale now and it took every reserve of strength she had left not to lean forward and take him in her arms. She wanted so much to end his pain. But that could never be. His perverted sense of duty to his brother and to his poor murdered father would destroy him and she couldn't stay around to see that. It would kill her too. She loved him too much to watch him do that to himself. She turned away without another word and almost bumped into Clive, walking out with Diana.

'The girls invited us to a party. Do you want to come?" Clive said.

Mick just stood there watching, feeling Maggie's glare from twenty yards away. He steeled himself and paced away, not wanting to hear the answer. He headed back toward Pat and McClean waiting for him in the car. They were as loyal to him as he was to them and the cause. There was no escape from the duty that had been thrust upon him. It didn't matter what he wanted. All that mattered was what he had to do. He walked on.

"You're leaving?" Melissa asked, her eyes on Mick as he walked away.

Diana was dragging Clive now, his arm outstretched, but he stopped in front of Melissa.

"You should come along," he said.

"There's no room in the car. Come on," Diana said before giving Melissa a look she'd rarely experienced before. "Leave that bitch here, did you not see her talking to that other fella? And look she's been crying too."

Clive stopped for a second, his face tight. "It was nice to meet you, Melissa. It seems like you've got a few things on your mind."

Diana dragged him along after her. The vacuum within Melissa's chest deepened as they walked away. Questions came like bubbles in boiling water. She went back inside to look for her friends. Why were the girls throwing themselves at those soldiers like that? And why was Mick talking to Maggie? Why would Mick go to a party that British soldiers, the IRA's sworn enemies, were going to? It was all so strange. She continued into the tussle of bodies inside.

Mick tapped on the car window. Pat rolled it down, and Mick got down on his haunches to speak.

"They're moving with the soldiers now, in a powder blue Vauxhall Viva. Shouldn't be more than a few seconds."

"Get in," McClean ordered. Mick felt the drag in his legs before his brother motioned to him. He opened the door and sat in the back. They waited in stony, terrified silence, their eyes like limpets on each car as it drove past.

Melissa found her friends quickly, but the questions still abounded in her mind. She could still feel the stabbing pain from seeing Mick. What had Maggie said to upset him so much and why would someone he knew be picking up British soldiers? And then she realized.

Outside, Mick was watching through the rear window of the red Ford Cortina as the soldiers packed into the Viva. Maggie was driving, with Clive already in the front seat. Norman was so drunk he could hardly get into the car, his body like putty. Robert was helping him, holding his head as he arched one leg inside.

Melissa ran outside and saw Norman squeezing into the back seat, and then Robert after him. She called out, but the roar of the engine cut through the air and the car pulled out. Melissa ran on, red-faced, her arm in the air, screaming after them, but it was too late. The Viva sped into the darkening night and up ahead a red Ford Cortina pulled out after it.

McClean lagged back a hundred yards or so, not seeming to care when another car pulled out between them and the Viva. Mick's heart was beating so fast he could almost see it rippling through the skin on his chest. Pat shifted in his seat, wiping sweat from his palms on the jeans he wore, fully aware of what was about to happen. He thought back to his training, and what they'd told him about the war. And it was war, he told himself. This was necessary. Sacrifices would have to be made. This was the only way to forge a better future. He was so nervous he felt like he might vomit.

The Vauxhall Viva pulled out onto the Ballykelly Road, back toward Derry. Darkness was absolute now and the hedges on each side of the road were horrific black green as if painted with shadows. The fields beyond stretched out into a terrifying unknown. Still the car ahead drove on. They stayed behind the Viva. Pat couldn't believe that the soldiers in the car hadn't noticed them. But then, they were drunk. This was going to be all too easy. They drove on past a farmhouse, all lights extinguished inside, and then another. The lights of the stars above were covered, the moon visible only in patches as the clouds shifted.

Another car passed on the other side of the road - the first they'd seen. Mick watched through the back window as it disappeared, its lights fading into the night. The hedge broke and they came upon a long stretch of fields to the side of the road. No houses. Nothing else other than the night. The brake lights in front shone red as the car pulled over. McClean turned the headlights off and slowed to the side of the road about a hundred yards behind. The engine cut, they could hear the drunken laughter as they stumbled out of the car, could hear each individual voice. McClean got out, making almost no noise as he opened the trunk. Maggie was shouting that she had to pee, and tramped off across the field into the void of darkness. She left behind the clink of whisky bottles and the roars of drunken laughter. McClean tapped on the back window, motioning to the boys to get out. He reached into the bag and handed each of them a Webley revolver, no word spoken. Mick felt the weight, passed it from left hand to right. A British soldier had likely used it in World War II. He looked to his brother but Pat didn't seem to want to make eye contact. McClean tucked the gun into his pants and strode toward the noise ahead, Pat followed. Mick hesitated, thought of his mother, his father, Melissa, before jogging after the disappearing figures of the other two men. This was his duty.

They were up on them in seconds. McClean pulled his pistol first. "How are we all doing tonight?" Maggie, who had just arrived back from being out in the field motioned to the other girls to stand back and the three women stood back in line, watching.

"What's this?" Clive said, the whites of his eyes clearly visible through the black of the night.

Norman was sitting on the ground, drinking out of a bottle, his brother Robert beside him. Norman barely seemed to register what was happening. "Who are these fellas?" he asked.

"Be quiet, Norman," his brother said, the fear evident in his voice.

Pat drew his weapon and pointed it at Clive, and Mick took his out too. His hand was firm as he aimed it. Much more so than he'd expected it to be.

"All right, let's do this quickly, humanely. We're not torturers," McClean said.

"Let's just talk this through for a minute before we do anything rash," Clive said, his voice infected with panic.

McClean walked the ten feet over to where the two brothers were sitting. Norman looked up and without any hesitation McClean shot him in the face. Robert screamed, cradling the bloody mess where his brother's head had been. Hair, skin, red gushing blood poured out over his hands as he began to wail.

"You bastard," he sobbed. "You killed my brother."

McClean motioned to Pat. "Do it quick," he said. Pat looked back at him, didn't move. "Come on. It needs to be done. You need to do it. Do it quick, humane."

"Just stop this now, there's no need for more killing," Clive spluttered.

Pat looked at his brother. Mick shook his head, the breath thundering out of his lungs. Pat stepped forward and held up the pistol, aiming it at Robert who didn't even look up as he held his brother's bloody, broken face to his shoulder. Mick wanted to speak, the words like barbs inside him, but they wouldn't come. Robert's whole body convulsed with tears. Pat stared at him, the seconds drawing out like years. The barrel of the pistol was only two feet from Robert's head. Pat let it drop, turned to McClean.

"We got one of them. Can't we…"

"Do it now," McClean ordered. "Making them wait like this is just cruelty, nothing more." Maggie and the others watched in silence. Mick took a step toward Pat, reaching out without words.

Pat raised the pistol again, aiming it at Robert's head. Robert raised his face and Pat fired, jerking his hand away at the very last fraction of a second. The pistol thundered, and everyone stopped, shock flooding Robert's eyes. It took Pat a second to realize he hadn't missed. The bullet had grazed Robert's neck, hitting the artery, and thick crimson-black blood began spurting out. Robert screamed in pain and brought his hand up in some vain attempt to stem his life's blood as it flowed out through his fingers onto his clothes, his brother and into the soil below. He fell backward, kicking his legs as if to some demented rhythm. He gurgled a few times and then went still.

Clive was white. He looked at McClean, who now motioned to Mick.

"Good and quick, now," McClean repeated.

Clive turned as Mick hesitated, running into the black of the field.

"Jesus Christ. Get him!" McClean ordered. "No wild shooting."

Mick turned and ran after him. Clive was about fifteen feet in front. Mick could just make out the color of his shirt through the inky black that had almost enveloped him. Mick slowed, and Clive got further out in front. He began to fade into the night as Pat came steaming up. Clive went down into the dirt as Pat tackled him. Mick ran to catch up, pointing the revolver at Clive's head as he tried to hit out at Pat.

"Bring him back here," McClean roared.

Mick reached down and grabbed Clive off of his brother and shoved the point of his pistol in his lower back, marching him back toward the car. Clive didn't make a sound. Maggie and the other girls were in the car as they arrived back, the engine running.

"Are we taking him back?" Mick asked.

McClean ignored the question. "Do it. Do it now."

Clive glared at Mick, his would-be killer, the hatred complete in his eyes. Mick turned to Pat, who didn't move, his pistol by his side. Mick raised the weapon to Clive's head but dropped it back down immediately.

"We don't have to do this. Can't we ransom him off? The British Army would pay a…"

The loud report of the Webley shook the air as Pat shot Clive in the head. The body crumpled onto the field in a clumsy heap. The shot echoed and faded out. No one moved for several seconds, Mick staring at the grotesque pile of corpses they'd created. McClean said something, gave an order and the girls drove off, leaving only darkness behind. No one spoke as the three men walked back to the car. They replaced the pistols in the trunk and drove off, leaving the freshly killed bodies of the soldiers where they lay in the dirt.

Chapter 13

Sleep came, but only with the passing of the dawn, and Mick felt like he had sand in his eyes as he woke just before noon. The house was still, the only sound a faint wind outside. The image of first McClean, and then Pat, shooting down the British soldiers was like a gash in his consciousness. The blood from the soldier's neck and the look of shock in the last soldier's dark eyes seemed imprinted on him now. He could barely see anything else. The darkness of that field the previous night had seemingly taken over his entire body, poisoning his soul within him. He felt changed, used, ill. He turned over to reach for the pack of cigarettes on the bedside table. The box was empty. He almost cried, crushing it in his fist and flinging it across the room. A lonely ember of the love he had for Melissa still glowed inside him, but the time for that seemed past. He lay there frozen for half an hour, replaying the events of the night, over and over, over and over. McClean had been happy, if not quite delighted, on the way home. He'd said that Mick wasn't a 'trigger man', but that was OK, that there were plenty of other ways to serve the cause. Pat had only glared, angry and distressed in equal measure when McClean had praised him. McClean dropped them off with an assertion that they should have been proud of themselves. Neither brother looked at the other as they went into the house and there wasn't a word exchanged as they each went to their separate rooms.

Pat heard the cigarette pack hit the wall in his brother's room. He hadn't slept at all, just wallowed in a pool of exhaustion all night. His blood-spattered shirt was in the corner where he'd flung it the night before. He knew he had to get rid of it and that his freedom depended on it, but he couldn't bring himself to look at it. The previous ten hours had been a hellish debate between the rational part of him, in utter disgust at his actions and the part of him loyal to the cause. Killing was a part of the war. This was a dirty war, not like the one his father had fought in. Without the IRA, there was no one to stand in the way of the British and their blood lust. More innocent people would die, and more families would be destroyed. The soldiers were unlucky, but must have known the risks. They knew that being in Northern Ireland was dangerous. No one had forced them to fight for the imperialists in Westminster. He and his fellow volunteers didn't want to kill. They had been forced. He told himself this over and over, and after a few hours he even began to believe it.

He heard a knock on the door.

"Come in."

Mick looked ill, the blood completely drained from his face. Huge black bags hung like bruises under his bloodshot eyes. He shuffled into the room and sat on the edge of the bed as Pat sat up.

"You gonna open up the shop today?" Pat asked.

"I hadn't even thought about that." Silence filled the vacuum between them for thirty seconds or more. "I suppose what happened last night will be in the newspapers tomorrow."

"Aye, I reckon it will."

Silence again, for another minute. Pat got out of bed and peeked through the curtains at the gray outside. He stayed standing by the window, Mick still on the bed.

"I can't get the picture of those soldiers out of my head," Mick said, his eyes on the floor.

"It's a war, Mick. We didn't start it. We didn't even want it, but we're in it now. Those soldiers who died last night are casualties of war. We're no more responsible for their deaths than Dad was for the Germans he killed in World War II. The real responsibility is with the politicians and generals who sent them here and the corrupt government in Stormont, only serving the Protestants."

"You believe that?"

Pat walked to the closet across the room and opened the door. He picked out a pair of jeans and began to pull them on. "Of course I do. Do you believe I would have done that last night if this weren't war?"

"Of course not. But..."

"But nothing, Mick. We struck a blow for the people of this community last night."

Mick thought of Melissa, thought of Paris, thought of the life they should have had there, the life that they deserved, that he'd passed up for this empty horror. "I want to thank you."

"For what?"

"For shooting that last soldier. I don't know if I could have...."

"I don't want to talk about that. Talking about what happened is useless and dangerous. You heard McClean last night – he's proud of us."

"And that's the most important thing is it? That's meant to surpass the guilt I feel, the shame?"

Pat threw his arms in the air. "I knew you weren't right for the mission last night. I knew you didn't have the stomach for it."

"Maybe you were right."

"I was right, and I'm glad I was right. Not everybody has to go on operations like we did last night. You heard McClean; there are lots of different ways to support our people and our cause. A smart guy like you could make a great intelligence man, a fundraiser, or a safe house operator."

"And what does that make you? You're a killer now?"

"I.... I just did what needed to be done."

Mick tried to reach for words that faded away as he opened his mouth to say them.

"I did what I was asked and I'll continue to do that." Pat continued.

"Do you think that was what the Paras said after they killed our dad and those twelve others in January?"

"Don't you dare compare me to them. I'm nothing like them. What we did last night was an act of defense. It was a defense of our people and our rights. What they did that day was murder."

"But the newspapers tomorrow will say that those boys last night were murdered and that our dad was a terrorist, shot down in the name of the government and the law."

"Exactly."

"I know that, so why do I feel like this? Why do I feel as bad as the day he died? I thought doing something like this would make me feel better, but I feel like I'm at the bottom of a deep black hole."

Pat walked over to the bed and sat down beside his brother. "I feel terrible too, but it will get better. This life we've been forced into will become easier, and we will win our freedom."

"What have they done to you, Pat? This isn't you," Mick said. Pat stood back, felt the jabbing pain in his heart as Mick continued. "We can't do this anymore, not after last night. We've seen it now, and we did our part, but we can't do this anymore. There's no happy ending to this story from here, only death and misery, horror and jail. It's the only way it can go."

"You knew what we were getting into."

"I thought I did, yes. But I was wrong. I was fooled into believing the republican bullshit just like you were. You know as well as I do that this isn't a war between the nationalists and the British government. This isn't a war against the imperialists. It's a war against the Protestants. There's no way we can win."

"There is an element of that old hatred driving some of the older members, I admit that, but that's not our motivation, that's not why we joined."

"We were fooled into believing that we were embarking on some heroic adventure, that we'd be greeted as conquering heroes. We're nothing more than common criminals, stealing and killing for our own ends."

"That's not it at all. How do you expect these people not to hate the loyalists when they've trodden on us for so long?"

Mick looked at his brother, taking in his words before speaking again. "Hatred isn't the answer. Our father never hated anyone."

"Leave him out of this."

"Why should I? He was the whole reason we joined in the first place."

"No, you're wrong. The reason we joined is because the Paras, who were working on behalf of the loyalist government in Stormont and the parliament in Westminster, murdered him, in front of us. We can't rely on them for justice anymore."

"There's got to be other ways. There's got to be a better way than murdering three unarmed young boys in a field by the side of the road."

"I wish there were, truly I do, but what? The civil rights movement in Northern Ireland is dead, killed by the Paras on Bloody Sunday."

"I know what happened that day. I saw everything you did. I saw them shoot down unarmed, innocent people, but if we do the same, we're no better than they are."

"You thought all this and still went on the operation last night? No one forced you to go."

"You're right. I went out of duty, and it took last night to show me what all of this is and I can't live with it. I can't live with the guilt of killing those boys."

"You didn't kill them."

"I didn't pull the trigger, maybe. But I killed them all right."

The words stopped Pat, forcing him to rethink what he was to say.

"So what are you going to do?"

"I don't know yet. I have no idea." Melissa was gone. He knew that, especially after what had happened last night. She wouldn't have any evidence that it was them, but she wasn't stupid. She knew. "Don't worry. I'm not going to turn anybody in. I'd rather kill myself than do that."

"Mick, please."

"I'm not about to do that either. If I died today, I'd go straight to hell, no doubt. I need some time to think, but I'm out."

'That's fine. You don't have to stay in. You've done plenty. Dad would have been..."

"Don't you dare mention his name now. Don't you dare sully his name by connecting him to this."

Mick got off the bed and walked out of the room.

He went to the shop that afternoon, opened it to get his mind off the horrors overwhelming him. The customers began to drift in as the evening progressed, and the whispers they brought with them were of the killings the night before. The story had been on the one o'clock news and had already been condemned by the British Home Secretary in the House of Commons, who said that the killings were deliberately carried out to encourage reprisals. A mighty surge of backlash was coming. Details of the soldiers' backgrounds were released. Mick couldn't watch the interviews with their families. The customers in the shop had different opinions. They greeted the news of the killings with grim satisfaction. It was a blow, a brutal, but significant blow toward winning their freedom against their Protestant oppressors in Stormont and Westminster. No one mentioned the soldiers themselves as if they didn't see them as truly human. Mick kept quiet, nodding his head as the men spouted off their opinions about what he knew had happened. He felt ill. There was no escape.

The funerals were in England three days later. Melissa sat at home watching the mourners carrying the coffins of the boys she'd met that night. Rallies were organized in Derry and Belfast, where The Reverend Ian Paisley led up to ten thousand people to the Cenotaph, many of them openly weeping. Dozens of wreaths were laid at City Hall in Derry, where a two-minute silence was observed. The mourners sang hymns before finally finishing with a rendition of "God Save the Queen." In Belfast, Ian Paisley demanded the resignation of the government in Stormont. The leader of the Unionist Party, and Prime Minster of Northern Ireland, Brian Faulkner, called for more troops to be stationed in the province, and condemned the killers as evil. Melissa was sick. It was hard to believe that Mick could have been involved in this. Could he have done this? She knew him, had seen his heart. Evil of this magnitude seemed beyond him. She didn't have any evidence. It was all circumstantial. But that would be enough. The unionist people of Northern Ireland were crying out for someone to pay. One word from her would undoubtedly be enough to have Mick interned, or worse. She needed to see him, to look him in the eye. He'd never lied to her.

Mick was in the shop, closing up. The news of the soldier's funerals was on the radio in the background as he swept the floor. He was numb to it. If anything, Pat had become more defensive in the days since the killings, insisting that they stick together, that if no one said a word they'd be safe. After all there were no witnesses, were there? No one would talk.

Mick felt the vise closing in on him. He needed to see her, to explain what had happened. She was the only link. But what would he say? Why should she forgive him? He hadn't pulled the trigger, but what did that matter? He hadn't done anything to stop it. He could have done something, tried something. The only chance was to convince her that he was finished with the IRA and that he was sorry for what he'd done. It all felt so hollow. He didn't deserve forgiveness, couldn't even forgive himself.

A knock on the door jarred him into the moment. Mick called out that the shop was closed. The knock came again. The person had their hood up but was plainly female. His heart ignited, and he paced over to let her in. Mick stood back as the door opened and watched Maggie pull the hood down to reveal the vicious scowl on her pretty face.

"What are you doing here?"

"Didn't think we'd meet again did you, John?" Her smile was like a weapon.

Mick was taken aback but stood his ground. "I asked you a question," he replied.

"We need to talk. I spoke to McClean. We're both concerned about the security of the operation the other night." She motioned to the seats the customers used. "Take a seat."

Mick did as he was ordered. Maggie pulled up a chair and set it opposite him. "First of all I should introduce myself. My name is Maggie. That's my real name. My surname isn't important. I'm an intelligence officer in the Derry Brigade of the Provisional Irish Republican Army, and as such it's my job to uncover opportunities to strike at the imperialist invaders occupying our country." Mick felt a cold sweat running down his back. Maggie seemed to be burning a hole in him with her eyes. "Another significant part of my job is to root out any potential informers, witnesses and any other rotten elements that could supplant or undermine our struggle." She had seen him talking to Melissa. He tried not to betray the raging sea of fear inside him.

"I'm no informer."

"Who said you were?" She stared back.

"You've no need to worry about me. I'd never rat out my twin brother."

"I know that. McClean testified to you and your brother's loyalty. I'm not worried about that. I don't see that as a possibility."

"Well then, to what do I owe the pleasure of this visit?"

Maggie's looked as if she'd just tasted something sour, and shifted in her chair. "The outcry of the loyalist community since the killings you took part in the other night has been more than we expected. It seems that when they kill thirteen of ours nobody cares, but three of theirs is a crime against humanity. Retribution is coming, and it's my job to make sure we all get through this unscathed."

"I'm here to help in any way I can."

"Good, I'm glad to hear that. Let's start with this. Who was that girl you were speaking to outside the pub in Limavady the other night?"

Mick's entire body stiffened. He had no idea how to answer.

"What girl?"

'The girl you had the conversation with outside the pub. The girl who knew you."

"She's no one, just someone I used to know."

Maggie gave a joyless smile, shaking her head. "I've no time for this. I saw the look on your face when you saw her. You looked like you'd seen a ghost. She knew you. She was inside with the soldiers, one of them stopped to talk to her as we led them out to the car. She's the only link between the killings and us. The RUC are going to turn over every rock and question every witness. The public wants blood. It's not going to be mine. Now, I ask you again. Who was that girl?"

The range of possibilities that opened up to Mick at that moment were like none he'd ever known before. His life, and possibly Melissa's life, depended on what he said next.

"She's an ex of mine. It's pretty embarrassing actually. She's a nut, completely out of her mind. I dropped her like a bad habit."

Maggie stared at him for several seconds before she began again. "And does this ex of yours have a name?"

"She doesn't know anything about me or what I do. I haven't spoken to her in almost a year."

"Don't make me repeat the question."

Mick was stunned by the harshness in Maggie's voice. It took him a second or two to regain his composure. He'd give her real name. She'd be able to tell if he were lying. It wouldn't go any further than this. That one truth would buy him the latitude, the trust to deflect her suspicions. "Her name is Melissa Rice." He spat out the words under the duress of her piercing eyes, regretting it as soon as he had.

"Why didn't you tell me that in the first place?"

'She doesn't know anything. I never told her my business."

"But you live here, don't you, in Free Derry, where everyone knows each other's business? That's what this place runs on. So to suggest that she'd have no idea that you're an IRA volunteer when half the people you pass by on the street know is patently ridiculous."

"She doesn't live around here."

"Where does she live?"

"I don't even know. I think she used to live in Waterside but..."

"Where does she live, Michael?"

Her usage of his name scared him, and she saw that.

"You think I don't know who you are?" She grinned. "I wouldn't be much of an intelligence officer if I didn't know who my own people were, now would I?"

"No, I don't suppose you would be."

"And I wouldn't be much of an intelligence officer if I couldn't tell when someone is trying to hide something from me, trying to protect someone." She inched her chair closer, the legs screeching against the floor as she moved.

"I'm not trying to protect anyone, Maggie. I've no one to protect except my brother and myself."

"Where does she live, Mick?"

"I told you…"

"Jesus," Maggie shouted, and all in one movement she jumped up and threw the wooden chair she was sitting on to the floor. "Whose side do you think I'm on? Why do you think I'm here? I'm trying to protect you. I'm attempting to protect your brother and your other comrades. You said you were going to help me, so help me. I saw the way you two were talking. I saw the look on your face. She wasn't the only one who was upset." She brought a hand to her head and paced around in a semi-circle before bringing the force of her glare back onto him. "That was no crazy ex-girlfriend who you were trying to get rid of. I need to know who she is. I need to know she can be trusted."

"I'm telling you the truth."

"No, you're not. Please don't make me get some people around here who will make you tell the truth, Michael. Don't make me do that, because I don't want to." She picked up the chair again and turned it around, so she was leaning her arms on the back as she faced him. "Listen, Mick, you seem like a nice kid." She was maybe two years older than him, but her face betrayed the horrors of what she'd seen and done. Right at that moment she looked twice his age. "I can understand how hard the other night was for you. I remember my first operation, back in '69. I was scared out of my mind, truly I was. My faith in the cause and belief in my actions got me through, and they'll get you through too, but you have to work with me. You need to realize that we're on your side. You showed your loyalty the other night, but being loyal isn't a one off. It's a lifetime bond."

Mick was trying to listen to her as the thoughts raced through his head. Could he run, and take Melissa with him? No, that was impossible now. She'd never leave with him. He could see the fear, the fanaticism in Maggie's eyes. He wondered what her story was, what had made her like this. What was the use in running? He had to protect Melissa. She was completely innocent. He'd dragged her into this. But how could he tell her the danger she was in? He focused back on the here and now of Maggie's piercing eyes. He had to make a decision, and he had to make it now.

"I admire your faith in the cause, the same as I feel. I'm just a little shaken after the other night. It's hard to see that for the first time."

"I understand that." Maggie's voice was less serrated now as if she were the good cop and bad cop all rolled into one. "It was a great blow on behalf of our cause. You should be proud. But the unionists are up in arms about it. There's a great whirlwind coming. We need to make sure we're watertight on this. I need that girl's address."

"OK, I understand. I just didn't want to get her involved, you know."

"Of course, but the truth is we're all involved."

"The address is 62 Clooney Terrace in Waterside. Her name is Melissa Rice."

Maggie stood up. "You did the right thing." She reached across to shake his hand, and he was standing too. "What do you think she knows?"

"I wouldn't say she knows too much. She's a complete scatterbrain if truth be told."

"Well, it's best we speak to her, just to be sure. How are you doing otherwise?"

"I'm just trying to adjust. It's a new life now."

"I know all about that but once the people in the south join us, we'll win this war."

"Soon, please God."

"Hopefully," Maggie said, moving toward the door. Just as she put her hand on the doorknob, she turned to him. "Any doubts in your mind? Any problems?"

"None."

"If you do, now's the time to say it. If the Brits do find us, they'll find you first. They'll put you under more pressure than most people could bear."

"I've already lived under more pressure than most people could take."

She hesitated for a few seconds, looking him up and down. "I think we all have. Just remember to keep that pretty mouth of yours shut." She closed the door behind her.

He stared after her for a few seconds as she walked down the street and away. His whole body began to shake, breaths slicing in and out of his lungs like razor blades. How long would it be before they realized that the address he'd given her was a fake? Would they go tonight? It was after six o'clock now. It would likely be the next day before they went to look for her. How long before they found her? And then how long before they came for him? The thought of running came to him again, but he dismissed it immediately. Why should he escape? He was guilty. She was completely innocent. His fate barely mattered anymore. He deserved this. He had to get over there, had to warn her. But then what was she going to do? Run? Go to the police immediately? If they connected him to the killings, Pat would be next. That couldn't happen. But she was his priority. He had to get to her first.

He ran to the phone in the corner and picked up the receiver. His hands were wet, shaking as he dialed the number. He held the receiver to his ear and listened to each torturous chime of the dial tone.

"Hello." It was her mother.

"Hello, Mrs. Rice. My name is Tom Adams. I'm a friend of Melissa's from college. Is she home?"

"I'm sorry, Tom, she's not. Can I ask her to call you back?"

Darkness fell across his vision. "Do you have any idea where she is?"

"Not really, Tom. And I don't know you, so I'd be slow to give out any information about that kind of thing over the phone."

"Any idea when she might be home?"

"She'll be home in time for bed."

"Thanks, Mrs. Rice. I'll call back later."

He replaced the receiver and sat down in a wooden chair beside the phone. Maybe they did only want to speak to her. He had no idea of what Melissa's intentions were. Would she want to go to the police about this? He thought of the words she'd exchanged with the last soldier they'd killed, the good-looking one. She knew him somehow, and he knew her, perhaps only from that night, but that might have been enough. Did she have any loyalty left to him? Did he deserve loyalty? He slumped back in the chair as the adrenaline in his body began to fade, and exhaustion swept over him.

Chapter 14

Pat arrived home from work at around six o'clock. Fergus, his boss, had asked him to go for a pint after but Pat made an excuse. He threw his bag down and went to the cabinet where they kept the booze. There wasn't much left. He picked up a bottle of whiskey, a quarter full, screwed the top off and held it to his lips. The amber liquid burnt all the way down, but somehow it soothed the agony. He felt the lightheadedness almost immediately, one step closer to leaving the reality he could no longer endure. The phone rang in the kitchen. Pat heard it and sat down, raising the bottle to take another swig. The phone was still ringing. He put the bottle down and hauled himself out of his seat, made his way into the kitchen and picked up the phone.

"Hello."

"Pat. Jesus, thank God you're there."

"What's going on, Mick? Is everything all right?"

"I had a visit from Maggie, the contact from the other night."

"What? Why?"

'There's something I didn't tell you about. I ran into Melissa outside the pub."

"Your ex?"

"Aye. She seemed to know those English boys somehow. Maggie saw me talking to her. She thinks that Melissa might go to the police. She came to the shop, put all kinds of pressure on me until I gave her up. She's going to go and see her."

"When?"

"She wasn't willing to share those details with me."

"Why didn't you tell me on the night? Why did you let us go ahead after you met her?" Pat felt his anger rising. "Why would you put us in danger like that?"

"It was all happening so quickly. I didn't...think it was going to matter. It just seemed like once everything had started there was no way to stop it."

Pat grimaced but regained his composure. "Where are you now?"

"I'm at the shop. Listen, I need you to do something for me. I need you to go and see McClean. I need to know what he knows. Don't be too obvious..."

"I know how to handle him. I'll see what I can find out. What are you going to do in the meantime?"

"I don't know. I need to warn her that they're coming. I gave them a fake address, but that won't keep them away for more than a day or so, not in a small town like this."

"Maybe there's no need to panic. They might just want to talk to her. She might co-operate and maybe not go to the police."

"You think they're going to take that chance? The whole unionist half of Ulster is baying for a sacrificial lamb. The RUC are going to break down every door, and question everyone in the city about this," Mick said.

"Would she protect you?"

"Why would she? She knows what I did. She must."

"You didn't do anything, Mick. It wasn't you."

Mick didn't answer. Pat let the receiver drop by his side before bringing it back up to his ear. "Right. I'll go to McClean and see what I can find out. You stay put. I'll call as soon as I can."

"All right."

"And Mick? You might want to say a prayer to that saint of impossible causes again because you've certainly got us into another."

Pat hung up the phone before his brother had the chance to say another word. The bottle was still in the living room where he'd left it. He took a deep swig, almost coughing out the burn. McClean lived about fifteen minutes walk away. Pat put the bottle down and went straight out the door. Mick had always been the more sensitive one, the better of them. Pat had been angry that McClean had brought Mick along on the mission, but once he'd realized what was going on it had been too late. What right did he have of denying Mick the chance to fulfill his duty? But Pat had known it had been wrong, had known all along. He'd hoped that Mick would see the war for what it was before it had a chance to leave a stain on his soul. He could accept the realities of the war himself, could bear the weight on his shoulders, but the thought of the effect it was having on Mick was like razor-wire wrapped around his heart. Mick was smart and romantic, not hard and practical like he was. He should have been inventing great things, wooing beautiful women and making babies, not killing unarmed men by the side of the road in the black of night. That was for the likes of him.

A brown Ford Cortina, not McClean's car, sat outside McClean's house. Pat slowed the pace of his footsteps as he approached, wary now. McClean's wife came out of the front door as Pat walked onto the driveway. She was carrying their baby daughter, holding their young son's hand. She smiled at Pat.

"Here for the meeting are ye? They're in at the kitchen table," she said, holding the front door for him.

"Thanks, Mrs. McClean. Off for a wee walk?"

"Just a few times around the block. Best to get out of the house with this kind thing going on."

"Who's in there? None of the top brass, I hope? I don't want to intrude."

"No, just some young blonde. Good looking girl, but serious."

Pat hid behind his smile. "Thanks," he said and went in. Mumbled speech came from behind the closed kitchen door. He turned around, leaving the door on the latch. His running shoes made no sound as he crept toward the kitchen door. He was about three feet from the door when he heard words that stopped him dead - 'Melissa Rice.'

He held his breath to listen. McClean spoke next.

"You know her?"

The next voice belonged to Maggie. "We did some reconnaissance on several of the local unionist councilors last year. We identified her father, Reg Rice, as a potential target. In evaluating him, we also investigated his family. I'd never actually seen her so I didn't recognize her from Saturday night, but as soon as I heard her name I knew who she was."

You said Michael Doherty seemed to know her."

"They knew each other. I've no doubt about that."

"And you spoke to him? Does he think that she can be trusted to keep her mouth shut?"

'Trust a Hun? A Hun who happens to be the daughter of a loyalist Councilor? Are you joking me?"

"You think she's a threat?"

"I don't know what she knows but is it worth the risk?"

McClean seemed to pause. "I don't like the thought of a civilian... and a young girl. It doesn't sit right with me."

"We could strong-arm her but what if that doesn't work?"

"She's not an eye-witness. She didn't see anything."

"Did you not see what the Prime Minister said today, and what Ian Paisley said? They don't need evidence. They want someone to pay for this. Do you want it to be you? She knows enough."

Pat heard the sound of a chair shifting and then silence for a few seconds. "So what do you propose?" McClean asked.

"A simple operation - one bullet. No pain. I'll do it myself."

"Are you looking for my permission?"

"Yes, but if you don't give it, I could go above your head. This needs to happen. We need to protect ourselves from this fallout."

A curtain of silence descended. All Pat heard was the sound of a teacup being put on a saucer and a loud sigh. "All right, but get it done quickly."

Pat's heart felt like a cold stone in his chest. He backed away from the door as silently as he could; aware of the most miniscule sound his shoes made on the carpet below him, praying that the kitchen door stayed closed. He got to the front door and stepped back outside. The street was empty except for a couple of young boys kicking an old leather ball against a massive mural of an IRA soldier in a balaclava holding an M-16. Pat took a deep breath and rang the doorbell. He pushed through the door and went back into the house, calling out as he went.

"Hello, anyone home?"

"Pat? What are you doing here? I'm in the kitchen," came McClean's voice.

Pat pushed the kitchen door open. McClean and Maggie were sitting at the table, their hands crossed in front of them. It would have been clear he was interrupting, even if he hadn't already known.

"Oh, I'm sorry. I didn't realize you had company. I was just passing by, and I had an idea...."

"We're in the middle of something here," McClean said.

"It can wait, it wasn't anything of vital importance." Maggie's eyes were like lasers on him. "I'll head off if you're busy."

"If you're sure it's not important," McClean said.

"I'm positive. I'll call over in the next few days. As I said, I was in the neighborhood."

Pat turned around and walked back down the hallway. He heard Maggie's voice behind him. She was standing at the kitchen door.

"Well done on the other night, by the way. You're a true soldier for the cause."

"Thanks," Pat nodded and kept on out onto the street. As soon as he was around the corner, he extended his stride until he was running. He had to get to Mick. They had to find Melissa, to get her out. He ran all the way back to the barber shop, praying with every stride that his brother was still there, that somehow he'd been able to get a hold of Melissa. Pat was wet with sweat as he banged on the shop door.

The sound of Pat's hand against the glass jerked Mick from the trance he'd fallen into, and he jumped out of his seat, running to the door.

Pat was red-faced, completely out of breath.

"Jesus, are you OK?"

"Did you get her? Did you speak to Melissa?"

"No, she wasn't in."

"Well, did you call her again?"

"I can't keep calling her house every five minutes. Why what's going on, what did you find out?"

"They're going to kill her. Maggie convinced McClean to let her kill Melissa. She's a complete psychopath."

"What? Jesus Christ." Mick felt his heart drop. "When? When are they going to do it?"

"I don't know. They just decided. I went to McClean's house, and I overheard them in the kitchen. We have to get to her. Have you any idea where she might be? We can't just wait around for her to arrive home. We need to find her right now."

Mick fought back the panic raging within him. "Yeah, I have some idea. I know some of the pubs she hangs out in. She's told me about all of her friends, although I've never actually met most of them."

"All right, let's sit down and work this out."

Mick ran into the back, emerging with paper and pencils. Pat was sitting at the small table they used to lay out the day's newspapers. The story on the front cover was about the Prime Minister asking for more British soldiers in Northern Ireland in the wake of the killings. He cleared the table as Mick laid out the paper.

"Wait a minute, what if she's already gone to the police? What if Maggie's too late?"

"Then we go to jail."

Mick spent the next ten minutes or so writing out the names of all the pubs they'd frequented together and the names of some of her friends. If they split up, they could do it.

Melissa stared out at the gray-blue expanse of the river Foyle and the trees on the other side, the Catholic side, where he was from. The clouds above blocked out any sense of the evening sun, and she crossed her arms to ward off the cold she was beginning to feel. She felt empty inside, numb as if she'd never feel anything other than this again. The love in her felt spent, squeezed out of her like toothpaste out of a tube. Nothing had ever hurt like this before. The conflict within her fought with the confusion, the responsibility she now had. The knowledge of what had happened to

Clive, to Norman and his brother Robert was destroying her. Every story in the newspaper was about the truth inside her, the truth that she was struggling to hold onto. She wished so much she'd never gone to Limavady on Saturday night. She wished she'd never met Mick. She wished they could be together, and away from all of this. She wished for so many things.

A couple strolled by, hand in hand. Melissa turned away and stared into the translucency of the river. There was no one to go to other than the police or Mick. Jenny and Victoria knew nothing, hadn't seen anything. Melissa was so used to the veil of secrecy over her relationship that she hadn't even told them anything of what she'd seen or who she'd spoken to outside the pub. Melissa had spoken to Victoria several times since the killings. She had listened to Victoria, and even held her as she cried away the stresses of knowing that she'd spoken to the men found dead the next morning, but somehow she'd said nothing. What would have been the point in telling her, and burdening her with the truth that she carried?

Mick was so sweet, so kind, and so wonderful. How could he have done this? Part of her refused to believe it. He might have been involved but did he know what the IRA was planning to do to those boys? Could he have killed them? Did she ever really know him at all? She brought a shaking hand to her face. She wasn't crying, not anymore. She was just numb now. She knew that she had the power over Mick's life. If she reported him, he'd be interned, and the RUC would break him. The thought of Mick in custody, or in jail, was almost too much. It was then that she realized that she did still love him, despite everything. But why should he and the other thugs get away with it, and who would their next victims be? If she didn't go to the police, their blood would be on her hands. The chasm of pain within her deepened.

"Melissa?" the voice behind her said.

Her heart almost exploded. It was him.

"What the hell are you doing here? Get away from me!" She stood up and started pacing away.

"Please, you've got to hear me out. I have to talk to you. Please," he implored. But she kept on walking, faster and faster until she was running from him.

Mick stood back for a second, watching her go, but the picture of Maggie's face came into his mind. "Please, Melissa, please stop. For your sake, not mine."

He caught up, grabbing her wrist and she struggled against him, trying to shake him off, but his gentle grip was too strong.

"Please, just listen. I know what you must think of me, and believe me it's nothing compared to what I think of myself."

"What the hell do you want from me? Come to finish me off like you did those soldiers? Tying up loose ends, are ye?"

Her words stung, but he collected himself. "Your life is in danger. I need to talk to you."

Her eyes widened. "What? What are you going to do?"

"Nothing. Nothing. I'm trying to protect you if you'll let me. Please, just give me that chance. I need to do something good again. I don't want to feel like this anymore."

She let her arm go loose, and he released his grip. "I'll give you one minute."

"OK, can we sit down?" He motioned toward the bench a few feet away. She nodded, and they made their way across. Months before, they'd sat almost on this exact spot huddled together against the winter cold, with nowhere else to go and nowhere else they'd rather have been. They sipped from a hip flask, numb lips and kisses in the darkness. She sat down on the other end of the bench as far away as it was possible to be. He went to move toward her, but she held up her hands, threatening to leave, so he backed off.

"What do you want from me? This had better be good, or I'll scream bloody murder."

"Just try to stay calm, you know I'd never do anything to hurt you."

"Do I? I thought I knew that, but now I look at you and don't have any idea who you are anymore. What happened to you? What have you done?"

Mick let his head fall into his hands, his body cold. She was the only one who told him the truth as he saw it now, who didn't hide behind the façade of duty or the war. He knew what he'd done, and knew and that atoning for that would be his real duty from now on. "I don't know. I don't know anything anymore. I remember a time when I was happy when I had my father, and my mother here. And I had you."

They were both facing out toward the river again. Her tears had come again and were flooding down her face. She wondered how she had any left.

"That's all gone now; there's no way that can ever be again," she sobbed.

"I know."

The weight of his thoughts made speaking difficult. He knew everything had to be perfect. He knew the rest of his life depended on this.

"I need to talk to you about what happened to those soldiers. I was involved."

"Of course." She didn't look at him. She couldn't.

"We were told we were needed to go on an operation, that they wanted some volunteers who weren't well known." His voice was dull, like a tempered blade. "Our active service unit leader picked us up and drove us to Limavady. We still didn't know what was going on. We had no idea what the plan was." He stopped to take a breath before summoning the strength to continue. "We were told three British soldiers were in the pub, that it was a place a lot of soldiers went to, and that there were IRA operatives inside with them. It was my job to make contact with the operatives inside, and that's when I met you. God, I wish you'd never been there. My heart almost went when I saw you in front of me."

"Why? Because you knew you might get caught?"

"No, not at all. I didn't want you involved. I had no idea what was going to happen next. The thought that they might have hurt you almost killed me."

"But killing those young boys in some field is fine, is it?"

"I thought we might ransom them or question them or something. I never thought we'd execute unarmed, off-duty soldiers like that. I had these notions of a noble fight, an honest war against oppression." His father came to him again as his words ran out. "I suppose I'm angry now, Melissa because I gave up everything for this…. cause, I gave up my future. I gave up you." He looked across, but her eyes didn't deviate toward his. "I did this to serve my community, to make my father proud. But I know now that if he saw what I did the other night, what we did, he'd be ashamed. He'd be ashamed of us, and that in trying to get some justice for his death, we'd just caused more misery and heartbreak for others."

"I need to know what happened in that field. I need to know if you murdered them."

Mick shifted in his seat and watched the Foyle flow past for a few seconds. It was so serene, so perfect. "I couldn't do it. It came to the last guy, the tall one with the brown hair."

"Clive. His name was Clive."

"I couldn't shoot him. I put my gun down. I tried to suggest we take him hostage or something else, something other than killing him, but it was already too late. The other two, the brothers, were already dead. It was too late. It all happened so quickly."

"So you didn't shoot them? You tried to stop it?"

Mick dropped his head, the weight of the memories inside too much. She was looking at him now. "I did, but I couldn't do anything. I couldn't stop it. I didn't move. I tried to say something but…." His voice was raw.

Melissa sat back. Of course, he would say this. No one would admit to shooting those boys, but she knew his heart, he'd shown it to her so many times that she knew he was telling the truth. He wasn't capable of killing like that. Deep down, she'd known that all along. Maybe that was why she hadn't gone to the police yet.

"Who did the killing?" He didn't answer. "I understand your loyalty to your fellow volunteers, but you can't let them just get away with this. The madness that's overtaken the city since your father died needs to stop. This could be our chance to stop it."

"Nothing's going to stop. Not now. Not after what happened to my father and the others. It's too late for this place now. This is going to go on for a long time, and a lot more people are going to die. This is only the beginning."

"No, there's got to be some hope left for us."

"I see it now. I see this war for exactly what it is. The people we killed were British soldiers, but most of the IRA men that I've met would rather go out and shoot a Protestant neighbor who was in the RUC or police reserve than an actual British soldier. When we joined up the local priest, the same priest who takes confession and says mass, swore us in. It was like a religious ritual, part of our faith. I believed that we were in a fight against British Imperialism. I believed that we were there to serve the community, but no one ever mentions the Protestants and what they want or even what's to become of them once we win our socialist paradise."

"I understand why you joined, why you did what you did. I don't blame you for that."

"I do blame myself for not having more faith in what we have, or had, but it was all such a daze then. I didn't know what to think. I had to support Pat. He seemed so sure. But he didn't actually know either, not then."

"Does he have the same doubts that you do?"

"I don't know. We don't talk about things the way we used to. I should have mentioned it to him, but I didn't want to seem disloyal, or weak."

"He probably feels the same way as you do." Her anger was abating, but the confusion was growing.

"It's the strangest thing – I've joined a Catholic defense organization and I'm not even a practicing Catholic."

"My religion barely matters to me, but it seems to define me to almost everyone I meet," she answered.

"The religion itself isn't important. It's the division that counts. Protestant is British and Catholic is Irish. They're the lines this civil war is being drawn with. It's just the name that counts, not the religion itself. So many people say that they'd never marry from the other community because their religion is so important to them."

Melissa thought of her father. "I've heard that a few times," she said.

"But it's not as if they care so deeply about the various rites of their religion, or that they worry which church they'd bring the kids to on a Sunday morning. None of that matters. All that matters is the prejudice and maintaining the division between the people of this province." Mick paused to take a breath. "My superiors know that we met on Saturday night. They saw us talking, and saw how upset we both were. I tried to pass you off as someone irrelevant to me, as a crazy ex-girlfriend but I couldn't."

"So they know about me?" she blurted, the terror rising in her.

"They do. I gave them a fake address, but it's only a matter of time before they figure that out."

"And when they do?"

"Pat found out what they're planning. He came to warn me." He turned to her. "They're going to... I think they're going kill you."

"What?" Melissa felt fear infesting every cell in her body as if she were drowning in it. She stood up and sat back down. Mick reached over and took her hand. It was frigid.

"I'm not going to let that happen. It's not going to come to that."

"How? What are you going to do?"

"I'm going to go to the police. I'm going to tell them that I killed those soldiers, that I acted alone."

"What? You didn't kill them, you just said you didn't."

"I didn't pull the trigger, no, but I'm still guilty." He squeezed her hand and let it go, staring out at the river in front of him. "It's the only way. I'll say I saw the soldiers get into the car with some innocent girls, and that I pulled them over. And then I'll tell them that I killed them."

Melissa searched for the words to express the confusion, the terror and the shock she felt, but they weren't there. "I don't know what to say. I don't even know what to feel. Are you sure? Is there no other way?"

"I deserve this for my part in the killings. I can't live like this. I can't live with the guilt inside of me, and I could never let anything happen to you."

A feeling of calm came over him. It was strange, but he felt better somehow as if a great weight had been lifted from his shoulders. "It's the only way to protect you, and to protect everyone who was on the operation with me, and to rectify the way I feel inside."

"Why are you so loyal to...? Wait, your brother was there wasn't he?"

"I'm not going to talk about that. I won't discuss any other details with you or anyone else."

"You're going to go to jail for the rest of your life."

"You don't think I realize that? I'm just glad that hanging is gone. I'd be dead for sure."

"Is there no other way? I understand the guilt you feel but if you didn't kill them...." She wasn't sure what she was trying to say.

"There aren't any other options. If I do nothing, they come for you. If they came for you, I suppose I could kill them, but that's not me. I've seen that. It's ugly. I could go to the police and sell out my fellow volunteers, but then I'd end up dead anyway."

"You could never do that to your brother, I know that."

"You could run, but why should you have to do that?"

Just for a second she thought about running with him, of going to Paris. Would it be so bad? Did she still love him enough to do that, to save his life?

"But those scenarios still leave me mired in shame, this guilt I have inside of me, and I can't live with it. I don't want to go through life like that. I can't. I have to atone for what I've done."

"Will they stop? Will the IRA stop coming for me?"

"Aye, if I take responsibility for the killings, alone, they will stop. There'd be no reason to come after you even if you are a Hun."

The word stung her, especially coming from him and he saw that.

"I'm sorry, but that's what they called you. It was as if calling you that made it easier for them to order your death as if that made you less of a human being."

They watched the waters of the Foyle drift pass. Mick hadn't told Pat yet. That was going to be hard, but his mind was made up. This was the only way. He'd never been so certain of anything in his life before - other than how much he still loved Melissa. He was still holding onto her hand, and he moved in closer. She looked up at him, his heart almost melting as he looked into her eyes again. The prospect of never seeing her again, of throwing away any final chance he had for happiness with her gave him pause, but the truth was he'd done that long ago. He'd lost any chance for some wonderful, halcyon life together when he decided to join the IRA.

"What do we do from here?" she asked.

"I need to make sure you're OK for a day or two at least before things die down. You'll need to call your parents. Tell them you're staying at a friend's house."

"Where am I going to stay?"

"You'll come to the house, with me and Pat. It's the only place I know you'll be safe."

"You can't do that. You can't expect one more quick one before you go off and do the honorable thing before you sacrifice yourself for me." She let go of his hand as if it were red hot.

"It's not like that. I just need to know you're safe."

"I never should have been in this situation in the first place."

"I feel exactly the same way, but we both got dragged in, didn't we? Kicking and screaming." He stood up, holding out his hand to her. "We should go."

Chapter 15

They walked together, across the bridge, and over into the western, Catholic half of Derry. They spoke little as they went, and then only of trivialities like the setting of the sun, the cold of the night and a bare recognition of the street they'd met on. Mick looked into the windows of the few cars that passed by in the mainly deserted streets, scanning for Maggie's face. She'd probably wait until the next day to check the address. They most likely had at least twenty- four hours, but he couldn't take that chance. He'd go to the police the next morning, and this would be his last night of freedom. He stared at the buildings on either side of the street as he walked past, taking them in as if for the last time. He felt as if he wasn't even seeing them, as if his very presence was already a memory. The memories of his life here seemed complete, as if he would never again walk these streets. Somehow that knowledge calmed him as if he were observing this from the outside and knew that things would be better now. Maybe it would be a relief to be away from all this. Maybe prison would be his escape. The thought of jail didn't scare him as much as the trial itself. He was to be the scapegoat for the tidal wave of anger that was sweeping the unionist half of the province. But he could accept that. He deserved their vilification. It was his mother's face that brought the hurt inside him. She had to hear this from him. She had to know the truth, or something close enough to the truth to offer her some scrap of comfort.

They hadn't spoken for close to five minutes when he finally broke the silence. They had passed through the checkpoints set up by both the British Army and the IRA and were in the Bogside. Only a few people drifted past them on the streets, and the only sound was that of cats wailing in the distance like ghosts in the night.

"I just wanted to say that I'm sorry for all this. You should never have been involved." She looked back at him but didn't answer. "You should never have been on that march, never should have seen what happened that day, what happened to my father. I feel completely responsible for that. I'm sorry."

"Are you apologizing for being with me? For our relationship?"

"I suppose I am. We were so convinced that we could be together if we wanted to be, and that everyone else was wrong. Maybe we were wrong, and they were right. We should never have gotten together. It could never have worked."

"No, Mick, you're wrong now. You're wrong, and everyone else was wrong too, and that's the problem."

They walked on, only minutes from the house, where Pat would be waiting for them. Mick had called him from a phone box along the way.

The words she'd said around inside him. He thought of running, of taking her with him. Was it impossible? Would she ever agree to it? Did he even have the right to ask? He looked across at her, holding her gaze for several seconds as they went. She'd never agree, and even if she did, he'd never subject her to the half-existence of living on the run. Her family would disown her. She'd have nothing left but him, and he knew that, until he atoned for his crimes, he wasn't worthy of that.

They passed into the house without a word; the street deserted outside. Melissa closed the front door behind her. She'd only been inside the house once before, on a stolen Sunday afternoon months ago, spent mostly in bed. This was very different. Pat came into the hallway, the relief of seeing them apparent on his face.

"Oh, thank God you're both all right," he breathed. "I tried those pubs you told me about, Mick. I got a few funny looks when I went asking after you, Melissa," he said, managing to smile. "I'm just so happy you're safe. We're going to work something out. I'll go above our battalion leader's head. I'll make sure nothing happens...."

"Let's go into the kitchen," Mick interrupted. "I know what needs to happen now, and I'm going to need your help."

"All right, whatever you say," he replied, holding the door open for them.

Pat made tea as Mick and Melissa sat at the kitchen table. No one was talking. Night had finally come, the kitchen window now a mirror in front of the black outside. Pat brought over the pot of tea, pouring for each of them before beginning.

"Where did you find her?"

"Somewhere I knew she'd be, somewhere I knew she went when she needed to think."

"And have you been thinking? Have you decided what you want to do?" Pat asked her.

"Pat, leave her alone. This is nothing to do with her."

"It's nothing to do with her, but she's involved now. We wouldn't have spent the last four hours scouring the city for her if she weren't involved."

Melissa began to get the impression that she was being interrogated. Perhaps that was it? Was this the ultimate good cop, bad cop routine? She picked up the cup of tea in front of her, her hands shaking.

"Pat, I've told you, leave her alone. This is for us to sort out."

"I just want to know what she intends to do. Your entire future depends on her. One word from her to the police and they'll haul you in. And that'll be it. You'll never get a fair trial."

"I'd get what I deserve, Pat. I'd get jail."

Pat rocked back in his seat, his face reddening. "I won't let you do this to him," he said, pointing a finger at Melissa. "You can't. You can't do this to him."

"I haven't done anything." She shouted. "I never wanted any of this. I didn't follow him to that pub. I had no idea he'd be there. I had no clue he'd do what he did that night."

"He didn't do anything. You got some fantasy in your head. He didn't do any of it." Pat wasn't shouting, but his words were hard as granite.

"This is going nowhere. I should have known," Mick interjected. "This needs to stop now." They both had anger in their eyes. Melissa was never one to back down, and Pat would die for him. Mick felt that loyalty as a crumb of comfort but nothing more. He'd need to deal with Pat himself. "Melissa, can you wait for us in the living room? I need to speak to my brother alone. I should never have brought you in here in the first place."

She stood up and went into the living room, closing the door behind her. Mick waited until he heard the television flick on before he began to speak again.

"Don't be so hard on her. I dragged her into this."

"She holds the power over your whole life, Mick. If we can get her to keep her mouth shut..."

"What? What happens then? Do we get out of this? I don't want to get out of this. I need to atone for my actions, to begin to forgive myself for what I've done."

Pat's eyes widened. "What are you thinking about doing?"

"The only thing I can do to begin healing, to leave all this behind. I'm going to turn myself in tomorrow morning. I'm going to take responsibility for the killings, alone."

Pat stood up. "No way, no way. That's not happening. I won't let it."

The sense of calm that fell over Mick now was unlike anything he'd felt since that day his father died. It almost seemed possible to feel peace again some day. He stood up, his movements slower than those of his brother. He reached over and hugged him.

"I can't go on feeling this way," he whispered. His mouth was right next to Pat's ear. He took Pat's face in his hands. "This is the only way."

"No," Pat shook his head. It was the first time Mick had ever seen him cry, even at their father's funeral. "I can't let you do that. I can't lose you too."

"It's the only way I can ensure Melissa's safety, that I can make sure that you don't go to jail, and that I can begin to find some peace."

"No, you can run. You could go down south. You could bring Melissa with you. She still loves you. She'll go with you."

"She won't, and I won't ask her." Mick's words were slow and assured. He felt in control. "And even if I did, even if I ran and she came, I can't escape myself and what I've done, what I was a part of."

"No way. Not going to happen. Are you mad?"

"I've no other option here."

"So you choose the option to spend the rest of your life in jail? You choose that option?"

"It might not be that long."

"How long do you think they'll give you for conspiracy to commit murder? And for these killings? Wake up, little brother."

"What would you have me do?"

"Run. Live."

"What about Melissa?"

"If she refuses to do what's best for her? I don't know. We can't force her to do anything."

"So she has to suffer because of my crimes? She has to suffer death or exile because of what I did because she happened to run into me?"

"She won't stay once she knows the danger she's in."

"Can't you see how wrong that would be, to force that upon her?"

"Can't you see that if you admit to this that you'll spend the rest of your life in jail?"

"I've no choice."

"You're not doing it and that's final."

"It's the only way. It's the only way to atone for what I've done and to keep her safe. She means more to me than you know."

"And you don't think she'll want you free, to continue your life with her?"

"I don't see how, not after everything that's happened."

"So you're just going to give up, you're going to give in to this, to sacrifice your entire life."

"I'll still be alive. That's more than we can say for those soldiers I killed."

Tears flowed down Pat's face in great swathes, and he was having trouble standing. Mick took him in his arms again.

"You didn't do anything. You didn't kill anyone. I did it. I killed those boys. It should be me going to jail, not you."

"You can live with this, Pat. I can't. That's the difference between us. The movement needs people like you. There's too much hatred intertwined with the cause and too many relics of the past controlling it. The people of this community need a leader, a strong leader like you. And you can't do them any good behind bars. They need you more than they'll ever need me. You were born to be a leader, not to kill unarmed soldiers by the side of the road. This is the way you'll make our father truly proud, and this is the way out mother will salvage some solace from my decision. You have to be the man you were born to be."

"I can't do anything without you. It's already too late."

"It's not too late. The other night was a horrible tragedy, something we'll have to live with for the rest of our lives, but our lives aren't over yet. There's still a lot we can do to make up for what we've done."

"Going to jail isn't going to bring those soldiers back."

"No, but it might bring me back. I can't go on living with the burden of this. I don't want to be the person I'm seeing in the mirror now."

Pat reached around his brother's back and embraced him, his tears leaving marks on his shirt.

"Earn this, Pat. Make me proud of you. Be the man your community needs, not some sectarian thug, killing and bombing to make his point. This land's already poisoned with them. It's time to begin to heal."

*****

Melissa heard little more than mumblings from the kitchen as she sat in the living room pretending to watch the television. Pat's involvement would be another reason for Mick to take responsibility for the killings. The bond they shared wouldn't stop short of going to jail for the other. Pat's posturing in the kitchen had startled her, but she knew she was safe, from him at least. And Mick would do anything to protect her. He seemed dedicated to everyone but himself. She brought her hands to her face, the feelings she still had for him like a noose sliding around her neck. The door opened, and they walked in. She stood up. Pat looked forlorn, Mick, strangely calm.

"I told him," Mick said, putting an arm on his brother's shoulder.

"You almost seem happy about it. Don't you realize what this is going to mean for you? You're going to spend the next thirty years in jail," she said.

"I realize, but what choice do I have? This is the best result for everyone. I think this is what needs to happen for us all to move forward."

'There is another way. You could run too." Pat said, staring at Melissa.

"Pat...." his brother hissed.

"I can't do that." She shook her head. "I can't just uproot everything I have for someone..." She couldn't finish the sentence. In truth, she didn't know how.

"That's not a possibility. I wouldn't allow that even if you wanted to." He was glaring at Pat now.

"Is that why you brought me back here, to pressure me into running away with you?" An icy finger of fear crept up her spine.

"No, that's not it. I swear it. Tell her, Pat."

"Why couldn't she run? She loves you, doesn't she? Why wouldn't she do that for someone she loves?"

Melissa drew her eyes downward, and Mick felt the anger burning inside him.

"Pat, leave it."

"I just don't see why she couldn't uproot herself for a few weeks?"

"A few weeks? You believe that?" Mick said. Melissa stayed silent her face tight and pale.

"I've already decided, Pat. It's done. I'm not just doing this for Melissa. I'm doing it for your sake too, and mine. It's the only way, really it is. One day this war will end, and when it does the prisoners of this war will be released. I'll just have to hope that day comes soon."

"Maybe that'll only be a few years," Melissa added.

Pat glared across at her, but her words soothed him. It seemed like a real possibility. He took a deep breath and nodded without uttering a word.

"Can you come back into the kitchen? We need to talk to you about how this is going to happen." Mick said.

They took their seats at the kitchen table once more. Pat began speaking. His voice was hollow. All the strength had gone.

"Mick seems to be determined to do this." He picked up the teacup, staring at it as he spoke. "If he does, we'll need to talk to our superiors, to make sure they know what's going on."

"The first thing we need to do is to make sure you're safe," Mick said, looking directly across the table at Melissa.

Another twenty minutes of fights, of arguments, led to nothing. No minds were changed, but Pat began to calm down. The rational side of him came to the fore again, and he realized that his brother's mind wasn't for changing, at least not tonight. He resolved to speak to him the next morning after he'd slept on his decision. He'd play along with Mick's madcap scheme for that night.

"We also need the higher-ups to think that you're doing this out of a sense of duty to the cause, not to assuage any guilt you might be feeling or to protect any witnesses," Pat explained.

"Why?" Melissa asked.

"Mick will meet all sorts of horrible people in jail. He's going to be famous. Infamous. There could be people who'd like to see him dead. He's going to need all the protection he can get, and there'll be none better than what he'd get from his fellow IRA men. So it's vital that he goes to prison as a hero of the republican cause, his head unbowed. Once he's inside he won't have to do anything or take part in any IRA operations, just keep his head down and wait until we can work on getting him paroled."

"It's going to be a long time," Mick said, his voice distant.

"Aye, it will," his brother answered.

All three fell silent.

"If you do go through with this, I'll get you out of there, I swear I will," Pat said.

"I should leave you two boys to talk. This is nothing to do with me now."

"No, please stay for a while. We can have a drink or something." Mick argued.

"No, I'd rather not. Now your time to be together. You have a lot to talk about."

"Let her go, Mick."

"All right, let's get you set up in the spare room." He said, standing up. It felt strange to call their parents' room 'the spare room.'

"I'll just need to call home first, tell them I'm staying out."

"Right. It's on the wall there."

"I know." She almost smiled.

She curled the telephone wire around the door so she could speak in private. They heard the murmur of her speaking to her mother and then, she hung up the phone. The door opened, and she was standing in the doorway. Mick drank her in with his eyes. The regret at not taking the chance he had at a life with her permeated to the core of him.

"Let me walk you upstairs."

She led the way, knowing exactly where to go. They stopped at the door to the bedroom as she held it ajar. The bed was perfectly made, the room spotlessly clean.

"This is it, then."

"I suppose it is," she answered.

The sorrow for him, and for what they should have had together was almost paralyzing. She stared into his eyes, the most beautiful she'd ever seen.

"I just want to say, I admire what you're doing. I don't blame you for what happened to me or for any of this."

"Thanks. That means a lot coming from you."

He wondered if he'd ever see her again. He might see her the next morning before he went to the local IRA commanders, but would he ever look into her eyes like this again? The deep longing was already beginning. Another period of mourning. It was too late for wishful thinking. He took a step backward.

"You'll be comfortable here, and when we get up in the morning I'll, go the local commanders, and then to the police."

"OK," she said, her voice barely audible. He took another step toward the stairs. She stood there, watching him go. He started down, stopping on the first step. She was still at the door. "I love you, Melissa."

Her face tightened as she forced a smile. He kept on down the stairs. It was only when he went into the living room that she finally replied, "I love you too" in a voice so low that she barely heard it herself.

Pat and Mick sat talking for an hour or two without enough booze between them to get drunk. Pat offered to go out and borrow some from the neighbors, but Mick refused. Tomorrow was too important to have the haze of a hangover sagging over it. His story had to be unequivocal. Lying had never come easy, and now he was going to have to lie to the entire country. More shootings and bombings would come to erase the memory of what they'd done. Two Protestant brothers had been found dead just that day outside Belfast. Speculation was that loyalist forces had killed them for having Catholic girlfriends. The public fury about the killings of the soldiers in the field would fade, but the feelings inside him wouldn't. There was no escape from himself. Even Pat understood that now, and he stopped trying to dissuade Mick from the decision that he'd already made.

They went to bed at around two a.m., trudging up the stairs one after the other. The sound of bedsprings from their parents' room told Mick that she was still awake. Her life would not be intertwined with his, as it should have been. He thought of her in another man's arms and pain tore through him. He didn't want to think about the life that he had in front of him; a life bereft of freedom and joy. But he felt the cold hand of fear and saw the real cost of his integrity for the first time. He had the thought to go into the room, to take her in his arms and beg her to run away with him, to leave the horror that was the daily currency of this war behind them. But he knew that could never be. He walked to his room and went to bed alone.

Melissa heard the boys going to bed. She sat up her heart hammering as she heard Mick bid Pat goodnight, and the slapping of backs as they hugged each other. Did she have the power to stop this? Mick seemed determined to turn himself in. It did seem like the right thing to do, but even after everything that had happened, the thought of never seeing him again tore at her. She closed her eyes, letting her head drop down to the pillow. Could she trust the rest of her life to him, who had been a part of the most gruesome killings of British soldiers in these Troubles so far? Would saving him be the best thing for him? Maybe he needed this as much as he made out. Maybe true atonement was his only salvation. She had been wrestling with these questions ever since the shootings on Saturday night. At least now he had taken the decision upon himself. That offered some relief. But still the fire raged inside her. Life, her mother had once told her, was about decisions, decisions made in moments of great turmoil, and it was these decisions that defined us.

She lay there for half an hour, maybe more. There was no clock in the room, and she couldn't make out the hands on her wristwatch. Sleep would not come, not when her mind was racing like this. She had to see him, just to be sure. She got out of the bed, only in her underwear. No way was she going in there like this, so she, pulled her jeans back on and slipped into the sweater she'd left hanging on the chair. She took a deep breath and opened the bedroom door. The hallway outside was completely dark. Even though there was no light coming from either room, she doubted they were asleep. Melissa didn't want Pat to hear her, didn't want him to know she was going to Mick. Her footfall was so light across the carpet that she barely heard it herself. The house was small, and, Mick's bedroom door was only feet away, just across the landing. She placed her hand on the doorknob and took a deep breath as she turned it. Mick was sitting up in bed, his curtains open, the silver light of the night outside covering his bare torso. He smiled as he saw her, the look of surprise fading from his eyes as quickly as it had appeared.

She closed the door behind her without a word. He looked so handsome in the moonlight that the words stopped in her throat. He turned his head away from her as she came inside and stared back out the window, motioning with his hand for her to sit down in the chair opposite his bed. He turned back to face her as she sat down.

"I don't know what I'm doing in here," she began. Nerves gripped her the way they had when she'd first seen him when he'd first asked her out.

"I'm glad you came. I couldn't sleep. I've just been staring out at the night, at the stars. I don't know how much of this I'll be able to see once I'm inside. I need to make the most of it now." He managed a smile.

She didn't know how to reply to that, couldn't imagine life without the stars. "I don't blame you for the things you did. I know how devastated you were by what happened to your dad. I don't know that I would have done anything different if I were in your situation."

"I think you would have."

"What do you mean?"

"I think you would have had more faith in what we had, and I think you would have chosen us, over a commitment to the IRA."

"I have no idea. I don't have an identical twin, another half of the person that I am. I understand that you wanted to support him and the commitment that he wanted to make to the Catholic community."

"Pat is a good man, very smart. He can do great things. If this is the impetus he needs to get out of the IRA and do something good with his life, then my decision will be justified."

"Is that why you're doing this, for him?"

"For him, for you. But like all human beings, I'm selfish at heart," he smiled. "I need to do this for myself."

She felt a rush through her like a stream of heat, and she blurted out the words bouncing around in her head. "But what if you didn't? What if I just didn't tell anyone? What if you went to your superiors and stopped the order to kill me?"

"You don't know the person behind all this. She's very dangerous – completely paranoid."

"She?"

"Yes. She's a woman, not much older than us. The hatred inside her must be strong enough to block out every other piece of humanity. The operation was her idea. There's no convincing her, no stopping her."

"What if you went to the police and told them about her, told them it was her idea, that she carried out the killings?"

"Then she'd just as likely tell them about me and the other volunteers who went on the mission, and I'd be a tout, an informer, and I'd end up dead."

Silence fell on them; the only sound that of a dog barking in the distance. The city was almost entirely quiet. She got out of the wooden chair and sat down on the mattress beside him, her legs touching his through the blanket. "What if we were to run? What if I went with you?"

"I could never ask you to do that. I could never suppose that you might even consider that, not after everything that I've done."

"But what if I offered? What if I said that I'd go with you, just like we planned when we were together?"

"Are you serious?" he said, leaning forward.

She put her hand on his muscular chest. She was smiling now. "Maybe," the smile melted and then came back. "I don't know, what do you think?"

"I think that you need to consider this very carefully, that you need to be sure before you make any promises."

"You said that you still loved me."

"I do. I never stopped. I never will. You'll have my heart forever."

"I love you too. I thought that I didn't anymore, that because of your joining the IRA it had died but I was wrong. I do love you, as much as I ever did."

She leaned in to kiss him, and he felt the feather brush of her lips against his as cool water in the desert his life had become. He ran his hand through the softness of her hair and held her against him, her hand on his chest. He knew no other feeling like this, but he still pulled back.

"I don't want you to make any rash decisions. I want you to be sure about what you're agreeing to, about what this is going to entail."

"I do know. This has been running through my head for days now."

"You'll have to leave everything behind. They won't come after you if we both disappear, but you won't be able to come back for years."

The excitement began to take hold of her and a smile burst onto her face. "We'll come back some day and if we can't, they can come to us."

Mick could see the love for him burning in her eyes, could feel it in the electricity of her touch. He should have been ecstatic, but he wasn't. The emptiness began to fill him again, the void inside expanding.

"Are you sure, I don't..."

"Stop," she whispered, and put her finger on his bottom lip. "Just stop talking now." She reached in to kiss him again, and he fell backward onto the bed, she on top of him. She sat up to pull the sweater over her head and to unclasp her bra. She was utterly intoxicated by him. The love that coursed through her was stronger than anything she'd felt before.

*****

When she awoke, he was gone. She ran downstairs, desperate to stop him, knowing already that it was too late. The house was empty. The note he'd left her was on the table.

Melissa,

I didn't want to wake you. I can't make you go through with what you said you'd do last night. It wouldn't be right to make you pay for what I've done.

You've got a wonderful life ahead of you. Please forget about me.

Mick

Chapter 16

The Long Kesh Detention Center, County Down, April 26th, 1974

The guard led Mick out of the hut. The sun shone over green fields still visible through the twenty-foot high wire fence. The outside tasted cool and clean, nothing like the squalid air inside the over-crowded cylindrical steel huts that he and the other republican prisoners lived in. Long Kesh had once been a Royal Air Force base, and the huts had been built to house airmen during World War II. The government took over the base in 1971 to house the detainees from the internments. The same internments that had given the IRA all the impetus it needed until the Bloody Sunday killings finally convinced the Catholic youth of the province that violence was the only answer. But Mick was not a detainee. He was one of the new breed of IRA political prisoners crowded in with them. Mick pulled the clean air deeply into his lungs, shuffling behind the guard as he led him toward the hut designated as the visitors' center. Mick longed to hear the sound of birdsong or to see a hare in the fields in the distance, any sign of a world beyond wires, guards, and bars. But there was nothing. Nothing to take him away from the grotesquery of the human world he was trapped inside, nothing to remind him of anything else but the rats that scurried under his bed at night.

"Lewis," Mick called out. "Any chance of a cigarette?"

The guard stopped walking and turned to Mick, a half-smile on his face. "Ever the smart-ass, Doherty." He shook his head.

"Yeah, but you like me. Come on, how about a smoke?"

"You've got a visitor. They'll have cigarettes for you."

"Aye sure, it's probably my Aunt Lisa, she never brings anything but that fruitcake she bakes me. I wouldn't mind if it had a file in it. Maybe I'd get out o' here."

Lewis let out a snigger and reached into his pocket. "Don't tell any of those other louts I gave you this, they'll be all over me."

"It'll be our secret, Lewis. Thanks. You're a good man. You'd be even better if you gave me a light though."

Lewis shook his head but still reached into his pocket. He handed matches to Mick, who lit the cigarette. "Let's get moving. We don't want to keep your visitor waiting, do we?"

"Certainly not," Mick replied.

They walked the two hundred yards to the visitors' center in silence. Mick was perfectly content. Good cigarettes were hard to come by. He intended to enjoy this one.

It was a Friday afternoon and the visitors' center was swollen with people. Some prisoners sat resolute, with straight postures and determined eyes. Others looked broken, on the verge of tears, pleading with their families to get them out at any cost. Mick thought of where he might fall, likely somewhere between the two. Lewis led him to an empty table, and Mick sat down, finishing off his cigarette. Lewis told him to stay put, but Mick knew the protocol. He had visitors most weeks. He looked around the room, catching eyes with Davey O'Byrne, also from Bogside. Davey waved across and introduced him to his family. Mick waved back. Davey was a good guy, in for seven years on a bomb-making charge. The bomb factory he'd been working in had blown up. He had been around the back taking a pee. The other two volunteers inside hadn't been so lucky.

Melissa walked in, her eyes immediately on him. The cold shock of seeing her again paralyzed him. She was radiant in her short skirt and dark blouse. Her hair was different, parted in the middle. She sat down; her face a clear reflection of her disgust at the place. The guard left her. Mick gazed across, not knowing what to say.

"Hello, Mick."

"Melissa, what are you doing here?"

"I just wanted to see how you are. It's been a long time."

"Almost two years."

"You're looking well. How are you?"

"I'm doing all right. It's not exactly a holiday camp in here." Just to feel the soft touch of her hair would have been more pleasure than anything he still thought possible. "You look wonderful."

"Thank you," she replied. Her gaze fell from his. "Does your mother come over to see you?"

"She came at Christmas. It's hard. She still lives in Paris."

"How did she take your confession?"

"Not well. I told her the truth. I knew I could trust her. I couldn't have her thinking those things that the paper said about me were true."

"You confessed to those things in court."

"Aye."

She smiled and reached into her bag for some lip-gloss but then thought better of it and focused back onto Mick. "Are you always allowed to wear your own clothes?"

"Yeah, I'm a political prisoner. I have Special Category Status. We're allowed to wear our own clothes, have more visitors, get packages from the outside, just as if we were prisoners of war."

"Is that how you see yourself, as a prisoner of war?"

"I try not to think about it too much. That's for the others to worry about. I'm just trying to keep my head down and do my time."

"A life sentence is a long time to keep your head down."

"Not according to Pat. He says he's going to get me out of here if it kills him."

"How is Pat?"

"Better than ever. He left the IRA and joined a new political party, the Social Democratic and Labour Party. I'm sure you've heard of them."

"The SDLP? Of course. I voted for them last year."

"Does your dad know you voted for a Nationalist party like the SDLP?" Mick smiled, leaning forward.

"No, he'd go through me. After everything I saw and what happened to you, their message of non-violence and civil rights for all resonated with me."

"I like what I hear from them, but they've got their work cut out."

"I suppose they do."

"How is your family? They didn't disown you, did they?"

"No, they didn't get the chance. They never found out a thing."

"They don't know about any of it?"

"Not a thing." She grinned.

"Ignorance really is bliss then."

Mick so enjoyed the sight of her sitting in front of him that he was slow to ask the question that lingered on his tongue.

"Melissa, I have to ask, what are you doing here? I haven't seen you since that night in my parents' house. The last conversation we had was about running together, about changing our lives. We…."

She cut him off. "I remember what we said and what we planned together."

Neither of them spoke for a few seconds while her eyes wandered around the dingy interior of the massive metal hut. His were fixed on her.

"I had some questions for you, questions that have been burning through my mind ever since you turned yourself in."

"I'm sorry I left without saying goodbye. I couldn't do that to you. I couldn't make you give up your whole life for some half-baked existence with me."

"Thank you for that. I've wanted to say that to you all this time."

"You're welcome."

"So many things remind me of you. The river, the stupid bloody river reminds me of you now. Whenever I pass it, I think about you, stuck in here and how it might have been."

"If we'd run together?"

"I know it's crazy. And I know you did the right thing. I was just so confused."

"I was too, for a long time, but I found the clarity I needed. That clarity led me here to this wonderful place." He held his arms out. "It's pretty awful here, but I don't regret my decision. Somehow I've found myself again, the real me, the person that I'd thought had died with my father. I've been able to resurrect myself."

"Do you think you'll ever get out?"

"Maybe one day when I'm old and gray, with a fake hip and none of my own teeth left." He clasped his hands in front of him, leaning forward to her. "According to Pat, I'm going to get out in 1982," he smiled. "He's obsessed. He's got all these plans to petition the Irish government, groups in the States, even the Queen herself. He's like a dog with a bone."

"You always did say how determined he was."

"He needed a cause. Now I'm his cause. Me and everyone in this world he's now determined to change."

"I'm glad." She looked down at the table between them, and Mick watched as a tear broke out and rolled down her face. It was hard to see her cry, but it lifted him, to see that she still cared enough to cry.

"I'm trying to make a difference in here. I can speak to the short-timers, the internees, to convince them to turn away from the violence that landed me in here. They listen to me." He reached across, took her hands in his. The feeling of her flesh against his was wonder beyond description. "Seeing you is amazing, so wonderful. I can't believe there's anything so beautiful as you in this whole messed-up world, but you need to leave here. You need to put me out of your mind and move on."

He contemplated getting up, telling her never to come back but didn't move. Telling her the truth - that she was with him every day - would have hurt them both.

"I need to know that you're not thinking about waiting for me," he continued. "I need to know that you're going to forget about me, that you're going to get on with your life."

"I am," she nodded. "I came here today to close this chapter in my life. I have to put what we had behind me. It's ridiculous. We were only together for a few months. We were nineteen and twenty, just kids. I shouldn't still be thinking about you. I shouldn't still have you in my heart."

Mick didn't answer, kept his feelings hidden. She needed this, and it needed to be her decision.

"You left your mark on me. I feel like I'll never love like that again, and that a part of me is locked up in here with you, that I'm paying for your crimes as you are. I need to feel whole again. That's why I came here today – to say goodbye. You can't move on unless you say goodbye."

A tear trickled down his face, but he didn't move, didn't speak.

"So I wanted to thank you for not waking me that morning in your house, for taking responsibility for those crimes that you aren't responsible for. I hope that you can forgive yourself for what happened that night and admit to yourself that it's not your fault that they died."

"I played my part."

"But it wasn't your idea. You wanted to stop it, but you couldn't. You thought you were honoring your father's memory, serving your community. You did play a part in that horrible crime. You did, but it's not your fault, and you're atoning for that now, in what you did for your brother and what you did for me."

"Pat had nothing...."

"Don't, Mick. Don't even start that. That's not why I'm here." Her tears were gone, her voice stronger. She was more forthright than he'd ever seen her, and she had always been strong. "I needed to see you for both of our sakes. We both need to put that appalling chapter in our lives behind us and embrace what future we might have left." She didn't smoke, never had, but wished she could now. "The times we had together were the happiest of my life. But that's over now. It's time for us to focus on the rest of our lives. You will get out of here someday."

He wanted her to say that she'd wait for him, that they'd be together again no matter what, that their age wouldn't matter. He wanted her to say that with every inch of his being, but never would have let her.

"Maybe, but you'll be married then, with a load of kids, or maybe even grandkids." He closed his eyes for a brief second, thinking about the void of his future. "Thank you for coming here and seeing me. You're the most wonderful person I've ever known. I only regret what being with me put you through."

She reached across and took his hand again. "Mick, I'm fine, really I am. You've nothing to regret. Being with you opened my eyes. I can see the situation in Northern Ireland for what it is now, and I know the way forward."

"At least someone does then."

"I know you think you caused me trouble and pain, but anything you indirectly led me into you got me out of. My life's as normal now as anyone I know. That's all behind me, thanks to you."

He sat back in her chair, letting her words wash over him.

She stood up. "I should leave."

He stood up too, the table between them. He tried to say something, but the words died in his throat.

"So, this is it," she said, managing to smile.

"I suppose so," he whispered.

She went around the table, and he took her in his arms. The smell of her and the press of her body against his was more wonderful than anything had felt in what seemed like a lifetime, and he held her there, wishing that the moment would never end. She drew away after a few seconds.

"Goodbye, Michael Doherty. You're a good person, loyal, honest and sweet. Don't let this place or wherever they put you change that. Stay just as you were. Thank you for what you did for all of us."

"Goodbye, Melissa. Live out the best life you can. You deserve that. Knowing that you're happy will get me through this."

"I am happy and I will be. You've given me so much." She thought to kiss him one last time, to feel his lips on her, but knew that would be too much, for both of them. "Goodbye," she said and motioned to the guard. Mick watched her as she left, the guard by her side until they both disappeared.

Chapter 17

The Maze Prison, County Down, February 6th, 1988

The suit was loose, and he felt a blister coming on his left foot already. The best part of sixteen years was nothing now, gone as if it had never existed. There were no memories to take; only the void where they should have been. A blank space left of time lost. The guards were smiling now, shaking his hand as they held the gate open for him. He was the last prisoner with Special Category Status to be released, the last of the old guard, and a 36-year-old relic of a time before political status for paramilitary prisoners had been revoked in 1976, before the blanket protests and the hunger strikes. The last of the first generation. He took one last look at the guards, and stepped through the gate. Pat was right there, one foot against the wall.

"How's the suit fitting ye?" The smirk on his face was wide as an ocean.

"It's a bit tight, and could you have sent me something a little smarter?"

"I would have, but I was saving it for a special occasion."

Pat got off the wall and threw his arms around his brother. They held the embrace, laughing and slapping each other on the back. The shining light of joy within him superseded the mourning over the time lost.

"Now, let's get the hell out of here," Pat said, as he led Mick over to his car.

It was the first time Mick had been in a private car since the night the soldiers had died in that field by the side of the road.

Pat was elated as he sat in the driver's seat, his brother beside him. He reached across to hug Mick again. Pat had visited him at least once a month, often more than that, but it was never like this. The feeling of seeing his brother, the other half of him, without guards watching, was almost too wonderful to take. He was overflowing, the tears beginning to well in his eyes. Pat pulled back, a smile etched onto his face.

"You're not going to start crying now, are ye?" Mick asked.

"You're only out two minutes and you're already annoying me?"

They pulled away and the prison faded into the distance. In seconds it had disappeared, sixteen years gone. Mick turned to his brother.

"You never stopped. You never stopped trying for me. You always were a pain in the arse, but I never thought anything good would come of it."

Their laughter filled the car.

"You always said you'd get me out, didn't you?" Mick continued.

"Aye," Pat beamed. "You know me, little brother, I'm like a dog with a bone. I never gave up on you, not for one day."

"Well, you said you'd have me out by 1982. I might be mistaken, but I believe that was six years ago. I could be wrong - prison time goes slowly. Maybe it really is 1982, and it feels like 1988."

"Ah, would you be quiet or I'll have you thrown back in there for good this time. Jesus, I'm wondering if the parole board made a mistake now. It just goes to show that if you ask someone enough times, they'll eventually say yes, just to shut you up if nothing else. And if you can get the right people to ask. The fact that you were the last official political prisoner left helped too. Your Special Category Status was awkward for them, what with all the other prisoners wanting it too."

The bitter memory of the hunger strikes stabbed at him; the ten dead men, all willing to give their lives for the political status he had. They died for something he gladly would have given them if he could. The courage they had in their own convictions had been startling and, just as Bloody Sunday before, their deaths had given the IRA more impetus at a time when public and political support had been waning.

"The fact that you were a model prisoner studying for your degree and all that, helped too," Pat said. "But who really cares? You're out, and that's all that matters. You wanna go for a pint? It's almost two hours back to Derry."

"Nah, there'll be plenty of time for that. I just want to get back and see everybody. How's the family?"

'They're great. They're looking forward to getting Uncle Mick home."

The lush green color of hedgerows and fields shot past them on either side. It had been so long since he'd seen anything like this, since he'd felt this sensation of movement. It was exhilarating, stupefying. It was amazing to know he could still feel like this. It was like emerging from a coma. They drove through the streets of Lisburn, a window into a new world. Clothes, hair, the people themselves, all looked so different. He felt like a relic from a bygone age, stuck in a time that no longer existed. Even the cars had changed. They were bigger and had multiplied. Pat asked him again if he wanted to stop, but he refused and they drove on. He didn't feel like dipping his toe into the ocean of the new society he saw out there, not yet at least.

Pat looked fit and handsome in his gray suit. Mick was thin and sallow, the cumulative effect of years inside.

"How's business?" Mick asked.

"Great. We hired another guy last week, which makes seven full-time now. There's plenty of work. It's not like the old days. You don't need to be Protestant to get work anymore. I have a shiny new job ready and waiting for you whenever you feel like taking it. Have you given much thought to what you're going to do?"

Mick paused and adjusted the seatbelt before he answered. The truth of what he'd planned lay heavy on him. He wished he could tell Pat. "Yeah, thanks for the offer. I may well take you up on that. I might keep up with the college stuff and get that Masters I always wanted."

"Are you gonna be one of those creepy older students, hanging out in the college bar, perving on the young girls?"

"I hope so."

"I wouldn't hold that against you, you've got a lot of lost time to make up for."

"Yes, I do. How's your work with the party?"

"We're in talks with our old comrades in the IRA at the moment. John Hume met Gerry Adams last week."

'That's progress. It would have been hard to imagine the leader of the SDLP meeting up with the head of Sinn Fein back in the 70's."

"We're trying to change things. It's tough though. The talks are torturous, and they haven't even mentioned the unionists yet. It's just a case of trying to convince them how futile all this violence is. The boys in the IRA aren't too keen on giving up the rifle in favor of the ballot box, but we're trying to persuade them, and we'll keep trying until they do."

"I campaigned for your lot in the last election, even though none of the people I spoke to about you were able to vote. They were all in jail."

"Unfortunately it's only actual, real votes that count, but thanks for the thought. Thankfully we didn't need your help in the end."

"No, you didn't." Memories filled his mind and he was back in the 70's again. It was easier to wallow in the only time he really knew. "It seems like a million years ago that we went through IRA training ourselves. I wish I could go back and tell my younger self…"

"I know. We were so young. I've tried to forgive myself for what we did. We thought we were doing the right thing, defending our community from the Imperial British Army." Pat's face tightened.

"You've made up for it since, Pat. I'm proud of you. Mum is proud of you, and if Dad could see us now, he'd be proud too. I'm sure of it. It's people like you that have given this province some kind of hope for the future."

"Thanks. It's just so much. Everyone seems like they'd rather kill each other -the republicans, the loyalists, the RUC, the UDR, the British Army. It seems like no one wants to be right."

"Keep fighting the good fight for us. We need you."

"Have you ever thought about getting involved yourself? We could use a smart guy like you?"

"A convicted IRA killer? Are you joking?"

"Just think about it."

"I haven't decided what I'm going to do yet. I'm just trying to get used to all these new cars and haircuts. I'm not sure I can live in a world without Led Zeppelin. You've had eight years to get used to that."

Pat smiled and paused a few seconds. "You heard about Paul McGowan?"

Mick cast his mind back, remembering his friend who'd been there with him on Bloody Sunday, who'd joined the IRA a few weeks before he had. "No, I haven't heard his name in five years. I know he did some time on a weapons charge down south. Is he out?"

"He joined the INLA a few years back."

"Why would he leave the IRA to join a splinter organization?"

"Who knows? Power maybe? To be a big fish in a small pond? Someone said it was out of sympathy with the INLA members from Derry who died in the hunger strikes, but I really don't know."

"So where is he now?"

"Dead. He was killed last year in a feud with the IPLO."

'The IPLO? Who the hell are they?"

"The Irish People's Liberation Organization – a splinter organization of the splinter organization. Rumor has it that they're more into drugs than anything else. They had a few cross words with their former masters in the INLA and started a feud. Paul got caught up in it. He walked out to his car one morning, and a motorbike rolled up. You know the rest."

"Poor Paul. He was a lost soul after the march. What about John Gilmore?"

"I don't know. He went to jail after he was caught with a weapons stash. He did a few years and got out. The last I heard of him was he was living in Australia."

"Why didn't you tell me about Paul when I was inside?"

"I didn't want to depress you. I can only imagine how hard it was for you in there."

"It's all such a waste," Mick breathed. "The IPLO? Who the hell are the IPLO?"

"I don't know. All I've heard about them is to do with killing other republicans in that feud." Pat reached into his pocket for a pack of cigarettes. He offered one to Mick, who refused.

"I always said I'd give up when I got out. It was easy to say that. I never thought I was going to." He laughed. "But today is day one."

"Good for you, brother. I won't have one either then." He put the cigarettes back into his pocket.

"It's hard to express how good it is to speak to you without guards and other prisoners listening in, without fear of saying the wrong thing or feeling the wrong way about something. It's almost too much for me right now. I'm getting into this freedom thing again. I've got a feeling I'm going to like it."

"You will. We'll make sure of that. Did the other prisoners know your feelings about what was going on outside?"

"They did and they didn't. The best way for me to get along was to toe the party line. I always promoted the cause of not killing people to whoever would listen although we didn't sit around having great political debates for hours on end."

"It took what you did to make me see another way."

"I'm glad something good came of it. I tried to show some of the younger prisoners the futility of the anger they felt and that the Protestants weren't behind all the evil in the world."

"I know you did. Your old cellmate, Sean Campbell's doing great. He's looking forward to seeing you at work."

"Sean's a good kid. He was lucky that he had you to give him a job. All the ex-prisoners you employ are."

They sped past a sign for Londonderry. All the street signs read Londonderry, the official name, changed by the British, hated by the Catholics who lived there.

"Derry's changed, certainly from what you knew. The last time you saw Bogside it was Free Derry." Pat stopped talking for a few seconds, staring out into the past. "That seems like a thousand years ago. It only lasted a few more weeks after you turned yourself in. The troops rolled in like it was an invasion, and I suppose it was. Everything changed. The soldiers and the RUC came back, but it didn't improve anything. Things only got worse."

"How is it now?" Mick asked.

"It's OK. It's not the beautiful utopia we all wish it were, but you coming back should improve the place a bit, for a few ladies at least."

"I'm very eager to improve the lives of any ladies I might run into, believe me." As he spoke Melissa came to him. He seldom thought of her anymore. He had trained himself to put her out of his mind but this time the picture of her stayed with him. He wondered what she looked like now. She could only ever be a different version of beautiful, and would be for the rest of her life, no matter how age tried to wither her. He wanted to ask Pat about her, even though he knew he'd have no clue. He wanted to talk to someone else who'd known her, just to mention her name in conversation. It was so ridiculous. He hadn't seen her in almost fourteen years, since she'd come to put an end to any thought of him in her life. He needed to forge his own way, to forget about the past, no matter how it tugged at him. There was a place for him in this new world, a place no one else could know about, not even Pat. Not yet.

*****

Flags and signs to welcome him home tinseled the outside of Pat's house. "Welcome home, Mick," Pat said. The sound of the car caused a tsunami of children to pour out of the house. It was hard to believe that they all could have fitted inside. Pat's oldest son, Michael, was first to reach Uncle Mick as he got out of the car. Mick took him in his arms. He was heavy now, almost nine years old. His younger brother Peter was right behind him, with Pat's daughter Siobhan toddling behind. The other kids were cousins, neighbors and children of old friends. None of them had been born the last time he'd seen this street. His mother was standing at the door and the tears began down her face as she walked toward him, her arms extended. He hugged her. She fit perfectly underneath his chin. She was older now, but her beauty remained undimmed. The thought of the pain he'd caused her was like broken glass inside him.

"I'm so sorry, Ma. I'm so sorry for what I did to you."

"That's all in the past now. We've got the whole rest of our lives to look forward to."

Her French accent warmed him. It sounded like home.

Pat's wife, Pamela, came through the crowd of kids and embraced him as she would have had they known each other properly. She was from Creggan, was three years younger and had been around when they were growing up and though Mick couldn't remember her, he always pretended to. Mick picked up his niece,

Siobhan. She was four. He'd met her only once. She squirmed in his arms, reaching out to her father. So many people mixed them up, but she wasn't going to be fooled. Pat tried to let her settle in Mick's arms, but she wouldn't. Pat took her, and she threw her arms around his neck, burying her face on his shoulder. Mick turned away. He shouldn't have felt the bitter sting of her rejection, but he did.

"Welcome back, Mick," Pamela said. "How does it feel?"

"God, I don't know yet. It feels good. It feels great. It's all so different."

"A lot of things have changed since '72," Pat said.

"I just hope I can catch up."

"You'll be okay. We'll make sure o' that," Pamela said, and hugged him again.

Several of his aunts and uncles were outside now. Mick hugged each of them in turn. They greeted him as a returning hero. They didn't seem to care what had happened, what he had supposedly done. His crime had been buried by countless other murders and bombings. So much had happened since then. Brutality had become banal. He was still officially IRA and scanned the crowd for fellow volunteers. He'd never done anything to revoke his membership. Despite his unspoken differences with them, the question of publicly snubbing the IRA had never been a realistic consideration. They had been his support system inside, his protection. He'd stayed away from the hardcore sectarians, and there had been plenty, but there were also many young men like him, caught in the fog of a dirty war. He had been a respected man inside. The older, hardcore IRA men admired him for the audacity of the murders he'd been convicted for, while the younger men looked up to him, craved the guidance he offered. He'd been valuable inside. He had negotiated for the hunger strikers in '81, had helped save some of their lives. What would he be here, on the outside?

Mick still had his arm around his mother as they went back into the house. He greeted Armand, her new husband, by shaking his hand at the door. He was tall and thin with gray hair and glasses. He'd never met him before, his own stepfather. It was hard to describe him as new – they'd been married for eight years, but he was new to him, and Mick suspected he always would be. But his mother was happy and that was enough. The inside of his Pat's house was foreign to him. He peered around, taking in the colors of the wallpaper, the lamp on the hall table, the carpet beneath their feet, the curtains rustling in the breeze.

Pamela had laid food out on the dining room table inside. He picked up a sandwich – the first non-prison food, other than packages, he'd eaten in almost sixteen years. Pat handed Mick a beer and their mother a glass of wine. She had her arm around Mick's waist as if it was stuck there. Pat got himself a drink and came back to stand beside them.

"Thanks so much for letting me stay with you. I know it's a bit of a tight squeeze here at the best of times with the kids. I'll get my own place as soon as I can. You don't need me in your hair."

"You stay as long as you want, little brother. It'll be a pleasure to have you around."

"You say that now. What about when I start walking around in my underwear and scratching myself?"

"Just give us a bit of warning on that and we'll at least try and get the women and children out of the house first. That kind of trauma could have a permanent effect on them."

They talked for a while before Armand came over. He was a businessman in Paris. He was smart and witty, just as Pat had said. He was scared of Grand-père too.

The afternoon faded into night. Mick's hand ached from shaking one hand after another. He'd spoken to as many people in the ten hours since he'd gotten out as he had in the entire time he'd been inside. His voice was almost hoarse. He wasn't used to talking this much anymore and felt that everything he said should have been profound or memorable. The kids outside were dragged home and Pat put his to bed, all in one room now, thanks to their Uncle Mick. But they didn't complain and even Siobhan made some kind of effort to hug him after her father forced her.

"Don't worry. She'll be used to you in no time," Pamela assured him before carrying her up the stairs. Armand took their mother back to the hotel they were staying in at about eleven o'clock. Pamela had already gone to bed half an hour before. Some of the uncles and cousins stayed another hour or so before leaving to stumble the walking distance home. Hardly anyone he'd grown up with had left Derry, other than those dead or in jail. With everything that had happened, they'd all stayed. Everything had changed yet was somehow completely the same.

Hours passed. They were alone in the living room. Pat rolled the whiskey around the tumbler he held in his hand, staring into it. Mick felt the gentle hand of sleep come over him, was barely awake now.

"Oh my God, this is incredible. I never want to get off this couch."

"We were thinking about getting a new one. That's getting a bit old now."

"Give this to me if you do. I'll pitch a little tent over it to keep the rain off. I'd be happy."

"You can do better. You'll be surprised at how comfortable the world outside of prison can be."

"This is one of many pleasures I intend to partake in over the coming weeks and months."

Mick was expecting an answer to his quip, but the room went quiet. Pat's head had dropped. He was staring out in front of him. There was no sound from upstairs. They were all asleep.

"Mick, I...just wanted...." Pat fumbled the words as if they were wet fish in a bucket. Mick raised his head. "I just wanted to apologize for all this. I feel like...I feel like I stole those years from you."

Mick let his head fall back and closed his eyes. "It's not your fault," he said and spiraled into the contentment of a deep sleep.

Chapter 18

Mick started work two days after getting out of jail. Pat had wanted to give him the week off, but Mick insisted on starting on the Monday. Something had broken within him and he didn't want to feel useless anymore. Sixteen years was long enough. The children would be gone during the day, even little Siobhan, still scared of her new uncle even after they'd spent Sunday together, would be in pre-school. Pamela worked part time in a local café. His mother and her husband had flown home the night before, with a promise from Mick to visit in the summer. The Doherty boys were up at seven and at the job site at half past, a new office block in the city center. Mick was installed as a laborer, at least until he enrolled in college at night and had a chance to use the degree he'd earned inside. He attacked the work. It felt good to be working toward something, not just counting hours. He didn't see Pat much during the day and had lunch with the other laborers. Several of the other laborers and plumbers were ex-IRA men. Pat made a point of hiring former volunteers trying to turn their lives around. Mick had met several of them inside.

Sean Campbell, a twenty-three-year-old from Bogside, who had spent three years sharing a cell with Mick, was sitting beside him at lunch. He lit up a cigarette before offering one to Mick, who refused with a smile.

"This beats the last place we were hanging out in," Sean said.

"Yes, it does, even in this weather."

The rain was spraying the windows in front of them, the wind rustling the tarpaulin over the gaps in the wall. The sandwich that Pamela had made for him tasted good. He reached for his flask of tea.

"Your brother was very good to me. He's been good to all of us."

"He's a great guy," Mick said, taking a sup of tea. It was too hot, and he blew on it, fluttering steam. "I'd never have gotten out without him and the lawyers that he hired. I'm sure that's where half the profits of this company went over the last few years."

"Aye, I reckon so." Sean had only been out less than a year, working for Pat around six months. There was no one else around, but he still lowered his voice. "Now that you're out, have you decided what you're going to do with yourself?"

"It's early yet."

"I mean have you given any more thought to what we talked about inside?"

Mick eyed him. "You haven't told anyone about that, have you?"

"Of course not. I would never." Sean looked insulted at the notion.

"If you told Pat...." A tiny spike of anger rose within him, but it disappeared. "I said those things without knowing that I'd ever get out again. At that stage, there was no prospect of me seeing the light of day for another ten years at least. I had no idea I'd be sitting here with you now."

"That doesn't change the things you said."

"No, it doesn't. What about you?" Your brother's still active isn't he?"

"Aye, he's in the thick of it. Still talking about the next big operation to blow this all open." Mick nodded; he'd heard it all before. "I have a girl now, Martina," Sean continued. "She's from the south. We're thinking about moving down there, getting away from all this."

"The weather's no better down there." Mick smiled.

"Aye, but there's no war there."

"I'm delighted for you," Mick raised his flask and tapped it against Sean's. "Here's to you and your girl and here's hoping I find one myself soon."

"You will, old man, you will."

"Right, let's get back to work," Mick said, raising himself to his feet.

Sean screwed the top back onto his flask and followed his friend across the floor to the wall they'd been working on.

*****

Days turned into weeks and weeks into months. It was June by the time Mick finally moved out. Every time he had mentioned even the prospect of moving in the preceding weeks, Pat and the boys had shouted him down, but he knew he had to leave eventually. The day came, and Siobhan cried, holding onto him like a life raft as he tried to say goodbye. Pat and the boys came with him to help him move into the new apartment in the city center; just a few minutes walk away. In truth, he barely needed them, as he had so little stuff to move, but the fact that they wanted to be there for him reinforced his sense of belonging, that he was somebody outside. They stayed for an hour or so after they'd moved in the mattress and the sofa that he'd bought himself until the boys grew restless, and Pat took them home. Mick hugged each of them, promising to be over for dinner the next day and then they were gone, only silence left behind.

The news report on his small television told of a bomb in Lisburn that had killed six off-duty British soldiers. They had been on a charity run when an IRA unit planted a bomb under the van they were traveling in. The other news story was of the murder of a member of the Ulster Volunteer Force in Belfast. It was thought that he'd been killed in retaliation for the murder of three Catholic civilians by the UVF in a bar in Belfast a few weeks before. Mick let his face come down into his hands, his warm breath rebounding onto his cheeks. The emptiness of knowing that nothing had changed spread through him. The killings he'd gone to jail for, so reviled at the time, had faded into an ocean of blood and misery. He'd wanted to make an example of himself, but no one had paid attention. They'd just carried on hating and killing. He thought of the soldiers murdered in that van, and the killings of the Catholic men as they drank a pint in their local pub a few weeks before. What had they achieved? What had any of the killings achieved? He was thirty-seven in a few weeks. The flower of his youth was gone, tossed away for nothing. Many of the republicans he'd known inside thought as he did. They saw the futility of the violence the province was soaked in, but they were a minority. But the majority came out even more committed to the cause than ever. And there were always more young boys and girls, disillusioned with their own lives and their treatment by the Protestants or the Catholics or whoever the other side happened to be. There was a steady stream of young people willing to destroy themselves for a cause that could never succeed.

The view from the window showed the street, a hundred feet below. He had to get out, had to do something to relieve the immense pressure building inside him. It was easy to make plans inside, but carrying through with them on the outside, in the real world, was a different matter. Did he have the courage to do this, to truly make a difference? Rain scattered down from above onto the street below, licking the window. It didn't matter. He had to get out. He picked up his jacket and hurried to the front door, slamming it behind him. The marble staircase was old, the steps worn from years of use, and he was on the top floor. The lift was out of order but going down was easy.

He'd been out a few times with girls he'd met. Several people had tried to set him up, but he'd always refused. He didn't want to disappoint anyone, didn't want to be held responsible for what might happen if he wasn't ready to settle down or if he wasn't ready yet for what Pat had.

It took a minute to reach the bottom of the staircase. The rain was still coming down outside but now as a thick mist. He stepped into it, felt the moisture wash against his face. After sixteen years with hardly any exposure to the elements, the rain felt almost as good as the sunshine. Wind felt nearly as beautiful as a rainbow. He looked forward to the coming of a cold winter and the layers of stunning white that it might bring. Without anywhere to go, he raised his collar as he walked into the wet. He just walked, up along Foyle Street and toward the Guildhall. It was ridiculous, but this area still evoked the memories of when he'd met Melissa. He could see her face as she looked that day as clearly as if she were in front of him now. He'd never seen anything quite so gorgeous as her. It was hard to believe that beauty like that existed, particularly in a town like this one. He remembered feeling comforted just at the sight of her as if merely seeing her was enough to change him. And then she dropped her wallet. It was like Christmas morning.

The rain thickened and he saw a pub a few yards in the distance. It never took long to reach a pub in Derry and he ducked inside, taking a seat at the bar. It was worn, but clean and well-maintained. The other patrons inside were mainly old men, barely passing him a glance in between sups of porter and puffs of cigarettes. The barman was in his forties and wore a thick black mustache. Mick ordered a beer and sat back, still thinking about Melissa. She had become his definition of beauty and happiness in all those years inside. Her image invaded his thoughts. She must have been married by now, with children of her own. She'd have no time for an old IRA man like him, nor should she.

One of the old men let out a raucous laugh that stirred Mick from his thoughts. Glad to be offered temporary escape, he lifted the pint glass to his mouth and took a gulp of beer. Beer had never tasted this good before he was in prison -another of the benefits of losing almost sixteen years of your life. The barman flicked on the television behind the bar. A special report on the killings in Lisburn was on. The IRA had already claimed responsibility, promising to wage unceasing war against all security forces in Northern Ireland. The barman shook his head. Mick looked out the window and into the rain. He thought back to the Remembrance Day bombing in Enniskillen the previous November when the IRA had set off a bomb in the middle of a crowd gathered to commemorate fallen soldiers from the world wars. He had sat in prison with his fellow IRA inmates, watching as live pictures of the scene came on the screen in front of them. Some of the IRA men were as shaken as he was at the callous nature of a bomb set off with little warning among a crowd of civilians. Others cheered the deaths of the ten Protestant civilians. The IRA dismissed the operation as a disaster, a monumental mistake. They'd set off the bomb too early and the death they'd brought to Enniskillen that day was inflicted on the wrong people. But although the botched bombing caused them to pause and apologize for the civilian deaths, it brought no cessation to the violence that they inflicted. No meaningful change occurred. They would continue to wage their ceaseless war. The realization hit him that day, after almost fifteen years inside, that the IRA, the organization he'd joined to protect and free his community, was the greatest scourge on the people of Northern Ireland. That night he made his silent oath to cripple them in any way he could, to do something to attempt to jar the endless cycle of death and misery. But it had been easy to make silent promises on the inside.

He picked the glass up, downed the remainder of the beer and made for the door. The rain had stopped, yellow sunbeams beginning to glint through the clouds above. He walked toward the Bogside, where the memories of his youth still ran along each street corner and hid behind every hedge. He continued toward the hulking gray of the Rossville flats, still there, still standing, but not for long. They were due to be demolished. The whole place was going to change. That was only a good thing. He stopped, looking down at the spot where his father's body had fallen, his blood spilling out onto the asphalt. There was no marker though his name was listed on the obelisk a few feet away with the other victims of the Paras that day. Mick stared at it for a few seconds and walked on, his convictions strengthened.

The burnt-out cars had gone with the barricades, all removed after the army had reclaimed Free Derry during Operation Motorman in 1972. The rubble barricade where Noel and the others had died was long gone. Few visible signs of that day remained, just random bullet holes burrowed into walls. He walked on, not seeing anyone he knew. He was glad of that. He didn't need to have his emotions stirred by some kind of false nostalgia now. The barbershop was gone, sold off soon after he went to jail. It was still a barbershop, just run by another family now. He didn't want to see it. Seeing it wouldn't serve any purpose.

It took him another ten minutes to reach the street where McClean still lived. A few boys were playing football outside, all wearing either the colors of Glasgow Celtic or Derry City. Mick stopped dead, all too aware of what he was about to do. McClean's front door opened and a teenage girl walked out. She didn't seem to notice Mick standing on the road opposite the house. Mick let her walk down the street before approaching the house himself. He rang the doorbell. McClean's wife answered the door.

"Hello, can I help you?"

"My name is Michael Doherty. I'm looking for Mr. McClean. I'm an old colleague of his." Mick was amazed at the level of calm that had swept over him.

She looked him up and down with suspicious eyes. "I'll let him know. Stay here." She shut the door behind her, coming back thirty seconds later.

"He'll see you in the kitchen." She opened the door for him, and he stepped into the house. "Take off your jacket and show me your belly."

Mick handed her his jacket and lifting up his sweater. Mrs. McClean seemed satisfied and motioned for him to walk through.

McClean looked much older than he reasonably should have, even with the sixteen years that had passed, with a graying goatee and little hair left on his head. He greeted Mick with a smile. "Welcome back, son," he said, hugging him. Mick forced his arms around him. McClean had never spent a day in jail, not for the killing of the soldiers outside Limavady, not for anything. "Sit down there," he continued. Mick sat in the kitchen chair. "I want to say how proud we were of you for doing your time like a man. You never opened your mouth once, and I know that can't have been easy."

"It wasn't, but I'd never do that. I'd rather die than grass." He hoped the line didn't sound practiced. McClean seemed to buy it.

"Well, just know that it was appreciated. I spoke to your commanding officer inside. He said that you were quiet but were an excellent mediator with the prison authorities and a mentor to the younger prisoners."

"I tried to help out where I could. It was us against them in there. I was in an unusual situation, being that I was the last prisoner with Special Category Status, the last of the political prisoners. It was difficult to handle sometimes, particularly during the tragedy of the hunger strikes."

"That was a terrible time for everyone in the republican community. We did gain a lot of political traction from it, however. Those men didn't die in vain."

"I knew them, each one of them." Mick saw their emaciated faces, their straggly, unkempt beards.

"I knew several of them myself. They're venerated heroes of the cause now."

"How is the fight against the imperialists?"

"I'm sure you see what everyone else sees on the news. We have successes and failures. The bombing in Enniskillen last year shook the entire organization to its core. The unit that carried out that attack was disbanded, but we have to move on. A worse tragedy would be if we gave up on the nationalist people of Northern Ireland because of one mistake."

Mick tried to think of an answer to what McClean had said, but couldn't. Nothing else remained to be said. "I want back in. I want to volunteer again."

McClean's face didn't change. "Are you sure?"

"I've had sixteen years to think about this. I'm very sure."

"A lot of people in your position would consider their debt to the cause paid in full. No one would hold that against them."

"I feel I've more to give. I'm not as young as I was but who is? I'm more experienced now. I know what I can and can't offer. I know the cause. I met a lot of great men during my time inside and learned a lot from them."

"You don't want this," McClean stated.

"With all due respect, you don't have any idea what I want. I want justice for the republican community of this province."

"What about your brother? Why don't you follow the direction he went in? He's not going to be happy if you come back."

"Pat's naïve enough to think that the Brits are going to listen to the SDLP's pleas for peace, that they pay attention to anything other than brute force. I wish we lived in a world where the SDLP held the key to a better future for Northern Ireland, but I know that's simply not the case. The future is in our hands."

McClean stood up and offered an outstretched hand. "All right. Give me some time to think it over. I'll give you a call in a few days to let you know what I've decided."

Mick leaned forward and shook his hand.

Chapter 19

The raw desolation of the landscape mirrored the stream of thoughts flowing through Mick's mind. He arched his body around a fallen branch, his hand on an archaic, dilapidated stone wall to keep his balance. Sweat beading on his brow mixed with spattering rain. Martin Heggarty, a twenty-five-year-old from Armagh whose brother had been shot down by loyalist terrorists a few years before, trudged several yards in front of him. They'd been walking through old disused fields, long since abandoned to the stones, and along rough-hewn country paths, hacked out of hedgerow for twenty minutes. Mick felt the strain, the bag on his back growing ever heavier but he kept on, never outwardly showing any sign of the tiredness that tightened its grip on him with every step he took. The strain of knowing that the contents of the bag would land him back in jail was the greater load to bear. They came to the end of a long hedgerow, and an old wooden sign. They carried on around the corner and saw the shed, the makeshift bomb-making factory. The landscape around the shed, picturesque as it was, seemed entirely devoid of life, absolutely barren. There was no other sign of human life in sight. The silence of the landscape lay thick in the air as if breaking it would anger some ancient god, slumbering underneath. The shed was about forty feet long by twenty feet wide, hidden away by hills and hedgerow, isolated and alone.

Martin's silence in the car had made the one-hour drive feel much longer. With no outlet, Mick had found himself trapped inside his own head, battling every instinct. He wasn't an expert bomb-maker by any means, but his unit commander, Bernard Quinn, had insisted he go along.

Martin looked to be in his mid-twenties, but by reputation was one of the most capable bomb makers the IRA possessed. Mick laid down his backpack on the large wooden table that dominated the shed. Cots lay along the walls, and a small larder sat in the corner filled with canned foods and water. Mick opened his bag and laid out the bomb-making kit: timing units, booby traps, watches, clocks, detonators, gelignite, and the IRA's most favored plastic explosive of all – Semtex. They had enough between them to make several sizeable bombs.

'This is quite a haul we have here," Mick said, just to make conversation.

"Aye," Martin grunted.

Mick walked the few feet back toward the door and stepped outside as Martin unpacked. The hills rolled green into the distance on every side, serene and beautiful. The place seemed sullied by what they were there to do, what so many had done before them in this same place. The gentle wind whispered through the hedgerow that surrounded them on three sides. Training for his re-entry into the IRA had been nothing like the first time. The higher ups had considered him already trained, and he'd been put on active duty almost as soon as McClean had called to tell him he was back in. Operations in Derry had been limited in the last few months, the exception being another monumental blunder in the Creggan. A local unit had booby-trapped the apartment of a local man whom they'd kidnaped, in the expectation that the security forces would search it. Some of his neighbors, worried that they hadn't seen the man in several days, tried to check on him by climbing in the window. Two Catholic civilians in their fifties were killed, with another man critically injured. Another mistake that the IRA recanted in their most apologetic terms.

The botched apartment bombing, which became known as the 'Good Neighbor Bombing,' changed the face of the IRA leadership in the city and the unit which carried it out was disbanded. A swift reshuffle followed and Mick's name came to the fore. McClean put him forward as a smart, experienced operative with a proven record of effective operations behind him. But more important was the fact that he hadn't talked. Nothing in the IRA's universe was more important. Nothing was more sacred than silence and Michael Doherty was a man who could be trusted. Despite the fact that he'd only ever been on one significant operation, he was earmarked for planning roles. His first had been the robbery of a bank in Monaghan - a much-needed fundraiser. Mick had staked out the place every night for two weeks before he'd come up with the final plan. He hadn't carried out the robbery himself or even been within fifty miles of the place when it went down, but the IRA netted almost £38,000.Mick had earned the trust of his commanding officer. No one had said it to him, but he was sure that this trip to the bomb-making factory was to be his last test.

Mick came back into the shed.

"Time to get started. We have a lot of work ahead of us," Mick said, trying to sound as officious as he could.

They worked through the evening and into the night, until, by flickering lamplight, they ate dinner heated over a portable stove and went to bed. They'd barely spoken the entire day, and then only in monosyllabic grunts. Mick watched Martin, mimicking his every move. There had been no need for questions. Martin was a gifted bomb-maker. Mick wondered what he might have amounted to in a world where bomb-making skills weren't valued quite so much. Martin fell asleep quickly. Mick sat up on the cot. The bombs they'd already made sat primed on the table. Neither of them had questioned how the bombs were to be used. It wasn't theirs to query the orders that came down. Grisly pictures from news reports he'd seen on television haunted him in the darkness, of the mutilated bodies and bloody remains left in the wake of bombs just like these that they'd made.

They got to work at eight the next morning, mixing fertilizer of the type Mick's mother had used in their garden with a pungent mixture of sulfuric acid and vinegar. Mick had little idea what he was doing, but Martin was in a more talkative mood than the previous day and was at least prepared to give him directions. Every time Mick asked him a question not related to the bombs Martin dismissed it with a razor-eyed glare. Mick felt like the young recruit under tutelage. He had no idea of Martin's background other than what Bernard Quinn had mentioned to him in passing about his brother's death in Armagh. Martin's eyes never strayed from the bombs. It was as if this man had no other personality and existed only to serve the cause. He was the perfect volunteer. His fanaticism was as dangerous as the glinting blade of a machete, his glare a constant illustration of focus and intensity. He was one of the most terrifying volunteers Mick had ever met, even in prison.

Mick glanced over at Martin, who was working on the detonating system for a large Semtex bomb he'd constructed the night before. How could he let these bombs get back to the IRA? He knew what they could do, the destruction they'd cause. Mick could destroy this mission, but what was to stop Martin from making these bombs somewhere else with somebody else?

"I need to take a break," Mick said, the pressure inside him building. He walked out and sat on the stone wall in front of the hut, which overlooked a barren green field, stones dotted across it. He thought of Pat and his family, his mother. He thought of his father, asking him for advice but no reply came, and there was only the silence of the field. The range of possibilities opened up in front of him. He could do nothing. He could make the bombs and transport them back to the safe house like he'd been ordered to do. If soldiers stopped them at a checkpoint, he'd do time again, but that seemed unlikely. There was nothing out here, and, without a tip-off the security forces would never find them. The shed looked like it'd been standing here for years, maybe even back to the civil war in the twenties. Dark thoughts began to spill into his mind. What would happen if he were to blow this place up, perhaps with

Martin in it? Martin's family would mourn his loss, but the IRA would miss his skills more. How many lives would Mick save by finishing his?

On perhaps the only occasion he'd strung more than three sentences together the day before, Martin had warned him about the dangers of the process and what chemicals had to be kept separate from one another. Mick had wanted to ask how long it would take once the chemicals were mixed for them to flame and explode. It was only a few feet to the door, and then only another few feet to the stone wall that would most likely be enough to protect him from the blast. It would be a risky move, not least for the flak that he'd get from the higher ups in Derry expecting the delivery of these bombs on Sunday night, but he could get around that. Bomb making factories were notoriously dangerous. Many IRA men had died in them. He'd known some of them himself. Would anyone question Martin's death here? It wouldn't be like killing those soldiers by the side of the road, there was a purpose to this - murder to prevent murder. He could feel the weight of Martin's glare even though he was facing the other direction. Mick got up and walked back into the shed.

It was evening when the chance came, Martin's shadow stretched long across the bare grass outside the hut, the smoke from his cigarette cascading into the air above him. Mick knew he had only minutes to do this. He picked up some rags he'd been using to wipe the table, bundling them into a pile. He took a vial of sulfuric acid in a shaking hand, knowing that the penalty for any mistakes here would be an instantaneous death. The pile of rags stood silent, waiting. Mick stopped himself. This idea was insane. It could explode instantly. Was this worth his life? Martin was still smoking, still facing out toward the field in front of them. Mick uncorked the sulfuric acid, which would immediately burst into flames as soon as he poured it into the petri dish. His breathing quickened, his heart racing like a piston, the acid in the beaker swishing back and forth like a raging sea. "No, no." He put the cork back onto the bottle. Outside the hut, Martin had thrown down his cigarette and stood staring at him.

"Everything all right in there?" he asked.

"Yeah, just fine, almost had an accident, but I caught it in time." His palms were wet, and he used a sleeve to wipe them off.

Martin didn't say a word, instead walking back to his place at the table and the timer mechanism he was building.

Mick stopped, his hands falling to the table momentarily until Martin sent one of his barb wire glances across at him.

"I think I need some air myself," Mick said.

Twenty minutes passed before his hands stopped shaking enough that he could come back inside and finish the bomb he was working on.

Night descended and Mick lay in bed, with Martin asleep on the other side of the room. The bombs they'd built were on the table, ready to be packed up and taken back to the safe house, ready to destroy more lives. His original plan to purposefully blow up the shed itself in an 'accidental' explosion was idiotic, a quick route to the morgue, if they found enough of him to bury. But there had to be something he could do, some way of affecting this. He could disable the bombs now, pulling out wires and tearing off timers, but Martin was meticulous and double-checked everything. Mick supposed that was the reason he'd survived so long as a bomb-maker. Mick peered over at him through the dark. There were no guns in the hut, but he could pick up a rock outside. A few quick blows and it'd be all over. It was miles to the nearest road or house.

Mick turned over in the cot to face away from the explosives, which were taunting him now. He couldn't call it in and he couldn't kill Martin. There was nothing to be done except report a successful mission to his superiors.

Mick was still awake as the dawn came. He got out of the cot, his limbs like icicles in the dim morning light. The explosives were just as they'd left them. Mick could hardly look at them. He wanted to get back to the city, away from the shame of what he'd done here. The local IRA units were much the stronger for having him as a member. Martin awoke with a snort. Mick told him they were leaving and within minutes they were packed up and ready to walk back to the safe house, several miles away. Martin took the lead, with Mick trailing behind him in the mist of the early morning.

That night he had dinner at Pat's house, taking his usual seat beside Siobhan, who always insisted he sit beside her. Somehow this existed in the same world where men trekked miles to sheds to make bombs to kill other men.

Dinner was roast beef, Mick's favorite. Pat sat a few feet away at the head of the table. Seeing his children getting to know Mick had been one of the greatest pleasures of his life. It warmed him every time Mick threw Siobhan over his shoulder or when he played football with the boys. Things finally seemed the way they should be. All Mick needed now was a woman of his own, and while Pat had enjoyed the stories of midnight liaisons with random girls, he was eager for him to settle down.

"So, were you away this weekend?" Pat asked.

"Aye," Mick answered. "I was away down the country. It was great. Very peaceful." It felt wrong to lie, but this wouldn't be forever. The chance to make a real difference would come, the opportunity to dull the pain of the guilt inside him that still burned after sixteen years inside.

"So, big night for you tomorrow night then, Mick," Pamela said.

"My debut as a student? Aye, it's something I've been looking forward to for a long time."

"You're not gonna grow your hair long and start watching Countdown are you?" Pat asked.

"Nah, it's different if you're studying for your Masters. We have to ponce around like we know everything and complain about government policy."

"You'd have plenty of people who'd listen to you around here."

"Aye, I reckon I would."

Mick smiled to himself, starting in on the meal. Pat had felt much the same pain he had, yet he'd been able to move on with his life. Why couldn't he? The paranoia within the IRA had reached almost manic levels since the supergrass trials a few years before. He was fully aware of the torture and death that lay ahead of him if he was caught. Was there no other way for him to be happy? What happened to the huge operation Sean's brother was planning? He reached over to Peter, ruffled his hair. Why wasn't this enough? Siobhan stretched over with tiny fingers and snatched a green bean off his plate, bursting into laughter as he feigned anger.

Chapter 20

Melissa studied her own face, trying to remember how she'd looked at sixteen, at twenty, at twenty-five, at thirty. It was hard to remember the passage of something that moved so slowly, yet went so quickly as time, and she flicked the mirror back up and got out of the car. The warmth of the day was beginning to fade as evening encroached. She was early as usual, and would have time to get a cup of tea before class started. A younger version of herself might have felt self-conscious showing up alone and sitting in a café wasting time. Considerations like that had dissipated. Some things did change. Not that she'd woken up one day as a different person. Getting older was as gradual as slipping into quicksand. She still felt the weight of men's eyes on her, but not like when she was younger. Back then, young men seemed to feast on her with lustful eyes. It was different now, more of a passing admiration from men of all ages, which, as in her younger years, she did her best to ignore. She kept the zipper on her jacket open as she walked up toward the student café on campus. She got a cup of tea and a scone and took a seat by the window, watching the students drift in for evening classes.

A young couple in their twenties stopped outside the window, a few feet away from where she was sitting. They were fighting. Melissa tried to resist the temptation of listening in, but with nothing else to do, her ears became attuned to their shrill voices. The girl, who had long red hair and piercing brown eyes, was complaining that she never saw the boy anymore. The boy, who had broad shoulders and thick arms, protested that he was too busy with training and that he was doing his best to juggle all the balls in life. Melissa smiled to herself. She knew how they felt. It had been hard after the divorce. Being a single mother was a lot more difficult. Even the paltry amount of help that John had given her when Jason was a kid had made her life a lot easier. But Jason was older now. Soon enough he'd be having arguments with girlfriends of his own. She just hoped that he wouldn't do it in quite so conspicuous a situation as this. The girl stormed off, leaving the burly boyfriend to scuttle after her.

Melissa finished up her tea and brushed the crumbs from her scone back onto the plate. She didn't recognize anyone around her as she walked toward the lecture hall. Night school wasn't like being an undergraduate, nothing like her first experiences of a student all those years ago. Life was more serious now and she was here for a purpose. She took a seat at the back, thinking about Jason and what he might have been doing in his friend's house, when Margaret, a woman in her fifties and one of the few people Melissa had ever spoken to in class, turned around to say hello. Melissa thought to tell her about her trip to Venice with David over the summer, but couldn't bear the thought of having to field any questions about their break-up, so she stayed silent. They were still talking as the professor came in and took his place at the podium. Margaret turned back and Melissa started jotting down the key points they'd covering. The topic of the class was the partition of Ireland in 1920.

Melissa's eyes flicked up as a door opened on the other side of the lecture hall, about twenty yards from where she was sitting. A man she thought she recognized stuck his head through the door and snuck into a seat in the back row. Most of the other people in the room who'd glanced up at the noise focused back onto their notes, but her eyes were like magnets on him. A glacier of shock ran down her spine. She looked over at the man again as he reached into his bag for pen and paper. It was impossible to believe. It couldn't be him – he was in jail. It was Michael Doherty. Her heart felt like it was about to implode within her chest, and the glacial cold turned into a hot flash, which ran through her entire body. He was looking straight ahead, seemingly hadn't noticed her. She unglued her eyes from him, but only for a few seconds, and they fell back onto him like pendulum returning. Was it Patrick? No, it was definitely Mick. He looked much the same. Maybe a little gaunt, a little more worn-looking but who wasn't now? Mick glanced around the room and Melissa immediately turned her head away. She waited a few seconds until it was safe to look back. He was staring down at the pad in front of him, taking notes, as she should have been. The lecture was well under way, but she hadn't heard a single word. She could get up and leave, but what would that achieve? She was going to have to take this class. She wanted to take this class. Why should he stop her? How was she going to take a class with him for the whole year? The pen in her mouth cracked with the force of her bite and Melissa drew it out immediately, checking for ink that wasn't there. She felt her face flame red. He was going to see her. There was no avoiding that, just best to get on with things.

Melissa kept her head down, her arm shielding her face. The eight minutes of the class felt longer than some years she could remember. She allowed herself to peek over a few more times, never catching his eye. He seemed oblivious. Perhaps it wasn't him. Perhaps it was Pat. She could tell herself that all she wanted, but she didn't believe it, not even for a second. The memories that she'd tried to suppress were in class with her. There was no escape in this town.

Her anxieties tempered like boiling water cooling off. She knew Mick, knew his motivations for what he did. He didn't need to know anything about her. She didn't have to tell him. A few words, a hello, wouldn't hurt either of them. Maybe he wouldn't want to see her. He didn't have to intrude into the life she'd chiseled out for herself. Seeing him here didn't have to change anything. The swirling frothy feeling in her stomach began to abate, at least enough to get out of the seat when the lecture finished. He was still sitting there, peering out into the space in front of him as the other members of the class filed up the steps toward the door. He hadn't moved. She waited until there were several people in front of him, blocking his view, before she got up out of her seat and made for the door. The feelings within her were like a relic of times past, how he'd made her feel all those years ago. She breezed through the door, looking as casual as she could, all the while eyeing every person around her. She whirled around, expecting to see him, suddenly disappointed he wasn't there. The thought to go back inside, to find him, just to see him, just to say hello, came into her mind. She stopped dead in her tracks, not prepared to look for him but not prepared to leave either. The other students brushed past her, her eyes trained on the door. Twenty seconds passed before something broke inside and swept her away, her footsteps ever faster until she was almost running away.

She made it all the way back to the car before she finally began to slow down. She cast an arm out to lean on the car, her heart pounding. Was she going to have to do this every week? That would make for a difficult year. A few simple words would suffice, little more than a hello in all likelihood. She couldn't leave like this, wasn't going to run away. Melissa put her books in the car and made her way back toward the lecture hall, almost sure that he wasn't going to be there. Surely he would have left by now, and she would have tried. The lecture hall was empty, and she turned back around, resigned to the fact that she was going to have to go through all of this again when the class met again on next week. She started back toward her car and was walking past the café when she saw him, drinking a cup of coffee alone. His eyes met hers through the pane of glass between them. She stood looking at him with no idea what to do next. He didn't move, not even to put down his coffee cup, shaking ever so slightly in his hand. Somehow her feet carried her over to the door and inside. He was standing as she came to him.

"Hello," she said, feeling the warmth inside come again despite herself.

"Hi. It's so good to see you," he said, his words slow, his eyes wide like a child. "Will ye join me for a cup of tea?" he motioned toward the empty chair opposite his.

"I don't know. I was going to leave pretty soon... I just wanted to say hello."

"You don't have to get something, just sit down maybe."

"All right." He was still so handsome, still the best looking man she'd ever seen. She let out a cough. Neither of them seemed to know what to say. Jason was on her mind. Protecting him had to be her priority.

"I saw you in the classroom," he said. "I was shocked. I didn't want to bother you...."

"You were shocked? I didn't even know you were out." She lowered her voice, looking around at the other people in the café who seemed completely oblivious to their presence. "I'm sorry, I shouldn't say that out loud."

"It's fine. I've spent almost half my life in jail, it's going to be difficult to hide that." Her beauty was transcendent. It carried him away beyond his pathetic life, beyond the murderous gray streets of Bogside and Derry, to some other place. She was more beautiful than she'd been inside his mind every day of those sixteen years. It had taken him the entire class to notice her and when he did the sight of her struck him like a thunderbolt. He'd sat there transfixed, unable to move for several minutes after everyone else had left.

"It's been a long time."

"Yes, it has. When did you...?"

"Seven months ago, back in February. I did fifteen and a half years of my life sentence."

"How did you get out?"

He picked up the cup, put it back down and took the spoon in both hands.

"A mixture of good behavior, pressure from my brother's lawyers, and political convenience."

"Well, it's good to see you. I should be going." Melissa went to get up, hoping he'd stop her.

"Can you stay a few more minutes? We're not going to be able to avoid each other. I'd rather be friends, wouldn't you?"

"Aye, of course." She sat back down, feigning reluctance to do so.

"I'm still trying to get used to things on the outside. The world's so different now. It's like the last sixteen years never happened. It's like I got into a time machine to the future. But I suppose I've changed too."

"You look the same."

"So do you." He stopped himself there, too afraid to venture further, not knowing where he'd be able to stop. "So what do you do for a living? I don't know anything about you."

"I'm a teacher. I teach sixteen-year-olds English and History."

"Sixteen-year-olds? How ironic."

"If I could get it into any of their thick skulls what irony is they might agree with you."

He laughed and took another sip of coffee. Someone behind him was smoking, and the thick scent of tobacco filled the air around them. The smell brought memories of jail. He ignored them. "You're teaching sixteen-year-old boys? I'd say you're popular."

She smirked, fidgeting with her bag on her shoulder. "You get used to the stares. They used to make comments, but not anymore. They know better."

"I wouldn't mess with you either, Miss Rice or is it Mrs. now?"

She thought about how to answer him. His eyes were so honest. She'd tell him as much truth as she could. "It was Mrs. for a while, but I'm back to Miss again now."

"Oh, I'm sorry."

"That's just the way things work out sometimes."

"Have you any kids?"

"Maybe I will get myself a cup of tea. Are you staying around?"

"I've nowhere to be. I've got nothing but time."

He watched her as she got up to walk to the cash registers. She had filled out, her body more womanly now. Other men's eyes flicked up as she drifted past them. The spikes of jealousy within him almost brought a smile to his face. She came back a minute later with a cup of tea in her hand and sat back down. It was hard to believe she was here. He'd thought about this so many times.

The teacup chimed as she stirred in the sugar. She thought she'd never see him again, that he'd be in jail for the rest of his life, that the fire he aroused in her was finally extinguished.

"So what are you doing with yourself now? What are you studying?"

"I'm studying for a Masters in Engineering. I'm only doing this course for a bit of a lark. I always wanted to study history, maybe if everyone did we wouldn't be in such a mess."

Melissa blew on her tea before taking a sip. "It's strange, but the students I teach were born after Bloody Sunday, years after the Troubles began, they've never known anything else. I'm trying to make them understand that there were times before this when we lived in peace or at least relative peace, and how avoidable this all was," she said.

"How do their parents feel about that?"

"It's a Protestant school, so there's a certain way they want me to phrase things, but I do have a decent amount of latitude. It's certainly no UVF training ground, but trying to get across the abuses the Catholic population suffered since the 20's is difficult."

"Ulster will fight and Ulster will be right, eh?" He remembered the old unionist saying from his own school days.

"A lot of the parents are still sticking to those old principles, but we're making progress. I've no doubt about that. Attitudes are changing. Anyway, enough about politics, that's what got us into this mess in this first place, that's what put you in jail."

"Aye. I've had a bellyful of all that rhetoric. I heard plenty of it inside."

"I can't begin to imagine what you went through." The truth of it was that she had imagined, or at least tried to imagine what jail must have been like for him many times, particularly in those early days. "What are you doing for work?" she continued.

"I'm lucky enough to have a twin brother willing to employ me. A lot of my fellow republican prisoners aren't so fortunate when they get out. You never answered my question."

"What question was that?"

"The one about children. Do you have kids?"

"I do. I have a son - Jason. He's fourteen."

Mick took a sip from his now lukewarm tea and placed the cup back down. "Fourteen? That wasn't long after I went away."

"He's a great boy, really smart and funny."

"He doesn't get involved with any...?"

"Oh God, no. He's not perfect, far from it, but he knows to stay away from all of that. I'd kill him if I ever got wind of him getting involved with anyone like that."

"I'm glad to hear it. I'd never have believed you if you told me back in '72 that this'd all be still going on now. I'd have thought we'd have come to our senses by now."

"Have faith, we will."

"Here we are, talking about politics again." Mick smiled, as much to see her smile again as anything else.

"Yeah, no matter how we try and wriggle away it always seems to drag us back in. What was it like inside?"

"It was bad. It could have been worse, I suppose. I was never directly involved in any of the blanket protests or the hunger strikes, just because I didn't have to be. I had the rights they were prepared to die for, just because of when I went to jail, but being out is definitely better."

"I suppose you appreciate freedom more than anyone now."

"I appreciate everything about the world. It's as if every sense in my body is heightened after being neglected for so long. I love the smell of the bakery and the feel of fresh bread as I break it in my hand. I love listening to the birds sing in the morning or sitting on a hill staring at the stars. I've spent nights awake just waiting for the sunrise. It's all so special to me now."

"That sounds wonderful, I'm so happy for you," she said, before realizing how it must have sounded. "I didn't mean it like that, I didn't mean going to jail was wonderful."

"I know what you meant," Mick said, smiling across at her.

"I'm glad you're able to appreciate what we take for granted."

"I appreciate life now, how fragile and wonderful it is. I intend to live mine well."

She felt energy spread from him and through her as he spoke. It took purposeful effort to look away from him, to stop herself from staring.

"You look incredible," he continued, his voice soft and wistful. "How do you look so young, especially chasing after a teenager all the time?"

"Thank you, you're very sweet. Not everyone agrees with you though. My boyfriend buys me skin treatments all the time. I think he's paranoid I'm getting wrinkly or something." She saw the twitch in his eyes as she mentioned the boyfriend she no longer even had. This was just too fast. She had to do something to stop this yet she couldn't quite force herself to get up and leave him. She was enjoying this far too much.

"He should count his blessings. He's a lucky man to be with a woman like you." He stopped himself from saying what would naturally have come next – that she'd be beautiful her whole life, that her eyes would never fade or the light within her would never dull. But he needed to slow himself. His heart was beating like a jackhammer and his palms were damp. He brought them down and rested them on his thighs, wiping the sweat on his jeans. The mention of her boyfriend had stung, but it was a boundary for him to respect, and he was used to boundaries.

"Where do you live?" he asked.

"In Waterside. It's a lovely house."

"So not all that much has changed then."

"Some things are different, but essentially we're the same people all our lives aren't we? I mean, our circumstances might change, our priorities sure as hell do but are we really that different?"

Mick let out a little laugh. "I've been through a lot and I can certainly say that my priorities have changed. But am I all that different? Probably not."

"Where do you live?"

"I have a small apartment in town, not too far from here. I walked over. I had no excuse to be late."

"Other than the fact that you're always late, that you'd be late for your own funeral?"

"Aye, you're right. We don't really change, do we?"

Melissa smiled, but it melted quickly. A spurt of panic shot through her. This was too much. She needed to make an excuse and leave. She picked up the teacup and held it to her lips, taking a small sip. She needed to leave, so why didn't she? His eyes were on her as she looked up at him again.

Mick reached down for his coffee. The cup was empty. He hadn't noticed drinking the last of it. He brought his hands back down to his sides, leaning back on the chair. He was glad she had a boyfriend, happy that he knew it. Harboring some kind of false hope that the dream of being with her again could be real would be too much for him. He thought of the IRA man he'd harbored on the floor of his apartment the previous week, the plans that he'd been tasked to come up with for another bank robbery. That was his mission now. There wasn't any time to think of anything else, not until he'd struck a real blow against them. The time for life and love and joy and happiness would come after that, and there were other women in this world, just none like her.

"How do you want to go forward?" he asked.

"What do you mean?"

"This is our first class together, the first of the year. We're going to be in the same room every Monday night for the next nine months. I never thought I'd see you again."

"I never thought you were going to get out of jail, let alone without a cane and gray hair sprinkled on your head. I don't know. I'm enjoying seeing you again." She cursed herself for saying that, instantly wishing she could take it back.

Her words warmed him. "I'm enjoying seeing you again, but where do we go from here? Are we going to be friends?"

Jason came into her mind. She wasn't prepared for this, hadn't had a chance to think things through. Was he the same sweet, gorgeous man she'd fallen in love with? Would there ever be a chance for them again? She knew him, knew his history, knew his motivations, his honor, and his shame. She knew it all.

"I don't know what happens from here." She reached down for the teacup, ran her finger around the circumference. "Let's take it slowly. I don't think I'm ready to be friends quite yet."

"I understand that."

"You're a good man, Mick. I know that. It's just that…. I wasn't prepared for this. I need some time to take it all in."

"That's fine. I'm not asking anything of you. Let's just wave for now. I'll sit on the other side of the class, and wave. You think you can handle that?

"I reckon I can handle a wave."

"And if you ever need notes, you'll know who to come to."

"All right. It's going to be weird, but all right."

"This whole thing's weird, but we deal with it the best we can," he said, getting up. He stood looking at her for a second or so before he spoke again. "I'll see you next week, from across the room."

"From across the room," she replied, and watched as he walked away. She sat there for several minutes alone. She had stopped thinking about this day years ago, had stopped dreaming that he'd come back to her in her twenties. How would Jason react to him if he knew who he really was? Mick was ex-IRA, the enemy of everything decent, yet she had always known he wasn't one of them. Going to jail had been the final act to prove that he wasn't a murderer, that his heart was true. She picked up the cup and drank back the last of the tea. It was cold.

Mick stopped as he reached the corner. The night was drawing in, the clouds blocking out the starlight above. His lungs gasped for the cigarette he refused to give them. He shook his head, trying to laugh off meeting her as if it was a joke, or an interesting story to tell, but it was more than that.

Chapter 21

Mick held up the pasta and watched as it lolled back and forth on his fork. He still relished every piece of non-prison food he ate, still couldn't comprehend the sheer choice and quality of what was available virtually everywhere he went. Pat sat opposite him, tucking into a steak. Mick hadn't mentioned meeting Melissa four days earlier, even though he'd seen Pat every day since.

"Are you all right?" Pat asked.

"Yeah, I'm okay. Why d'you ask?"

"You've had your head in the clouds all week, with that big dumb smile on your face."

"This big dumb smile?" Mick said, using the fork to point to himself.

"That's the one. You've had that plastered on your face all week."

"Maybe I'm just happy, brother."

"I'm glad. I'm delighted. Is there anything going on? Did you get laid or something?" Pat smiled. "Or is it more? Wait a minute, did you meet someone?"

"What makes you assume it's a woman?"

"What else is gonna make you smile like that?"

Mick put down his fork and picked up the teacup in front of him. He rolled the tea around inside, watching it splash on the side. "No, it's nothing like that. I'm just happy to be out, enjoying my food, enjoying my life."

Pat didn't reply for a few seconds and sat back in his chair, his arms folded across his chest. "Come on, spill the beans, you can't hide it from me. I have your DNA. I know what you're thinking. I can reach inside that mind of yours."

"Why are you asking if you can see inside my mind?"

"Come on, I'm married twelve years, share a little excitement with an old guy would you?"

"There's nothing to share, not yet at least. I'll tell you all about it when there's something to tell."

"OK, I can take a hint. There's something else I want to talk to you about."

"It's not my outrageous love life is it? Because I already told you..."

"No, it's a little more serious." Mick put down his knife and fork and sat back in his seat. Pat sat forward, motioning for his brother to do the same. Pat looked around, making sure no-one was listening to them. "It's about Sean Campbell. I know you've taken him under your wing."

"To some extent. He's a big boy though."

"I've heard he's involved again, that he's joined an active service unit in the city. Did he mention anything to you?"

Mick's blood went cold. He forked more pasta into his mouth, doing his best to hide behind it. It didn't feel right to lie to him, but Pat wouldn't understand what they were trying to do. It was too early to tell him. Mick shook his head. "No, I don't know anything about that. I know about his brother..."

"We all know about his brother." Pat picked up his teacup but didn't drink from it. "His brother Tony's a dangerous man. He'd bring us all back to the bad old days if he could, back to when we were in."

"The bad old days?"

"OK, the worse old days. Worse than now, which is saying something."

"I don't know anything." Mick's nerves jangled inside him. If Pat had found out about Sean, then what was to stop him finding out about him, and his so-called involvement with the IRA again? Thoughts crackled through his mind like sparks spat from a flame. Maybe Pat would help him if he let him in. Keeping this from him was alien to anything he'd ever known, felt alien in every way. Pat was looking at him across the small table. Mick brought his hands down to rest on the vinyl tablecloth. It was too soon to tell him. Mick would need to speak to Sean first, to figure out a plan. Things were changing. The picture of Melissa drifted into his mind. Was she more than just a complication? Would she be a reason to leave this all behind?

"Are you all right, brother?" Pat asked. "You don't look so good all of a sudden."

"Yeah, I'm fine, just a little upset that Sean might have joined up again. We've all done so much to try to turn that kid around."

"Have a word with him. Find out what's going on. I don't have confirmation that he's active, yet. Try and find out where his mind is."

"I'll speak to him, find out what's going on."

"Good man." Pat brought the cup of tea to his lips and took a sip. "Is there anything else you want to tell me? Anything at all?"

"No, no. There's nothing. I'll find out."

Mick began eating again, trying to avoid eye contact with his brother for a few seconds at least.

Sean was alone on the second floor of the worksite when Mick found him later that afternoon. Sean glanced up as he sat down beside him.

"I had a conversation with Pat about you at lunch today. He knows. Somehow, he knows."

Sean turned to him, his blue eyes blazing like gas fires. "What does he know? What did he say?"

"He knows you're back in. I have no idea how. I don't know who told him."

Sean put down the drill in his hand. His movements were slow and deliberate, as if he were searching for extra seconds to think about the information Mick had just given him. "What about you?" he finally said.

"He didn't mention anything about me, but if he knows about you…"

"Then there's no reason for him not to find out about you too."

"I thought to tell him, to admit what I was doing."

Sean shot panicked eyes at him.

"I wouldn't mention you. I'm not taking this lightly. I know what it would mean if this got out. I'll pull the plug on this before I put you in danger," Mick continued.

"Those are very sweet words, Mick, but you'll forgive me if I'm not completely reassured."

"I'll handle my brother, Sean, and I'll handle this. You just need to keep talking to your own brother, keep gaining his trust and find out about this big operation he's planning that no one else in the Derry Brigade knows anything about it. I'm starting to wonder if we're risking out lives for nothing."

Sean paused, his eyes flicking back and forth.

"There's no one around. I checked," Mick continued.

'This little crusade was your idea," Sean hissed, struggling to stay within the bounds of his whisper. "I was ready to leave this behind and get on with living."

"Who's stopping you? You can do whatever you want. I would never have known anything about this massive operation your brother was planning if it weren't for you. Is it genuine?"

"Yes, it's genuine."

"How do you know?"

"Because he's been talking about it for nine months now, and because he's completely disillusioned with the direction he perceives the IRA to be going in now. He's disgusted by the talks with the SDLP; even the mention of peace without absolute victory is a stab in the back to him. He's serious. He's very serious."

"But you don't know when or any details."

"He hasn't mentioned any specifics yet. I don't think he knows himself."

"So we're risking our lives for something that might never happen."

"You knew all of this already, but you don't know my brother. If he says something, he means it."

"He'd better. I made bombs last week. I've helped them rob banks in the south. I'm helping the cause I'm trying to destroy."

"Now who's the one who wants out? We can finish this, get out while we still can. This was an insane idea. They're completely paranoid, obsessed by informers. We're going to get caught."

"We're not going to get caught if we stay smart."

Sean closed his eyes, raising a gloved hand to cover the terror on his face. Was this a person that Mick wanted to risk his life with? Sean was tough. He'd proved that much in prison, but this wasn't his war, not any more. He'd done his time. Mick put his hand on the younger man's shoulder.

"Things are quiet now. Apart from that botched bombing in the Creggan there's not much happening. This could be a good time for you to step down, unofficially at least. All you need do is keep talking to your brother. You don't have to be an active member."

"That won't work. He's only talking to me again because he thinks I'm one of them. I only earned his respect once I went to jail for the cause, before that he told me nothing." Sean reached into his pocket for a pack of cigarettes. "What about you?" he asked.

"I don't know. I think I need to stay in. If I'm to affect anything I need to be on the ground when it happens. I can't stand the thought of working with the RUC, or the British Army, the people who killed my father." The mention of his father's name drew a black veil over Mick's vision. He closed his eyes to try to wipe it away.

"What about the Gardaí? You could go over the border, talk to them." Sean suggested.

"About what exactly? I'm only a bit player at the moment. It'll take us years to get back in to the extent where we have any truly meaningful information to give. I'm not risking my life to give up an arms dump or to stop a bank robbery in the south. I can't do this for how long it would take to climb the ranks and become a full time member. I don't think I'd make it."

Sean held the pack of cigarettes up to Mick, who shook his head.

"How did I ever let you talk me into this?" Sean said.

"I didn't talk you into anything. You did this yourself. And you can get out anytime. You know that." Mick knew that Sean looked up to him; probably still felt he owed him after looking after him inside. "You don't owe me anything. I'll do this without you. If you feel like I've forced you into this..."

"You didn't force me into a thing. You just showed me what this all is and what needs to be done." Sean placed the cigarette between his lips. It flamed red as he lit it.

"We need to hang in, just keep in touch with who we can and learn whatever we can learn about what's coming up. If we could have done something to stop that 'good neighbor' bombing a couple of weeks ago, that would have been worth it."

"That's tiny compared to what my brother's talking about. He wants this operation he's talking about to be a defining moment in the Troubles so far, this generation's hunger strikes or even Bloody Sunday."

"We can't let that happen." Mick felt the motivation rising within him once more. "Who would we be if we did nothing?"

"I don't know who we'd be, but we'd be alive," Sean answered, staring out the unfinished window in front of him. The smoke from his cigarette drifted upwards, gray into the air.

"There are worse things than death in this world," Mick said and got up.

*****

The weekend was notable only for his thoughts of her. Her invasion of his consciousness was under way, like nothing had changed. Was she filling in a gap in his life? Was the dearth of any other meaningful relationship in the sixteen years since they'd broken up forcing these feelings upon him? It felt real. He hadn't dreamed about her in years, not since the early eighties at least but seeing her once had implanted the picture of her back into his subconscious. When he saw her in his dreams, it wasn't as the woman she was now. It was as the girl he'd known back in the seventies, the carefree, beautiful girl who'd loved him as much as he loved her. The girl who snuck out of her parents' house to kiss him under the streetlights. Was she still even the same person? Would he even find out? Now that her curiosity about him was quenched would they ever even speak again? It was good that she had a boyfriend, useful. Her boyfriend would be the wall, the wire fence to keep him away. A boundary marker, and he was used to those. And she had a son, too young to be his but very close. She was a mother now. The girl he'd known was gone forever.

Monday came, the time in work an utter irrelevance. The day seemed to have no other purpose but to see her again. Mick came home from work later than usual, arriving at his apartment just before six. He showered and changed, staring out the window at the golden orange hue of the evening sun outside. This city was choking him. This mission, this crusade he'd put himself on, dragging Sean Campbell along with him, would end up killing them both. He needed to find himself a new life, somewhere where there were no Catholics or Protestants, no IRA, UVF, UDA, INLA, UFF, UDR, no British Army. Somewhere where there was no Melissa Rice, tugging at his heart. He went to the fridge and took out the leftovers from last night's dinner at Pat's house. He picked up the plate, peeled back the aluminum foil, and placed it into the microwave Pamela had made him buy. The buttons made their obnoxious pinging sound as he programmed it to warm up his food. The light came on inside, the food bathed in ethereal yellow. Mick took a deep breath. He had to get a hold of himself; he was becoming obsessed. Melissa had been very important to him at one time. He thought she was the love of his life, the last woman he'd ever be with. His time in prison had robbed him of the time it would have taken to get over her, to move on with his life and be ready to find someone else. Seeing her was the last thing he needed. He began to wish they'd never met up again, that she was married, that she'd refused to see or speak to him. The microwave dinged, and his dinner was ready.

"I don't have to go to college," he said out loud. "I'm not even doing history." He was only doing the course to escape the loneliness of the flat, the silence and the malaise of a single life he'd never anticipated. After almost twenty years of sharing a room and almost sixteen years of sharing a cell, the last three with his friend Sean Campbell, being alone was almost impossible. The important courses, the ones for his Masters were Tuesday and Wednesday. They were the ones that would get him a job, not this history course he was taking with her. He could drop out, but why should he? They could sit in the same room as one another. He wasn't a child, wasn't some horny teenager with no self-control, at the mercy of his hormones. It was possible to sit in the same room as your ex, even if you might still have feelings for them, particularly if they weren't interested or available.

He laid his dinner down on the small kitchen table and sat down. The thought of giving up a course he wanted to pursue only because of her was ridiculous. He would sit away from her, avoid her, not even looking across. And if she wanted to be friends, they could talk, there would be no harm in that. He didn't need her, didn't need to be with her to find truth and beauty in this world. She was a friend now, nothing more, and he had more pressing concerns to engage his mind. Why was it that she dwarfed all of his other thoughts and dominated his mind? He sat there chewing his food, trying to think of something else. Eventually, he succeeded.

267

Melissa gazed at the clothes she'd laid out on her bed. Why was she doing this, dressing up for him? It was ridiculous. She wasn't even planning to speak to him. Was she making all this effort to wave across a classroom at someone? She'd barely given this much thought to any date she'd ever been on. She laughed out loud at herself, more of a teenager now than her own son. She moved to the bed and picked out the outfit in the middle, pretending that she was doing so at random, that it wasn't the one she liked best. She put on the skirt and blouse and applied a little eyeliner with a touch of lip-gloss before she heard the knock.

"Ma, we'd better get moving. You're going be late for your course," Jason said through the closed door. She was a mess, embarrassed in front of herself. Her teenage son was hurrying her for her own college class.

"I'm coming now, just give me a second. The door's open, you can come in."

Jason pushed through the door. He was still in his school uniform. He looked more like his father with each passing day.

"Are you wearing your school uniform to Ian's house?"

"Aye, I don't mind."

"Why don't you get changed, love? You'll be more comfortable. Put on a t-shirt and a pair of jeans. Go on now."

"All right, give me a minute."

She looked at her son as he left the room, watching him walk down the hallway and into his room. What was she doing? How would he react to this, whatever it was? The ink on her divorce papers was barely dry and now she was contemplating this? Or was she? How would Jason react to Michael? He'd been through so much and bringing him, of all people, into his life could destroy him, or them both. This wasn't a good idea. There was no doubting the fact that Mick coming back into her life, into Jason's life, was a bad idea. But wasn't he finished with the IRA? He was finished with them even before he went into jail, so he must have still been finished with them now. Jason came back out of his room.

"Are you ready to go now, Mam?"

"Yeah, I'm ready, don't forget your homework."

They walked down the stairs together and Jason picked up his school bag where he'd left it beside the front door.

It was a warm evening outside, the light of the sun casting deep shadows. They were in the car when Melissa started talking again.

"So, how's your dad?" It didn't feel right to give John that title now. He'd done little to earn it in the first place, and certainly didn't deserve it now, not that he wanted much to do with Jason anyway.

Jason didn't look around as he answered, just stared out at the road in front of them. "I don't know. I haven't heard from him in a while."

"Are you going around to his house next weekend?"

"No, he's over in London."

"What's he doing over there?" Melissa asked, trying to keep the anger buried within her.

"I don't know, going over to see some girl, some graduate student."

"His girlfriend?"

"I don't know, he didn't tell me."

Melissa's knuckles glowed white on the steering wheel as she drove. John had canceled the previous month too, had been in Edinburgh on business that weekend.

It was five minutes to Jason's friend's house and Melissa kissed him on the cheek as she let him off. "I'll see you later," she said, her voice jingling with the nerves teeming inside her.

"Are you OK, Mam? You look pale."

"I do?" she raised a finger to her cheek and looked at herself in the mirror. "Yeah, I'm fine, you get your work done and I'll see you later."

She waited in the car, watching Jason as he strolled up toward the front door and then inside. She closed her eyes for a few seconds, gripping the steering wheel in both hands. She started the car and made her way toward the University campus. It was a ten-minute drive, over the Craigavon Bridge and into Cityside, past the Guildhall and on to the University. Memories of the night he'd found her by the river, staring into nothing, wondering if she was going to turn him in or not, spun through her. She remembered every word he said, every movement and gesture he made and the night they'd spent together in his house. It had been easier to believe his essence was gone forever.

She parked her car in the same spot as the week before. A stream of students moved past. She didn't want to meet him out here, didn't want the awkwardness of that. A wave across the class and nothing more was definitely the most sensible course of action, for now at least.

She got out of the car, aware of everyone around her as she made her way toward the classroom. Dozens of faces flashed past her on the way to the classroom, but not his, and she felt a strange mixture of relief and disappointment as she took her seat. The seat he'd been in last week was empty. She let her eyes slide around the room, but didn't see him. Margaret took a seat in front of her and Melissa gave her a cursory smile as she said hello. The professor came to the front and began speaking. Melissa heard the sound of the door on the other side of the classroom opening, and knowing it was Mick, refused to look up. She held her gaze at the notepad laid out on the desk in front of her, but wasn't writing anything, the words of the professor lost to her impervious mind. She took a deep breath and looked across. He was laying out his book, pen in his mouth. He looked over and she stayed to catch his eye. Mick raised a hand, a diluted half-smile on his face. Melissa waved back and focused back onto the professor, finally able to focus enough to immerse herself in the subject matter once more.

Mick let his hand drop to his side as Melissa turned back to face front. Seeing her seemed to release something inside of him and he leaned back in his seat and wrote the heading of the lecture on the cover of his notepad.

The IRA 1926-1969

He glanced over at Melissa one more time, just to see what she was wearing, how she was looking. She had turned away from him, no doubt deliberately. Her boyfriend was a lucky man, he said to himself, finally able to settle into the lecture and happy that the most anticipated wave he'd ever made in his life had gone according to plan.

Chapter 22

Mick chewed his sandwich slowly, savoring the sensation of every mouthful. He was sitting by the window of the office building they were working on. The sun was laboring to break through a thick layer of clouds. The ground was freshly wet. It was Monday. It was May 1989. Melissa was part of his life again and he was a part of hers. Their Monday night meetings had begun in earnest just before Christmas. At first it had been whenever he'd ask her to join him for coffee, and that was every third week or so. But, as time wore on, the lure of each other grew impossible to repel. Without telling anyone else in their lives, they'd met every Monday for the past three months. Their meetings were theirs alone and, until they worked out what they were to do, would remain so by tacit agreement. They both understood that no one else would understand. The consideration that they might be hurting each other by meeting was brushed aside in favor of the joy of being around one another. It was a simple routine of coffee after class. Her son was the one thing she never talked about. That was the one area of her life Mick could never stray into. She'd told him about her marriage, her divorce, and the terrible father that John had proven to be, particularly after their breakup. Mick felt he knew every intricate detail of people's lives he never touched, people like her sister, her parents, and her best friends. She would talk about anyone but Jason, but that was enough. And now she knew him too, knew about everything he did and almost every part of his life. Still, some things remained that he couldn't tell her, hidden in the dark corners of his mind. She hid her son and he hid his dealings with the IRA. In his mind, that made them even.

Their Monday nights together became the thing he looked forward to most, his cloak against the clandestine part of his own life.

His food finished, he went over to the waste chute, balled up the sandwich wrapping paper and threw it down. The end of the school year would hail the end of their excuse to see one another. The safety net of their college course was almost gone, and worse, Melissa was moving to pursue her studies, to Dublin or London, she wasn't sure which yet. But one thing was certain: their meetings were soon to end. The cold hard world outside would soon encroach on the fantasy they'd constructed for themselves. This pseudo-friendship they'd cocooned themselves inside couldn't last. It would have to end or change. They'd have to decide which. Neither of them had spoken of it much, and Mick had reacted as a supportive friend would when she talked about leaving. Jason would follow her, and she'd find a good school for him wherever they ended up. That was all Mick knew, all she'd tell him.

She never mentioned a boyfriend. She bemoaned her lack of social life as much as he did, as if she expected him to say something, to solve her problem of not having anything to do on a Friday night. But he never did. He didn't want to infringe on her life outside of what they had. In many ways, their Monday night meetings were perfect, with no pressure and no intrusion from the outside. It had always been perfect when it was just the two of them. It was the rest of the world that seemed to do whatever was necessary to keep them apart, which had always been the problem. For the first time since they'd known each other they had a time and place to be together, comfortable and unafraid. It felt natural to be fearful of losing that. He berated himself for not manning up, of course, for not asking her out when she seemed to experience the same longing that drifted through him, but it was hard. The buffer of the end of the school year would force both of their hands. He would be a qualified engineer come the summer. He could leave, could support her and Jason both as she pursued her PhD. He just hadn't had the courage to mention it out loud yet, but it was all he thought about some days. Still the thought that his feelings weren't reciprocated lurked dark in the recesses of his mind behind some door he dared not open. Soon he would know.

The grit on the floor hissed under his boots as he stood up. The sun was breaking through again outside. The weather was an endless fascination, a mystery constantly being unraveled. Mick wondered where Sean was. He'd missed their usual lunch together. Mick had considered telling him about Melissa several times, but had always stopped himself. Admitting his behavior to a man twelve years younger would have been patently ridiculous, like a father chattering to his teenage son about the absurd thoughts and dreams he harbored in his own mind. And about a Protestant girl, from the time before he went to jail no less? Sean asked him about women often, and had tried to set him up several times. It was best to decline with a soft smile, to blame time and a fear of commitment.

Mick leaned on the unfinished concrete windowsill and peered down to the street below. Three soldiers stood checking people's ID's as they passed a British Army checkpoint on the road.

The sound of footsteps behind him jarred Mick out of the sanctuary of his thoughts.

"You finished your lunch?" Sean said.

"Aye, just finishing up now. Where were you?"

"I had to go down the road to pick up some pipes with a few of the others." He walked up behind Mick, putting a hand on his shoulder. "You got a minute?" His stern face lent weight to his words. The city had been quiet since the killing of two British soldiers on the Buncrana Road in March. Six others had been wounded in the blast, a massive landmine set off by remote control. Although they were still active volunteers, neither Sean nor Mick had heard anything about the bombing until after it had happened, when they saw it on the news like everyone else.

"Aye, of course. What's going on?" Mick replied.

"My brother called over last night."

Strong rumors swirled around the city that Sean's brother, Tony, was responsible for the Buncrana Road bombing, he and a small unit of volunteers loyal to him, but, as usual, no one admitted to anything. No suspects were arrested and the RUC let the case go, dismissing it as another unsolved atrocity to add to the litany of such acts carried out in the name of freedom for some on behalf of a dwindling minority.

"I'd say that was a real hoot. What did he want?"

"He wanted to ask me if I knew anyone reliable, someone I'd trust with my own life."

Mick turned to face him.

"I told him that you were the best I knew."

"Did he say what he was talking about?"

"He didn't. But he wants to meet you, tonight. Can you come, after college?"

"Where and when?"

"He said he'd pick you up on the corner of Rossville and Fahan Street at ten o'clock."

"All right. I can make that."

"Aye, I already told him you would. I'd better get off. Just say what you need to say to get his trust and we'll get this done." Sean's eyes burned.

Mick was calmer than he'd anticipated being. "All right, I know what to say. I'll get everything set up."

Sean nodded and walked away. Mick looked at his watch. Five hours until he saw Melissa and three more until Tony.

Mick's own recent IRA activities had been limited to monitoring RUC men's movements, trying to find regularities in their schedules to provide a convenient time to kill them. Of course, Mick never found any patterns, never opened a window for the murderers to swoop through. His commander seemed unfazed by his lack of tangible results, happy to wait for the right time and place to strike. It was a slow war; a war of grinding intelligence and everyday life interrupted by occasional murder. Weeks, or even months, might pass where an active volunteer like Mick would live an entirely normal life, not called upon to do anything. But then the call might come, and he would have to answer it, just as he had in 1972. The worry that he might have to be involved in something he couldn't get out of, couldn't sabotage without being found out by the other IRA men, hovered black over him like a savage wraith. Discovery as an informer, or a 'tout' as the IRA called them through gritted teeth, would mean death. It hadn't happened yet, but if he did this for long enough…. Tony Campbell's next operation needed to be the big one he'd been talking about all this time. Tony must have known Mick wasn't a killer. Everyone else did. But then, they didn't need him to be. There were always killers, always young men with a thirst for revenge against other young men they never actually met, yet who inspired terrifying bloodlust within them. But Tony could use an experienced man he could trust, and that was where he could use Mick. Mick had met Tony a few times now and he was a terrifying individual, completely obsessed by the sectarian madness that had possessed him all his life. Sean and Tony's father had been old IRA, before the split, before the Troubles began in Derry, back when the truest of the hardcore obsessives had kept the republican cause alive, back before the British soldiers came in and young men like his sons were swept in along with so many other disaffected young men and women. Mick's brief meetings with Tony Campbell had taught him one thing; he had to be stopped.

Melissa hugged Jason a little tighter than usual, and felt him squirming to escape her grasp. She leaned back, granting his wish as she pushed back a stray lock of hair that had fallen down across his forehead from his cowlick above. The first of Jason's A Levels were days away.

"You're going to study tonight?"

"Aye, Mam, of course I am. I'm taking this seriously."

"Your entry to college depends on the results of these exams. You need to take them more seriously than anything ever before." He was a good student; more interested in sports, but had always done well. "Don't get complacent, I'm depending on you."

"I won't let you down," he said, and reached over to hug her voluntarily. She couldn't remember the last time he'd done that.

"I know you won't," she whispered.

He got out of the car and bounded up the driveway to Jessica's house. She was pretty. She would soon be a memory to him. Melissa felt the tug of guilt inside at uprooting him. She watched him as the front door opened. Jessica's father waved out at her, a huge smile on his face. He went to walk out to her, but she waved him back inside. She had to get to college, didn't have time to sit and smile, making polite conversation.

The car hummed into life and her mind immediately turned to Mick. The red light at the end of the street gave her a chance to pull down the mirror and check her makeup. She'd never worn makeup to college until a few months ago. Now she wore it every week. The light went green and she pushed the mirror back up. The nerves began inside her. It was so ridiculous. What chance could they have together? College was over in a couple of weeks and she was leaving. The feelings she had for him were an irrelevance, no matter how strongly they gripped her. They had to be. Jason was the most important thing. The flirtations she and Mick were pursuing with one another were nothing more than that. It felt good to appear attractive to someone as attractive as Mick was. But she knew it was much more than that. It was the wonder of just being around him, to have him in her life again. Talking to him was like no one else. Perhaps if her family could sit down and talk to him, they could love him as much as she did.

The setting sun was coloring the city orange, red, and gold. She pulled into her regular parking space ten minutes early so she waited in the car. It was hard to think about anything other than him. The feeling that she was about to lose him again choked her inside. She couldn't go through that again, could she? But what was the alternative? How would Jason react? How would Mick react? She'd kept anything about Jason from him, afraid of what she might say or reveal if she spoke openly. Perhaps Mick could be a father to him. This could be the chance they'd be waiting for their whole adult lives. She tried to shake the visions of a future with Mick out of her head but they seemed stuck like limpets on the rocks of her mind. This would be their last Monday together. She knew he was thinking the same.

Mick arrived late and took his seat. He glanced over at Melissa several times in the first few minutes of class, but never found her eye. Each time he found her looking straight ahead, her gaze a picture of sharp focus. A few minutes passed and he gave up trying. The class ended on time and the professor stood to receive a round of applause from the students, each standing to show their full appreciation. It was only then that she looked over at him, but not with the smile that he was hoping for. The applause faded and died. The class began to leave. Mick darted up the stairs, waiting for her at the door. A watery smile greeted him as her eyes met his. He ignored the outward signs and motioned toward the café. They walked together. Her beauty was dangerous now, like the flash of a drawn blade, ready to slice into him.

"Are you doing all right?" he asked.

"Yeah, I'm doing fine." She lied and he wondered if he was going to have to go through the charade of asking her multiple times before she actually told him how she was feeling. They went on in silence, entering the café together in their practiced fashion. The impending meeting with Tony Campbell began to weigh on him and it was hard to know if the nerves he felt were about that or what he knew he had to say to Melissa. The cash register rang behind him and Melissa made her way over to their usual table. The cappuccino machine behind the counter seemed to take an age and she was sitting there for a couple of minutes alone before he arrived to join her. Neither of them spoke for a few seconds as he sat down. Her eyes squirmed around, eager to look anywhere but at him.

"So this is it," he began.

She looked up at him at last. "I suppose it is."

"Are you ready for the exams next week?" he asked, and as soon the words sounded he berated himself for making the conversation too easy. He knew she was ready, and it was no surprise when she said so.

"Aye, I'm a bit long in the tooth to be away off drinking when I need to get study done." She ran a hand through her hair, patting it down though it was perfect. She was wearing makeup again, but this time she'd gone to even more trouble for him, had taken even more care over her already immaculate appearance. Knowing that she cared was enough to swell his heart.

They spoke about nothing for a few minutes: the content of the course, some of the vagaries of their fellow students, the professor. Melissa felt her body grow tenser with every passing minute. She'd tightened up as soon as she saw him, having no idea what to say or even what she wanted. It was she who finally said something real after twenty wasted minutes.

"This is our last class together."

"I don't even want to think about that," he said, the words slipping out of his grasp like water through his fingers. "I've been dreading the end of the course, the prospect of not seeing you anymore." His eyes were completely earnest and she immediately felt her skin hotter, her breathing confused.

"I know…. I enjoy meeting with you so much."

"It's been fun. I don't think anyone else in our lives would understand though."

"God knows what my parents would say."

"It's good you're not a teenager anymore isn't it? I look forward to these Monday night meetings more than just about anything else in my life. Does that sound pathetic?"

"Yes," she replied and they both laughed. "You need to get out a little more." It took them a few seconds to settle down. There was so much to tell him. "No, it doesn't sound pathetic, because I feel the same way." She shrugged. "Maybe we've become two sad old middle-aged bores together."

"That sounds just fine. Now that I'm thirty-seven I don't care what people think about me anymore – one of the benefits of getting older."

"Oh, I didn't realize there were benefits."

"Come on now."

She brought the teacup to her mouth and drank some back. "No, I agree with that. I don't care what most people think either."

"Most people?"

"Well, there are certain people I'm wary of all the time, certain people whose feelings I have to take into account."

"Your son, your family?" He didn't like where this was going now. It felt like the bad news was coming. He had the sudden urge for a cigarette, but fought it back. "What are you getting at?"

"I don't know. I really don't."

"I want to see you. I don't want this to end. This shouldn't end just because our excuse to see each other is gone," he said.

"It's not as simple as that."

"You don't think I know that? Nothing between us was ever easy except the time we spent together alone. That was the only easy part. I know you've got a son. I know you're leaving soon." The intense danger he was putting himself in came front and center into his mind. Could he go through with that and continue seeing Melissa? If she found out, they'd be finished. If

Tony found out his true intentions, he'd be dead. One thing at a time, he told himself.

"So what do you suggest?" she asked.

"I don't want to stop seeing you. We've always been good together. You have to admit that."

"Of course I do," she said. "It destroyed me when you went inside. I remember watching you on TV, reading about you in the newspaper, knowing the truth, knowing that the things they were saying about you were wrong, that the things you admitted to were things you didn't do. You were in my mind for years. You never left me." She surprised herself at the candid nature of her comments. If he was shocked he wasn't showing it. He just raised the coffee cup to his lips and took a sip before replacing it without saying a word. He looked on, waiting for her to continue. "I think it's obvious that if there were no extenuating circumstances...."

"What about your son?"

The question cut her off, knocking the wind out of her lungs. Jason. She thought of him, thought of Mick and Jason together like she had so many times. She tried to come up with some kind of deflection where there was none, and knew she'd have to speak about him now at last. It was right.

"Would you like to meet him?" Her voice was weak, almost as if half of her was trying to hold the words back.

"I would love that."

She nodded and brought the cup to her mouth to cover her quivering lips. The teacup rattled as she put it back onto the saucer. She brought her hand to her head and stood up, pushing the metal chair back with a screech on the marble floor.

"This was a mistake. All of it," she said. Her voice fortified somehow, even though she was just as confused as she had been all night, all week, ever since she'd met him again. "You can't meet him, you can't come into my life, there's just too much, your history, my family. We can't do this." She turned to walk away.

His heart crumpled in a heap inside him and he sat motionless for a few seconds before gathering himself to bounce out of the chair and after her. He caught her just as she was walking out the door. Several people were looking at them.

"You're making a mistake," he told her.

She looked back at him through damp eyes, but didn't speak, just continued out the door into the darkness of the night. He went beside her.

"This isn't going to be easy, but nothing worthwhile ever is. What we have is special. It always was," he continued.

She stopped and turned to him. "What do you mean what we have? We meet for coffee every week, nothing more," she said and walked on.

He realized she was deliberately trying to hurt him. It was the natural thing to do, to dismiss this. He wasn't going to let her.

"You're wrong, and you know you're wrong."

They walked together for thirty seconds in silence. She was desperately trying to hold herself together in front of him. The pain within her was the sort that only he could bring, and she reverted to the memories of how she'd felt seventeen years before.

Tears were rolling down her face as they reached the car. She reached into her bag for her keys but dropped them to the ground, cursing out loud. He was still standing there as she righted herself. His eyes implored her, his face so honest in every movement.

"There's a lot more on the line for me than you. Are you going to come to London with us?" He opened his mouth to answer, but she didn't let him. "I need time to think, to sort out my feelings for you. Let me just think it over. We'll be in the same place next week for the exams. Give me your phone number. I'll call you if I need to talk."

He nodded his head, taking a pen and piece of paper out of his bag. He wrote his address and phone number down before handing it to her. She took the slip of paper from him and placed it into her purse.

"All right, you have my number, so use it." He forced a smile.

"OK. Come here." She reached out and put her arms around him. He brought her into him and held her against him. The feel of her, the smell, and the brush of her hair against his cheek. It was the first time they'd touched in seventeen years. She drew back and away from him, managed one last smile and got into the car. He stood still, watching as she drove away. He had to meet Tony in ten minutes.

Chapter 23

Mick reached the corner of Rossville and Fahan Street just before ten o'clock. The street was dark, quiet. Most people were home on a Monday night. Sean had prepared him, had versed him on what Tony wanted to hear. He was ready. Minutes drifted past. It was a clear night and Mick looked up at the night sky, each star like a tiny diamond on an immense black velvet cloth. The spot where his father had died was less than a hundred yards from where he stood. This city offered no escape. The ghosts of the past were always close. He brought his eyes down from the calm above the earth to the mural of a British soldier smashing down a door with a sledgehammer and wondered what the stars thought of all this, all that this city had been through.

The lights of a parked car flicked on a hundred yards down the street and started advancing toward him. It pulled up and Tony Campbell rolled down the window, motioning for him to get in the passenger seat. Tony was a huge man, well over six feet tall, his face thick with black stubble. He was around thirty, heavy and muscular, like an attack dog bred specifically for one purpose. Mick took a deep breath in through his nose and opened the door. The car smelled of cigarette smoke, the ashtray overflowing with gray filth and half-smoked butts.

"Get in." Mick did as he was told. Tony's tone didn't invite more conversation and he put the car into gear with a tattooed arm before pulling out. There was no traffic, no one on the streets. Tony didn't look around, didn't speak as he drove. The radio was off, an oppressive silence in the car. Tony drove for a minute or so before pulling off onto a side street Mick and Pat had played on as children, where Jimmy Kelly, who died on Bloody Sunday, two months short of his eighteenth birthday, had lived. Tony turned the engine off, leaving the car on. He flicked on the radio, a ridiculous pop song by an Australian soap opera star bouncing around the confined space of the car.

Tony turned to him. "I hear you wanted to see me."

"Sean told me you needed good, reliable men, looking to make a difference in the fight against the British imperialists." He hoped his lines didn't sound too practiced.

Tony took a few seconds to digest what he'd said before he replied. "We can always use committed soldiers. You're an active member at the moment, aren't you? What makes me so special, why do you want to see me?"

"I'm afraid. Attitudes are softening. People are forgetting what happened to my father and so many others in this city. The subjugation of the Catholic population has lessened just enough for people on the street to lean toward talk of a peace that would bring us back to a time where we had no rights, where we were hardly better than slaves to the ruling Protestant classes. I'm afraid that the work that I've done over the last twenty-odd years, the work that I've dedicated my life to will all be in vain."

"Sean said that you were a good man. You were cellmates for how long?"

"Three years." Mick thought back to the day Sean had come into his cell. Sean had been a different man then, young and delusional; hypnotized by the propaganda he'd been fed his whole life. But Mick immediately saw the good in him, knew there was hope. It was difficult to harbor such hope for his brother.

"He's a good kid, needs a little help finding his own balls sometimes, but a good kid."

"He's an excellent volunteer, someone who wants to make a difference, committed toward building a better, socialist future all the people on this island." It felt bizarre to say those words, to have them come out as his voice.

Tony offered a cigarette to Mick, before lighting one up for himself. The smoke seemed to fill the air in the car like water, permeating every space almost immediately. Mick thought to open a window, to try to catch a breath, but decided against it.

"He's got a big mouth is what he has. I suppose he's told you about the fact that I'm planning something."

"Aye, but no details. I just wanted to…."

"He doesn't know any details. This operation is too important to be put at risk by touts." Tony almost spat the final word; tout - the slang word for police informants.

"I'm no tout, and neither is Sean." Mick's indignant tone caused Tony's eyes to flicker like a flag in the wind, but only for an instant.

"I never said you were, mate, and I know my brother's not."

"So what are we doing here?"

"We're getting to know each other, Mick, just getting to know each other. What about your brother?"

"What about him?"

"I know he has his prisoner rehabilitation program, his outreach with ex-loyalist paramilitaries. I know he was in once too, back before you went inside."

"He does his thing, and I do mine. We're twins, but we're not attached at the hip. He's taken his path, and I've taken mine. He doesn't concern himself with my business."

"And what about you? Are you going to set up your own prisoner rehabilitation program? Are you reaching out to UVF butchers?"

"Pat has his way of helping the community and I have mine. He knows nothing of what I do. He doesn't want to. We both want the same thing - peace and justice for the people of this province."

"Peace." Tony shook his head as if the word was a curse he'd caught a child using. "There's too much talk of peace these days. Our masters in the IRA are talking with your brother's lot in the SDLP. Sinn Fein has recognized the government in the south and their candidates are standing in elections. It's all a distraction, a waste of time and energy. That's what my mission is, Doherty, to wake up the Catholic people of this province, and to bring the other Irish, the people in the south, back into a war they've dismissed as an irrelevant irritation. The Protestants and the Brits don't understand anything but brute force. That's the reason

I asked to meet you on Rossville Street. I wanted to remind you of what we're up against. I wanted you to be in the place where they murdered your father and all those other poor delusional marchers in 1972."

Hot, bare anger poured through Mick as he listened to Tony speak of his father. Mick stared out at the darkened street in front of the car and thought of how disturbed his father would be that those who worshipped at the same altar of insane violence that killed him were holding him up as a martyr. Mick bit down on his lip so hard he almost drew blood. Tony seemed not to notice, wasn't looking at him and kept on talking.

"Until our final victory, there's no place for peace in this struggle. Peace without victory is surrender," he continued, taking a long drag on his cigarette. His gravelly voice was harsh, every word delivered as a denunciation. "And if I can instill that thought in people's minds then I'll be remembered fondly by future generations of republicans."

"So what do you intend to do?" Mick asked. Just sitting in the car with this man was enough to make him feel changed. He'd met hundreds of IRA men in his life. Some of them were vicious killers, some of them were misguided young men with sincere intentions and pure hearts, but he'd never met anyone quite like Tony Campbell. The level of hatred in him was frightening to behold, as if it was all that sustained him, was all he had to live for. Mick wondered about his life outside the IRA. Sean had mentioned that he had a child, a three-year-old girl, with an ex-girlfriend. It was hard to see him as a father, impossible to imagine him showing love or compassion. Yet Sean had told him that he saw his daughter every day, that he was an excellent dad. It just didn't seem to fit.

"I intend to give this generation what it needs," Tony continued. He was finally looking at Mick, his eyes two black marbles in his face. "Your generation had Bloody Sunday, and we're eternally thankful to those martyrs who died that day."

Mick had to hold himself back. His father died for nothing. He knew that. The memorials were kind and it was heartening to know he'd not been forgotten but all his father's death, as well as the deaths of the other people that day, had promoted was more violence, more death and despair, more broken lives and heartache. But people like Tony Campbell would never accept that, would never accept that his father had never intended to die that day on 1972, and wasn't killed because of his religious beliefs or the love he felt for his community. Meaning only existed where and when it was inferred and that's what made the idea of martyrdom so dangerous. All that had happened that day was murder and the men who'd murdered his father would never see the inside of a jail cell. The only justice was moving on, striving for a better life, and in the rejection of the insane violence that had killed him.

"My generation had the hunger strikes," Tony continued. "And the outpouring of national sympathy that occurred after that. What this generation needs is something to pin our colors to, and something to inspire young people throughout the country, north and south, to get up and join the cause. That's what will bring us the final victory. You can mark my words."

Mick was almost speechless and just stared back at the void of Tony's eyes. No feeling was perceptible there, and he knew that if Tony discovered his true intentions there would be no mercy.

"You want to inspire the people of the south to join the war, to bring them in on a full war footing?"

"That's what it's going to take to finally win this war. I've heard whispers of a ceasefire within the ranks of our fellow IRA volunteers. The hard truth of it is that they're getting soft. They're too old. They're living in the past. Our bombing campaign now is little more than an irritant to the politicians in Stormont and Westminster. We need to take it upon ourselves to escalate this conflict into a full-scale war, to clear out the negative elements in our communities and to finally win after twenty years of treading water."

Mick supposed that Tony's 'negative elements' were the Protestants, the hardcore loyalists at a minimum.

"I couldn't agree with you more. We need to bring this war to the population at large, the people avoiding it here, the people down south, the immigrants abroad. We could garner huge support from America. They seem to realize the nature of things here." Mick felt the smile come to his face. His acting was good. "Its refreshing to hear a man with big ideas, who's not willing to sit back and let the status quo rule. It's men like you who began this struggle, who won the freedom in the south they now take for granted, that we have to earn. These are the types of ideas that people like Padraig Pearse and James Connolly had, sentiments of the kind Robert Emmett or Wolfe Tone first came up with. These are important ideas, and I'd love to be a part of this, to be there as history is made, or perhaps even to play a part in it."

Tony stubbed out his cigarette and turned to face front again. "I'm flattered that you'd mention me in the same breath as Irish republican heroes like Pearse and Connolly, Wolfe Tone and Robert Emmett, and I'm glad that you can see that it's those type of ideas that I'm aspiring to. People within the IRA will call me a dissident or a separatist. Some may even call me a traitor for going behind my superiors' backs in planning this, but when they recognize this as the inciting incident for our generation, the incident that leads to the transformation of our struggle, they'll be erecting statues to me all over this country."

Mick did his best to swallow the shock inside him. "What are you planning to do?"

"There's no need to quibble over the details, not yet at least, but rest assured that this is going to be happening soon. Provisions have been made and the process has begun." Tony turned to him. "I've enjoyed meeting you, Mick. You're exactly what my brother said you were: a committed republican, not bound to the existing power structures within the IRA, someone willing to do whatever it takes to advance our cause."

"I'm glad we see eye to eye," Mick said, proffering a hand which Tony almost crushed as he shook it.

Tony reached past Mick to open the passenger door to the street. "This is where we part ways. I'll be in touch. Don't leave town in the next few weeks, but more importantly, don't talk to anyone about anything you heard tonight. I despise touts, Mick, more than the

Brits, more than the loyalists, more than anything in this world." Tony's eyes burned like black coals as he spoke, each word a threat.

"You and me both," Mick answered, but his words stopped there. He stepped out of the car and onto the street. Tony stared at him for another second from the car before reaching over to shut the door. The car started and Tony drove off, the headlights scything through the darkness as he went. Mick stood still for a few seconds after he'd gone, his only movements that of his breathing. He had to tell someone, Pat, the RUC, the IRA leadership, someone. The IRA would never approve of the type of mission Tony was talking about. Even they had their limits. Surely they'd stop him, but what if someone told Tony who'd leaked the information to them about the operation? And he had no details. He couldn't go to the RUC with stories of a massive operation to escalate the war, he'd be laughed out of there, and the news would be just as likely to leak back to the IRA as if he'd gone to the leadership themselves. If he told his active service unit leader or someone higher up in the Derry brigade, Tony would find out and once that occurred his life span would be measurable in hours. Tony Campbell was the type of psychopath who volunteered to kill informers, who'd torture them just for his own pleasure. He could drop out, just pretend that he'd never had this meeting, but then what if Tony's fantastic plans came to fruition? It was impossible to see his plan of bringing the people in the south into a massive, full-scale war to determine some future victory, but Mick had no doubt that a lot of people would die. It was probably a bomb, much like the type Tony had used to kill the British soldiers on the Buncrana Road in March, an operation lauded throughout the IRA as exemplary. Tony was a skilled killer. That much was beyond any doubt.

Mick began to walk. He had no idea what to do and, without Pat to confide in, felt half a person. Pat's house was about ten minutes walk away and, without making a conscious decision, he began to make his way toward it. The pressure behind his eyes was building, his brain felt set to explode. He couldn't do nothing. This was what he and Sean had rejoined the IRA for. Maybe Tony wouldn't even want Mick involved, maybe he'd just read about the operation the day after it happened, see the news reports on the TV. Maybe he'd never see Melissa again. Maybe all this time, since he'd gotten out of jail, had been wasted. He knew he couldn't tell Pat; telling him would only endanger him, yet he longed to give into selfishness and reveal his secret life to his brother.

He walked on, the street lights above him pouring yellow light onto the quiet streets below. Mick tried to listen for his father's words, attempted to search his mind for his father's voice, but it wasn't there. He was thankful his father had met Melissa, even if it was only hours before his death. Somehow that had always validated her further in his mind. No other woman could ever come close to knowing him the way she did. But he couldn't make her love him, couldn't make her reciprocate the feelings he knew he had for her. He'd always known, had just tried to block them out. He felt the absence of her and wished beyond anything that she would have been waiting for him when he got home, that he could slip into bed beside her, making sure not to wake her as he flicked the light off and settled down to sleep. It didn't seem too much to ask.

He found himself at Pat's front door, not quite sure how he'd gotten there. It was almost eleven o'clock, but the light in the front room told him his brother was awake. He couldn't account for the half hour since Tony had dropped him off. It was only a ten-minute walk to Pat's house. The time had just evaporated, just as whole years of his life had disappeared, had faded into nothing like ripples expanding in water. They'd meant nothing, not even to him, had only been leading to this. Mick tapped on the living room window and stood back to wait for a response. The curtain ruffled and he saw an inquisitive look on Pat's face as he looked out. Pat opened the front door for his brother a few seconds later.

Pat's initial happy expression changed as soon as he laid eyes on him and Mick knew he'd have to tell him something. "How are you doing? You don't look so great, is everything OK?"

"Yeah, I'm all right." Mick pushed past his brother and inside the house. The television was on, but there was no other sound. Mick went into the living room without another word and flopped down on the couch.

"Can I get a drink?"

"Of course," Pat replied and went to the cabinet in the corner, taking out a bottle of whiskey with two tumblers. He poured a couple of fingers into each before handing one to Mick. They clinked their glasses together before each took a sip.

"So, what's going on?" Pat inquired. "I'm always happy to see you, but I wasn't expecting you at this time on Monday night, looking like that." He pointed. "You were fine this morning."

Mick ran fingers through his hair. Coming here was a bad idea but staying away was impossible. Escape was out of the question now.

"I'm fine. You were right; there is a girl. A woman. There's a woman in my life."

"Somehow it doesn't seem like things are going well."

"Not really. It's complicated."

"One of the great things about being your own boss is that you can stay up late on Monday nights listening to your brother's women problems without the worry of coming in late the next morning - I've got time."

Mick pushed out a heavy breath and raised the tumbler to his mouth. The whiskey seemed to fire his throat as he swallowed it back.

"Yeah, the girl's Melissa Rice."

Pat's face fell almost to the floor. "Melissa Rice from when we were kids, who was on the march on Bloody Sunday with us?"

"That's her. I can't seem to shake her." He grinned, trying to force a laugh that wouldn't come. "I met her again last September. She was in my college course. Monday nights with Melissa soon became the highlight of my whole week. It must sound ridiculous now."

"No, of course not. Is she available? I thought a girl like her would have been married off long ago."

"Divorced, with a son. He's fifteen or so, maybe fourteen. She doesn't mention him much. We talked about everything but him."

"Are you seeing her now?"

"No," Mick took another sip of whiskey. "It's much more pathetic than that. We chat, every week. We've met up after class for coffee for the last eight or nine weeks in a row. I haven't even kissed her."

"But…"

"But I love her, and class is over now. The exams are next week and I don't know if I'm ever going to see her again after that." Mick shifted in his seat, suddenly uncomfortable. He longed to tell him about being in the IRA, about Tony and his insane plan to plunge the city back into the bloodbath of the early seventies once more, but he couldn't and it was destroying him inside. "I'm pretty sure she has feelings for me, although she hasn't said it. She said she needed time. I gave her my number."

"She'll call you, don't worry about anything, little brother. She knows a good thing when she sees it. It's difficult for her, with her background, and your history, but she'll come to you. Mark my words."

"There's something else – she's leaving, going to college in Dublin or London. She's not sure yet. Her son, Jason's going with her. They're all set to leave in the next few months."

Pat sat back in his seat, taking a long sip of the amber liquid. "She'll come to you and when she does, you should go with her. New place – new start. There's too many ghosts here, too much history dragging us back. I sometimes wish I could live in a place with no memory, where the reminders of everything I've seen and done in my life aren't all around me every day. You should go. Everyone here deserves a chance to start over, and this could be yours."

Chapter 24

Weeks drifted past with nothing from Tony. Sean assured Mick that his brother had been complimentary in the brief mention that he'd given their meeting on that Monday night in Bogside. Speculating on what Tony might have been planning became a near obsession. Sean thought that he might have been planning to assassinate a loyalist politician. Perhaps James Molyneaux, the leader of the Ulster Unionist Party or even Ian Paisley, the more radical and substantially more hated leader, and founding member of both the Democratic Unionist Party and the Free Presbyterian Church. But that didn't seem possible. Getting to either of those two men, the most powerful unionist politicians in Northern Ireland, seemed beyond the capabilities of Tony Campbell or indeed any IRA man. Killing one of them, particularly Ian Paisley, would enrage the loyalist population and would be a call to arms for hundreds, if not thousands, of disaffected Protestant young people all over the province. Mick didn't think that even Tony Campbell would be audacious enough to attempt that. He guessed that Tony's attack might be on the Guildhall, the seat of the local council in the city and symbol of Protestant domination. The 300th anniversary of the siege of Derry was coming, a massive event for the Protestant, male-only, Apprentice Boys of Derry society, and the unionist community that supported them. Tension during that march in 1969 had caused the Battle of the Bogside. That had led to the formation of Free Derry and the arrival of British troops in Northern Ireland, which most people recognized as the beginning of the Troubles. Hitting that would be equally insane, and be just as likely to ignite smoldering hatreds and lead the province into a firestorm of violence. He'd told no one and neither had Sean. It was their responsibility alone.

The summer sun was bathing the city, illuminating everything as spun gold as Mick walked home from work. He thought back to the night he'd told Pat about Melissa. Pat had asked him about Melissa several times since, but the truth was that there'd been little to tell. She'd been there at the exams, but somehow they'd regressed. They didn't speak and hadn't spoken since. Seemingly it had all been too much for her – not that he could blame her for taking the easier option. How could she tell her son, a young boy from Waterside, that his new stepfather would be a convicted IRA terrorist? Melissa knew the circumstances of his time in jail, of course. She knew the real story but would that matter? People still remembered the killings and would remember his name. Finding out who he was wouldn't be difficult, but living with him after that certainly would be. The time they'd had together had been a beautiful distraction, but only that. He'd sacrificed his own happiness many years ago. It seemed a high price to pay for the folly of youth.

It was a Monday night. Mondays didn't seem the same anymore, and probably never would be again. The flat was empty, and he didn't want to be alone, so he drifted into a pub, took a seat at the bar and sat there among strangers for a couple of hours. Just a few cursory words about what was on the television and the weather outside constituted conversation as he sat there. It was awful, but still preferable to the loneliness of his apartment. He should have called over to Pat. He could have played with the kids and sat down with them to dinner, but somehow the feeling of always being with someone else's wife and children was beginning to weigh on him. It seemed like his chance had passed. It seemed that his only worth now was to disrupt Tony, to be a protector of people who'd likely as not openly despise him, and who'd certainly never show him the least bit of gratitude. He picked the beer off the bar and finished the rest. The barman glanced at him, but he got off the stool, shaking his head. This had to end. He needed to get over this. There was still life left to live and still causes to fight for. The night air was warm and sticky against his skin as he stepped out, the light of the sun still high in the June sky. It was almost nine o'clock, almost their time. He thought back to the last time he'd seen her. The pathetic wave she'd given him had told him all he'd need to know. They only saw each other once on each of the two nights the exams had lasted. That was it. No tearful goodbye or painful breakup, only the void left inside him, only the useless love for her he still felt with every passing breath.

It was five minutes back to his apartment, but he walked so slowly it took him twice that. Two soldiers were checking cars and pedestrians at a security checkpoint at the end of the street he lived on. It had been two weeks since he'd spoken to his mother and he resolved to do so when he arrived home. He passed through the checkpoint. Checkpoints were a fact of life; he barely noticed them anymore. So many places existed in the world without armed soldiers, murals, and faded terrorist flags blowing in the wind. So many places existed without the daily possibility of a bomb going off on a crowded street or the soldiers at the checkpoints opening fire. He thought of Melissa and wondered if it was time that he should get out too. Maybe a fresh start was what he needed, somewhere that people wouldn't remember him, somewhere that people weren't divided by loyalty or religion. He came to the door of his apartment building and heard the sound of someone getting out of a car behind him. He whirled around; paranoia grabbing him like hands around his throat. It was Melissa, dressed in sweater and jeans, the makeup around her eyes smudged from tears. He stood frozen as she came to him.

"Where the hell have you been? It's Monday night, isn't it?" She managed to smile as the words came.

"I didn't know. I was in the pub having a drink. Were you waiting long?"

She looked at her watch, wondering if she should tell him the truth, before deciding against it. "A few minutes." Her heels clacked on the pavement as she moved from foot to foot.

The warmth came again but he was utterly confused, even about what to say or do next. He caught himself staring at her, not saying a word.

"Would you like to come up to my apartment? It's not exactly palatial but...." It was a mess. He remembered the remnants of this morning's breakfast, still on the table.

"I'm sure it's great, but I thought we might go for a walk. It's a beautiful evening."

"Yeah, of course." Relief coursed through him as she led him away from the apartment.

"I didn't think I was going to see you again," he began. "After the exams...."

"I didn't think I was going to see you again either."

"What made you change your mind?" The words drifted out of his mouth as if he were in a dream.

"You." She glanced over at him as they walked, a half-smile on her face, which subsided to a sigh almost as quickly as it had come.

The instinct to ask her about the exams, about the college course, about something other than what she was here to talk about came to the forefront of his mind, but he fought it back. The time for wasted time was past now.

"I'm so happy to see you again. It must sound crazy to you, but I've missed you so much the last few weeks. It's as if there was a hole in my heart that only you can fill. Do you understand what I mean?"

"Aye. Perfectly, almost too much so."

He tried to look at her, wanted to take in the full beauty of her face, to lose himself in the eternal green of her eyes, but she looked straight ahead. They came to a cross street and waited for the traffic to come to a stop. The silence between them, necessitated by an old man standing next to them walking his dog, seemed to last hours though it was thirty seconds at most. Mick reached down to pat the dog, a chocolate Labrador. Melissa's face was stretched tight as a snare drum, her eyes closed as they waited. The light changed and Melissa paced across the road, leaving the man and his dog trailing in her wake. It was amazing how quickly she could move in heels. Mick had almost to jog to catch up with her. They walked along Shipquay Street, down past the Guildhall and toward the river and Waterside beyond it. They hadn't spoken since they'd stopped at the lights. Mick longed to reach out to her and take her hand, to pull her to him.

"Where are we going?" he asked. "Can you slow down a bit? I thought this was meant to be a leisurely stroll. I didn't know we were training for the fifty-kilometer walk in the next Olympics."

She dropped her pace. "I'm sorry, I just wanted to get away from that old man at the light."

"I know. I don't really know why you're here," he replied. "What's going on right now?" She glared at him and then straight ahead again. This wasn't how he'd imagined this being. He would have to lead if she wouldn't. "When the college year ended, it felt like I was losing you all over again."

"This hasn't been easy for me. I have more to lose than you do. There's more for me to consider."

"I know you have your son."

She turned to face him. The leaden expanse of the river was in front of them now. "I...." She stopped, struggling to find the words.

"You don't have to say anything." He moved to her, resting his hands on her waist. He was inches from her now.

"I do have to say something."

"I love you, Melissa. I have from the first moment I saw you, just back over there." He pointed back to the spot. "I'd never seen anything as beautiful as you in my whole life, and I know now I never will. I've loved you every minute of every day since. I know now...."

"It's not as simple as that," she said, the tears coming now. His hands moved up to her shoulders and then to the smoothness of her face. She put her hand on his as he cupped her cheeks. "My whole life was set before you came along. I was single, but doing fine. I was happy."

"You told me you had a boyfriend," Mick interrupted.

"I lied, so sue me." She wiped away a tear before continuing. "Jason was doing great. I was getting ready to move away, to start a new life, for a while at least, and then I look over and see you in the bloody classroom, waving back at me."

"I didn't wave the first class. The waving came later."

"Thanks for the correction," she said, not rising to the joke. "You turned everything upside down. Jesus, if my son could see me now, crying on the riverfront like some teenager, and over you."

"Melissa, if you don't love me then just...."

"Of course I love you, you idiot. Why else would I be back here, subjecting myself to this? Only someone in love can act as stupidly as I am right now."

She looked into his eyes as he let the bliss of her words sink in. He leaned down and kissed her on the mouth, but only as a peck. The time wasn't right, not yet.

"It's not as easy as that."

"I know about your family and my past. Surely...."

"It's not even that," she said, stepping back away from his touch. "It's Jason."

"I'm sure that once he gets to know me..." His words trailed away.

She took a deep breath, the gravity of what she was about to say having its full effect on her.

"I haven't been honest with you. Jason's not fifteen. He's sixteen. He was born on March 21st, 1973."

The realization scalded him like boiling water. She didn't even have to say it.

"He's your son. Jason's your son, Mick."

He stood there motionless for a few seconds, feeling his insides implode. He leaned back against the railing, his legs uneasy. Melissa was staring at him, watching him as he scanned for a bench, somewhere to sit before his legs gave way entirely. The weight of his body forced him down until he was on his haunches, his hands out in front of him with sweaty palms bonded together.

"All this time?" he said, his voice tired and thick. She didn't answer, just reached down a hand to him. He shook his head and used the old iron railings behind him to help himself back up onto his feet, before turning to lean out toward the Foyle, just like that night he'd found her on the other side in 1972. "It was the night before I went to the RUC, wasn't it?"

"Yes," she replied in a whisper.

"You're sure it's me, you're sure I'm the father?"

"I'm sure, Mick. I was a virgin before we met. I'd never been with anyone else. You know that," she snapped.

"I think I'm within in my rights to inquire." He fought the anger back, tried to focus on the love surging through him, the opportunity in front of him. And the anger faded. He understood. He understood why she hadn't told him. It was the only thing she could have done. Melissa was leaning over the railing looking out, close enough to touch.

"I wanted to tell you about Jason. I wanted to tell you in 1974 when I came to you in jail, but I just couldn't. What would have been the point? I thought you were going to be in there for the rest of your life. What would my parents have said? 'Oh Mam, Dad, you'll never guess who the father of your first grandchild is – the guy on the news, yeah him there, the one who shot those soldiers last year.' How could I do that, Mick?"

Mick felt a wry smile come to his face. "Ok, but you could have told me earlier, you could have said it to me in September when we met up again."

"I had no idea you were going to be there or how you would have reacted. Jason has had a father all his life, or at least he had a man who he thought was his father. I didn't want you to show up and confuse him. I had to look after Jason. He was always my first priority."

"So why are you telling me now? I could have lived out the rest of my life without knowing. Jason need never have known either. Why did you tell me?"

Melissa closed her eyes and shook her head. She kept her eyes closed as she spoke. "I realized. It took me a while to realize, that I love you, that there's no one else in this world for me but you, and there never has been. All the problems with John and anyone else were always because I was comparing them to you."

"What, the convicted IRA murderer?"

"That's not who you are. You know as well as I do that you're not that person." She moved to him, touching her arm against his and his turned his body to face her. "I've seen inside you too many times to think that. I've seen your heart. You were never that person." Her hands were on his chest now. "I'm sorry I couldn't tell you about Jason; it was just too risky."

"But it's not risky now?"

"Of course it is," she raised her voice before realizing where she was. An old couple sauntered past them, hand in hand. Melissa waited until they'd moved past to continue. The maelstrom had faded from her eyes now; the certainty of what she was doing giving her the courage to continue. "This is one of the riskiest things I've done since I started seeing you. You're the biggest risk I've ever taken, and, apart from a few obvious things, I might be yours too."

"Did you tell Jason about me yet? Does he think that John is his real father?"

"I haven't told him. I needed to speak to you first. I'm not going to tell him until I figure out where we're going from here, and yes, he thinks that John is his real father."

"Does John know himself?"

"He always knew that he wasn't the father. I don't think he wanted to know who Jason's real dad was. I told him it was a one-night thing."

The wind gusted off the river blowing her hair across the smooth skin of her forehead. Mick moved gentle fingers to correct it and brought his palm down to her cheek again. She leaned into the warmth of his hand, drawing herself closer, their hips touching now, her mouth inches from his.

"I don't know what we're going to do. All I know is how much I love you," she whispered and he brought his lips down to meet hers, felt the velvet touch of her kiss, the intoxication of her, all over again. The years melted away and they were kids again. They were back in a time before his father died, before those soldiers were shot down, before his time in jail, when all that mattered was that they loved each other. He drew away from her thirty seconds later, assured of something in his life at last.

"I want to meet our son."

She nodded and leaned into him, her ear on his heart as it thundered inside him. They stood there for a few minutes and kissed again before he led her back from the riverside and past the Guildhall toward his apartment. They spoke little as they went, moving back through the city and the timelines of their lives laid out in the buildings and streets they passed on their way. They walked hand in hand past the place they'd first met and through the old city walls, which snaked around to hover like a school bully over Bogside and Rossville Street where his father had died. They moved through everything they'd ever known together. The story of Derry was woven into their own like fingers interlocking. The story of the city, and the sadness and violence it had visited on the people like an abusive, yet loving father, was theirs too. But another story was coming sharply into focus. If Jason would accept him, to some degree at least, only his promise to Sean, and his commitment to Tony remained. Without a word to one another they floated up the stairs, barely touching the ground on their way into the bedroom.

Chapter 25

They were all thankful for Siobhan. She latched on to Jason as soon as they'd met, and insisted on holding his hand as they walked from the cars to the restaurant and then on sitting beside him at the table. Her instantaneous fascination had melted away any awkwardness that might have arisen, and given them all something to laugh about. It had taken the boys longer, but by the end of that evening in July, they were all out in the garden behind Pat's house together. Jason was playing football with them as Siobhan looked on with adoring eyes. Jason was smaller than Mick had been at that age and had his mother's hair, but apart from that, Mick could have been looking at a picture of himself. The very thought of Jason's existence perplexed him. He had always been there, through all the times he'd had inside, through all the times when it didn't seem like there was any light left to break through the darkness. He'd existed as his and Melissa's son. It was almost too extraordinary to contemplate. Pat's son, Michael, went to slide tackle him, but Jason side-stepped out of it and flicked the ball over his cousin's prostrate body before volleying past seven-year-old Peter in the tiny goals.

"He's a showboater, just like his dad," Pat smirked and took a swig of beer from the bottle he was holding. All four parents were standing at the kitchen window, watching the children playing together. He wondered how Jason would react, how he would react himself. Even the word 'parent' lay slack on him like an ill-fitting jacket.

"When are you going to tell him?" Pamela asked.

Melissa reached over and took Mick's hand, interlocking her fingers in his as he began to speak. "I figured tonight would be the night, but I almost don't want to spoil it now. He's no idea what's going on, thinks that I'm his mother's new boyfriend from Bogside. He's never even been here before."

"How was he about coming over here?" Pat asked.

"Fine, there were no problems about that. He's a good boy, not like some others. I always tried to instill that in him," Melissa said.

"Have you had much of a chance to sit down and talk to him yet, Mick?" Pat asked. Siobhan was playing with the boys now, running around in circles with the ball in her arms.

"We've spoken, but he's guarded. It's going to take a while to break through with him. It's going to be a lot to take on."

"He's still hurting from the divorce," Melissa interjected. "I'm sure he likes Mick, but I just don't know how he's going to react. He's too old to wait very long. That'd only make things worse."

"How are you going to explain where you've been all his life?" Pamela asked.

Mick took a few seconds, silence filling the vacuum where his words should have been. "I don't know yet. I have to be honest with him. It would kill him if he found out from someone else, and we might even be able to keep it from his grandparents if he's in on it."

"Is he close to them?"

"Aye, he is," Melissa answered. "And he has cousins on my side too, my sister Jenny has a boy and a girl."

"What age are they?" Pat asked.

"Johnny is six, and Lily is four. They're great kids. They live over in Waterside, not too far from where we grew up."

"And when are you off to Dublin?" Pamela asked.

"A month or so. Mick's help was greatly appreciated last weekend when he came down with us to check it out. It gave him and Jason a good chance to spend some time together too."

"That's great," Pat said and reached across to put an arm around his brother's shoulder. "How was Dublin, Mick? It's been a few years since I was down there myself."

"It was fabulous," he replied, swallowing a mouthful of beer. "No checkpoints, no soldiers, no terrorist flags anywhere, just people getting on with their lives."

"It'll be like that again some day. People are sick of the endless cycle of violence. Even the IRA is beginning to see that peace and the ballot box are the only real answers," Pat added.

The specter of Tony still lurked in the shadows of Mick's mind. Mick hadn't met him since that night in May but had received dispatches through Sean. The plan was very much in motion, but Tony wasn't giving any details away. Mick and Sean knew nothing. Tony was playing it the right way, the smart way. The more people knew the details, the more chance of an informant giving it away. Mick and Sean knew that they were on standby for something huge, something that would blow this all open again. That was all. Mick watched as Jason picked up Siobhan, holding her high in the air.

The light of summer deceived them all, and before they realized it, ten o'clock had crept up. The kids wailed as Pamela went out to take them off to bed, Jason smiling as they each waited their turn to hug him goodnight. Mick stood back, let Jason's mother take him inside to say goodbye to Pamela and Pat, before pointing him in the direction of the car out front. Melissa said goodnight to Pat. He'd accepted her as quickly as he had the first time, and now as they hugged, they seemed like old friends. Melissa made her way out to the car.

"I'll follow you out," Mick said and hugged Pamela.

"I'll leave you two boys to talk, I've got to put the little ones to bed." Pamela made her way up the stairs. The three children were in the bathroom where Siobhan was attempting to bark orders at her brothers, who were busy ignoring her.

Pat broke into a smile as soon as she'd gone. "Come here." He embraced his brother. "I'm proud of you and everything you've done since you got out, and before that. You've got a great woman now, and a ready-made family. You've just got to go out and claim it. You going to be all right?"

"I think so." Mick's skin was cold now, the claw of nerves sunk deep into him. He hadn't felt like this since he'd turned himself in.

"You're going to be fabulous. Get out there and lay claim to the rest of your life."

"Right then, let's do this."

"Good luck, little brother."

Mick strode out of the house to Melissa's car and got into the front passenger seat with Jason in the back.

"What d'you think of my family?" Mick said to Jason as the car pulled out.

"They're fantastic. I had a great time."

"Yeah they're a good bunch, I lived with them for a while myself." Melissa looked over at him through the corner of her eyes.

"I think Siobhan wants to start your fan club," she added.

Jason laughed. "She's a cute wee thing."

The words came to Mick but stopped in his throat, teetering on the precipice of a new unknown that would begin as soon as he uttered them. Jason turned his head to look out the window. Mick felt Melissa's hand on his. The memories of his youth were all around them in the houses and streets of Bogside. The murals held their own stories, but his was the fabric of the city itself. They passed Free Derry corner, now preserved as a stand-alone wall as the original buildings that had made it a corner had been demolished. The mural with the faces of those who'd died on Bloody Sunday loomed a hundred yards away, the spot where his father had been gunned down just across the road. He so wanted to bring Jason to it, to tell him about the grandfather he'd never know, who'd been taken from all of them that day. He longed to tell him about Jimmy and Noel and what they could have become had their brief lives not been wrenched from them. They were only a little older than Jason was now when they'd died. Jason glanced up, catching eyes with Mick in the rearview mirror.

"I've enjoyed getting to know you over the last few weeks, Jason." The answer Mick hoped for didn't come so he continued, the nerves raw inside him. "As you know, your mother and I knew each other when we were younger, and that's why we've seen so much of each other so quickly."

Jason turned away from the window, plainly expecting something that he didn't want to hear.

"I told Jason how we've been talking for almost a year now, that we took the decision to get together very seriously," Melissa interjected. "There was an extra reason that we took so long. We were together before you were born before I ever met John. We were a couple."

Jason had never heard his mother refer to the only man he'd ever known as a father as John before. The night was darkening, and the windows were mirrors enclosing them now. He looked at his reflection and then at the man sitting in the front seat, a man whom he'd never met a month before, and he knew. The pain spiked inside him and spread down through his entire body, dragging anger in its wake like fire on a string.

They came to a red light as they came from the Craigavon Bridge. Melissa looked over at Mick, tension in her movements, her eyes. They were only a few minutes from the house.

"We never wanted to break up, but times were different back then, even harder than they are now. The fact that I was Catholic made things difficult for us, and when my father died on Bloody Sunday, I thought that leaving your mother was part of my duty to my community."

"Why are you telling me this?" Jason's tone was sharp. Melissa's immediate instinct was to cut him down, but she let Mick continue instead.

"Your mother was a crucial part of my life, someone I could never leave behind, no matter what life and the Troubles threw in our way."

Mick stepped back from the precipice, fear gripping him. He knew what the next words had to be, and what effect they'd have. They drove on for another thirty seconds or so, Melissa hurtling through the amber light to get to her driveway. The car pulled to a halt, but no one moved to get out. They both turned to him, his arms crossed over his chest, his face cold as stone.

Mick continued. "I was away when you were born. I was away your whole life. But I want to be there for the rest of our lives together." Jason's eyes dropped, but Mick kept talking. "Your mother never told me about you, for your sake. She never told me that I was your father. She was trying to protect us both."

"But I don't have to anymore," Melissa began. "Mick is a wonderful man, Jason, and I love him with all my heart, almost as much as I love you.

"What about my real dad?"

"If you're referring to John, then the answer is that nothing changes. If you want to see him, you can." She resisted the temptation to twist the knife into John, to remind Jason of what an awful father he'd been. Mick would have to prove himself. Nothing was going to be solved tonight.

Mick didn't speak, was still turned around to look at his son. He wanted to tell him he loved him, but the truth was they were almost strangers. He felt some innate warmth toward him but love? It was too soon to say.

"Is that it? Can I go inside now?"

Mick saw the irritation in Melissa's eyes but held out a hand to calm her, letting it fall into her lap. She turned back around to face front and let her seatbelt out.

"Yes, you can go inside. You have your key?"

"Aye," he said and got out of the car.

Neither adult moved. The sound of the door slamming behind Jason reverberated in the confined space of the car after he left. Mick undid his seat belt and turned to her.

"On the scale of great to awful, it was somewhere in the middle. It's a start."

"Give him time. It took us nine months to get our heads around this, and he hasn't even asked why you were away his whole life."

"We'll move one mountain at a time."

"It's probably best off you don't come inside. I need some time alone with the boy. You want me to call you a cab?"

"No, it's a great night. I think I'll walk. It's only twenty minutes. It'll be just like the old times when I used to throw stones up at your window, running home afterward." The excitement he'd felt came as a memory, the waves of joy.

She felt the smile appear on her lips despite herself. "We did the right thing, didn't we?"

"Telling him? Of course."

"And everything else, getting back together?"

He reached over and kissed her. "I've never been so sure of anything in my entire life. And in a few weeks or a few months, Jason will be right there with us, and then there'll be nothing in our way, nothing to hold us back."

She reached forward and kissed him, the grin full on her face. "You're right. Best not get too carried away right now with your kisses. Jason might not appreciate you taking advantage of his mother in the car outside the house."

"I wouldn't if I were him," Mick said and got out of the car. Melissa got out to give him one last kiss, but he was already walking away, and she let him go, making her way inside to deal with Jason instead.

Mick ambled down to the river and made his way along the bank. He tried not to pay any particular attention to the place where he'd found Melissa back in summer 1972, attempted to consign the past to memory, to focus on the shining future almost within reach. It was too much to resist analyzing how breaking the news to Jason had gone, and he went over each sentence in his head, wondering how he could have played it better. But the truth was that he'd done all he could. The rest would happen in time. It would be up to him to prove himself to Jason now. The commitment to Sean gnawed at him. The one thing he and Sean both agreed on was the date that Tony was likely to hit. The 300th anniversary of the siege of Derry, when the Protestants under King William withstood the barrage of the Catholic King James, and one of the biggest loyalist parades of the year, was coming on August 12th. Violence during the same parade in 1969 had marked the beginning of the Troubles. Tony had an eye for history and knew the level of outrage any attack during the parade would cause. How he intended to do it, and on the grand scale he'd mentioned, was the question, a question he and Sean still had no answer to. But there was more than just his pledge to Sean to consider now. Could he leave Sean to do this alone? He'd been the one who'd convinced Sean to do it, and what if Tony was the harbinger of war and death that he aspired to be? Could he live with himself knowing that he could have prevented it? Would Melissa live with him if he carried through with it? She knew nothing of his personal crusade. It had been easier to hope it would never happen, that they could leave together without having to foil Tony, or be tortured to death by him. He knew that if it did come to happen that he'd tell her. He couldn't die and be a mystery to her. He couldn't bear the thought of her never knowing what his intentions were. She might think he'd conned her and that he might have been a regular IRA volunteer and a dissident madman at that. And what of Jason? What would he think? He wasn't a child and had his opinion on the Troubles, even if he hadn't mentioned them out loud yet. Everyone did. Choosing Melissa and Jason was the easy option, the sensible option, but he knew he couldn't do it, couldn't desert Sean or the people of the city whether they were his people or not. The burning dark in Tony's eyes was real.

The night seemed to close in around him like a great black cloak. He walked out onto the Craigavon Bridge. The wind off the river was cool, even in July and he rolled up his sleeves to feel it on his wrists, to let it filter into him through his veins. His movements were slow, mechanical as he approached the checkpoint in the middle of the bridge. He didn't look at the soldiers as they questioned him, their words as inconsequential as a sneeze or a cough. His mind faded into memory as he tried to remember his father, the smell, the feel of him as he held him as a child or shook his hand in Bishop's Field the day he died. He wanted to remember him as the man he was, not as the name on a memorial visited by tourists and exalted by Republicans as a martyr to a cause he never wanted to be a part of. His mother, his father, he and Pat. He tried to remember the times before any of this when his father was alive and his mother was here. Before all of this had destroyed them. Back when their lives had been attached, inseparable, like paper cutouts torn apart by the British soldiers, the IRA, UVF, UFF, INLA, Orange Order, the Apprentice Boys. What was the difference in the end? They were different versions of the same polarizing force that had been tearing this province apart for generations.

The different versions of his father came to him, the young man with muddy knees and grey-white shorts who'd taught him to play football. The man who'd walked through dew coated country meadows with him as he ran his hand through the long grass looking for fat stalks to pull and pick and blow on between his thumbs. He was so many men at so many different times. So why was it that the only one he ever thought of was the one lying on his back on Rossville Street, the NICRA flag an impromptu shroud, stained with his blood? The man who'd taken him to work when he was fourteen, who'd let him sweep up straggly hair as it fell on the floor at the weekend for a few extra coins, came to him. The father who'd caught him stealing beer from the cabinet and clipped him across the back of the head without telling his mother. Mick remembered the man who'd come home from work at night with a smile on his face and a kiss on the mouth for his wife. Every dinner they'd had together, every time he'd played with Pat on the floor as Dad read the paper, as Mam did the knitting or made the tea, all seemed wasted now. Those moments were like gold dust slipping through his fingers. It didn't seem possible that anything might be more precious than that. She was gone now too, without him to keep her here. He'd lost both parents that day, even if he still wrote to her and saw her at Christmas. Losing him was losing her both. The soldier who'd fired that the bullet had done more than just kill his father. He killed everything he'd built too.

The river sang to him in a low hum as he passed through the checkpoint. The sensation that he was one with the city, and that it wasn't whole without him or he without it came to him, but he immediately shrugged it off as the yoke it was. He was leaving – with Melissa. He was leaving with his son and Jason would never see him gunned down in the street, holding a white handkerchief, trying to be the last comfort to a dying man. Life beyond this did exist. Mick stopped at the end of the bridge, pausing to look back across and then at the gray spread of the Foyle stretching out both sides in front of him. How could this city be wonderful and full of love yet callous and unforgiving? So much had happened here, so much that could never now be undone. Was there no one else who could stop Tony? Mick wished for a cigarette though it had been many months since he'd touched one.

He'd loved Melissa all his adult life, but had written his feelings off as a burden. They were something to be disregarded as he set out on his personal crusade for atonement that almost no one else would ever know of, let alone recognize. Sean had come to him a corrupted youth, a polluted stream, choking to death on the hatred he'd been filled with his whole life. It had taken Mick years to reveal himself to Sean inside; the walls of the cocoon he'd built around himself were too thick to break through any quicker than that. The fire of hatred within Sean had taken even longer to suffocate. But by the time Sean got out, a year before Mick, he was unshakeable in his new conviction that peace was the only victory and that the way of his family would ultimately destroy them.

Mick turned away to continue home, the confusion reigning in his mind undiminished. Scenarios ran through his head like tiny movies where he got out free after foiling Tony's plan, where he left without doing anything and nothing happened, or he left and failed to prevent a massacre. And, of course, the scenario whereby Tony caught him and tortured him was the main attraction in the movie theater of his mind. Would any of this be worthwhile if Melissa found out and left him again? Was any of this worth it without her? Was his own personal happiness more important than the lives of other people he'd never know, would never meet and who'd likely despise him if they met him anyway? Would he even be able to prevent the mission Tony had planned? He'd told no one. No one seemed to know a thing. Mick had dropped hints as subtly as one could when inquiring about the possible movements of a rogue dissident to other IRA men, but they were completely oblivious, or magnificent in their efforts to appear so. Sean had invited him, and Tony was the brains, but, apart from that, Mick didn't even know who else, if anyone, was connected with it. Tony was smarter than he'd given him credit for, perhaps too much so for them to stop him. But only he and Sean would have the chance. A light rain began to fall, warm against his face. He walked on.

Melissa trudged back into the house, knowing that Jason was already in his room. The idea to leave him, to speak to him the next day came to her, but she swatted it away like a mosquito. The time to talk was now. She couldn't bear the thought of the pain and confusion he must have been in. He'd left the door on the latch. She pushed it open. Silence reigned inside. No TV, no stereo blasting music, no movement or noise of any kind. She went to the kitchen and poured herself a glass of water, readying herself. She drank it back in two gulps and turned to go up the stairs to Jason's room. Golden light spilled out from underneath his door. She knocked with the knuckle of her middle finger; three short taps. No answer came, so she rapped on the door again.

"What do you want?" His words bled through the wooden door, low and distant.

"We need to talk, let me in." She tried the handle, but he'd locked it. She heard the sound of the key turning, and she pushed the door open.

Jason was sitting on his bed, still fully clothed, the lamp in the corner spraying yellow light all over. The stereo on the desk was silent for once. He looked like a child again. She sat down beside him, putting her arm around his shoulders and venturing to kiss him on the cheek. He only flinched a little as she kissed him. She had to wait for him to begin, had to let him direct the conversation. This couldn't be a case of her trying to appease him.

He began about fifteen excruciating seconds later.

"So are you in love now? Just like you two were when you were kids?"

"What do you think of him?"

"I can't believe you'd do this to me. I can't believe you'd bring this person into our lives, just as we're about to leave."

"What if he came with us? He wants to be a part of our lives. I want him to be a part of our lives."

"So, you are in love with him."

"As much as one person can be with another, but you knew that. You're still the number one man in my life though, and you always will be."

"I'm finding that hard to believe right now." He finally looked at her, his eyes raging torrents. She put her arm around him again.

"I've loved you more than anything in this world since the first time I laid eyes on you. You're the most beautiful, wonderful thing in my life, and if you don't want Mick in our lives, he won't be, but you shouldn't make that judgment yet. He deserves a chance."

Jason leaned forward, hunching his back, his elbows on his thighs. Feelings crashed inside him like waves on the rocks, over and over. He turned around to look at his mother's loving, earnest face. The touch of her hand on his back was warm and welcome. He closed his eyes, searching for the right way to feel.

"Who is this guy? Why haven't I ever met him before? If he's so interested in being my dad, where's he been for the last sixteen years of my life?"

Melissa leaned back, her spine cracking ever so slightly. The question bounced around inside her head. She'd done her best to keep Jason away from the rhetoric her father still espoused from time to time at awkward dinners and trips to the countryside. But there was no doubting that Jason was a Protestant from a unionist background. Most of his friends were as non-political as he was. But there were some who spoke of the 'Fenians' and the 'Taigs' in the Catholic community, who leaned toward prejudices that she had tried to hide him from. Shielding a child was impossible.

Guidance was all that she could provide. But Jason had to accept that Mick was his father, his judgment had to be colored by that one inalienable fact. It was better that he found out from her. Now.

"He was in prison."

Jason turned his head to her in a flash, his eyes wide. "What?"

"We met in 1971. Things were different then. That was the worst time to meet a Catholic boy, even more so than now, and we had to see each other in secret. I met his family for the first time in January 1972, on the civil rights march that led to Bloody Sunday."

"You were there? On Bloody Sunday, when they shot down the terrorists?"

Melissa raised both hands to her face, rubbing her eyes. Jason's words were like needles. "They didn't shoot terrorists, only innocent people. I was there. I saw it with my own eyes. The soldiers just mowed them down, for no other reason that I could see than asserting their control or as some kind of perverted sense of punishment for daring to challenge the government. Mick and Patrick's father, Peter, was one of the people killed that day."

"Why did Mick go to jail then?"

"He and Pat waited for the official report on the march to come out but when they saw it and the whitewash that it was they joined the IRA. They did it to serve their community. They saw it as no different from joining the army to defend your country in a time of war."

"And you were still with him then?"

"I was, but we broke up when I found out. It was too much for me to take."

"What did he go to jail for, did he kill someone?"

Melissa blew out a breath, deep and hot from the pit of her lungs. Did he need to know all the details? But what if he found out himself somehow? If he got a hold of old newspapers or spoke to someone? She'd take the chance.

"Something horrible happened and Mick stepped forward to take responsibility for it, to ensure that his brother and everyone he loved stayed safe. He sacrificed his freedom and turned himself in for a crime he didn't commit."

"Why didn't he tell the RUC he didn't do it?"

"It was his brother and his friends, and there were threats toward people he loved. Everything happened so quickly. He didn't feel he had any other choice. Pat swore to leave the IRA after that and has been working to promote peace ever since with his prisoner rehabilitation program and his work with the SDLP. Mick, your father, went to jail for sixteen years. I didn't even know he'd gotten out until last September when you were fifteen. I didn't think he ever would. I thought he was lost to you forever. I didn't see the point in either of you knowing about each other. I thought it'd only be fuel to the flames of the pain within you both."

"What did he do?"

"He didn't do anything. He didn't commit the...."

"What was he sent to jail for?"

"The murder of three British soldiers."

She stopped dead, the silence deep and full. She was staring at the side of his face as he leaned forward and away from her, looking for some emotion. But there seemed none there.

"This is who you want to be with? An IRA murderer?"

The words stung, but she understood and pressed on. "He never killed anyone. He made some mistakes, but he left the IRA as soon as he realized who they were. It was a different time then. Catholics thought the only recourse they had was joining the IRA. He and Pat saw their father die in front of them, shot down by British soldiers. Try to understand. He's finished with that life now. We all are. This is the time for us to be happy. He's going to come to Dublin with us, to get a job as an engineer. He wants us to be a family. So do I. I love you more than anything in the world, but I want you to be happy for me."

He turned to her and saw the tears running down her face. He put his arms around her, felt the warmth of her against him, trying to imagine his own father in the IRA. It was just as well they were leaving. If some of the boys he knew found out about this, they'd kill him themselves. But maybe it was time for his mother to be truly happy, not the carbon copied, diluted happiness she'd pretended to have with John. He'd never seen her like she was around Mick, not in his whole life. He hugged her closer, her breath caressing him to calm.

Chapter 26

Weeks passed with still no word from Tony. Mick and Sean sat mostly in silence at lunch now; too afraid to talk about what they knew was coming, unable to go to anyone but each other for a grain of comfort. Fifteen thousand marchers were readying themselves for the Apprentice Boys parade. Mick thought back to the same parade when he was a boy, the bottles and stones thrown at the marchers, back and forth, back and forth. No point to any of it. It still went on and it always would. Young men marched with their fathers and grandfathers. The indoctrination of young Protestant males was seen as a priority. The Catholics had their parades too, but the Protestants, the loyalists, were the ones who invested most in these shows of power and pride in the face of what they saw as republican aggression. This was their way of showing solidarity with one another and proclaiming their loyalty to a government in London who'd likely be rid of them, and everything else associated with Northern Ireland, if it could. But that was politically impossible, so the loyalists marched, inflaming old hatreds, reinforcing prejudices, all in the name of protecting their way of life and their precarious hold on power in this in-between place.

The call came on Thursday the 10th of August. Mick felt all the strength draining from him as Tony's words came through the receiver as if his true fate was finally being revealed. Somehow he knew that he wasn't going to survive this, that his plans to move to Dublin with Melissa and Jason would never come to be. The Troubles would take him, as they'd taken his father and those British soldiers by the side of the road who still haunted his dreams. Tony didn't say much on the phone. He would meet him on the corner of Fahan and Rossville streets, same as last time. Mick kept the phone to his ear after Tony had hung up, frozen in the reality of the moment and of what he'd committed himself to do. Why couldn't he have left this behind? What redemption was there in an agonizing death at the hands of a psychopath like Tony Campbell? He went to the window of his apartment, put his hand against the cold glass of the window and peered down onto the street below. He tried to imagine his father, tried to see him in his own eyes in the reflection in the glass. He took a deep cold breath down into the pit of his stomach, breathing condensation onto the glass in front of his face. He had only minutes to get to the rendezvous with Tony.

His whole body was shaking as he left the apartment. The bottom of the stairwell came, and he pushed his way out into a warm sticky night. The thoughts in his head were devoid of love or hope. Melissa seemed like a dream from another life. He came to the phone booth just down the street from his apartment. He thought to call Sean, to see what he knew but didn't risk it. Who knew if he was being watched? The five-minute walk seemed like hours, and he felt physically ill as he arrived. The car moved to meet him as before, the window rolling down to reveal

Tony's face. Mick got in, and they drove in silence for thirty seconds before they pulled over.

"This is it." Tony's words were tinged with excitement. "We're nearly there. Everything's in place, are you ready?"

"Ready for what?"

"Never you mind for now."

"How am I meant to know if I'm ready for something when I've no idea what it is and when it's taking place?"

"We're going tomorrow night. I'll need you ready at nine o'clock. I'll meet you here again."

An icicle of fear slid down Mick's spine. "What's the operation? What are we going to do?"

"I'll brief you fully when you need to know," Tony smirked. "Don't take it personally, it's not that I don't trust you, it's that I don't trust anyone. This is too important, and I've put too much into this to have it destroyed by some tout."

Mick had to work hard to hide the river of frustration flowing through him.

He'd hoped for some information here so that he wouldn't have to go on the operation, but what choice was there now? Only to take this upon himself or to deny it, to pawn it off on someone else or to hope that the dead could forgive him.

"All right, I'll see you back here tomorrow night."

"Wait and see, we're going to be held up as heroes for this."

Mick nodded, although he doubted there'd be any streets named after Tony Campbell. "I'll see you here tomorrow night then." He thought to ask about Sean but decided against it, climbing out of the car into the warm night air instead. Tony drove away, and he was alone once more.

His immediate instinct was to go to her, to tell her, to seek counsel or comfort, but, before he realized, he was walking back toward his apartment again. His feet were oblivious to the turmoil in his mind. He passed the monument to those killed on Bloody Sunday, right on the spot where he, Pat and Melissa had cowered together, twenty feet from where his father had been murdered. He looked at each name in turn, pausing on Jimmy and Noel's names before coming to his dad at the bottom, the last person who'd died that day. Nothing had changed. This was his chance to do something. It didn't matter if no one ever recognized him for it. His father would.

A fitful night of sleep ended with the dawn, and his limbs were heavy as he hauled himself out of bed. She was the first thing he thought of, but it wasn't long before the creeping fear followed in her wake, pushing her out. He made his way to the bathroom mirror, examining his face. The wrinkles around his sunken, gray eyes were like tiny lines drawn in the sand of his skin. He tried not to think too much; thoughts would only lead to worry and worry was a waste of emotion. He brushed his teeth. A single line of red blood stained the bristles on his toothbrush. He washed it off and placed it back.

The worksite was a fifteen-minute walk away, but he made it there in less than ten, immediately searching for Sean as he arrived. Robbie Morris, a former IRA man who'd done time on kidnapping charges, was on the first floor putting a window frame in place.

"Morning, Robbie, have you seen Sean?"

"He called in sick," Robbie said without looking up. "Your brother was asking for you a few minutes ago though. I think he's up on the second floor."

"All right, thanks," he murmured as he turned away, an enormous pressure building within him. He had to speak to Sean. The stairwell was empty as he made his way up, and Pat was there, working on a wall in the corner. He put the hammer down as he saw Mick.

"Jesus. You don't look good, brother. Rough one last night?"

"Nah, I didn't sleep much is all."

Pat turned back to work on the wall again. "Well, we need all hands on deck today, Sean called out sick." Mick nodded, trying to keep it together. "I've got to get out of here in a bit, and I'll be gone all day, but how about a drink after work? I've been missing you all week."

"All right, I'll talk to you later."

Mick walked away from his brother, each foot like lead. He made his way back downstairs to begin the day's work. Sean had called out sick. Had he run? Was he on the mission already? He'd said nothing when Mick had seen him just the day before, had given no indication that anything was amiss. The prospect of facing down Tony without Sean was something he'd never contemplated. Had Sean done the sensible thing? Maybe he'd found out what the mission was, and had called the authorities already. A phone box sat two hundred yards down the street.

"I'm popping out for a minute," Mick said to nobody in particular though several of the men wandering in heard him.

As soon as he was out of sight, he began to run, pushing past morning commuters on their way to work and soldiers idling on the street, their automatic weapons lazy in their arms. The phone booth was covered in graffiti, the glass scratched with teenagers' initials and hearts with arrows through them expressing loves likely long forgotten. He reached into his pocket for a coin, dropping it in his haste to shove it into the slot. He got another and dialed the number. Sean lived with his girlfriend in Creggan. She worked as a nurse, mightn't be home. The number rang and rang. He hung up and dialed again, and then again. The cold realization that he was alone saturated him, and he hung up the phone with a shaking hand. How could he do this without Sean? Ragged breaths pushed in and out of his lungs, and the panic inside was almost unbearable. People stared as they shuffled past, but no one stopped. It took him several minutes to calm down enough that he could return to work, and once he did, holed up the corner speaking to no one.

Time drew out more slowly than he thought possible, each minute like the cold drip of water torture on his forehead. He tried Sean's phone twice more but the result and his conclusion, was the same; Sean had run. Perhaps it was the thought of betraying his brother. Perhaps it was the same fear that was infesting

Mick like a swarm of locusts. Either way the result was the same. He was gone, and Mick was alone.

Mick was upstairs, the light of the evening sun casting his shadow long across the unfinished floor when Pat found him.

"You ready to knock off? Up for a pint? We won't have too many more chances before you leave to go down south."

Mick nodded, knowing that this might be the last time he'd ever see him. "Just give me a few seconds to clean off my hands." They were out on the street making their way toward the pub when Pat began to speak.

"Are you all right? You've been off all week. I've meant to speak to you, but you've been hard to get a hold of. Everything good with Melissa?"

"Yeah, everything's great."

"What about Jason? Baby steps, right?"

"Yeah, he's starting to come round. We're almost back to how it was before he knew I was his father. We have a ways to go yet."

"You'll make it. I'm sure of that. He's a great kid, he just needs time."

"We all do."

They made their way into the pub, packed with after-work drinkers, and some who'd been in since lunchtime. The mahogany-brown wood panels of the walls shone brightly behind them, and the smell of smoke and stale beer hung thick in the air. They found a place at the end of the bar beside some young student types. Somehow Mick managed to conceal his feelings for an hour as they talked about football and the kids and work, but every minute was a minute closer. Glossing over it in his mind was not escape.

Mick excused himself to go to the pay phone in the corner. Sean's phone rang off again. He tried Melissa, wanted to see her.

"Hi," he said.

"How are you, stranger? I was wondering when you'd call." Her voice was like ice water on a deep burn. "Are you coming over?"

"I just wanted to stop by for a little. I'm pretty tired. I'm going to get an early night. I'm just having a pint with Pat and I'll be over around seven or so. How's Jason?"

"He's getting there, little by little."

Mick said goodbye and hung up the phone. Pat greeted him with a smile and a fresh pint as he came back. Mick so wanted to tell him. Pat's innocent eyes were too much to take. "I just wanted to thank you, Pat, for everything you've done for me, taking me in and giving me this job and for all the support you've given me. I'd be nothing without you."

Pat paused for a second. "Of course, what else would I do? You're my brother, the other half of who I am. I had to do something to make up for what I did to you." He tried to hide the crack in his voice, but Mick turned around to face him as he heard it.

"What are you talking about, Pat?"

"For everything that's happened to you. It's all my fault."

"I made my own choices."

"You went along with me, to support me. You never should have been the one to go to prison. I was too much of a coward to take responsibility for what I'd done. You atoned for my sins, gave your life for mine." The tears came so quickly that Pat barely had time to turn his head, ashamed of himself in front of his brother and the strangers bustling around him. He felt Mick's hand on his shoulder. "I'm sorry, I just lost the run of myself there for a second."

"No, it's fine. We've been through a lot, and with Jason now."

"It's just that...." It was hard to find the words. He'd hidden them so deep that they were hard to retrieve. "I know that everything that's happened to you is because of me. If it weren't for me, you'd be living with Melissa and Jason and probably your other kids now. If I hadn't...."

"That's enough of that," Mick said, the tears welling in his own eyes now. "It's time to move on. Everyone has a past. That's what we are, but it's our future that counts more, what we aspire to be. That's all we can control."

They stood there for a few more minutes, drinking their pints, only a few words exchanged. Mick looked at his watch, knew it was time to leave. "I got to go, brother." The urge to tell him about Tony, to ask for his help was like a wild animal unleashed inside him, tearing him to pieces. He put the empty pint glass on the bar. Pat opened his arms and hugged him.

"I love you, Mick," he said. It was the first time either of them had said it.

"And I love you too, Pat. This isn't your fault. None of it is."

Pat nodded his head, bringing his gaze down to the floor to hide the tears bulging through.

"I'll see you soon, all right?" Mick said. "Tell Pam and the kids I love them too."

"Aye, of course," Pat said and watched his brother push through the crowd and out of the pub.

Forty-five minutes later, Mick was at Melissa's front door after the quickest shower, change and taxi ride he could remember. The sensation of seeing her as she answered the door was like an oasis in the desert of his despair. He held her tight for several seconds before drawing back to kiss her again.

"How's Jason?"

"He's doing fine. He's upstairs if you want to see him."

"Will he come down for dinner?"

"Aye, of course." She looked concerned. "Are you OK? You don't look so good."

"I'm fine." He pushed past her and inside the house. "I'll wait a few minutes before I see him, give him some time." Nerves raced electric in his veins and though he'd only walked from the taxi to the house, he was panting. "What's for dinner?" he asked in a conscious effort to draw attention away from himself.

"Are you sure, you're OK?" Melissa asked again.

"Yeah, of course. I'm just feeling a little off." Cold sweat swam down the skin on his back.

She led him into the kitchen where she'd lit candles and laid out pretty ornate place settings, the good china. This was somewhere place settings, china and candles were still important. She went to the fridge and got him a beer. Time ticked out loud in his mind. He had to meet Tony in ninety minutes. Dinner would be ready in ten. Pushing past the sliding glass doors, he walked out into the tiny back garden. She stayed in the kitchen, happy to leave him alone while she finished the dinner. He sat on the step, staring into the evening sky, trying not to drown in the immense fear that was overtaking him. Melissa called him inside when dinner was ready and he was sitting down when Jason came to the table.

"Hi Jason, how are you doing?" Mick asked.

"I'm doing all right."

He took a seat beside Mick.

"How d'you feel about the big move next week?"

"I'm gonna miss my friends."

"You'll make more, and it's not forever," his mother interjected.

They ate for several minutes, Mick barely noticing the words coming out of his mouth as he made conversation. Each word felt lost as soon as he said it. Jason spoke too, even laughing as Mick made a joke. Jason helped him clear the dishes away after they'd finished. They were at the sink together, Mick washing and Jason drying when Mick asked him the question.

"What do you think of me coming to Dublin with you?" His eyes flicked up to the clock on the wall as he waited for the answer. He had forty-five minutes.

Jason didn't look at him as he answered. "If you want to come with us, I can't stop you. Mam seems to want you to come."

"Jason, I...." The words stopped, the fears within him choking them back. They finished the washing up in silence and joined Melissa on the couch. Mick poured her a glass of red wine, taking water himself. They talked about the move, the house they'd chosen to rent in Sandymount and where Mick might live himself. They weren't selling this house, just renting it. They could still come back. Mick tried to convince himself that he'd get through this, that he wasn't going to die before he made it to Dublin with them. The desire to tell her was so strong that it almost overtook him and he knew that if he stayed any longer he would. He got up, making an excuse about being tired and kissed her before he went to the door. There was no ceremony about his leaving, just a smile, and a promise to see them soon and then he was alone in the driveway once more, the taxi he'd called already waiting for him. He had twenty minutes. He heard the door opening. Jason ran out.

"What is it, son?" It was the first time he'd referred to him as that. "Is everything all right?"

"What are you trying to do to us?"

"I don't know what you're talking about."

"Why are you coming to Dublin? We were fine before you came."

Mick reached a hand out toward him, six feet from where he was standing. "I want to be with your mother, with both of you." The contradiction between what he was about to do and the words forming in his throat clouded his mind, and he began to question everything within him. "I want to make up for the time we lost, to be there for you. I need you, both of you. My whole life's been destroyed by a war I never wanted any part of, that dragged me in. There's not a day that goes past that I don't wish we'd never gone on that march, or that I'd stayed in France with your mother, that I'd chosen her love over what I thought was my duty at the time."

No one else could stop Tony and the mass murder he had planned, but this was his son, and the woman he'd loved all his adult life. They were here, waiting for him, all he had to do was stay, to let the Troubles take their course. He'd live and he'd live well, away from all this. What duty had he left on this personal crusade that even Sean had forsaken? More deaths would come whether he prevented this or not. But their blood wouldn't be on his hands. The blow he'd been dreaming of taking against the violence, against the death and misery of this useless conflict, was waiting to be dealt. Real redemption awaited him, after all these years of darkness, guilt and pain. Jason was staring at him and Mick stepped forward and took him in his arms. Jason spread his arms around him and Mick held him there, the tears starting to come.

"There's something I have to do, for my father. For myself," he whispered. "I can't let it happen, not when I know that I can do something. I hope you'll understand. I love you."

He broke away from his son and turned to get into the taxi. Jason was still standing there as the taxi took him away, back to Bogside, and back to Tony. He had ten minutes.

Chapter 27

The car was waiting as Mick arrived. Mick opened the door with wet palms. Tony was smoking a cigarette, one hand on the wheel and turned to face him as he got in. Mick recognized the man in the back of the car as he got in. It was Martin Heggarty, the bomb-maker.

"Where the hell is Sean?" Tony snarled.

"I was hoping you'd be able to tell me. He wasn't at work today, isn't answering his phone." He turned to Martin in the back seat. "How are you, Martin?"

"You two know each other?"

"We've worked together before," Mick replied.

Tony slammed his fist down on the steering wheel. Curses flew from his mouth, mixing in the air with the swirling smoke in the confined space. He took a breath, his knuckles white as he gripped the steering wheel as if choking the life out of it.

"Right, we can still do this. I'm going to need you more than ever, to make up for that bloody useless brother of mine," he said turning to Mick, who nodded in reply. "Let's get out of here for starters. We don't have much time."

He started the car and they sped through the narrow streets of Bogside, taking a small side road to avoid an army checkpoint ahead. No one spoke. Mick felt his heart hammering so hard in his chest he could almost see it coming through his skin. Martin's face was stoic, bereft of any emotion as if carved from granite. It had been Martin who'd built the bomb Tony had used to kill the soldiers in March. That operation had pleased their IRA superiors, but Mick was certain this operation, whatever it was, hadn't been approved. Could he use the IRA itself to stop this? Would they step in if he could somehow get a message to them? But with absolutely no details, what could he tell them? He would have to go along for the ride a while yet.

They drove for ten minutes, out to the Buncrana road, which led to the border with Donegal and the Republic of Ireland, just a few short miles away. The sun was darkening now, the light fading into night. After a few minutes, Tony leaned forward and flicked on the radio. The latest manufactured pop hit from England filled the otherwise soundless air in the car. Without any signal, Tony turned off down a side road to a secluded country house and pulled up alongside a white van parked outside. Tony opened the door and ordered the other two men out. Mick wondered how much Martin knew. He certainly wasn't talking, not that he ever did. Tony walked around to the trunk of the car. He opened it up and pulled out three balaclavas, directing each man to put one on as he pulled on his own. The two men, their faces now hidden, followed him up to the small, unkempt house. Flecks of red paint were peeling off the door, like old skin hanging off an onion, and the windows were unwashed and gray. Tony pushed a key into the lock and led the others inside. The lights were off, but the muffled sound from inside told Mick they weren't alone. Tony led them into the living room where he flicked on a light, instantly revealing the figure of a man in a blue jumpsuit, tied to a chair. The gag across his mouth was wrapped tight, forcing the flesh on his face back. He hadn't been beaten or tortured, at least that Mick could make out. The man's eyes brimmed over with terror as the three men came in, his manic breathing the only sound in the small room. Tony went to him, leaning down into his face until he was only inches away.

"All right, Terrence, I'm going to take off your gag now. Remember, we know where you live, and I'll be taking one of these charming gentlemen with me to pay a visit to your family as soon as we leave here. If you say anything to anyone, especially any British soldiers or police you might happen to encounter, we're going to start with your daughter, Tracy, then move onto young Thomas. We'll save your wife, Jennifer for last. It's amazing what two, otherwise completely civilized, motivated young men will do. The good news is there won't be much left of your family to bury and you'll be able to save on the price of coffins, stuff all the remains into one."

Terrence's hysteria spread from his eyes, his whole body bouncing up and down in the wooden chair. His own weight forced him over and Tony let out a laugh before reaching down to right him with strong arms.

"I'm going to untie the gag now. You're not going to say anything, are you, Terry? I can call you Terry, can't I?"

Terrence shook his head from side to side almost as if he was having a fit. Tears ran down his cheeks, dabbing the navy blue gag dark.

"I can't call you Terry? Or do you mean you're not going to say anything? I'm confused, Terry. Oh sorry, I mean, I'm confused, Terrence."

Terrence seemed to be shouting under the gag, the words coming through as an incomprehensible muddle. Mick was standing frozen, not quite able to believe what he was seeing.

"Now, joking aside. I'm going to take off the gag. Don't make a sound. Not one sound."

Terrence nodded and Tony reached in and took it off. Terrence pulled massive breaths into his lungs. He looked in his mid-forties, balding, with a mustache. There was nothing remarkable about this man. Mick had no idea who he even was. If Mick could talk to him, find out who he was and why Tony wanted him, he might have some chance of stopping this.

"Calm down, Terry. The calmer you are, the better it'll be for your family. Here's what's going to happen. You're going to make your usual delivery tonight, just as though nothing was out of the ordinary. My friend here's going to take you, and then hold you until everything's over. If you keep your head and do what we say, you'll have an exciting story to tell your friends about your bravery in the face of republican thugs. If you don't, you'll be burying your entire family next week. Do you understand?"

Terrence nodded.

"I want to hear it, Terrence. Tell me."

"I understand, just don't hurt my family."

"That's entirely up to you."

Tony turned away from Terrence, still sitting in the wooden chair.

"The kegs are out back, in the shed. I'll need you two to move them. I'll be out to help you in a minute. Take the real kegs out of the van and replace them with the ones in the shed. He knows what I'm talking about." Tony pointed at Martin.

Mick followed Martin outside into the gritty air of the late evening, the leaves on the trees around the house whispering and shuffling in the summer wind. An old shed stood beside the house, an unlocked padlock hanging from the closed door. Martin pulled the door open to reveal about twelve steel beer kegs, stacked up one top of each other in two rows. Martin gestured toward them and picked one up. Mick did the same and followed him out to the van. They began unloading the van, packing the real kegs into the shed, no doubt to be sold later. Tony came out to join them and ten minutes later the van was empty. Without pausing, they reloaded the van with their kegs, packing them in. There seemed no difference between the kegs they'd taken out and the ones they'd loaded.

Neither Mick nor Martin had spoken since they'd arrived at the house. Tony broke the silence again, wiping beads of sweat from his brow.

"I'll go get our boy inside. Martin, you OK to go down there with him?"

"Aye," Martin answered.

Tony walked inside. Questions flashed through Mick's mind - questions he didn't dare ask.

"Where are you going with this lot?" he ventured.

Martin replied by flicking his eyes at him and then away. Tony reappeared with Terrence, who'd calmed down some.

"All right, Terry, business as usual, my friend here is going to accompany you. "Sorry pal," he said to Martin. "You're going to have to lose the balaclava, the other member of our gang not showing means we're down to a skeleton crew."

"That's OK," Martin muttered and took off the balaclava. "If this bastard rats me out, I'll have his family killed."

"It's not going to come to that though, is it, Terry? Your family are getting out of this healthy, aren't they?"

"Yes, please, please."

"No need to beg. Just get into the van and do your job. Let us do ours."

Tony took Martin aside and whispered something to him. Mick stared at Terrence, trying to figure from looking at him where the hell they were going. There were no markings on the van, nothing on his jumpsuit. He thought to look in the van for a list of merchants they were visiting, pubs or restaurants he delivered to. But as soon as the idea spawned in his mind, Martin came back and climbed into the passenger seat. Terrence got in beside him and started the van. Tony waved them off and the van was gone.

"Time for us to make a house call. Take the mask off before we get in the car."

Mick didn't reply, just did as he was told. Melissa and Jason came to him, but only as a ripple in the dark water of his mind and he focused on controlling the nerves boiling inside him. Tony led him over to the car and both men got in. There had to be something in those kegs other than the beer Mick had heard swishing around. Martin was a gifted bomb-maker, but turning kegs into bombs? It was unheard of. But then this was no ordinary operation.

Without knowing the destination, he was powerless. The van would probably arrive by the time Mick got to a phone, and besides, there was no one he could call to have a van stopped. The RUC wouldn't do that because of an anonymous tip. He had to find out where it was going. Tony started the car and drove back toward the city. Again, the men traveled in silence, the pop music on the radio the only sound. They passed through an army checkpoint with no issues and continued for the ten minutes it took to get back to the city. They went through Bogside and across the river into Waterside, before stopping at a house close to where Melissa lived. Republican sympathizers were scant on this side of the river. Tony went inside for two minutes before emerging with a black plastic bag bulging under the weight of the contents inside, sickening in its familiarity. He placed the bag in the trunk of the car and got back in the driver's seat.

"Now we're ready," he said.

"For what? I've still no idea what's going on."

"You're doing great, just hang in there."

They drove south along the river for a few minutes, shadows joining to form the darkness that was now all around them. Tony turned off into an estate marked off by union jacks flying from the lampposts and red white and blue painted on the sidewalks. Without warning, he pulled off to the side and turned to Mick.

"Here we are. See that house?" He pointed to a red detached house at the end of the street. "That's where our friend Terrence lives and that's where we're going to be for the next few hours, to make sure he keeps his word. Follow me and don't put the balaclava on until I do."

The street was empty except for some kids playing football against a wall a few hundred yards away. Many of the men marching in the parade the next day would be from the houses around them. Were they the targets? Was he going to hit the parade itself? Tony ambled beside him, black bag in hand until they came to the house. The lights were on in the front room and Mick could see a woman and teenage girl watching television through the window. Neither seemed to notice as they ducked around the side of the house. Mick followed as Tony climbed over the gate and then crouched down behind him as Tony inched toward the back garden. Tony moved as if he knew exactly where he was going, as if he'd practiced this before. He stopped as they reached the end of the back wall before it extended into the garden. The houses around them were quiet. Mick didn't know if he wanted anyone to see them or not.

Tony stood up and raised a finger to his lips before drawing keys out of his pocket. He moved around the wall to the back door and slid a key into the lock. It made a tiny clicking sound only they could have heard, and he pushed the door open. He motioned to Mick to put the balaclava back on and they crept inside, the black masks over their faces. Tony reached into the bag and pulled out two revolvers. He handed one to Mick. It wasn't loaded. It was hard to tell if Tony was incredibly smart or incredibly paranoid. In all likelihood, he was both. Before Mick had the chance to protest, Tony was whispering again.

"They're in the living room. I think the boy's up in bed. You get him."

He burst through the kitchen and into the living room, the gun drawn. Mick could see Tony's smile peeking through the mask.

"Hello, Jennifer. Hello, Tracy."

They both screamed, the girl scrambling to hide behind the armchair she was sitting in. She was about thirteen. Petrified tears ran down the wife's face as she pressed her whole body back against the armchair, her eyes wide with terror.

"Shh, stop that now. If you keep that noise up someone's going to get hurt. Come out from behind there," he said to the girl. "Get the boy," he said to Mick. The lights were off on the top floor and Mick felt his way up the stairs. He tried one door and then another before he found the child, around five years old, asleep in bed. Mick held the door open, watching the child's breath push his chest up and down in perfect rhythm.

Tony was still standing in the middle of the living room aiming the gun at Terrence's wife and daughter as Mick came back in.

"The boy was asleep. I figured it was best to leave him up there."

"You're probably right."

"What are you doing here?" the mother said, pushing the words out through quivering lips.

"Are you going to kill us?" the daughter asked.

"Not if your dad does as we ask him."

"What could you possibly want with Terrence?"

"I can tell you one thing this isn't and that's a question and answer session. You will shut your mouth. You will not say one word. You make one move to call the police and the girl dies." Tracy squealed. "And you, if you scream one more time, I'll kill your mother, do you both understand?"

They nodded in perfect unison.

"Now, what's on the telly?" Tony said as he sat down on the couch.

"What's the meaning of this?" The mother asked.

"I thought I said no questions." His tone was almost jovial. It was as if he knew them, as if this were some big joke. Mick stood by the door, watching in silence. "I will allow that one. We're here to make sure your husband, your dad, does us a favor. If he does that favor, we'll release you unharmed. We'll just walk out the door and you'll never hear from us again. If you try to mess us around or if I hear word that he does, well, let's just say that things might get violent." His words were like razor blades.

The young girl jumped up in her seat. Tony fixed a glare on her.

"What time does the boy get up at?"

"Usually around seven," the mother replied.

"Will he sleep through the night?"

"Yes."

"All right then, let's plan on being in this room until at least then. In the meantime, my colleague here, who you can call Shay, will take you to get some blankets. You can call me Billy." He directed the mother to get up, waving the barrel of the gun at her. "Shay, make sure she doesn't try to make a phone call or shout for help."

Mick followed the mother out of the room and up the stairs. They went in silence, Mick's heart beating faster with every step. He had to find out where that van was going. She must know. He could call it in himself, but how? Tony had given him an unloaded weapon. The mother's legs were rigid as she walked. They were inside the bedroom when he shut the door behind them. She looked at him with the petrified eyes of a child, stepping away until her back was against the wall.

"Calm down, I'm not going to hurt you," he whispered. "I'm not like him. I'm trying to stop him. I'm working undercover."

Her face changed, the fear in her eyes mixing with confusion. He put the gun into his pocket, holding his hands out.

"I don't want to hurt anyone. I just need to know why he took your husband. I need you to tell me so we can stop this. I know it must be hard for you to believe, but I'm on your side. I'm trying to stop whatever he's got planned, but I need your help."

Her face slackened as she tried to take in what Mick had said. She opened her mouth to speak but then shook her head.

"He said that if we try anything, that if we tell anyone…"

"He won't know. Dozens of people are going to die if we don't do something."

They both heard the sound of footsteps coming up the stairs. They had only seconds left.

"Where was your husband going?"

The door handle turned and Tony's face appeared, the daughter by his side.

"What's going on here? Having a chat? We need to get back downstairs. Get the blankets and let's go. Before we go, you two take the chance to use the toilet."

They picked up the blankets and walked out. The daughter went into the bathroom, closing the door behind her.

"What were you two discussing?" Tony asked.

"She was asking me to let her go. I told her she'll be free to go tomorrow." The mother's face constricted with the lie. It was tight as a guitar string.

"Maybe. I certainly hope so," Tony replied.

The daughter came out and the mother shifted in past her. They stood and waited for a minute or two before tramping back down the stairs into the living room.

Hours passed with no words spoken. The mother and daughter huddled together on the couch with Tony and Mick in the armchairs on either side. The late news was on. There was no mention of any bombs or terrorist activities. The Apprentice Boys parade would officially begin at midnight with the firing of cannons from the city walls, then continue the next morning with the parades throughout the day. It would end at around four when the highest ranking marchers returned to their headquarters at Memorial Hall, not ten minutes walk from Bogside. Memories of throwing stones and shouting abuse at the marchers as they passed along the city walls overlooking Bogside came to him. Everyone else had done it, even Pat, so he did too. Their parents would have killed them had they known. Hitting the parade would have to wait until the next day, but where would be bombs hidden in the kegs be placed? What pub could they hit that the marchers would be congregating in, or passing by? Dozens of pubs would be filled with marchers and non-marchers, some Catholics interspersed among them. It was a Saturday night. Mick stared across at Tony as he watched the television, trying to pierce into his mind.

"I'm going to the toilet," Mick said. Tony looked at him with lazy eyes before focusing back onto the glowing screen.

Maybe there was some kind of paperwork, some sign of where Terrence was meant to go to deliver those kegs. Mick slipped into the kitchen, the phone beckoning him on the wall. He rifled through some papers left out on the table, a few bills, a letter from the bank and a postcard from Terrence's mother. He moved to the windowsill, poring through old checks and letters from school. He looked at his watch, aware of every second he was gone. Tony was as likely to shoot him, as he was Terrence's wife or daughter. If he aroused any suspicion, he was as good as dead. There was nothing in the kitchen and there probably wouldn't be anything anywhere in the house. It was a routine delivery. That's why Terrence had been taken; he was a part of a routine no one would suspect. Mick poured four glasses of water, carrying them into the living room on a tray he'd found in the corner. He gave one to each person and settled back into his seat, the yoke of tiredness beginning to bring itself to bear upon him. The key was to stay awake, to wait for his chance to get the mother alone again and then to make the call somehow. He would wait for his chance. It would come.

Chapter 28

His father came to him, holding out his hand. He was still alive, had been all these years, living in Belfast. Mick asked him why he'd left, why he'd never told him, but his father had no answer and they found themselves fishing on a lake, and Pat was there and their mother too. Mick was a child again and dipped the end of his fishing rod into the water before casting the line far out into the expanse of the water spread out like a carpet of deep blue beyond. His father turned to him with a smile on his face and put his arm around him, drawing him in tight. Melissa walked down to the water and sat down beside them. They watched the sun come up, casting yellow, red, orange, gold light all over so that nothing else was visible, only the glowing beauty of its aura.

Mick awoke with a jolt. Dawn was leaking in through the curtains. His eyelids felt as if they were stuck together. It took him a few seconds to figure out where he was, the unfamiliarity of the surroundings jarring him before the far more horrific remembrance of the reality he was in formed in his mind. It took him a second to shake off the haze of sleep. The TV was still on; the talking heads of the breakfast show well dressed and smiling. Tony was asleep. His eyes were closed, his chest heaving in time with each long, heavy breath he took. His hand was on his chest, the gun out of reach underneath. The mother and daughter were asleep too and had been since about one. The last thing he remembered was checking his watch at five and Tony had been awake then. It was almost seven fifteen now. The boy upstairs would be awake soon.

Mick took his leg off the arm of the chair and placed it on the carpet as gingerly as he could. It was no good Tony being asleep if he still didn't know where the van had delivered the kegs. He glanced over at the couch and saw the girl staring back at him. Mick's heart jumped inside his chest, but he remained still. He held the girl's eyes. A few seconds passed before he put his other leg on the floor and raised a finger to his lips. She watched him as he stood up and moved toward her. The door was closed. Mick had no idea how heavy a sleeper Tony might be but knew that opening the old wooden paneled door risked stirring him. He pointed over toward the door before bringing his hands together to plead with the young girl to follow him. She didn't move. He went to her, hovering over her on the couch.

"I want to get you out of here while he's asleep," Mick whispered. "You've got to trust me."

She took a few seconds, looked over at Tony and then back into Mick's eyes. "OK," she whispered. Mick helped her off the couch and led her to the door.

"Where are you off to?" The voice came from behind them like a cold blade slicing into his back. Tony was sitting up, the gun in his hand.

"I was taking her to the toilet. The young boy is going to be up soon too."

"Can we leave him in his room?" He directed the question toward the girl.

"Not for long, he's going to need his breakfast." She answered.

"We all will. I'd murder a nice fry up. Sound good?"

"Yeah, definitely," Mick answered.

"Bring her to the bathroom and then get the kid. We'll be in the kitchen waiting for you."

The mother opened her eyes and sat up on the couch, emerging from the sanctuary of sleep into the nightmare of her real life. Mick put his hand back on the door handle. It didn't matter how much noise it made now as he opened it. He left the door open, hearing the sounds of Tony and the mother making their way into the kitchen as he and the girl trod up the stairs in silence. It was impossible to know how much time he had, but the parade was beginning in less than two hours. The bombs could explode at any time after that, and, with no warning time to evacuate, his call to the police would be useless. He had little time to play with if he were to affect this. He knew that Tony wasn't going to slip. The mother, or even the girl, would be the key, and he was with the girl now, walking up the stairs behind her. They reached the top of the stairs and Mick motioned toward the bathroom. The sound of the young boy's voice came through the door of his room, calling for his mother.

"Go to the bathroom, and then we'll get him," Mick said, his voice soothing and soft. The girl did as she was told, her blue eyes stricken with red streaks, the skin below swollen from tears. She closed the door behind her and Mick waited, listening to the boy calling over and over. The sounds and smells of Saturday morning breakfast drifted up the stairs. Mick realized just how hungry he was when the girl opened the door.

"I need to speak to you," he whispered. "We don't have much time." The boy was banging on the door now.

"Get that kid and get down here!" Tony roared from the kitchen.

"That man is using your father to deliver what I think are bombs." He reached out to the girl, gripping her wrist like a baby bird in his palm. "I'm trying to stop him, but I need to know where your father was delivering to last night. They intercepted him and replaced the kegs of beer in the back of his van with kegs of their own, kegs with bombs inside. I need to know what their destination was. Who does you dad work for?"

"He works for the brewery." Her voice was soft as crushed velvet.

"Have you any idea where he was going last night? Was it somewhere to do with the parade today?"

"The other man said he'd hurt us, if we...."

"I'm not going to let that happen. Please, where was he going?"

"I...I don't know. I know he mentioned it, but I don't remember."

"You have to try. Does your mother know?"

"Probably, I can ask her...."

The banging on the door was louder and louder and Mick heard heavy footsteps pounding out of the kitchen toward the bottom of the stairs.

"Get the kid and get down here!" Tony shouted.

"All right. She was taking ages in the bathroom," Mick called down the stair before turning back to the girl. "Let's get your brother."

The boy recoiled at the sight of the stranger in his house, but the girl calmed him down. She took him in her arms, she brought him downstairs to the kitchen where her mother was at the stove. Tony was sitting at the table. The light of the morning was flooding in through the kitchen window.

"Pull down the blind," Tony ordered and the mother complied, leaving a chink at the bottom to let the light in.

The daughter let the boy, who seemed on the verge of tears, out of her arms and he took a seat at the table. The mother poured him some cereal and kissed him on the head. Tony was at the head of the table, with the girl at the opposite end beside her brother. Mick sat beside them, the mother in between him and Tony.

"When are you going to let us go?" the mother asked.

"We'll have a few more hours together. Plenty of time to get acquainted."

The mother served sausage, bacon, and fried eggs to her captors, sitting down with them to eat. No one spoke; the only sound was the harsh scratching of cutlery on the plates. Even the boy was petrified into silence. After breakfast, the mother made them tea. Tony made no sign that they would be moving back into the sitting room, seemingly happy with the new surroundings and ordered the mother to turn on the radio. It was the girl who broke the silence first, perhaps half an hour later.

"Tommy likes drawing. Can I get some pens and paper and we'll draw some pictures together?"

"Why not?" Tony said as if acknowledging the question was below him.

The girl left, returning less than a minute later with a small bucket of pencils and crayons as well as several pieces of both colored and white paper. She laid them out and the two children began drawing pictures of houses and farms, animals, and green fields. Mick watched them as they drew, all too aware of the ticking clock in the corner and the impending massacre. There must have been two hundred pounds of explosives in those kegs. Martin must have rigged them somehow that the barrel was split into two, with beer at the top covering the explosives in the bottom half. It would be impossible to detect, particularly after getting them from a scheduled beer delivery. If the barrels were in place, the only thing that could stop them was a malfunction in the timers, but with that many kegs the chances of them all being faulty were miniscule. It was all down to him. The clock on the wall said nine-thirty. The parade was under way. The marchers would be making their way around the city walls in their dark suits and white gloves, their purple sashes draped over their shoulders, the cacophony of their marching drums and the union jacks flying. The bombs could be primed to go off anytime.

The girl poked him in the arm, staring at him with huge eyes. She handed him a drawing to examine. It was of her father in the delivery van, his name on the side. A rush of adrenaline shot through Mick's body.

"Do you want us to draw you another?" she asked.

"Yes, please," Mick whispered, his heart thumping in his chest.

Tony looked away, his arms crossed as he stared out through the gap under the blind into the back garden.

Mick watched her as the girl drew a large building with tiny colored stained glass windows dotting the walls. She drew marchers in the parade walking toward it and the name, Society Street, as a sign on a wall and Mick knew. The kegs were being delivered to Memorial Hall, the headquarters of the Apprentice Boys of Derry, where the leading clubs met after the day's marching. The horror of Tony's plan spread through him like death itself, rendering his entire body stiff and cold. He knew the building well. It was only about a mile from where he'd grown up, half a mile from Rossville Street. He had thrown eggs at it as a boy, shaking his fists and cursing the Prods before running back to the safety of Bogside. The heads of the Apprentice Boys would all be there after the march, all of the principal clubs in one place. A bomb going off there would cause unknown carnage, would enflame every militant unionist in the city and cause unthinkable retribution. Loyalist anger from this would be unparalleled. Dozens would die today, untold hundreds more from the whirlwind of violence that this would create. Tony still stared out into the garden, doubtless dreaming of the civil war he was trying to start.

Mick picked up the drawing. "This one's not your best," he said, crumpling it in one fist. "Try to draw me something else. Have you ever been to the zoo?" His voice was shaking. Tony was sitting beside the phone and was no doubt planning on keeping them here all day, or at least until the parade ended at four and the clubs made their way to Memorial Hall. That was six hours.

The mother got up.

"My sister will be calling over in a few hours. She comes for lunch every Saturday, and what if the kids' friends call to the door?"

"Call your sister, tell her no lunch this week, and if the kids call, we just won't answer," Mick said.

"No funny business when you're on the phone," Tony warned.

The mother made the call, her voice calm and even, and sat back down after she'd hung up. Tony seemed satisfied and resumed his position staring out the window. Mick thought of the marchers at Memorial Hall. Most had families just like this. Would Terrence have been out there himself today? There were no union jacks in the house, no pictures of King Billy or Ian Paisley. It was a house like any other, like the houses in Bogside, or Creggan. He thought to try and reason with Tony but dismissed that idea immediately. He was beyond reason, only sustained by hate. Even being around Protestants, people only different from him because of their political beliefs and the religion they happened to be born into, was probably repugnant to him in every way. He probably felt dirty.

Two hours passed, Mick's nerves growing with every second that passed. Apart from the mother taking the boy to the bathroom an hour before, no one had moved, or even spoken. He had Tony's trust now. He knew he'd passed some unspoken test in his mind, breached some threshold. Tony had visibly calmed, was smoking a cigarette at the table and reading the newspaper as if this was his house. All Mick had to do was wait for his chance to get to that telephone on the wall above Tony's head.

Mick got out of the chair to stretch out the muscles close to cramping in his lower back. Tony didn't take his eyes off the newspaper. Mick excused himself, walking out of the kitchen to the bathroom. He was at the washbasin rinsing off his hands when he thought of climbing out the window, or even running out of the front door to the nearest pay phone. This was a loyalist area. Tony would never chase after him waving a gun, or would he? Tony didn't seem to care. Would calling the police put the mother and children in danger? Time was trickling away. The afternoon sun was high in the sky. It would be a good day for the parade. No one he knew had ever paid it any attention before, other than throwing coins and bottles at the marchers when they were kids. Yet thousands of people marched in it every year in this city of just ninety thousand. He went back downstairs where the boy was eating lunch as his mother read to him. Tony seemed almost in a trance. He'd barely moved in hours.

"Billy, are you all right?" Mick called to him.

"Just beautiful, Shay. Waiting for the fireworks to begin." He smiled.

"How about we have our other colleague bring Terrence back to his family now?"

"And have them see our comrade's face too?" Tony made sure to use the correct, socialist term. "I don't think that would be a good idea. Just sit tight. We'll be out of here in a few hours."

The mother's eyes flicked up and then back to the pages of the children's book she was reading to her son. She read to the end and placed it back down on the table, picking up another to begin.

Tony applauded and got out of his seat. "That was great. If you'll excuse me for a minute –call of nature." He closed the kitchen door behind him, Mick's pulse racing. Mick listened for Tony's footsteps, holding his finger to his mouth to shush the woman as she read. The bathroom door closed and Mick jumped out of his seat, running to the phone.

"What are you doing?" the woman asked.

"Calling for help. We can't let this happen."

"What are you talking about? He'll kill Terrence."

Mick dialed the confidential police hotline, heard the phone ringing on the other end.

"Don't do this, please," the woman screamed. "Stop! He'll kill my husband!"

"He won't, you didn't do anything," he said to her as a male voice answered the phone.

"No, you can't," she said, running at him, grasping at the phone in his hand. Upstairs, the door opened and Mick heard the footsteps thundering down toward him. He pushed the mother back as she flailed at the phone, holding it out of her reach with his other hand.

"Hello? There are several bombs in Memorial Hall." She scratched at his face as he put his foot in front of the door. The handle turned, the wood bulging from the pressure Tony was exerting from the other side. Mick put his full weight against the door, pushing the woman away. 'The bombs were delivered last night, disguised as kegs of beer, delivered by Terrence Turner. I'm at the Turners house right now...."

The door crashed open and Mick felt his body flung onto the kitchen floor, the phone ripped out of the wall, coming down on top of him. The woman retreated into the corner, shielding her children with her body as Tony aimed the gun at Mick's prostrate body on the floor.

"A tout? You're a bloody tout? Oh Jesus," he said kicking Mick in the side. Pain shot through him.

"Don't hurt them, they tried to stop me," Mick moaned.

"Oh no, please, no," Tony said, with tears in his eyes and his hands on top of his head. He kicked Mick again. "Three years. I was planning this for three years," he roared. "You're gonna pay for this." He brought the black of his boot down on Mick's face and the world went dark.

Chapter 29

Sean poked at the food on his plate, threw his fork down and picked up the glass of whiskey. Martina, his girlfriend, reached across the table to him, but he moved his hand away. This was all her fault. How could he have told her about their plans? What was he thinking? How could he have let her convince him to run, without telling Mick? He'd deserted him, his best friend. Surely Mick hadn't gone through with it without him. It had been hard to make out the news report in the pub, but there had been no news of any large-scale terrorist activities. There was only a small breaking news story about some bombs discovered in some beer kegs or something. The parade had gone without a hitch. Why hadn't Mick answered his phone? Why wasn't he home? No republicans would be out in the pub tonight. All but the most staunchly republican pubs would be wall-to-wall orange. He got up from the table, pushing past the waiter as he made for the phone booth by the men's bathroom. Martina was crying as he left, the tension from the previous twenty-four hours spilling over, but there wasn't time for that. He called Mick's number again, then Tony. Neither answered. He cursed out loud, slamming down the phone. He tried Pat, the phone ringing twice before Pamela picked up. He coughed as he spoke in an attempt to wipe the frustration from his voice. Sean changed his mind about telling him several times in the ten seconds it took Pat to get to the phone.

"Pat, it's Sean."

"Hi, Sean, how are you doing? You don't sound too good."

"Where's Mick? Is he with you?"

"I haven't seen him since yesterday evening. I thought he'd probably be in hiding like the rest of us Fenians," Pat laughed, but his tone dropped as his quip was met with only silence. "Are you all right, Sean?"

"No, I'm not all right. I'm very far from all right. Mick and I were meant to go on an operation with my brother today."

Pat laughed but then stopped. "You're joking? This is a joke isn't it?"

"I wish it were. Tony's been talking about this massive operation to change the face of the war. We figured we could stop him."

Pat felt his entire body go cold, anger and terror taking a hold of him with icy fingers. "What was it? What the hell are you guys doing mixed up with him?"

"We were trying to stop it. He didn't say what it was, just that it was going to be huge."

"Was it the bombs they found in the beer kegs, in Memorial Hall? Was that it?"

"I don't even know. Probably."

"Oh my God, he's taken Mick, he's taken my brother." Pat's skin was cold as marble. He attempted to swat away conflicting thoughts, the fear creeping across him. He tried to focus. "Where are you? Have you any idea where they might have taken him?"

"I'm over the border, in Manorcunnigham. I had to get out. I couldn't take it. I left him alone. I left him...."

"Oh no," Pat said. Pamela and the kids were in the TV room just a few feet away. "Where is he?"

"I think I know. He's mentioned a house on the Buncrana Road, called it his personal safe house. They might be there. Can you call the police?"

"And say what? That an IRA man is torturing another IRA man somewhere on the Buncrana road? They'd laugh down the phone at me. And today? Half the force is down at the Memorial Hall. No, Sean, this is up to us. I'll go over to his apartment and call his girlfriend to make sure. You get on the road. Call me from a payphone in half an hour when you're back in Derry. Leave right now."

Pat slammed down the phone. He felt like he was drowning.

"What is it?" Pam asked as she walked in.

"Nothing, just a personal problem Sean Campbell wants to see me about."

"What? On a Saturday night?"

"I don't know anything right now, let me speak to him first," Pat snapped.

Pamela held her hands up, walking away. Pat ignored her, focusing on finding Melissa's number. It was written on a pad by the phone.

"Hello," came Melissa's voice.

"Hi, it's Pat. How are things?"

"Fine, yeah. You haven't seen that brother of yours around, have you? I've not been able to get a hold of him all day."

Pat's blood ran to ice as the decision to tell her or not was forced onto him.

"No, I haven't. I was hoping he was there with you, to be honest."

"Is there something going on?"

"Nothing's going on. Everything's fine. I'm sure he's out having a few drinks somewhere. Did you have plans with him?"

"Nothing substantial, but I was expecting a call. Why were you looking for him?"

"No reason, just wanted to ask him a question. I'll catch up with him tomorrow, I'm sure."

"All right. Make sure to come over and see us before we leave next week."

"Sure, yeah, we'll organize something," he said and hung up.

The sound of the TV drifted through the door, his family there. He could stay in with them. Mick was probably fine, must have been walking or in the pub. "This is probably nothing," he said out loud, but he knew something was very wrong, felt it inside him. He'd check Mick's apartment, he might have been asleep on the couch or had the TV on too loud. Pat stuck his head into the living room to say goodbye. Pamela and the three kids barely acknowledged him, their eyes caught by the glare of the TV screen. He shut the door behind him and made for his car out front. The crisp night air hit him like water in the face. It was just after eight and the traffic in the city was getting back to normal after the reroutes and gridlock caused by the parades earlier in the day. He was over at Mick's apartment in minutes. He pressed the buzzer with no reply, ran up the stairs to knock on the door, but nothing. He ran back down the stairs and pushed into the nearest pub, wading through the crowd as he searched, calling out through the smoky air, his voice raw and torn.

*****

Mick felt the wet first and then the searing pain as he wrenched his eyes open, stung by the light. He heard the broken sound of his own breathing; felt his arms curled around his back tied together, tied to the same chair Terrence had been in. His ribs burned from where Tony had kicked him, the pain slicing through him as he tried to move his torso. Warm blood sluiced down his face onto the mess of his t-shirt below. Several teeth felt loose, his entire face raw. He was alone? Or was he? Tony came into view through swollen eyes. He was sitting on the couch opposite, smoking a cigarette and reading the newspaper. He hadn't noticed that Mick had come to. Mick thought back, remembered the morning and the family, Terrence and the kegs. Faint remembrances of being bundled into the back of the van outside Terrence's house came to him but then faded into nothing like dark clouds disappearing over the horizon. He remembered the fists, pummeling him in the chair. Tony and Martin hadn't even bothered to ask any questions. It was hard to believe that level of hatred existed. He wondered what they'd done with Terrence. They must have let him off at his house when they picked him up. The comfort of that quelled the fear and pain he felt for a few seconds at least.

Tony flicked the newspaper down to reveal his sneering face.

"Wakey wakey, eh? The tout has risen" He stood up and punched Mick full force in the face, breaking his nose. Mick's eyes filled with water as his vision faded and the agony felt like fire spreading through him. "Was it worth it? Saving all those Huns? Those filthy unionist pricks who wouldn't piss on you if you were on fire?" The blood gushed down Mick's face, drenching him all the way down to his jeans.

"What about Terrence?" Mick gasped.

"What was that? I didn't quite catch that," Tony said, stubbing the cigarette out on Mick's hand. Mick screamed almost vomiting as the stench of his own burning flesh filled his nostrils. He rocked back on his seat, but the wall was only inches behind and righted him almost immediately.

"What about Terrence and his family? What did you do to them?"

"It's touching that you're so concerned about those orange pricks. I suppose I owe them a debt too. If it weren't for that dumb bitch, I'd never have known that it was you who called in the warning on the bombs, that it was you who ratted me out."

Martin walked in from the kitchen, a cup of tea in his left hand, the saucer in his right.

"Are they OK?" Mick repeated.

"They're fine. Killing them would have been more of a hassle than it was worth. Killing you is going to be a pure joy, however. A pure joy that I'm going to prolong for days." The light above his head cast down deathly shadows, darkening every hollow in his face, his beard black as night.

Mick closed his eyes, anything to try to block out the pain. He attempted to conjure the picture of Melissa, of his mother, of Pat, of his son, but the images were garbled and even trying to think was like a dagger through his brain.

"When is our guest arriving?" Tony said, turning to Martin, who was standing in the corner.

"Any minute now," Martin replied.

"Good." Tony leaned down into Mick's face. "We have someone coming to see you, someone very eager to make your acquaintance again. And once they're through with you, things are going to get nasty around here. What we've done to you so far is going to seem like flirting once we get the blowtorches out."

Tony punched him again, strong and hard in the middle of his chest, and Mick passed out.

*****

The wash of panic had set in. Pat felt it, spreading through him. A part of him was still trying to shake it off, to tell himself that nothing was going on, that it was a coincidence that Mick had gone missing after the operation with Tony. But these thoughts were counter-productive now, a waste of time and energy. Time was against them. He knew Mick wouldn't see the morning. Where was Sean? He cursed as he arrived back at his house, somehow hoping that Sean would be there. He slammed down on the steering wheel as he brought the car to a halt, the pressure inside him building, the pain wetting his eyes. He took deep breaths, in through his nose and out through his mouth. Getting Mick back, if they found him at all, might be just the beginning of their problems. He shook the premonitions of death and torture from his mind and stepped out of the car, smoothing down his hair and wiping his face as he went into the house. Pamela greeted him in the living room with a smile, the distress etched onto his face hidden in the half-light. He sat down, picking Siobhan off the seat she was slumped in and placing her onto his lap. She lay back, the softness of her hair lapping down onto his chest. He took each of her wrists in his hands, rubbing his fingers along the smoothness of her skin.

Michael lay on the floor in front of them, propping his head up on his hands, his legs wiggling in the air above him. Peter was beside his mother on the couch, his head against her shoulder. No one said a word; the only sound other than the television was Siobhan's soft breath. Pat reached down and kissed the top of her head. The phone rang. He lifted her off his lap, feeling the absence of her as soon as he stood up. He patted Michael on the head as he passed him and sat down on the couch with the others, the phone still ringing. Pamela gestured to him to get it and he kissed both her and Peter. He closed the door behind him, no one turning to watch him go.

"Hello," he gasped.

"It's me," Sean said. "Did you find him, has anyone seen him?"

"No, nobody's seen him all day. Have you heard anything?" Pat asked even though he knew the answer.

"Not a thing. Tony must have him...out in the house." Sean coughed, his voice heavy, weighed down with sorrow and regret. "We have to get him."

"Where are you now?"

"Just over the border, in Bridge End, about ten minutes away from the house."

"We've got to get over there right now. If he's still alive..." Pat's words faded out.

"I'll meet you at the end of Branch Road, where the roundabout is. It's just down there."

Pat looked around, bringing his voice down to a whisper. "We can't walk in there with just our good intentions. We're going to need some serious hardware."

"I know. There's a dump pretty close to there. I know where to go. I'll have something for both of us."

The words hung in the air for a few seconds, as if neither of them wanted to proceed.

"All right then," Pat said. "You ready for this?"

"I am."

"I'll be there in twenty minutes."

*****

The feeling of someone tapping his cheek, again and again, dragged him out of semi-consciousness. The black veil lifted from his eyes as the room came into view. The pain was everywhere now, his chest a rickety, broken mess, his face a blood-sodden marsh of lacerations across bruises and raw flesh. Tony was in front of him; the smile on his face like the muzzle flash of a gun.

"Hey, hey," he said, still tapping Mick's cheek.

Mick lifted his head, groaning by way of an answer. Martin was standing behind Tony, and there was someone else just beyond his view, a shadow in the corner he couldn't make out.

"We've got someone here who wants to meet you. You should be thanking our guest. She's the only reason you're still alive or at least able to still answer questions. She wanted to speak to you, to ask you about a few things before the inevitable end. And, as it turns out, you're old friends. Funny old world, isn't it?" he laughed, as the shadow in the corner took form as a human being and he heard her voice.

"Hello, Michael," Maggie said. "It's been a while."

Mick lifted his head as if it weighed a thousand pounds. He spat blood on the floor.

"It certainly has," he answered. "Seventeen years. But not nearly long enough. So you're the brains behind this operation then?"

Maggie's face turned, the hatred blazing through every pore. "We were planning that operation for three years, and it would have been a massive success, would have given us back the impetus to finally go on and win this war. If I'd known you were involved...."

"Killing dozens of innocent people is your idea of success?"

"Who are you protecting? Those orange pricks who march through our neighborhoods with their flags and drums and bowler hats? The same bastards who killed my brother back in '69? You're protecting them? Our enemies?"

'They didn't kill your brother...."

"I'm done listening to you..." she spat. "I just need to ask you a few questions. If you answer, I'll make the rest of your miserable life quick, get Tony to go easier on you. I promise you that you won't see the dawn if you answer. Otherwise, the agonies these boys have planned for you could last days. I'd almost object if you didn't deserve every ounce of the pain they're going to inflict on you."

"Get on with it," Mick coughed. "Stop wasting my time."

"Were you alone? Did Sean Campbell work with you?"

"No, I was alone." Mick's eyes brightened and he managed to raise his head upright. "Sean didn't know anything about this. You're the intelligence officer for the Derry Battalion, aren't you? Still, after all these years?"

"Never mind me..."

"Because I'm positive that this operation wasn't mandated by the higher ups. The Army Council would never have approved something of this size directed against a non-military target. Associating with these two dissidents..."

She slapped him hard across the face, blood spattering on the floor. "Don't think you're talking your way out of this. I know who I am. I know each of the members of the Army Council of the Provisional Irish Republican Army, and each one of them would approve of your death." She wiped his blood off on the last clean part of his jeans, round by the calf.

"You really believe that, Maggie? Really? What you do to me doesn't matter now, you're all going to die," Mick spluttered. "There's no way the Army Council is going to tolerate this. You'll be in the grave with me soon enough."

Martin turned to Tony, whose face was burning, his fists clenched, digging fingernails into flesh. But Maggie's eyes didn't change. The cold concentration remained. "Was Sean with you? You shared a jail cell for three years, worked together for almost two, had lunch together, drank together. You never talked about taking down his brother's crazy scheme to kill as many loyalists as possible, to kill dozens of innocent people? You two never wanted to repay the debt you owed to society, to yourselves, to atone for the past? Did you convince him to help you exorcise the demons of those soldiers you killed in that field in 1972, Mick? Or did you even tell him about that?" She moved in, just inches from his face. "Did you just tell him it was the right thing to do? Did you tell him that you weren't just using him for your own selfish means, that you were willing to risk his life so you could finally sleep at night?"

Mick didn't speak, just stared back into the depths of her dark blue eyes.

Maggie waited a few seconds before she continued. "Sean didn't do anything. He just ran, but Tony deserves to know who his brother is, whether he can be trusted."

"Sean wasn't with me. I don't know why he left."

"We could be here for a while." Maggie turned to Tony. "Light the fire. Maybe a red-hot poker will loosen his tongue."

*****

Sean waved him to a stop and Pat got out of the car. The light was fading to dark, the sun dying in the sky. There were no other cars and few houses. Sean looked as if he was about to cry as Pat went to him.

"I'm so sorry, Pat. I should have told you...."

"There's not time for that now. Where's the house? Did you check it out yet?"

"I haven't had the chance. It's half a mile away, back over there." He motioned with his hand.

"Do you have the guns?"

"In the back."

"Let's go then."

*****

The fire was the only light in the room now, blazing and crackling in the corner. Mick stared into the orange-yellow flames, running his eyes up along the intricate decoration on the fireplace and then to Tony, sitting opposite him, staring into space as if he was waiting for a bus. Steel pokers stuck out from the flames like deadly spines. Martin pulled one out, examining it.

"Are we ready to go with that?" Tony asked.

"Just a couple more minutes," Martin answered. "The fire's not quite hot enough yet."

Maggie glanced through the open door from the kitchen, cup of tea in hand, sipping, waiting. It wouldn't be long now. He'd talk. They all talked.

*****

Sean drove with the headlights off, still able to see without them in the murk of the gray dusk falling. The hedgerows around them seemed like green shadows jutting out of the earth, the evening air gritty, as if they could feel the texture of it against their skin as they got out of the car. Sean opened the trunk to reveal two AK-47 rifles. He picked one up, handing it to Pat.

"You know how to use this thing?" Sean asked.

Pat felt the weight of the rifle in his hand, the first time he'd held a gun since the night the soldiers had died. The model was unfamiliar, the principal the same.

"I've never used one of these before, but I'm familiar enough."

"All right. Let's go."

The night was desolate, not a sound in the air as Sean led Pat a hundred yards to an opening in the hedgerow. Two cars sat in the driveway of a small house. The door on the shed to the side was ajar, the gleam of silver just visible inside. Light flickered in the front windows, licking the glass with flutters of gold, bouncing back and forth in time with the flames from a fire. They moved in stealthy silence, past the cars and to the front of the house. They crouched down, underneath the small old-fashioned front windows. Pat motioned to look inside and raised his head, edging just high enough to see in. His blood froze as he saw Mick, head down, covered in blood, tied to a chair with Tony opposite. Another man was at the fire and drew out a poker, looked at it and placed it back in. A woman he couldn't quite see poked her head in from what seemed to be an old kitchen before retreating. The black shape of a handgun was visible on the table beside Tony and the man by the fire had a pistol in his belt. Pat motioned to Sean to take a look, as he slumped down onto the grass below the window. Sean looked in and sat back down beside him. Pat motioned to follow him and they made their way around the back of the house. The darkness had descended and, with no stars above, they fumbled through the long uncut grass, following the chinks of golden light from the back door. Pat peered in through a small window. The woman was gone, had walked back into the living room. Pat tried the door. It opened. He closed it back over and nodded to Sean before they retreated to the cars, hiding behind a Ford Escort.

"We've got to cause some kind of a diversion, get them away from him," Pat whispered. "Have you got a lighter?" Pat asked. Sean nodded and took it out. "Take off your t-shirt," Pat continued, pointing to the vest Sean was wearing under his shirt. Sean did it without question and handed it to Pat, who tore into several strips. Pat unscrewed the car's fuel cap and placed several pieces of the torn vest down the fuel line and into the tank, the end protruding like the fuse on a bomb. He took a deep breath, fighting the nerves inside. He knew they didn't have much time.

"I'm going to go around back. When I leave, count to a hundred. Then light the shirt. Get well away from the car and make sure that whoever comes out of the house doesn't go back in. I'll use the back door. No killing unless we absolutely have to, agreed?"

"Agreed."

Pat scuttled into the night, the darkness enveloping him. He counted as he went, reaching the door at about forty. The woman was in the kitchen again, staring into space as she leaned against the narrow table. The seconds seemed like days as the count in his head went on, eighty-seven, eighty-eight, eighty-nine... His palms were so slick that he was worried he might drop the gun when he burst inside. He put a hand on the back door handle, braced himself.

*****

Martin took the poker out of the fire, smiling as it glowed hellish red. Tony bounced out of the seat, grabbing it out of his hand like a child unwilling to share. Mick raised his head, saw the red-hot metal, felt the searing heat as Tony held it inches from his face.

"Wait a minute," Maggie said, walking in from the kitchen. "Give him one more chance." She waved fingers at Tony, who withdrew the poker. She leaned down to Mick, looking into his bloodied eyes. "I'm going to give you one more chance before this gets really gruesome. You know how much he's looking forward to this, and what he's going to do. So, I ask you, did Sean Campbell know about your little plan to disrupt the operation? Was he working with you?"

The taste of blood was sweet on Mick's tongue. "I've already told you, he didn't know anything. I did it all myself."

Maggie paused and then drew her face back. "Do it," she ordered, and Tony advanced. Tony moved the poker toward Mick's face, relishing each second. Suddenly, a massive explosion rocked the entire house and the front garden was bright with fire. Tony dropped the poker and went for his gun on the side table as Martin ran out the front door. Maggie shouted to stop him, but he was gone. The back door thundered open and Pat ran through the empty kitchen, rifle in hand. Tony spun around and let off a shot, which sliced through the air by Pat's ear, sending wooden shards through the air like shrapnel. Pat closed his eyes as the shards of wooden daggers rained down on him but dropped a few inches, his finger tightening on the trigger. Tony held up the gun to fire again as Pat squeezed the trigger, pouring three bullets into him, the sound reverberating through the room like thunder and Pat thought his ears would burst. Tony's chest erupted crimson blood and his lifeless body fell back onto the floor, the gun falling from his hand. The sound of more AK 47 rounds came from the front of the house, and then silence. Smoke hung in the air, thick with death. Tony was lying still on the floor, a pool of blood emanating from the garish holes torn in his chest. Maggie was standing, frozen in the middle of the room, her mouth open as Pat turned the gun on her. No one spoke. Mick coughed, looking up at his brother.

"Don't kill her, Pat," he spluttered.

"Go easy there," Maggie whispered.

Sean burst through the front door, his rifle raised. His eyes fell on the body of his brother on the floor and he dropped the rifle to his side. "Oh, Tony," he said, shaking his head.

"Sean Campbell," Maggie said, her eyes wide.

"Untie my brother," Pat ordered, the rifle still pointed at her.

Maggie moved to Mick, moving her hands around to the ropes behind his back to untie him. Sean kept the gun on her as Pat moved to Mick, taking him in his arms.

"We've got to get out of here," Sean said. "We've only got a few minutes." Pat laid his brother out on the couch, tears in his eyes.

"What have they done to you, little brother?"

"I didn't do that to your brother," Maggie insisted. "I only questioned him. It was the other two who did that. Him." She gestured to Tony's body on the floor. "You'd better run now, boys. You just killed two highly decorated volunteers, men with glittering records, men who served their whole lives for the cause you've forgotten."

"Another one's not going to make any difference then, is it?" Sean said, raising the barrel of the rifle to her.

"Don't do it," Pat said. 'Tie her up. Killing her won't help us, and that's their way, not ours. We'll call this in. The RUC will find her here and we'll have bought ourselves some time." Pat knew that this was far from over, that it had barely begun.

Maggie sat in the chair, still wet with Mick's blood. She flinched as Sean tied the knots tight around her wrists.

"This isn't going to make any difference. You've only killed yourself now too, Pat," she said. "The Derry Brigade isn't going to let this go. They'll find you."

Pat wiped the blood from his brother's face and lifted him into his arms. Mick squirmed as the shock of pain ran through him. Pat stood up, carrying his brother out of the house and into the night, Maggie's words ringing in his ears.

Sean went to his brother. He touched his face, closed his eyes, remembering a time before the poison of the violence and hatred.

Sean stood up, looked at his brother one last time and walked out. The flames of the burning car illuminated Martin's lifeless body on the asphalt drive as they moved past. They only had a few minutes now. The police would be on their way. Someone would have seen the explosion, heard the shots.

Mick opened his eyes. "I'm sorry, Pat. I wanted to tell you."

"Don't say that, brother. There's no need for sorry. You saved those people today. You've nothing to be sorry for." He had tears in his eyes. "We're not out of trouble yet though, Mick."

"How bad is he?" Sean asked, putting his hand on Mick's chest.

"I don't know, but we need to get him to the hospital right now."

"We won't be able to protect him. They can get to him there."

"We're not going to be able to protect him anywhere unless we sort this out," Pat replied, as they reached the car. Sean opened the back door and Pat laid his brother down on the back seat. Sean started the car as Pat got in the front.

"What now?" Sean asked.

"Get back across the border, back to Martina. At least you'll be safe from the RUC there."

"What about the IRA? They'll get me as easily there as here. Maggie would have called in the information as she got it before she went to the house. They'll know."

"I know that," Pat said. "They only know about him, not you." They pulled up alongside Pat's car. "Get back over the border. I'll sort this out. You'll be safe."

"How are you going to do that?"

"Never you mind, just get out of the area and stay away. Call us in the next few days and one of us will let you know what to do next."

Sean got out to help put Mick in the back seat of Pat's car.

Mick's eyes were closed, blood running along the slit of his eyelids.

"I'm so sorry I left you, Mick," Sean said. "I panicked. I'm so sorry."

"You came back for me. You came back," Mick gasped.

"Get him out of here," Sean said, hugging Pat. "And stay safe, they're going to be coming for all of us now."

"Get rid of those guns and get over the border, I'll look after everything else."

Thirty seconds later Sean was gone and Pat started the car, the broken body of his brother in the back seat and the burden of all their lives on his shoulders.

Chapter 30

Mick tried to sit up but fell back down like a rag doll, coughing out a spurt of blood as his head hit the leather again. His vision was dimming, the yellow flashes of streetlights hurting his eyes.

"Are you OK back there?" Pat asked. "Hang in there, brother, we're going to get you some help."

Mick tried to answer, but the words came as a jumble of sounds, blood, and saliva. It was no use. He felt the car slow and pull over, heard the front door opening and felt the waft of air come over the exposed flesh of his face. The door beside his head came open and Pat was over him, his eyes imploring him to get through the next few hours.

"Mick, are you awake?"

Mick couldn't open his eyes, but managed to squeeze out the words, "Yeah, I can hear you." Each word spoken was a minor triumph.

"All right, I need to tell you a few things. You know that your life's still in danger. The IRA can get to you in the hospital, and once they find out what happened tonight, they won't hesitate to go after either of us. You're an informant, and two full-time IRA volunteers are dead. That's more than enough to condemn all three of us to death. I'm going to take you to Melissa's house. Dr. Kimberly will meet us there. We just need to get through the next few hours and then we'll be OK. I'm going to sort everything."

Mick tried to speak, to ask him how he was going to sort this mess out. But the words came as a cough, and more blood spluttered up from his lungs and out the side of his mouth.

"Don't speak. Just stay here. There's a phone box by the car. I'm going to call Melissa and then have Dr. Kimberly meet us. Just hang in there."

Mick nodded and took Pat's hand in his. "Thank you," he said. Pat hesitated, placing a tender hand on Mick's forehead and went to the phone.

They were just outside the city now. Pat closed his eyes, wondering if he should bring Mick to a hospital or not. He was in bad shape. The blood coming up from inside him could have been internal bleeding and the injuries to his face had rendered him almost unrecognizable. What was the use in saving Mick from being tortured to death just to have him die on Melissa's couch? But it was a risk they'd have to take. If the IRA got a hold of him, they'd both be dead within hours, and Sean too. The range of options seemed to be narrowing by the minute.

He picked up the receiver and called Dr. Kimberly, an old friend from Bogside. Dr. Kimberly picked up on the second ring and listened without interrupting as Pat explained their situation. He gave the doctor Melissa's address and told him to meet them there in twenty minutes. Pat thanked him and hung up. The next call would be harder. He dropped the coins into the phone and dialed Melissa's number.

"Hello," she answered.

"Melissa, it's Pat."

"Hi, Pat, what's going on, what has you calling at this hour?"

"It's Mick. I found him, but he's been severely beaten. He's not in good shape."

"What? What happened?"

"I don't have time to explain right now. I need to take him somewhere safe, away from Bogside, where the republicans wouldn't think to look for him."

"What are you talking about? I don't understand what's going on."

Pat ignored her question. "I've arranged for a doctor to meet us at your house in about twenty minutes. I can't take him to a hospital; it's too dangerous."

"Why would they do this to him? What did he do?"

"Saved about thirty people's lives. I don't have time to have this conversation now. We can talk when I get him to you."

"How are you going to get past the checkpoints if you get stopped?"

"I'll say I'm taking him to hospital. I need to make my way to your house now. Please be ready," he said and hung up.

Mick had managed to sit up as Pat came back to the car.

"It's all set. Dr. Kimberly is meeting us at Melissa's house."

"Help me into the front. In case we get stopped."

"It's not going to make any difference with the state that you're in. Just sit back and we'll get you there."

Mick didn't reply but stayed propped up; his eyes open as slits between the deep swelling. Pat got back into the car. No one would be able to tell they were twins now. Fresh anger swamped him, igniting his entire body. He started the engine. The bright lights of the city came into view within seconds, the Foyle snaking dark beside them, drawing them in. Pat turned to his brother, reaching back to him as they waited at a red light.

"I just wanted to tell you, Mick, that you're the bravest person I ever met. What you did today..." He shook his head as the tears started to come. "I just wish I had it in me to do the things that you've done. I just wish I had your goodness, your love within me, but I don't. I'm not like you."

"We're the same," Mick gasped.

"No, no we're not." The car was moving again, the street lights flashing past. "My answer was always to fight, to take control. People said I was a leader, but I'm not. All good in me is because of you. I don't know what I would have become without you. I would have been one of them."

"I am so proud of you, of what you've done," Mick whispered.

"You know how diamonds grow, Mick? How they become?" The tears were rolling down his face as he spoke, the words coming like water gushing through breaches in a dam. "By adding microscopic layers of crystals bit by bit, day by seemingly inconsequential day, over millions of years. It's the sum of all those days that makes them whole. That's how we grow, each experience adding another layer, turning us into the people we become. That's why none of us are the same, even though some of us look like we should be. We might have the same DNA, but we're different people. You've grown differently to me, into the brightest diamond of them all. I've been living in your light all this time."

"No, no." The words came as a moan.

"You gave your life for Melissa and for me. You tried to atone for that horrible thing I did to those soldiers, for my actions. I killed them, Mick. It was me and I was the one who should have gone to jail for it. You were too good though. You shone too bright for that. You gave me a life I never should have had. You gave me a wife and children, and the opportunity to run a business and to try to give back to this city. It's all because of you. I'd probably be dead or rotting away in jail the rest of my life if it wasn't for you."

"You did those things, not me."

"I'd never have done any of it except for you."

"Well, you've paid me back now, in full," Mick coughed.

"No, I haven't, not quite yet, but I will. I have the chance now and I'm not going to waste it. You deserve the best life anyone's capable of living and soon you'll have it. I'm going to make sure of that."

"What are you talking about?"

"Never mind the details. You just need to concentrate on getting better."

They were back in the city now. The soldiers on Craigavon Bridge let them through, persuaded by Pat's story about a motorcycle accident, and, minutes later they were pulling into the driveway at Melissa's house.

Pat was careful, making sure not to attract any undue attention as he lifted him out of the car, his arms around Mick's shoulders as they stumbled to the door together. Melissa ran out, Jason by her side, her face stricken with panic. Mick was drifting in and out of consciousness, like a light switch flicking on and off, as they laid him out on the couch. Melissa wiped down his face with a wet cloth.

"Why did this happen?" she sobbed.

"He found out about the bombing planned in Memorial Hall through a friend. And Mick being Mick, he called it in. I heard he was being held and managed to get him out of there." Melissa looked at him and knew not to ask any more questions.

"Is he still in danger?" she asked.

"Yes, but they won't find him here." Pat turned to Jason where he was standing back in the corner, inviting him forward with a wave of his hand. "Your dad needs you now."

Jason came to his father's side, took his hand.

"Hello, son," Mick breathed. "I'm so sorry, Melissa."

"There you go trying to save the bloody world again, you stupid idiot, this is what you get." The tears were streaking down her face.

Dr. Kimberly arrived a few minutes later and sat with Mick for an hour or more, cleaning and bandaging his wounds.

It was almost midnight and Mick was asleep, his face almost entirely obscured by blood-tinged bandages when Dr. Kimberly took Pat and Melissa aside.

"He's lost a lot of blood and could have internal injuries. His face is going to need more stitches once the swelling goes down and several of his ribs are broken."

"Can we keep him here the night? Will he make it to tomorrow afternoon?"

"Yes, but he does need hospital treatment. I've done all I can for him."

"Thanks, doc," Pat said and walked him out.

"Your dad's a hero, Jason, directly responsible for saving dozens of people's lives today," Pat said, as he walked back from the front door. "But no one can ever know. Telling anyone might endanger his life."

"I understand," Jason said, still holding his father's hand. Jason moved away as Pat hovered over his brother for a few seconds, and though Mick's eyes were closed, he still spoke. "Goodbye Mick, you'll be okay here with your family. I just wanted to say that I love you and that I hope that I can make you proud." He turned to Melissa. "I don't think he can hear me. Let him know I said that, will you?"

"I will, Pat."

He hugged Melissa and Jason before stopping to stare at the figure of his brother laid out on the couch. He knelt down beside him and kissed his cheek, his tears solid and thick, leaving tracks of silver down his face.

It was fifteen minutes home and Pat's house was absolutely still as he went inside. Nothing had changed here, although he knew that it could never be the same again. Only the hall light was on, his family all in bed. He slipped up the stairs and into bed beside Pamela, who was completely oblivious to anything that had happened. She stirred with a grace he'd only ever seen in her, arching her back gently as she lifted her arms up to envelop him. She didn't speak as she brought him into the warmth of her, didn't notice the tears in his eyes. He wanted to tell her but knew the impossibility of that. They would have this night together. This would be theirs. No matter what was to happen.

The sound of the children downstairs woke him at around eight and, just for a few seconds, it seemed like an ordinary Sunday. It seemed that he'd go downstairs and make breakfast before taking them to the country, to football or to see their cousins. Pamela was already up, already in the shower. He waited for her to come back and they made love, laughing at Peter shouting at the neighbor's dog, telling it to shut up as they lay there. She got dressed and went downstairs to the children. He had a shower and came down to join them, kissing each one in turn. Siobhan came to sit on his knee and he bounced her up and down, raining kisses on her cheeks as she laughed out loud. He waited until breakfast was over to call Melissa. The news was good. Mick was fine, there'd been no need to call Dr. Kimberly overnight, but he was still going to require hospital care, and soon. Pat nodded his head and told her to look after him and hung up the phone.

Pat waited until the kids were outside to tell Pamela the same story he'd told Melissa the night before. Pamela was shocked, wanted to call the police, wanted to go straight over there and bring him to the hospital until Pat explained what doing either of those things would mean.

"If we go the police, he's dead. We can't take him to the hospital either. It's not safe for him there. Not with everything still up in the air as it is now."

"I don't want you getting involved in this."

"I'm already involved, in everything he does. I need to fix this for him and for the other boy too. No one else can. If I don't, he's dead. They both are. It's only a matter of time."

"They could run."

"To where? The IRA would find them, like it finds informants all the time, in Canada, in England, in Australia, in the States. There's nowhere for him to go. And what's the point of him running without Melissa and his son? That's no life for him. He deserves better than that. He should get a medal for what he did yesterday. Have you any idea of the retribution the loyalists would have taken if those bombs had gone off? Or the number of lives he saved?"

"What about us, Pat? I don't want anything to happen to us, to what we have," she wept.

"I'll be fine, they're not going to do anything to me." The lies tore at him inside, but he knew there was no other way. "I love you, Pamela. I have from the first moment you threw that drink in my face." She forced a smile as he continued. "You and the kids are more than I ever deserved, but I need to do this, for my brother, and for myself." He put his arms around her again held her tight to him. "I love you, but I have to go while there's still time."

"Don't do anything stupid. I don't want a hero for a husband."

He smiled as he pulled away from her, his fingers lingering on hers until finally he let go and strode into the house, fear and regret permeating every part of him.

It was almost noon. The IRA would be out looking for them soon, first Mick, then Sean and him. Pat knew that if they'd killed Maggie no one would have ever known that he was there. But Mick would still be in just as much danger, and he'd be a murderer, just as bad as they were, and that was something he'd never be again.

It was a five-minute drive to McClean's house in Creggan, the same house he'd gone to seventeen years before. But the situation was different now. The IRA didn't take prisoners; there would be no jail time they could serve. Pat pulled up a block away. Maggie would be in custody until tonight at least, with no opportunity to tell McClean or any of her other superiors what had happened until then. He rang the doorbell, knowing that within seconds there'd be no turning back. Every part of him screamed to run, to go home to his family and hope that somehow this would turn out right, but he didn't move. Just waited. McClean's wife answered the door, an inquisitive, suspicious look on her face.

"Is Mr. McClean around? My name's Pat Doherty."

She nodded and disappeared into the back, re-emerging a few seconds later to invite him through to the kitchen and out into the back garden where McClean was waiting.

"I certainly didn't expect to see you today," McClean began.

"All sorts of strange things are happening," Pat replied, his voice quivering.

McClean clenched his teeth together, his jawbone jutting out through the unshaven skin on his face. He shook his head and looked away, turning his back to Pat.

"We can't talk here. Come with me."

Pat followed McClean through the house and to his car parked out front. McClean held the door open for him and Pat got in. It felt like he was being arrested though he knew that if there were to be some kind of trial, McClean would be judge, jury and executioner. A thousand thoughts appeared and disappeared in his mind. His words would never be more significant. His life depended on them. McClean got into the car beside him, cast a sideward glance. No words were exchanged as he started the car. The city faded. The Foyle followed them until that receded too. They drove in silence until all signs of civilization had disappeared and only the green surround of the countryside prevailed.

Pat was visibly shaking, his skin pale, deathly white as McClean finally began.

"I heard what happened yesterday. I still can't believe it. Mick? A tout?"

"He was never a tout. He never betrayed one sanctioned IRA operation. That unsanctioned, dissident action yesterday was insane. The blowback would have been more than any of us could have handled. It was a deliberate attempt to usurp the status quo and mobilize the loyalists, to cause a full-scale civil war."

It had been years since they'd spoken. McClean was an old man now, worn down by the war. He looked much older than his sixty-two years.

"You should be thanking Mick for what he did, for stopping that insanity."

McClean stared back into Pat's eyes. "I always liked you, Pat, your brother too. He served his time inside honorably. That's why I'm so upset about this."

"He did his time for the cause. You should see what they did to him last night. He's an absolute mess. There's been enough death. He was just trying to protect his people, and his fellow volunteers, from the inevitable retribution that would have come about as a result of this operation."

"If he was so unsure about the operation, why didn't he come to me, or to one of the other officers?"

"Tony was careful, he didn't give Mick any details in advance. Mick didn't even know where they were hitting until the afternoon of the march. By that time, it was too late to call you. He did the only thing he could, which he never planned on doing. It was a last minute decision, a knee-jerk reaction."

Green hedgerows seemed to close in on each side of the car, the road narrower and narrower as they went. They were entirely alone.

"I'm not a monster, Pat, but what would you have me do? Two IRA volunteers were found dead in that house last night, another taken into custody. I've not spoken to the volunteer in custody yet, but I'm pretty sure I know who they're going to identify as the person who sprung Mick last night."

"Aye, it was me. What else could I have done? Let them torture him to death?" Pat was looking at the side of McClean's face, searching for a chink in the harshness of his eyes. "You know what he did was right.

The IRA is going to embrace the steps toward peace soon. You know that. This would have derailed all of that, thrown us back to 1972 again like it was when I joined up. When we went to Limavady together. Don't punish Mick for saving us from those times again."

McClean pulled over to the side of the road, by an old stone wall, built up piece by piece with no cement or modern tools. Pat looked over into the field beyond it, unkempt grass leading toward a craggy wood.

McClean turned to him and reached into his pocket for a pack of cigarettes. He placed one in his mouth before offering one to Pat, who refused.

"That's all very well, but it still leaves me with the fact that two volunteers were killed last night. Someone has to pay for that."

"Why?"

"What do you mean 'why'?" McClean's face looked like he'd tasted something bitter.

"The men killed last night were not on a sanctioned IRA mission. They were dissidents and, as such, should not be afforded protection."

McClean stared out into nothing. "I can't let this go. Those men had friends, had outstanding service records. Someone has to pay for this."

"Just let Michael and Sean go. I was the one who did the killing last night."

McClean looked at him, the end of his cigarette flaming red as he pulled smoke into his lungs. "Why didn't you come to me last night, Pat?"

"There wasn't time. They would have killed him. Do I have your word that my brother will be safe, that he'll be allowed to leave the city?"

McClean paused, stubbing out the cigarette. He rubbed tired eyes. "Aye, you do."

"And what about me?" Pat asked, his voice thick.

McClean shook his head, his voice low, flecked with regret. "I'm sorry, Pat. It wouldn't wash with the higher ups. They'd have assassins looking for you both within hours of Maggie getting out tomorrow. I'll be able to give Mick the pass. I'm sure of that." McClean reached over to him, put his hand on his shoulder. "He owes you his life. Sean Campbell too. I'll do it myself. I promise it'll be quick."

Pat nodded, unable to speak.

If it were to end here, there would be no final words to loved ones, no advice to carry forward into the expanse of the vastness of their lives as his contracted into nothing. Goodbyes had already been said. The life Mick deserved would finally be his. The price for that would be his to pay. The fragility of his life came into focus, the fleeting, ephemeral nature of anything he'd ever done, the influence that he'd had. Mick would live on and that would be enough.

"I'm going to have to ask you to get out of the car," McClean said. His tone was almost mournful. Pat's body was ice cold. As if he were dead already. Pat opened the door and stepped out into the wash of the fresh country air, looked over at the field.

McClean got out of the car. He made his way around to the back and opened the trunk. A secret compartment held a handgun and McClean took it, gesturing to Pat to climb over the three-foot wall and into the field. Pat's pulse raced through him as his feet came down on the squelch of the mud. He begged his body to relent, to allow him to greet this passing with the serenity he'd always imagined. His heart beat on, air rushing in and out of his lungs, his skin clammy, his gait stilted and stiff.

A whisper of wind came through the trees. The tender hiss of the grass in the wind. The sun peering through the gray clouds above, gilded beams cast down. The warmth on his face, the cold soil beneath. They walked for thirty seconds in silence, Pat's mind sprinting though what cards he had still left to play, what could save his life. McClean motioned to him to stop. McClean spoke, doleful and bleak, murmured that he was a good man, and that this was a tragedy, but Pat wasn't listening. Pamela was smiling, her arms languid and slow around him. Peter was in his arms, and Michael laughing with him, with them all. And Siobhan came to him, her arms out, the mystery of life dancing in her eyes and expressed perfectly in every movement, every step. They were together. And nothing could be more perfect. Pat fell to his knees, his head up, back straight.

Each breath Pat took was to be his last, yet another and another followed in its wake. Pat felt McClean behind him, knew he had the gun drawn. He looked down, saw the shadow of his would-be executioner, and stood up.

"What are you doing?" McClean asked.

Pat turned to him. The fear washed away. His heartbeat was solid and even. "You don't have to do this." His voice was calm.

McClean brought a hand to wipe the pain from his eyes. "We've been through this already. There's no other way."

"Of course there is. Who else knows about this? Did Maggie tell anyone?" McClean didn't answer, held the gun higher, aiming it at Pat's face. "Then this is your decision, no one else's. You can say I came to you, that you sanctioned what I did, in the name of progressing the real cause. My brother is not a danger. No IRA men will go to jail because of what he did. He saved the lives of hundreds of Catholics. He gave us a chance for peace after years of misery and death. I know you don't want this. You remember what he did for you back in '72, you remember how he took the heat for what you did when the whole unionist side of the province would have strung you up if they could. You OK'd the hit on Melissa. He kept her innocent blood off your hands. You owe him."

"I do owe him, and that's why he's going to live. You can't. You have to go, Pat, for killing those volunteers."

"They weren't IRA volunteers when I killed them. You know that. I'm not a danger to you or anyone else in the IRA." Pat stepped forward to him. They were three feet apart now, the barrel of the pistol inches from his face.

"Stand back."

"You don't have to do this. If someone needs to pay for this, it should be the one person left who almost caused this catastrophe, not the people who stopped it."

McClean didn't speak. He took his finger off the trigger and slid it back on.

"This is wrong. You know that," Pat said.

McClean let the gun drop to his side.

"They were dissidents," Pat continued. "They had to be stopped. We were just the ones who had to do it. You would have done the same thing in my place. If it were your brother...."

"I know, and you're right, but I just can't let you away with this. Not completely free. I'm sorry, Pat."

The roar of the pistol shook the air around him. Pat felt the bullet cut into his flesh. The pain sliced him down, his body crumpling to the cold ground below, his hands clutching the soil in clumps as he tried to drag himself back to the car, back to life.

Chapter 31

August 2nd, 1999

A noise from behind spun Mick's head around but then receded into nothing. The fears had faded over time, but the instincts were still with him and the flutter of nerves inside took a few seconds to ebb away. He kept on, up the hill, further into the City Cemetery, each step propelling him further into a past that felt like a dream from which he'd never awoken.

Sean had moved back to Derry in '96 with Martina and the baby, but Mick had stayed away, haunted by the ghosts of the city he still loved. He brushed past the Republican plot, past the graves of Tony Campbell, Martin Heggarty and Maggie Heffernan, all dated within days of one another and all still alive in the darkness of his dreams. Maggie had died at the hands of her former comrades, her former masters. The story at the time had been brief, a two-line mention on the nightly news. He kept on, determined that they would not sully this moment. His breath quickened as he saw his father's name chiseled in black into the gray headstone. The words caught in his throat as he tried to coax them out.

"It's been a while, hasn't it?" He tried to laugh. "Things are good down in Dublin. I'm sorry I haven't been back, it's just that with everything that happened...." The words stopped as if he'd come to a wall inside of himself. The others were behind him. He hadn't noticed. Tears rushed down his cheeks as he felt a hand on his shoulder.

"Come on, Dad, you don't have to do this," Jason said. Melissa stood behind him but didn't speak.

"Thanks," Mick said, trying to gather himself. "I'll just be a minute. Make sure your sister's all right," he said, motioning to five-year-old Jenny, bent over to smell fresh flowers by the grave. Jason bent down and picked a pink carnation, sticking it behind her ear and the sight of them was a gleam in Mick's heart, saturated with love. He coughed, felt Melissa's arms envelop him, her face resting against his back. "It's peace now. They're saying the war's finally over. Maybe what we did had something to do with that." Mick's voice began to break as tiny droplets of rain spattered down from above, wetting the names on the grave. "Melissa says that you'd be proud, that you'd have done anything to protect your family and your community. She says you'd be proud of the lives me and Pat have lived since you died. I hope she's right."

The sight of his brother coming up the hill, hobbling on his cane, refusing help from Pamela or the kids, brought a broad smile to Mick's face. It had taken Pat ten minutes to make his way up and he was panting as he came to Mick, standing at the grave.

"How's the knee?" Mick asked. Pat hadn't walked without a cane since McClean had settled for the traditional IRA punishment of kneecapping in that field ten years before.

"It's better than that face o' yours. A fine pair we are," he smiled and put an arm around his brother.

Green hills rolled across the river, the football stadium just in front. They cast eyes over the city to the old walls, and rows of houses threaded together, interspersed by cathedral spires, Catholic and Protestant. The sun emerged from the blanket of clouds, and they made their way back down the hill, back to the streets of Bogside, gleaming from the rain as if sprinkled with diamond dust.

Author's Note

After the most expensive legal inquiry in British history, the Saville Inquiry into the killings on Bloody Sunday was published in 2010. It exonerated the victims that day, laying the blame entirely on the Paras who did the shooting. The British Prime Minister, David Cameron, issued an official apology to the victims and their families on behalf of the British Government.

Thank you so much for reading THE BOGSIDE BOYS. It was incredibly rewarding researching and writing this book. Meeting some people directly affected by the Troubles in the north of Ireland, particularly the IRA man I interviewed, who'd spent twelve years in jail, and the son of one of the victims of the Bloody Sunday massacre, was an amazing and humbling experience. Please check back on amazon for my other books.

Thanks again,

Eoin Dempsey (It's pronounced Owen by the way!)

83590325R00243

Made in the USA
Middletown, DE
13 August 2018